'The present a . . . . the initiation of mili. . . . . .ons to remove, if necessary, any th. . . . rom this direction forever.

'The aim will be to destroy Polish military strength and create in the East a situation which satisfies the requirements of Germany's national defence. The Free State of Danzig will be proclaimed a part of the Reich territory at the outbreak of hostilities.

'It will be the task of the German army to destroy the Polish armed forces. To this end a surprise attack is to be aimed at and prepared.

'The plans of the German army and the details for the timetable must be submitted by May 1 1939.'

(Extract from 'Case White', the top secret document relating to Hitler's intention to destroy Poland as a nation.)

ESCAPE TO LONDON

Mary Jane Staples

CORGI BOOKS

ESCAPE TO LONDON
A CORGI BOOK : 9780552151108

First publication in Great Britain

PRINTING HISTORY
Corgi edition published 2007

5 7 9 10 8 6 4

Set in 11/12pt New Baskerville by
Kestrel Data, Exeter, Devon.

Corgi Books are published by Transworld Publishers,
61–63 Uxbridge Road, London W5 5SA,
a division of The Random House Group Ltd.

Addresses for Random House Group Ltd companies outside the UK
can be found at: www.randomhouse.co.uk
The Random House Group Ltd Reg. No. 954009.

The Random House Group Limited supports The Forest Stewardship
Council (FSC®), the leading international forest certification organisation.
Our books carrying the FSC label are printed on FSC® certified paper.
FSC is the only forest certification scheme endorsed by the leading
environmental organisations, including Greenpeace. Our
paper procurement policy can be found at
www.randomhouse.co.uk/environment

Printed and bound in Great Britain by Clays Ltd, St Ives PLC

ESCAPE TO LONDON

Chapter One

March 14, 1938.

In a poorly furnished apartment of a workers' block on the east side of Vienna, two men were talking. One had just arrived, and it was he who, at the wish of the other man, answered a light harmless-sounding knock on the apartment door. Opening it, he was confronted by two members of the German Gestapo. He knew them by their black raincoats, their wide-brimmed hats and their look of impassive omnipotence. He effected something of a miracle in being quicker than they were. He slammed the door shut before they could burst in, and at the sound the other man disappeared into the bedroom.

It took the Gestapo men only a few seconds to blow the lock and to crash the door open. They rushed in, their revolvers fitted with silencers. The living room was empty, and they hurled themselves into the bedroom. From behind the battered apartment door, the man who had slammed it shut emerged and slipped quietly out. He sped along the corridor and down the stairs to the ground floor, making for the rear exit.

In the bedroom, the Gestapo hunters saw an open window. Reaching it, they sighted their quarry. They recognized him. He was edging his way over the roof of a warehouse below. One Gestapo man took aim. They had authority in Vienna, members of the German Gestapo, for Hitler had just annexed Austria.

'Wait,' hissed the second man, 'wait. Himmler wants him alive.'

Their quarry looked up and saw them at the open window. He scrambled over the roof to the gutter.

'Halt!' Both Gestapo men shouted the command.

The hunted man looked up again, face white and teeth gritted. He made a gesture of defiance and contempt, then peered over the gutter, looking for a way down. Sighting carefully, the first Gestapo man fired. The bullet, intended as a warning, ricocheted and struck the quarry's foot. He jerked and fell. He disappeared and they heard his anguished cry.

'Idiot!' spat one Gestapo man to the other.

The man who had slammed the door in their faces came running into the street. Hidden by the warehouse, he saw the fallen man, huddled and broken-bodied. The street was otherwise empty. He sprinted fast, reached the fallen man and bent over him.

'My God,' he breathed.

Glazing eyes opened. A hand lifted painfully.

'In my pocket – take it.' The hand fell, the eyes closed. The stooping man searched the jacket pockets quickly and found a white envelope. He extracted it, hesitated a moment in compassion, realized nothing could be done for a man who was dying, and broke into a new sprint, travelling fast.

When Himmler's men reached the street seconds later, they saw him. In a light coat and brown hat, he disappeared fast as he negotiated a corner that took him into a busy thoroughfare, where people were streaming to join thousands of others awaiting the arrival of the Fuehrer of the Greater German Reich.

There was only a body for the Gestapo.

It was not long, however, before they took up the hunt again.

The Fuehrer was standing in the open, slow-moving black car, acknowledging the hysterical welcome of the citizens of Vienna with upraised right arm, palm turned flatly back. His expression, naturally, was one of triumph. His contempt was masked. He despised Vienna, and the Viennese. During his time there, from 1909 to 1913, he had never been appreciated, never been much more than a down-and-out. It was the German people who had seen him as a man of genius and accepted him as their Fuehrer.

The Austrians thickly lining the streets had either forgotten or were unaware of their erstwhile neglect of him. He was their Fuehrer too now, and they greeted him deliriously, with a forest of saluting arms and Nazi flags. With him were his closest associates, and following on were column after column of his Stormtroopers, standards flying.

Baroness Anne von Korvacs stood rigid as the cavalcade of cars approached. She was among the few in the teeming streets who did not like what was happening and what might come of it. She shared with her mother a nostalgic love for the stateliness of old and Imperial Austria which, compared to the corrupt and blood-letting politics of the post-war era, had had so much to commend it.

In a car containing leading Austrian Nazis, Anne saw her ex-husband. Count Ludwig Lundt-Hausen, in his black uniform, his dark emaciated face looking ravaged rather than exultant. Anne knew him as a fanatical Nazi and a sour, embittered creature.

She watched him pass by, she watched the moving cavalcade. She felt stifled by the pressure of people around her, and smothered by the roar of their voices. She also felt shocked by the hysterical nature of their welcome to the High Priest of the Nazi religion. Some people were verging on frenzy in their adulation. She alone did not have an arm raised in salute to the Stormtroopers. No, there was someone else, a man in a light coat and brown hat. He materialized beside her out of the crush. She glanced at him, feeling his eyes on her. He gave her a little smile of recognition, which slightly startled her since she was sure she'd never met him. About thirty, he had a pleasant if somewhat rugged countenance. His brief further smile seemed an acknowledgement of her glance and the fact that they alone stood apart from the hysteria. On her other side, a youth wearing a miniature Nazi flag in his buttonhole had his right arm stiffly raised. His shouts of 'Seig Heil' were beginning to crack his cords. Aware that Anne was not sharing his enthusiasm, he dropped his arm and turned on her.

'What are you?' he demanded. 'A Communist? A Jewess?' Receiving no reply, nor even a look, he said aggressively, 'You aren't welcoming the Fuehrer, are you? Why not, eh, why not?'

Anne tensed. The moment was dangerous. In a crowd as intoxicated as this by the arrival of the Great One, an altercation provoked by her indifference to his glory could result in her being beaten and bruised.

'I'm not immune to events,' she said quietly and truthfully.

'What's that? What's that?' The young bruiser, who looked no more than eighteen at the most, considered her comment unsatisfactory, and he was quite sure her attitude wasn't what it should have been. 'Why aren't you—' He broke off as the man in the light coat pushed in. 'Here, who d'you think you're shoving?'

'What are you wearing that for?' The man's German was accented, his manner just as aggressive as the youth's. His finger poked at the little flag. 'That's the symbol of German greatness, and its invincible architect has just gone by. Yet all you can do is make improper advances to a lady. You need six months in a labour camp to get your priorities right and to improve your manners.'

The youth, flustered, said clumsily, 'Now you look – you wait a minute – don't you talk like that to me.'

'I'll report you,' said the man sternly. 'I'll report you for flouting the arrival of the Fuehrer by insulting behaviour.' He cast a glance over his shoulder, then eyed the youth threateningly. The two of them, with Anne, formed a small island of irrelevance in the sea of surging Austrians. The disconcerted youth simmered and muttered. The crowd pushed and swayed. The man glanced at Anne again. She gave him a faint smile, knowing he had interceded on her behalf. Amid the tumult and the making of history, they silently shared a less enchanted view of events than most of Vienna.

Anne was forty-one, but her clear skin, her wealth of fair hair and her blue eyes made her look much younger. She carried herself well, in the way of her kind, and her refusal to let adversity and disillusionment impart a droop to her shoulders or her mouth, placed her among the people who had been brought up to meet misfortune with dignity and pride. Her cream-coloured raincoat and blue hat favoured her looks and her colouring. The man beside her allowed frank admiration to surface for a moment.

He cast another glance over his shoulder. He glimpsed two men in black raincoats and dark hats elbowing their way through the massed banks of people. He sighed, then addressed the glowering youth again, letting him know a second time that improper advances to a lady on such a day as this could get him into serious trouble with the new Nazi forces of law and order. The youth blustered, but the man turned away, brushing against Anne as he did so. He did not look at her, but she caught his whisper as he began to shoulder his way through the crush of people still paying their tributes to German leadership.

'Forgive me, Baroness.'

That startled her again. She had discarded her married name and title after Ludwig had divorced her. She reverted to her maiden name and title. This man's use of the latter confirmed he knew her, although she was still sure she had never met him.

She decided she too did not want to stay longer. A second inquisition from the unmannerly youth had no appeal for her at all. She began to make her own exit, noting faces that seemed like shining masks of exaltation. Mouths gaped and eyes looked feverish. It was not easy to work her way through. She caught sight of the pleasant man, shouldering a path for himself. There were two men in black raincoats not far from him, and they too were using their shoulders, pushing vigorously in his direction. They suddenly separated, one continuing forcefully on, the other turning to advance on the unpleasant youth, who was once more shouting 'Seig Heil' along with thousands of other people. Stormtroopers were still marching by.

Anne freed herself from the crush and reached the clear section of the wide pavement. She had to turn left for home. Her friend of the moment was walking briskly in the opposite direction. One of the raincoated men was running after him. The other appeared, bursting from the mass and dragging the protesting youth with him. Anne suspected then that the men in the raincoats were members of the secret police, the kind who had come into being the moment Hitler had proclaimed the Anschluss. The first caught up with the pleasant man to detain him, and the youth was being roughly propelled towards them by the second.

Yes, she thought, overnight Austria has sprouted its own Gestapo. What happened to people they arrested she could only guess at. What would happen to the man who had interceded for her, she didn't like to think about. He had sounded like a foreigner, his accent reminding her of another's. Yes, that of her brother-in-law, James Fraser of England. Was this man from England too? Appearing to be quite unmoved by being apprehended, he seemed to be making a good case for himself in his conversation with the raincoated men, of whom there were three now, the third in a dark blue trilby. If he really was from England, the Gestapo would have to tread carefully with him. It was Hitler's policy to present Nazi Germany as a benevolent dictatorship to the Western democracies.

Anne turned then and went on her way. It was odd about the youth. Why had he been dragged out of the crowd? His idolatrous welcome for Hitler and the German troops could not have been faulted. Was he suspect because he had been seen talking with the pleasant man? The Gestapo wanted the latter, that had been obvious. Did they also want every person seen talking with him? Would they have detained her if they'd seen him talking to her? She suspected they would. In not saying one word to her, apart from that whispered aside, he had perhaps been generously thoughtful on her behalf. She hoped he was not in serious trouble, for his chivalry awakened memories of the gallantries of pre-war Vienna.

She walked on, passing only a few people. Almost everyone seemed to have gone to welcome Hitler. In following that raucous Pied Piper from Berlin, she felt the Viennese were committing suicide. Perhaps they wanted to, for their city was only a ghost of its former proud self. Gone were its years of splendour, gone its gaiety and its emperors. The post-war apartment blocks, elbowing architecture handsomely baroque, were ugly to her eyes, for she shared with her mother a love of old Vienna. And with her father she shared a detestation of Hitler and his National Socialist Party. That organization, her father maintained, had its brains, its power and its purpose entirely in its jackboots.

Anne accepted, however, that the comparisons one made at her age were governed by the conviction that everything had been better in the old days. But life then had been lovely for her and her sister Sophie. True, theirs had been a privileged existence, but even so, even so. Sophie lived in England now, married to James Fraser, an Anglo-Scot whom she had met in the summer of 1914. It was unforgettable, that beautiful but fateful summer, when Sophie was falling incurably in love with James, and brother

Carl had seen the future as an exciting continuation of the present.

She walked on, through streets that seemed deserted, as if even the houses were empty of people. The Communists would be lying very low. Their time in Austria was up. The Nazis would smash them. How strange that they hated each other when they had so much in common. Both were monstrously intolerant of even the mildest opposition, both believed the State to be the supreme arbiter, both encouraged neighbour to denounce neighbour, children to denounce parents.

As for Ludwig, her ex-husband, he had been amiable and fun-loving as a young man. He married her in 1915 when on leave from the army. Subsequently wounded and taken prisoner by the Russians, he literally disappeared from her life until the war was over. On his return from his years in a primitive prisoner-of-war camp, he was acid-tongued and dark-souled. She tried, desperately at times, to love and understand him, but his darkness always shut her out. She conceived no children, for he never made love to her, insisting on separate bedrooms. She felt he merely tolerated her.

Not until Hitler came to power did Ludwig find something that animated him, the formation of an Austrian Nazi Party. He committed himself to its ideals and purpose like a dead man given new life. But its brutality typified for Anne all the violence and misery Austria had suffered at the hands of political extremists since the demise of the Empire.

Ludwig had divorced her a year ago on the grounds that she was having an affair with a man called Josef Meister. Herr Meister was a Jew, a cultured man and a friend of the family. She had sat in court listening to Ludwig impassively lying his head off, and a Nazi colleague of his corroborating the lies. Herr Meister made the mistake of trying to defend his name and hers. He was torn to pieces by Ludwig's counsel. Anne herself refused to plead. When she left the court, a divorced woman, she drew a deep breath of fresh air. She cared little for what Ludwig had sought to do to her character and reputation, for her family and friends would know what was true and what was not. Her brother Carl had said cheerfully, 'Well, you and Ludwig both acquired something today. You acquired sweet freedom, and he acquired the distinction of being the biggest liar in Vienna. I think yours far the better acquisition, so let's go home and take a bottle of champagne with us.'

Anne reached the handsome family house on the Salesianergasse. It had been converted into apartments, lofty and spacious. Her parents lived on the ground floor. Brother Carl, his Italian wife Pia and their two children occupied the first floor. She herself had rooms on the second floor, where there was also a suite used by Sophie, James and their children whenever they visited from England.

Two old family servants were still in residence, Hanna and Heinrich. They had been with the family since they were young, and were husband and wife. Heinrich was sixty now, but still efficient.

Anne, letting herself in, saw him in the hall, polishing a gilt-framed mirror.

'Heinrich, haven't you been out to wave a flag?' she asked with a smile. Heinrich, sporting silvery mutton chop whiskers of a bygone era, replied that the only flag he would ever wave was the Imperial one. 'I'm afraid that's just a relic now,' said Anne.

'Not to me, Baroness,' said Heinrich firmly.

Anne entered the drawing room, which had been the family gathering point for many years. Large and square, it was bright with colourful English chintzes. The furniture, chosen for comfort, was well preserved, polished daily. Here and there a spring was apt to creak, but not without a subsequent sigh of apology.

Anne's parents sat beside the fire, her mother at work on some fine embroidery. Her father, Baron Ernst von Korvacs, was seventy-two, but still a man with a straight back, although his mane of white hair was thinning a little. He conducted himself with dignity in a world he neither liked nor understood. Austria had been defeated in a catastrophic war, but why it had surrendered its nobility he would never know. He had served Franz Josef, and been willing after the war to serve the Republic, his love for Austria being greater than his dislike of the new order. But the Socialists preferred to make political appointments, not intelligent ones, and had forced him into retirement at fifty-two. They had given him a modest pension and told him he was fortunate. He would have had to sell the family house if his son-in-law James had not persuaded him to accept a large batch of shares in the Fraser car company when it launched a European offshoot. The offshoot boomed, the shares went sky-high, the baron sold his and was suddenly well off again.

His wife, Baroness Teresa, four years younger, still had an opulent Edwardian figure, although her fair hair was turning silvery. She dressed stylishly, but in muted colours, sharing with her contemporaries a sad regret for the passing of the Empire. However, she still found some pleasure in life, mainly through her family, and would have liked to see more of her daughter Sophie and son-in-law James.

Modern Vienna held little interest for her. It lacked grace and manners. Today, it was entirely out of favour with her. What had happened to its citizens that they were crowding the streets to welcome a man who encouraged acts of godless thuggery? She had switched off the radio after listening to the commentator for only a few minutes.

She and the baron looked up as Anne came in. Anne had insisted on going out to discover just how Vienna would greet the German Fuehrer.

'We are blessed,' said the baroness.

'Are you, Mama?' said Anne. 'How so?'

'We feared you'd be swept away,' said the baroness. 'Our fears came from listening to the radio. What was it like?'

'A heathen circus,' said Anne, 'but I've a feeling that today's performing clowns will turn into tomorrow's ravenous jackals.'

'You saw the entrance of the ringmaster?' enquired the baron drily.

'He's actually the prodigal son, isn't he?' said Anne. 'Dear Lord, how mortifying to know Austria gave birth to him, and how frightening to realize Austria is the fatted calf.'

'He has what he wanted,' said the baron, 'and perhaps, when he's devoured the Communists, he'll leave the rest of us alone.'

'Do you think Sophie and James will come now?' asked the baroness.

'Mama, of course they will,' said Anne confidently. 'They always come at Easter, and won't be scared off by Hitler.' About to recount the incident involving the aggressive youth and the chivalrous man, she decided to keep it to herself. 'Darlings,' she said, 'must we live under our new masters? Shouldn't we think about going to England, to live near Sophie and James? I am going to find the Nazis intolerable myself, and Carl can't stand the sight of them. But I should not go without you.'

'To England?' said the baroness.

'Yes, Mama, to join Sophie and James, and your grandchildren, Victoria, Paul and Emma Jane. I've been thinking about it, and am sure England would not say no to some nice old-fashioned Viennese, would she?'

The baron gave the suggestion deep thought. The baroness considered it with warm interest. Anne knew how much her mother liked James, who cherished Sophie and had done so much to bring a badly wounded Carl home to Vienna at the end of the war. He had brought a beautiful

Italian girl too, a girl with an extraordinary devotion to Carl and now his wife.

The baron said quietly, 'Could we bring ourselves to leave Vienna, Teresa?'

'Ernst,' said the baroness, 'we could bring ourselves to think about it.'

'I am wondering if we can bring ourselves to stay,' said Anne.

The door opened then, and a grey-headed man entered. Dark-suited, his white shirt and grey tie immaculate, he had a long face and soft eyes.

'I'm so sorry, Baron,' he said, 'I was unaware you had a visitor.'

'It's only me, Herr Meister,' said Anne, smiling at the man named by Ludwig in the divorce court.

Herr Meister peered at her.

'Why, of course. How are you, my dear friend?'

'Suffering the torture of feeling invaded,' said Anne.

'Ah, so?' said Herr Meister, and looked sad.

'Anne,' said the baron, 'Herr Meister is staying with us for a few days.'

'Fortunately,' said the baroness, 'his wife and family are in London, and Heinrich went out an hour ago to send them a cable, telling them to stay there.'

'Mama?' said Anne.

'Now that Austria has sold its birthright to the ogre,' said the baron, 'it's wiser for them not to return.'

'Oh, my God,' said Anne involuntarily. Hitler. The Gestapo. The Jews. Josef Meister and his family were Jews. 'Yes, I see. I'm so sorry, Herr Meister.'

'There are compensations, Anne,' said Herr Meister quietly, 'the compensations of having friends.'

'Herr Meister's stay with us is a private matter, Anne,' said the baron.

'Yes, Papa, I understand,' said Anne, and smiled again at the gentle-mannered Jew. 'I'm going to your gallery later today to look at Mariella's exhibition. I don't want to go just yet, not while Hitler's jackals are still marching, but when I do shall I give Mariella your regards?'

'Perhaps,' said Josef Meister, 'perhaps it would be better, for her own sake, not to let her know where I am.'

'I understand that too,' said Anne. 'Mama, if you're about to order some tea, I'll come down and join you, shall I? I must just freshen up first.'

'Yes, do join us, my dear,' said the baroness.

Anne went up to her apartment. It was there that she found something in the left-hand pocket of her raincoat. A small stiff envelope, unsealed. In it was a film negative of a very small size. She knew at once how the envelope had found its way into her pocket. It had been slipped in when the protective gentleman brushed against her. Very obviously, it was something he badly needed to get rid of at the time. But what was the point of passing it on to someone he might never see again?

Correction, she thought. He knew her. He had pointedly told her so when using her title. And that, perhaps, meant he would get in touch with her. Unless the Gestapo disposed of him. She fervently hoped not. She would have to wait and see. Carefully, she put the negative back into the envelope, and tucked it away in a shoe.

Chapter Two

It was a fiasco. It was the very first day of her very first exhibition of real importance, and the gallery had not seen more than ten visitors, and these had all been elderly. They had lingered and looked, but in a fidgety way, as if they felt they ought to be elsewhere. Mariella Amaraldi guessed what was on their minds, the entry of Hitler and his Stormtroopers into Vienna. It was elderly people who most disliked the thuggery of the Nazis.

She talked to some of them, and they were either awkward or garrulous in the way of nervous people. She herself was disgusted rather than nervous. An odious megalomaniac had been allowed to embrace Austria, and that embrace was going to crush to death all opposition. His arrival had spoiled for her the excitement and pleasure of presenting her work to the public in such a famous gallery as this.

She painted, basically, to please her own artistic sense, but liked people to find her pictures interesting enough to discuss. It had been a struggle to achieve her first sale, but when it happened, when one of her paintings, showing in a shop window, attracted a buyer, she experienced delight.

When Josef Meister approached her some months ago to offer her his gallery for a week in March, she was rapturous. Herr Meister was a respected dealer and connoisseur, and she knew it was a great compliment to be invited to hang her canvases in his superb salon. But the exhibition had opened on the day when the people of Vienna had massed on the streets to acclaim the man who styled himself the Fuehrer. Such acclaim, she thought, was a sad thing.

At thirty-one, Mariella Amaraldi was Latin-dark, her rich beauty almost sultry, her figure endowed with Latin splendour. Fellow artists had begged her to pose for them. She asked in what way? Most suggested as Aphrodite rising from the foam. Her answer was no. She had no desire to be a model, only a recognized artist of God-given talent.

If her blood was warmly Italian, her inclinations were Austrian. She had been born an Austrian subject in the Tyrol, had developed a very young love for a certain Austrian and for Austria itself. Nothing could keep her from eventually moving to Vienna. At the age of twenty-one she made her home there. Her sister Pia, married to Carl von Korvacs, also lived there.

The gallery by mid-afternoon was empty. Perhaps everyone, simply everyone, except herself, was welcoming Hitler. No, not everyone, after all. A man and a woman entered. The man was tall, mature and distinguished, wearing a grey Burberry coat and a light grey trilby hat. He removed the hat, a gesture of good manners that pleased Mariella. She had a preference for mature and civilized men. Painters were expected to be Bohemian, to exist with little regard for social conventions or people's opinions, and no regard at all for filthy money. To Mariella, that meant painters were expected to achieve immortality by starving to death in a garret, surrounded by unsold masterpieces. She did not conform to that kind of idiocy herself. God gave life without commanding any man or woman to foolishly relinquish it.

Seated at a little table in a corner of the gallery, she studied the visitors. The woman, in a pale blue coat and dark blue hat, was very fair and looked to be in her forties. The man, thought Mariella, was in his early fifties, and so fine and personable. They made a striking couple. Moreover, they were neither fidgety nor nervous. In their survey of paintings, they seemed entirely unconcerned with what was going on elsewhere. Mariella wanted to talk to them, but felt they were entitled to some minutes of uninterrupted viewing.

They referred from time to time to the catalogue they had bought at the door, and finally became extremely taken with a particular canvas. The man murmured something, and the woman smiled and nodded. They approached Mariella, and she came up from her chair.

'Fräulein Amaraldi?' said the gentleman. His deep and mellow voice and his very masculine presence struck an instant response in Mariella. She had never seen a more distinguished-looking man. His thick brown hair and moustache were tinted with flecks of gold. His grey eyes were worldly and direct, his face brown and weathered, as if he had known burning summers and biting winters.

'Mein Herr?' Mariella smiled, and the smile enriched her colouring.

'A moment, while I refer,' said the gentleman. His German was fluent, but Mariella felt he was neither German nor Austrian. He consulted the catalogue. 'Yes, number twenty-seven. *English Cottage*. My wife likes it.'

'It's a little more than that,' said the fair lady. Her German had a softly thick accent. Her smile and her tranquil brown eyes gave her a serene look. It was a deceptive look. 'I have fallen in love with it.'

'It's for sale, I believe,' said the gentleman.

'You are thinking of buying it?' said Mariella, showing delight. She was very demonstrative.

'My wife insists,' he said. He smiled. It further commended him to Mariella. Smiles cost nothing and were the sun on the faces of people. Well, some people.

'Yes, I would like to have it, please,' said the fair lady, her hair a shining gold beneath her hat.

'Shall we look at it together?' said Mariella, naturally inclined to discuss the merits of the painting, and experiencing warm pleasure that here were two visitors able, on this fateful day, to give priority to an interest in art. With her, they studied the canvas in question. *English Cottage* had been painted when summer was verdant. Mariella had tinted the shadows, and the tints reflected the colours of the cottage and the foliage. The cottage itself, which its owners would have said was of light brown stone, had been treated to delicate dashes of greens, blues and yellows. Mariella belonged to the Impressionist school, and considered Turner and Watteau to have inspired the origins of Impressionism in Monet. She had spent a year in England, where she fell in love with Turner's genius, and where she often stayed with Carl's sister Sophie and husband James in their Warwickshire cottage, the subject of the painting.

'Is it correct for me to say it's charming?' ventured the fair lady.

'It's correct to say whatever you feel about it,' said Mariella. 'It's correct, if you don't like a painting, to say so. I would never myself buy a picture I disliked, whoever had painted it and however much it appealed to others.'

'Where did you find the subject, Fräulein?' asked the gentleman.

'In England, naturally,' said Mariella. 'Do you know England?'

The fair lady laughed.

'We should,' she said, 'our home is there. We are in Vienna only as visitors.'

'You're English?' said Mariella.

'My husband is. I am Russian.' The fair lady smiled. 'But not a Bolshevik.'

'Bolshevik?' said Mariella. Few people used

that word these days. Bolshevism had become Communism.

'No, never a Bolshevik.' The fair lady smiled again. 'They are all terrible people.'

'Ah, so?' said Mariella, and thought that, despite the smile, a sudden little glint of steel briefly gave the lie to serenity. A fascinating woman. 'Friends of mine, relatives of my brother-in-law, used to live in that cottage. I painted it twice. The first I gave to them. This is the second. If you wish to buy it, you will make me very happy. The price is in the catalogue.'

'It's a very reasonable price,' said the gentleman. 'Very reasonable, since I'm told you're a genius.'

'Oh?' Mariella's rich laugh bubbled. 'I'm sure I'm not, but may I ask who told you I was?'

'The gentleman who owns this gallery, Herr Meister.'

'He is prejudiced in my favour,' smiled Mariella.

'Very well, remain modest, Fräulein, and wait for time to tell.'

'Ah, time, mein Herr, is not always kind to artists. Some have only known posthumous recognition. How sad, don't you think?'

'Too sad to happen to you, Fräulein. Why not accept now that Herr Meister is right?'

'How kind you are, how encouraging,' said Mariella.

'I only know we both like the painting very much,' said the fair lady. 'A cottage, yes, only a cottage, but so atmospheric.'

'Of England?' smiled Mariella, delighting in these people.

'Yes, of England,' said the fair lady. 'And there, look.' She pointed. 'That one I find very moving.'

In the catalogue it was called *Alpine Soldier*. It depicted an officer of the Imperial Austrian Army, seen in a snow-covered Alpine village. His arm was around the shoulders of a young girl. Her head was bent, her face in profile, the profile a hazy outline, suggesting adolescent anonymity. He was looking down at her, his peaked cap casting a shadow that softened the hard lines of his deeply tanned face. The colour of his eyes was indeterminate. A hazy blue-grey, perhaps. Mariella had not attempted to capture their true colour, an intense blue. She had captured something far more meaningful to her, an impression of soldierly compassion for the young and innocent, for a girl sick and feverish. The background of Alpine whites was splashed by streaks of blue, and lightly daubed colours speckled the officer's pale blue greatcoat and the girl's dark winter coat.

'It pleases me that it touches you,' said Mariella.

The gentleman, referring to the catalogue, said, 'It isn't for sale, I see. Is it a depiction, then, of people you knew?'

'It's an impression, a memory, of my childhood, when Austria was at war with Italy,' said Mariella.

'And you found something that meant a little more to you than the war?' suggested the gentleman, viewing the painting with fresh interest.

Because she liked this striking couple so much,

Mariella said impulsively, 'That, mein Herr, is a depiction of love being born.'

'A mutual love?' said the fair lady.

Mariella smiled and shook her head.

'Unrequited,' she said.

'Painfully so?' said the gentleman.

'At times,' said Mariella.

'Ah, but strangely, one simply won't give up that kind of pain,' said the fair lady. She glanced at her husband, a teasing smile showing. 'One suffers it and hugs it, all in the hope that a man who is blind will one day see.'

'Sometimes a knock on the head saves all that waiting,' smiled the gentleman. 'May I pay you for the picture, Fräulein Amaraldi?'

'Thank you, mein Herr,' said Mariella, 'and I really am very happy to sell it to you and your wife.' She accepted banknotes from him. 'May I have your name for the receipt and the record?'

'Kirby,' he said, 'John Kirby. And this lady is my wife Karita.'

'Karita? That is Russian?' said Mariella.

'Crimean,' said the fair lady firmly.

'You are both a great pleasure to me,' said Mariella, 'and I'm very happy to have met you. You don't mind that the painting is to remain until the exhibition is over at the end of the week?'

'Not at all, Fräulein,' said John Kirby, whose years of work in the field for British Intelligence had made him an agent of unequalled resourcefulness. Before the war and during an assignment in Russia he had even become involved with the ill-fated Imperial family of

Tsar Nicholas, and his relationship with Grand Duchess Olga, the Tsar's eldest daughter, had been an extremely intimate one. The murder of the whole family shattered him. His wife Karita, whom he had met during his time in Russia, had a temperament that belied her serene look. She had been known to throw plates at him. She had never allowed him to go off on any mission without her, and since she owned a mind as sharp as his, she became his ex-officio assistant. That is, she was not on the Government's official payroll, but she did have her place in the British Intelligence files and in Kirby's expenses account. 'It's the usual thing, I believe, for all canvases to remain until an exhibition closes.'

'I am only happy that *English Cottage* will remain as ours,' said Karita. She and her husband were not in Vienna as visitors, but observers, and they had indeed made their observation of the entry of the man British Intelligence regarded as Europe's greatest threat to peace.

Mariella, marvelling that nothing had been said about Hitler, found the gallery very quiet again after they had gone. Two young women wandered in at four thirty, but stayed only a few minutes. Then a tall slender man in a black overcoat and dark blue trilby hat came in. His inspection of the paintings was cursory, although he finally lingered at number forty-two. *Linden Tree*. He called her over.

'Mein Herr?' she said.

'Quite pretty, Fräulein,' he said, eyeing her Latin beauty impassively. 'Even promising.' Mariella's response was to give him a look of disgust. He noted it without changing expression. He had fine features, if somewhat ascetic, and she thought him in his forties. 'I'm speaking, Fräulein, of this painting.'

'Then look at it, mein Herr, and not at me,' she said.

'I suggest your brushwork isn't bold enough.'

'You mean I should attack a canvas?'

'Boldness achieves definition, Fräulein Amaraldi.'

'For some, perhaps,' said Mariella.

'You're of Italian extraction?' he said.

'I was born a subject of the Emperor Franz Josef,' said Mariella, 'and therefore I am Austrian. By birth and by wish.'

'I did not say you weren't. You don't favour definition in painting?'

'There are different forms of the art,' said Mariella. 'I think your kind of definition is for those who see their subject uncompromising of shape and in light that's constant. But light is very variable, so much so that it can introduce several changes of colour to a tree in only an hour, and variable light and changes of colour can produce changes in shapes.'

'I'm a simple man – '

'Are you?'

'I repeat, I'm a simple man, Fräulein. I like a tree to look like a tree and for its leaves to be green.'

'But there are many different colours to be seen, not green alone. One can see reds and yellows.'

'In autumn, in autumn.'

33

'In summer too,' said Mariella.

'There's the argument, then,' he said. 'Is a tree a tree, or is it something else?'

'That's an argument I thought was over, mein Herr. It occupied the critics for years at the turn of the century, but the techniques and individualism of the Impressionists are accepted now, aren't they?'

'By some,' he said, 'not by everyone. It was always a degenerate trend, a betrayal of true art. A directive, perhaps, will be issued.'

'A directive?' Mariella was onto him now. A man of the new government. How quickly the Nazis went to work. 'What kind of directive?'

'One that will define how trees should be painted,' he said. He had deep grey eyes and looked intelligent but austere. 'Ah, where is Herr Meister?'

That put Mariella right on her guard. Josef Meister was of the religious fraternity loathed by the Nazis. He was also an intellectual, and Hitler despised the breed. Additionally, Herr Meister, although shrewd, was kind and gentle. A friend of Carl's parents, he had appeared in a divorce court once to deny he had ever been the lover of Carl's sister Anne.

'Herr Meister was here this morning, but left at noon,' she said. 'I've no idea where he is now. You know Herr Meister?'

'I know of him,' said the inquisitive man. 'I understand he prefers Impressionists to traditionalists.'

Mariella supposed this implied Herr Meister also preferred degeneracy. The Nazis believed

34

all culture should be based on Teutonic thunder and lightning.

'Herr Meister is a connoisseur, with an appreciation of all methods and every kind of artistic talent,' she said.

'Including yours, Fräulein?' he said, inspecting her as if her chief talents lay in her splendid bosom. 'Do you appreciate his appreciation?'

His was the classic approach of the investigative Nazi to people who had Jewish friends. Mariella was very much on her guard.

'Do you mean am I in love with him?' she said. 'Well, I do find older men more attractive and more civilized than young men, but no, I'm not in love with Herr Meister.'

'That must be a disappointment to him.'

'You're quite mistaken, mein Herr,' said Mariella coldly. 'Herr Meister is happily married.'

'Is he?' There was a suggestion of scepticism. 'Then why has his wife left him to go to London with his children?'

'You are mistaken again, mein Herr. Frau Meister is English, and her parents live in London. She and the children have simply gone to visit them.'

'I'm surprised, Fräulein, that in knowing Josef Meister as well as you obviously do, you were not told where he was going when he left the gallery this morning.'

'He merely informed me he was going out,' said Mariella, 'and I'm not as inquisitive about his movements as you seem to be.'

'My inquisitiveness relates to my work, Fräulein.'

'What work?' Mariella refused to be intimidated. 'Who are you?'

'My name is Voegler. I am Kommissar Voegler, and have the authority to ask questions. Especially about Jews.'

Mariella felt sick. Her knowledge of Nazi officialdom was sketchy, but she knew at least that German Gestapo officials of a certain rank bore the title of Kommissar. She supposed the Austrian Gestapo had come into very active being now, and that they wore the plain clothes of the secret police, although they were also members of the SS.

'Herr Meister is a good and kind man,' she said.

'Is that possible?' said Voegler. 'We shall see. It seems a pity, by the way, that you're exhibiting so many pictures when there are so few people here.'

'Just you at the moment,' said Mariella.

'It could be put down, I suppose, to the excitement of the events elsewhere. So many shops shut and other galleries closed for the day. You and Herr Meister resisted the temptation to close this one?'

'It was a temptation, naturally,' said Mariella. 'One can't expect to see the Fuehrer every day. But this is my first exhibition of real standing, and I'm sure you understand what that means to a struggling artist. So I begged Herr Meister to open up.'

'Where is he?' The question came abruptly.

'He was here this morning,' said Mariella. 'Where he is now, I've no idea. Perhaps caught up with the day's excitements. Or perhaps he's at home.'

'No, he's not at home.'

'Then he must be in the streets, waving a flag with everyone else,' said Mariella.

'Not everyone is waving a flag, Fräulein. You are not, for instance, and there are others, no doubt, who are too preoccupied. With worries, perhaps, and uneasy consciences.'

'Ah, so? You are telling me why you aren't waving a flag yourself?' Mariella carried the fight audaciously to the opposition. 'It's because the arrival of the Fuehrer is a worry to you? You have something on your conscience? If so, you must solve your own problems, mein Herr. I beg you not to confide in me.'

His brief smile was not unpleasant.

'I was talking, Fräulein, not confiding.'

'Even so,' said Mariella, 'whatever your troubles are, you must keep them to yourself. I don't wish to inform on you.'

'I said nothing about any troubles.'

'I naturally inferred, from what you did say, that it was safer for you to be here than on the streets. In any event, I can't help you, nor would it be fair of you to ask me to.'

Again the brief smile, but slightly caustic this time.

'You are very specious, Fräulein. I'm here only in the hope of seeing Herr Meister.'

'I'm afraid you're out of luck,' said Mariella.

'I'll take a look at his office.'

'I suppose I can't stop you,' said Mariella, hiding worry. She was certain now that this man had not come merely to see Herr Meister, but to take him away. The round-up of Jewish persons had actually begun yesterday, the day when the Anschluss had been officially proclaimed. Herr Meister was now a candidate for a labour camp, no doubt. One did not get to know a great deal about these camps, only that the Germans used them for the incarceration of Communists, Jews and other people of whom the Nazis disapproved. Such places would be built in Austria, and quickly.

Another man appeared, putting his head round the door. Voegler made a dismissive gesture, and the head withdrew. Mariella watched as Voegler then walked to the door of the office at the end of the long gallery. At that moment, the place was invaded by a dozen young people. They were noisy, excited and high on adrenalin. Wearing miniature Nazi pennants, they swarmed to view the canvases and to make their comments loudly but by no means disparagingly.

Mariella joined them and found they were students. They were in favour of Hitler, but not yet fully indoctrinated as young Germans were, and therefore they were also in favour of Mariella's Impressionist technique. They discussed this enthusiastically with her. Voegler came out of Herr Meister's office and left without any further words. He did not bother to hide the fact that he took with him papers removed from Herr Meister's files.

The students left in the same way they'd entered, in an excited rushing group, much as if they might be missing something by staying. The gallery was empty again. Mariella sighed, and in her worry for Herr Meister she entered his office. The cabinet of files showed every sign of having been ransacked. When she came out, a man was in the gallery, coat over his arm, hat in his hand. He was making a study of the first paintings.

Mariella's brown eyes glowed.

'Carl?'

Her brother-in-law turned. His light brown hair was showing a little grey, and there were slight smudges of tiredness under his eyes. He was in his forty-seventh year, but to her he was still Austria's most attractive man.

Major Carl von Korvacs, in command of an Austrian mountain regiment during the war, had lodged in the Tyrolean house of Mariella's parents during one of the regiment's rest periods. Her sister Pia, fiercely Italian, resented his presence, but fell in love with him, all the same. So did Mariella herself. But Pia was nineteen, and she was only twelve. So Pia was the one who married him. Years later, in Vienna, when Mariella was twenty-six, she took a lover in a desperate attempt to cure herself of her hunger for Carl. The affair was doomed from the outset. It incurred Pia's anger and disapproval, it lasted only a short time, and it did not cure her. It was not her fault she was in love with her sister's husband. It was one of life's bitter little quirks. If he had been married to anyone else other than her sister, she would willingly have become his mistress. She told him so. He laughed. He could not take her seriously. But Pia had her suspicions and her moments of hot Italian jealousy.

Carl, watching Mariella swooping towards him, took note of her radiant smile and her surging advance.

'Stand off,' he said, smiling.

'Carl, how lovely to see you.'

'I'm hardly a picture,' said Carl.

'You are you,' said Mariella. 'Carl, am I not to receive a kiss?'

'No, you are not,' said Carl. 'With you, my cuckoo, one kiss will lead to another. How has your first day been?'

'Very quiet but very pleasing,' said Mariella. 'I sold a painting of James and Sophie's cottage to a charming couple.'

'Congratulations,' said Carl. 'I'm familiar with your work, of course. I own two immortal canvases of yours.'

'They're far from immortal,' said Mariella, 'and you bought them for quite the wrong reasons, out of kindness for a starving artist.'

'I bought them because I liked them,' said Carl, 'and might I point out you've never looked starving?'

'You've noticed I have a figure?' said Mariella. 'I'm delighted. Will there be any advance on that?'

'Behave yourself,' said Carl, and studied other pictures.

'Yes, I must behave, I suppose, or Pia will kill me,' said Mariella. 'Isn't that terrible, my life at so much risk from my own sister?'

'And mine from my own wife?' said Carl.

'*Mamma mia*, would she take an axe to you too?'

'Quite definitely, if she thought I was having an affair with you,' said Carl. His attention was caught by *Alpine Soldier*. 'Hello, have I seen that picture before?'

With a faint flush, she said, 'Oh, that's just an impression of a memory.' And she wondered if he would remember the moment. He did.

'You were walking home from school, sick with tonsillitis.'

'And you caught me up, took me to the doctor and carried me home,' said Mariella. 'I was twelve years old. I had no idea that a girl of twelve could fall in love.'

Carl regarded the painting silently, so silently she wasn't sure if he was really seeing it. He looked strained and tired. She knew how much he had disliked the militant politics that had plagued Austria for years. She knew too that he found the Austrian Nazis totally repellent. Then there were the responsibilities of his job. He headed the production team of the car company called Austro-Fraser, the factory having been built and financed by Sir William Fraser, father-in-law of Carl's elder sister, Sophie, in 1920. It was an Austrian offshoot of Sir William's huge British business. Carl was a technical executive, and a very good one. He had helped to design, build and race the Austro-Fraser Comet, a joint Austrian and British effort for the international circuits. Even now he could still hold his own as a racing driver, and was the idol of Austrian fans. He had been working long hours recently to ensure the Comet Two was ready for the 1938 season. He hoped to have two cars in perfect

41

shape for a race at Brooklands in England, in May.

'You've made a sale, Mariella,' he said, 'but it hasn't been a good day for you or for Vienna, has it?'

'It hasn't been a good day for the whole of Austria,' said Mariella.

'Austria,' said Carl, 'hasn't had a good day since Sarajevo.'

'A man has been here asking to see Herr Meister,' said Mariella.

'Josef? What kind of a man?'

'Do you really need to ask that?'

Carl sighed. Mariella understood his feelings. He had fought all through the war, he and other men, and they all deserved more than Austria had given them. Above all else, they deserved peace. But for years they had only known bitter and violent politics. And now they had Nazi jackboots pounding their streets, and the Gestapo at their backs.

'There's a way out, Mariella,' said Carl. He smiled at her and her nerves tingled. 'How would you like to exhibit in London?'

'London?'

'It's a city of many galleries, and its dealers and connoisseurs have few equals. Mariella, it's time the whole family left. You too. Austria disappeared today. Today, it became a minor province of the Greater German Reich. As an artist, you love freedom, don't you?'

'I cherish it,' said Mariella.

'Well, you've just lost it,' said Carl, 'and so has everyone else in this country. To make anything of life now, it's necessary to join the Nazi Party. Even then we shan't be able to prevent Hitler dragging us into another war.'

'Another war?' breathed Mariella. 'Holy Mary, he's as crazy as that?'

'A madman whose associates have helped him rob the German people of their sanity,' said Carl. 'I've been speaking to Anne recently about moving to England. It's a natural choice because Sophie and James live there. Anne agrees we must all go.'

'Well, I for one would hate to be left behind,' said Mariella, 'even if the English aren't the same as Austrians.'

'Sophie doesn't find their insularity a great problem,' said Carl. 'You'll come with us, then?'

'Nothing will stop me,' said Mariella. 'London and its galleries and museums? Even its winter fogs with their ghostly lamplights have a strange appeal to an artist. My dear Carl, I can hardly wait. My lovely Vienna is suddenly a prison.'

'Mariella? Carl? Hello.'

Anne had arrived. Mariella flew, embraced her and kissed her.

'Anne, how exciting, Carl has been telling me we must all leave Vienna and go to England. Well, I've had a threatening visit from the Gestapo, a Kommissar Voegler, who's looking for Herr Meister because he's a Jew.'

'If he doesn't find him, he'll come back for Mariella,' said Carl. 'That's the way they work.'

'Then, yes, we must all go to England,' said Anne.

'As visitors,' said Carl. 'Then we'll apply for resident permits.'

'I am very agreeable,' said Anne, 'and Mama and Papa are thinking favourably about it. We must win them over.'

'What has Pia said?' asked Mariella. Pia was due to leave for Italy soon, with her daughter Lucia, to visit her mother in the Italian Tyrol. She would be back for the latter half of the Easter holidays.

'She isn't taking the suggestion seriously at the moment,' said Carl.

'Well, I am taking it very seriously myself,' said Mariella.

'Are we being impetuous, Carl?' asked Anne.

'Running too soon?' said Carl.

'Before we know which way the wind will blow?' said Mariella.

'I know which way it will blow,' said Carl.

'Yes, so do I,' said Anne.

'And I,' said Mariella. 'On top of everything else, I don't think Hitler is going to like the way I paint.'

Anne answered her telephone later that evening.

'Yes?'

'Baroness von Korvacs?' The voice was masculine, the German slightly accented. 'Baroness Anne von Korvacs?'

'Yes.'

'Bear with me, please. I'm a British freelance journalist, lately specializing in European affairs. You and I came face to face today.'

'So you are that gentleman,' said Anne.

'Gentleman? Thank you.' A warm little laugh reached her ears. 'My name is Gibbs, Matthew Gibbs.'

'Excuse me?'

'Gibbs.'

'Ah, Gibbs, yes, I have it. You were very helpful to me, Herr Gibbs. But how did you know who I was?'

'I was in a civil court here in Vienna about a year ago. The case had an interesting note for a foreign observer of what was happening in Austria. A husband had filed a divorce petition, on the grounds that his wife was having an affair with a Jewish gentleman.'

'Oh,' said Anne.

'I sat and listened, and I watched the lady with a great deal of interest.'

'I see.' Anne became cool. 'I was a subject for a sensational story?'

'Not in my book,' said Matthew Gibbs emphatically. 'I don't write those kind of stories, and certainly not about a lady of grace and dignity.'

'Herr Gibbs—'

'That was how I saw you. I asked a friend of mine about you, an Austrian journalist. He made me realize your family is quite well known in Vienna, and much admired. I'll not tell you what he said about your ex-husband, or what I myself thought of him at the time. Today—'

'Herr Gibbs, are you English?' asked Anne.

'Yes. Does it count against me?'

'Not in the least. How could it when I and my family know England so well, and I have an English brother-in-law who is dear to all of us?

No, I must correct that. His mother is English, his father is from Scotland.'

'An Anglo-Scot?'

'Yes, that is it,' said Anne.

'It's a small world, Baroness. My two children are Anglo-Austrian. My wife, looking after them at home, comes from Salzburg.'

'I'm happy for you, Herr Gibbs,' said Anne. 'Now, you wish to speak to me about this afternoon?'

'Indeed I do,' said Gibbs. 'I was guilty of using you.'

'Yes, you slipped an envelope into my coat pocket,' said Anne. 'But you also saved me from some unpleasantness. Thank you. If I'm not mistaken, you were arrested a few minutes later.'

'Detained, questioned and searched, Baroness. I'm speaking from a public telephone box. I've a feeling phone calls from my apartment are being monitored. Austria's in a sad way. My passport has been temporarily confiscated, and I'm being followed. There are two grey-looking gentlemen on my tail now. I wish to apologize deeply for using you. It wasn't the best thing I've done in my life, and I'm afraid you need to take care. The oaf who was bothering you was also detained, and made a complaint that I'd wrongly accused him of insulting you. They took no notice of that, and he's still under detention, I believe. We were both thoroughly searched, but they failed to find what I'm certain they were looking for.'

'Yes, because I had it,' said Anne.

'Yes, I'm damnably sorry, Baroness,' said Gibbs. 'A moment of panic.'

'I don't think it was panic, Herr Gibbs,' said Anne. 'It was very ingenious. Also, how thoughtful of you to have avoided speaking to me during your argument with that very unpleasant young man. Yes, and clever too from every point of view. Are you sure you're only a journalist?'

'A journalist, yes, and also a biographer. Nothing else. But journalism has led me into dark corridors recently. I'm desperately worried that in slipping the envelope into your pocket, I may have stored up trouble for you.'

'I shall do my best, Herr Gibbs, to present an innocent front.' Anne was not a timid woman. She had lived through the devastating war, the post-war troubles, and the years of an impossible marriage. She had acquired resilience and an ability to face up to whatever else life could throw at her. She had known this man, Matthew Gibbs, only for a few minutes, but by instinct she was prepared to trust him.

'Baroness, you must get rid of the envelope,' he said. 'I've managed to make what I think will be safe arrangements for you to pass it on.'

'It's something of great importance?'

He hesitated a little before replying.

'Yes. I'm told it could mean exposure of the anti-Christ when decoded and published.'

Anne knew he meant Hitler.

'Please continue, Herr Gibbs.'

'Baroness, if you can, please be at the Opera Theatre at noon on Tuesday. A man will meet you there. Simply say that you have something for him.'

'How will he know me?'

'He'll know you. Hand him the envelope, and then forget all about it. At the same time, forgive me. I must ring off. The two grey-looking gentlemen are—'

The phone clicked and went dead.

Chapter Three

'Now,' said Mrs Sophie Fraser in businesslike
fashion, and her children lined up with their
backs to the handsome bow window that gave
such a pleasant view of her beloved garden.
Whenever her children needed to be organized,
Sophie insisted that they present themselves in a
tidy row. It avoided the kind of disorder that
could make three fast-growing offspring sound
like a small mob. Of course, they all considered
themselves far too old for the ritual, but they
obeyed because Mama was fussy, eccentric, and
therefore to be indulged.

There were two girls and a boy.

Victoria Teresa, called Vicky, was eighteen,
had dark brown hair as lustrous as her mother's,
and brown eyes that could look unsure of
what was before her, because of myopia. Still
at college, she was an attractive and shapely
young lady who found life fascinating, was
given to quaint turns of speech and to making
frequent appeals for new clothes. Her mother
could say no to her, her father found this
impossible. Accordingly, Vicky sidestepped her

mother and beguiled her father.

Emma Jane, fourteen, was auburn-haired, piquant of face, round of eye, slightly plump and quick of wit. Her interests were many and varied, and short-lived.

Paul William was just seventeen, slim, agile and mechanically minded. Black-haired, he had a ready smile and an amiable disposition. His interests were radios and cars. He was very fond of Lucia, the adopted daughter of Uncle Carl and Aunt Pia. They wrote to each other, and Lucia had recently promised to look at the engine of her mother's old car with him. Her mother kept saying it needed looking at, and her father, who lived with cars daily at the Austro-Fraser works in Vienna, kept turning a deaf ear.

'We're assembled, Mama,' said Vicky. 'You may proceed.'

'Thank you,' said Sophie. She was in her forty-fourth year, a fact which caused her to use the bathroom scales daily. Although her weight was both reasonable and constant, one never knew what tricks might suddenly be played by advancing years. 'Now, children—'

'Steady, Mama,' said Paul, alarmed in case this generalization might be carelessly applied at the wrong time. One liked to be considered fairly manly by a pretty cousin. 'I'm not children.'

'I'm even less not,' said Vicky. 'Or is it more not? Well, whatever, I can say with confidence I've long been adultified.'

'Here, what sort of a word is that?' asked Emma Jane. 'You're showing off again, Vicky. I suppose it means this is just going to be between you and me, Mama.'

'It's between all of you and all of me,' said Sophie, thus putting herself in a winning position. 'Now, I know the three of you are bursting with energy, so Paul will make sure all his shoes are cleaned and polished before he finishes packing, and Vicky and Emma Jane will finish theirs immediately. I have nearly finished packing for your father and myself. Your father should be back from the garage any moment, when we shall have an early lunch, and show him how earnestly we are preparing to catch the afternoon ferry. Remember, everyone is to be ready by noon. There are to be no failures of any kind.'

'No, Mama. Yes, Mama. No, Mama.' It was a dutiful chorus. Mama's rounding-up of them, and her instructions, were on similar lines every year, with the result that the annual Easter journey to Vienna by road and cross-Channel ferry was often begun miraculously on time.

'Mama, Maisie's promised to help finish my packing and Emma Jane's,' said Vicky. Maisie was the live-in servant, a cheerful woman of whom the young people took full advantage. There was also a gardener, George Potts, who supplied the family with fruit in the summer and vegetables all the year round. The comprehensive nature of English gardens had been a source of delight and wonder to Sophie during her first years in the country.

'Maisie is far too busy,' she said. Her perfect English still retained a suggestion of a Viennese lilt, enchanting to her bilingual son and daughters. 'Vicky, where are your spectacles?'

'Mama, I only need them when I'm trying to read bus numbers or signposts,' said Vicky, 'not when I'm preparing to go to faraway places.'

Vicky considered myopia should never have been invented, and certainly not for growing girls. The shock of discovering, six months ago, that she could not clearly read a blackboard or distinguish the numbers of oncoming buses, made her write a protest poem.

'What can the world be coming to,
When cruelty it surpasses
By giving me myopia
And a pair of horrid glasses?'

Sophie expressed admiration for the poem and sympathy for the condition.

She said now, lightly, 'Yes, darling, but do remember to take them with you. You like to read the map for Papa.'

'But Daddy knows the route all the way,' said Emma Jane.

'Dear me, oh dear me,' said Sophie, 'you know Papa likes Vicky to make sure for him.' She ignored the fact that the children always called their father Dad or Daddy. They called her Mama because she insisted. James, however, did not insist on being called Papa. 'Now let me see. Have you all taken baths? Good. It simply isn't the thing to enter France looking grimy. Remember Waterloo and how clean and grand the English and Scots looked to Napoleon.'

'Clean and grand?' queried Paul, more inclined to believe the troops were all pretty filthy and a bit flea-ridden into the bargain. 'You sure?'

'Of course,' said Sophie, 'and I'm also sure it unnerved Napoleon.'

'Mama, that could have been the Scots' kilts blowing in the wind,' said Vicky.

Paul burst into laughter. Emma Jane giggled. Sophie kept her face straight.

'Shoo,' she said, and they scattered, laughing, exuberant and excited. It made her very happy, the fact that they loved spending Easter at her parents' home in Vienna. She and James were in the twentieth year of their marriage, having met in Vienna in the summer of 1914. But the war came, and instead of a wedding there was a bitterly quarrelsome parting, with James returning to England to fight against Germany and Austria. She thought that would kill her love, but when he reappeared in Vienna immediately after the war, she fell into his arms. They were married in January 1919.

She did not know where all the years had gone to since then. They spent the first twelve in Warwickshire, in a country cottage some ten miles from Coventry, where James worked for his father, Sir William Fraser, an industrialist and head of the Fraser Automobile Company. Although James had not been enamoured of cars, thinking them a dubious benefit to civilization, he had a natural talent for design. He worked hard to provide a good living for his family, very conscious of the fact that Sophie was the daughter of a cultured Austrian baron. Her mode of life in England was governed by what he earned as head of his father's design department. Sir William was generous up to a point, but never inclined to set aside the principle that what a man received should be decided by what he gave. James gave a great deal of his natural talent and a variety of good results.

He and Sophie ran a car of their own, but their especial delight during their years in Warwickshire had been a pony and trap. In the latter, Sophie explored the tranquil beauty of the countryside, and every Sunday she and James rode to church in it.

They were uncompromisingly in love during their time in Warwickshire. They had lost four years because of the war, and were often urgent to make up for that.

Victoria Teresa was born in the autumn of 1919. Paul William and Emma Jane followed at intervals. Sophie was very content with that. Three children and a husband were manageable. She managed them very well. It helped, of course, the importance she placed on having time for all of them. In return, she asked for James to have time for her. She made it clear from the beginning that he was to be her husband, lover and chief companion. She flatly refused to let him make a habit of working late at the Coventry plant. He was married to her, she said, not to his father's factory, and both he and his father must understand there were certain priorities to observe. James agreed she was his first priority, so instead of staying late at his work, he brought it home with him. There were nights when he was still up long after she'd retired to bed. Sophie began to express outrage. James unwisely suggested they had single beds, so that he wouldn't disturb her when he finally came up.

'Single beds?'

'It might be practical, Sophie.'

'Practical? What kind of a word is that?'

'It's just a suggestion you can kick around.'

'James, we are not going to have single beds. Single beds divide a husband and wife. I don't care how practical they are, they have nothing to do with marriage.'

'Well, as long as you don't mind being disturbed.'

'Disturbing me must stop. James, you obviously have too much work to do. You need a qualified assistant. Speak to your father.'

'I have, and a qualified man is being taken on.'

'There, you have done it, James. Good. You can come to bed now.'

'I'll just finish—'

'Now, James.'

They had been lovely years, exciting years. They were in calmer waters now. Sir William had opened a new plant in Weybridge in Surrey eight years ago, for the production of a sports car that would add new prestige to the name of Fraser. James was put in charge, and at last received what Sophie considered was no more than his due, a salary that made them feel affluent. At the same time, the racing car, the Austro-Fraser Comet, emerged from the Vienna production team headed by Carl. It became well known on the Brooklands and Continental circuits.

Sophie and James, with their children, moved from their Warwickshire cottage to a large and lovely house in Shepperton, close to the river, and there the peaceful flow of the Thames seemed very much in keeping with the calmer flow of their lives. Every Easter they went to Vienna. Every summer, Carl and Pia came over with their children, and so did Anne. But never Anne's husband, Ludwig. She had come last summer, not long after her divorce.

The visit to Vienna this year had suddenly taken on worrying overtones. Hitler had annexed Austria under the guise of unification. Sophie was appalled. Just as she considered the people of her beloved Austria to be easy-going and whimsical, so she considered the people of Germany to be orderly but Prussian-ized. All too easily they had now become slavish adherents of a demented political animal whose jackbooted troops were presently in occupation of Vienna. Sophie, however, backed up by James, was not going to abandon the annual visit.

Vicky entered her parents' bedroom, where her mother had just finished packing.

'Mama, I find I'm in desperate straits,' she said, her horn-rimmed spectacles perched on her reluctant nose. With her white blouse and brown pleated skirt, they gave her a studious look, appropriate to her final year at a college for young ladies. 'I don't know if I can finish my own packing. I've reached an impasse, an impasse of despair.'

'Darling, you alarm me,' said Sophie. 'How can I help?'

'It's too late for help,' said Vicky, 'we're leaving this afternoon.'

'So?' said Sophie.

'Don't you realize I've nothing to take with me except some old rags?' said Vicky.

'No, I don't realize that, my love,' said Sophie. 'You have some very pretty clothes, and your party dress is new.'

'New?' Vicky clapped her forehead dramatically. 'New? I've worn it countless times.'

'Twice, I think,' said Sophie.

'Mama, I'm not eight, I'm eighteen. At that age, twice is as good as countless.'

'Well, we can't have your packing left unfinished because of this impasse of despair,' said Sophie. 'I'll take you shopping in Vienna and we'll buy you one or two very attractive outfits. Will that help?'

'Mama, I'm constantly amazed at how indispensable parents are,' said Vicky. 'Some are quite ripping as well.'

'Ripping?' smiled Sophie.

'Helpfully nice,' said Vicky.

Emma Jane yelled on the stairs.

'Daddy's home, everyone! Jump to it, everyone!'

Sophie heard her husband's voice.

'Where's the fire, minx?'

'It's sort of invisible,' said Emma Jane, and entered the bedroom with her father a few

57

moments later. Fifty, he was tall and lean, and his five o'clock shadow along with his thick black hair, not yet touched with grey, often reminded Sophie of the images she had once conjured up of dark Balkan brigands.

The family car having been serviced for the journey, James had just collected it from the garage.

'Daddy, we're all packed,' said Emma Jane. 'Well, almost.'

'I suffered an impasse,' said Vicky, 'but it's been taken care of.'

'So go and finish,' said Sophie. 'You too, Emma Jane.'

'I must first say, Daddy, I've just discovered I like having parents,' said Vicky.

'I see, your mother and I are in favour at the moment, are we?' smiled James.

'Very much,' said Vicky, 'especially Mama.'

'Oh, do come on, Victoria, and stop gassing,' said Emma Jane. 'I want to know if you've got room in your case for some of my shoes.'

'You'll be lucky,' said Vicky, leaving the bedroom with her sister.

Sophie regarded James thoughtfully. Yes, she was still glad she had waited for him all through the war. She had few complaints about him as husband, lover and companion.

'Tell me, James, where have all the years gone?'

'Nowhere out of sight,' said James, 'they're all visible.'

'Are they?'

'Yes, every day, in the persons of Vicky, Paul

and Emma Jane. They're our years, Sophie. Of course, I daresay you could include our double bed.'

Sophie laughed. In a jersey wool dress of impeccable style, her appearance could not be faulted. Just as her sister Anne had the natural elegance of her kind, so did Sophie, and with a little extra flair. James always thought Sophie could have made something of herself even in sackcloth.

'Sometimes you find quite an inspired answer to a question,' she said. 'Now there's the question of how my family can possibly live happily under the Nazis. Can you find an answer to that?'

'I rather fancy Carl could find a better,' said James.

'Hitler has arrived in Vienna, and I hate the thought of the swastika flying over the city,' said Sophie.

'I spoke to the old man yesterday—'

'James, I've told you before, you are not to refer to Sir William as the old man. It's quite the most disrespectful thing.'

'It's—'

'Yes, an English thing. But I won't have it. Heavens, I should faint if Paul ever came to refer to you as the old man.'

'He probably does, Sophie,' said James. 'If not, he probably will, one day. Anyway, let me say I spoke to my respected father this morning. I wanted to find out if he knew exactly what might be going on in Austria's deeper waters. As you know, he does have contacts in Westminster and Fleet Street. There was just one thing that seriously concerned him. Hitler's police are laying heavy hands on Jews, Communists, opposition leaders and all people known to have publicly or privately expressed a rejection of Hitler and the Nazi Party. Sophie, your father is well known in Vienna. Has he ever publicly expressed his views on Hitler's brand of National Socialism? I know he considers Hitler an illiterate, and that he sees most Nazis as thugs.'

'James, my father is a diplomat of distinction,' said Sophie, 'too much so to ever be indiscreet outside his home. Dear God, Austria was mad to allow all this to happen. But we're going, aren't we? The family will be so disappointed if we don't.'

'Yes, we're going,' said James.

'You're resolute? Good,' said Sophie.

'Well, I want to see exactly what's happening in Vienna, and to confer with Carl on the Comet Mark Two,' said James. 'Most of all, I want to see how things are with your family. They're my favourite Austrians.'

'Tell me,' said Sophie, 'are you worried?'

'A little,' said James.

'So am I, a little,' said Sophie.

'It frankly concerns me,' said James, 'that Vienna, of all cities, has become a place in which men like Ludwig will exercise power and women like Anne and your mother will belong more and more to the past.'

Sophie winced.

'I thought we agreed that the name of that SS pig should not be mentioned in this house,' she said.

'Not in front of the children,' said James, 'that was the agreement.'

'I may soon ask not in front of me, either,' said Sophie. 'Now, will you please tell Maisie we'd like lunch served in ten minutes?'

'Will do,' said James.

Chapter Four

'Is there nothing at all on him?' asked SS Standartenfuehrer (Colonel) Ludwig Lundt-Hausen, former husband of Baroness Anne von Korvacs, and head of Vienna's SD, the Security Service of the SS.

'Nothing except the information he gave us about his career as a journalist and biographer, and of course our knowledge of his recent association with Staffler,' said the plain-clothes Gestapo officer. His name was Hans Voegler, and he had the finely austere look of an intellectual.

'We're still holding his passport?' said Ludwig, glancing up from his desk.

'Yes,' said Voegler. 'He's made representations to his embassy, and we've informed them he's under investigation. They don't like it.'

'I don't suppose they do,' said Ludwig sourly. 'The British have an arrogant belief that their country is an example of incorruptible rectitude, forgetting that they nurture the most extensive collection of corrupt Jewish bankers in the world. Gibbs's link with Staffler, how was this discovered?'

'By accident.' Voegler, a high-ranking officer of the Austrian Gestapo, the secret police arm of the SS, was compelled by the official nature of the interlocking relationship to give full assistance to all investigations launched by Colonel Lundt-Hausen, a bitter and cold man with whom it didn't pay to argue.

Voegler had all the information the Colonel needed at his fingertips. 'It was thought by the Berlin authorities at the time that Gibbs was American, since he was accredited to a New York magazine. Staffler himself wasn't under suspicion. He'd been a trusted member of the Fuehrer's secretariat for years. One of our German colleagues spotted him with Gibbs in a second-rate Berlin restaurant several weeks ago. He thought it strange, a man as important as Staffler dining in a restaurant no-one would recommend to anybody, but put it down to the fact that members of the American Press Corps will eat anywhere, as long as there are beef-steaks on the menu. Also, Dr Goebbels has always insisted on maintaining a cordial relationship with the American press. It's been a matter of policy for all representatives of the Fuehrer to go along with American eccentricities, here as well as in Germany. It's resulted in the German Reich receiving fairly favourable notices in American newspapers. Americans on the whole are likeable but gauche.'

'You're speaking of a people famous for their vigour and enterprise,' said Ludwig caustically. 'Why are you giving me a history of their country when the subject is a damned Englishman?'

'Because, as I've already mentioned, it was thought at first that Gibbs was American,' said Voegler. 'To continue, our colleague in Berlin credited Staffler with no motive but that of being agreeable to Gibbs.'

'So?' said Ludwig impatiently. His right leg was throbbing. It always gave him trouble until warm weather arrived. It had been severely wounded during a campaign against the Russians in Galicia in 1915. Captured, he had something to thank a Russian army surgeon for in the saving of his leg. But the post-operative treatment had been minimal. Discharged far too soon, he was freighted with other captured Austrian soldiers to a prisoner-of-war camp while his leg was still in a bad way. The treatment at the camp was almost non-existent. The flesh of his leg had wasted. It was still not much more than skin and bone, and it made him a limping man. He could not do what other men could in the heat of summer, put on swimming trunks and bathe in a pool or in the sea. His leg looked skinny and ghastly. He hated Russians, and he hated the Austria that had allowed him to suffer and linger in a prisoner-of-war camp. The hatred embraced all people who had supported the old haughty and autocratic regime of Franz Josef, the regime that had done nothing for its soldiers held in primitive conditions by the Russians.

'However,' said Voegler, 'our Berlin colleague mentioned the incident to his superior when Staffler's name came up in conversation a few days later. He mentioned it in passing, not in suspicion, but his superior ordered an immediate investigation.'

'A correct decision,' said Ludwig.

'Discreet surveillance was arranged and a thorough search made of Staffler's apartment while he was at work,' said Voegler in his dry manner. 'Nothing incriminating was found, but unfortunately Staffler obviously suspected a search had taken place, and he slipped the surveillance team. He disappeared. But he was seen in Vienna later. So was Gibbs. Berlin had been in touch with us, letting us know they'd discovered that a copy of a highly secret document was missing from a file in Staffler's office. His presence in Vienna was reported to Berlin by our underground organization, and also the fact that Schuschnigg's security police were giving him protection. Schuschnigg ignored Berlin's request to extradite him, but he also ignored Staffler's request for safe conduct to Hungary. That would have put him one step away from Poland, the country relevant to the top secret document. Schuschnigg, obviously, wanted to use Staffler in some way. He knew a meeting with the Fuehrer was inevitable, since the Fuehrer had made it clear he was not going to indefinitely tolerate Schuschnigg's hostility towards the Austrian National Socialist Party.' Voegler paused and drank some water. 'I suggest Schuschnigg hoped to go to the meeting with a card up his sleeve, a card supplied by Staffler. It didn't work. The Fuehrer isn't a man to be blackmailed by someone equating with a priggish schoolmaster. It's no wonder Schuschnigg was despatched to a concentration camp. We had kept watch on Staffler, and had orders from Berlin to arrest him as soon as Schuschnigg's security police had been dispossessed of power following the unification of Austria and Germany. The power was ours then. Two of my men broke into Staffler's apartment, but the idiot leapt to his death.'

'Correction, I think,' said Ludwig, dark face sardonic.

Voegler, not a man to be easily discomfited, showed a faint smile.

'Certainly, a warning shot was fired from the window,' he said. 'Which caused him to leap or fall from the roof.'

'Which in turn caused him to die and keep his traitorous secrets to himself,' said Ludwig.

'An unfortunate outcome, Herr Colonel.'

'Very, since nothing of importance was found on him or in his apartment,' said Ludwig.

'But a man seen running was followed and eventually caught,' said Voegler. 'It was Gibbs, who we then discovered was British, not American, an observer of and commentator on European affairs. He was detained, questioned and searched. It's suggested he took something from Staffler before he began his run. But nothing was found on him. However, as you know, we impounded his passport and are watching him. He won't be allowed to leave the country, and the phone in his apartment has been tapped.'

'Have you thought about how he came to be on the spot when Staffler fell from the warehouse roof?' asked Ludwig.

'Naturally,' said Voegler. 'Staffler had something to tell Gibbs or to give him or sell to him, and we know he was in the apartment and that he must have slipped out when my men were at the bedroom window.'

'In which case, his presence was carelessly overlooked,' said Ludwig.

'Carelessness, Herr Colonel, is not commonly practised by the Gestapo,' said Voegler, never inclined to show the fault of resentment, irritation or impatience. 'It's our firm belief that Staffler did pass something to Gibbs, either when they were in the apartment together, or outside after Staffler's fall. In some way, between the time my men saw him running and the time when they were able to detain him, he must have got rid of what he received from Staffler. I have to say, however, that he was not seen to do so. On the other hand, we're still holding a young man seen talking with Gibbs just before we arrested them both. Nothing suspicious is known about him, and he claims to be a supporter of the Party. He's given us no information. He swears he has none to give, that he had never seen Gibbs before. He also swears Gibbs was abusive to him, accusing him of improper advances to a woman in the crowd.'

Ludwig, silently suffering painful throbs in his cursed leg, said, 'Now why should a man, knowing himself wanted and pursued, concern himself with something stupidly irrelevant at a moment when your men were closing in on him?'

'An attempt, I suggest, to make irrelevance

seem like the action of a man bothered by nothing except the behaviour of a young man.'

'You think so?' Ludwig looked sarcastic. 'Interrogate the young man again. Drag out of him all he can tell us about the woman. And irrespective of whether he can tell you much or little, find her.'

'I take notice of that, Herr Colonel,' said Voegler. 'Incidentally, our attempts to locate Josef Meister are still proceeding. '

'Ah, yes, you went to his home and then his gallery after you were compelled to release that damned Englishman,' said Ludwig bitingly.

'By your order, Meister was to be brought in that day,' said Voegler.

'You got as much out of Mariella Amaraldi as you did out of Gibbs, precisely nothing,' said Ludwig, who knew Mariella was the sister-in-law of Carl von Korvacs, the latter a member of a family he had come to despise as archaic relics of a decadent and lost Empire. 'You can interrogate her again too. She knows where the Jew is, I'm damned certain she does. Let her know her face can be spoiled.'

'I take notice of that also, Herr Colonel,' said Voegler, eyes reflecting nothing of the fact that he entertained an acute dislike of Lundt-Hausen.

'They're here, Ernst,' said Baroness Teresa von Korvacs happily. The hall was alive with the sounds of arrival. After many hours on the road and two overnight stops, the Fraser family had reached the house on the Salesianergasse just before noon on a crisp and sunny morning.

Heinrich, knowing he would be overtaken by the energetic young people unless he was quick, left it to Hanna to help with the removal of hats and coats, and accordingly won the annual race to the drawing room. All too often the young people succeeded in preceding him, rushing in on their Austrian grandparents. It was a matter of correct protocol to Heinrich to announce all visitors before they entered the presence of the baron and baroness. He only won by a whisker on this occasion. Then Vicky, Paul and Emma Jane poured into the drawing room, where their maternal grandparents received them with an affection that led to a demonstrative exchange of hugs and kisses.

Sophie and James entered less noisily, but Sophie was quick to embrace her mother, then her father.

'Mama, how well you look,' she said. 'And you look quite splendid, Papa.'

'Do you say so?' smiled the ageing baron.

'Of course,' said Sophie.

'For myself, I think the excitement has given me a flush,' said the baroness, and turned to receive a very affectionate greeting from James, which included a warm kiss on each cheek. She responded with an unreserved smile and an endearment. She could never forget how much invaluable help the family had received from him at the end of the war.

James shook hands vigorously with the baron,

69

and they exchanged some informative conversation without any mention of the Anschluss being made. Not in front of the children, Sophie had said.

Vicky, Paul and Emma Jane calmed down after a medley of enthusiastic comments, and Heinrich then brought in a tray of refreshments. Over it everyone talked at once.

A girl, vividly brunette, came in. The adopted daughter of Carl and Pia, Lucia was fifteen. She had been orphaned at the age of two by the death of both parents in an avalanche. They had been immediate neighbours of Pia's mother, and as Pia and Carl were there at the time, a process began which led to the adoption.

Lucia already had an Italian lushness, and Paul considered her a stunner.

'Oh, hello, you're here,' she said in English. She was as fluent in English as in Italian and German.

'Who's this?' asked James.

'Uncle James, it's me, you know it is,' said Lucia.

'Well, I'm suitably impressed,' said James.

'So am I,' smiled Sophie.

'So fast some girls grow these days,' said the baroness.

'Oh, good morning, Grandmama, good morning, Grandpapa,' said Lucia, 'good morning, Aunt Sophie, Uncle James and cousins. How pleased I am to see all of you.'

Sophie, knowing the girl had a crush on Paul, smiled at the effect of her entrance in an apple-green dress obviously new.

'Lucia, you look delightful,' she said.

'We're all positively enchanted,' said Vicky.

'Are we?' said Emma Jane. 'Oh, yes, I suppose we are.'

'It beats me, what happens to girls,' said Paul. 'Advance and be recognized, Lucia.' Lucia presented herself to him with a visible blush. How sweet, thought Sophie. 'Well, now I know that it's really you, Lucia,' said Paul, 'let's get busy.'

'Excuse me?' said Lucia.

'Goodness me, yes, busy at what, might we all ask?' said Vicky, eyes bright behind her clarifying spectacles.

'A pertinent question,' smiled the baron.

'Oh, it's just that Lucia and I have arranged to look at the engine of her mother's car,' said Paul. 'If it's in the garage.'

'Yes, it is,' said Lucia, delighted that Paul considered her qualified to inspect a car engine with him. 'We can go there now.'

'Are my ears deceiving me?' asked Sophie.

'Is there a problem, Mama?' asked Vicky.

'You bet,' said Emma Jane, looking at Lucia's new dress and stockings.

'It's only a car engine, Mama, not a bomb,' said Paul.

'I forbid it,' said Sophie.

'Can you forbid a car engine?' asked James. The baroness smiled. She was happy that she and Ernst were now so conversant with English that they could follow all the little nuances that were part of a Fraser family dialogue.

'I am sure, James, that I have no idea myself how to forbid a car,' she said.

'Nor I,' said the baron.

'I am being mocked,' said Sophie, who badly wanted to speak to her parents in private about the annexation of Austria. 'Paul, I forbid any attempt by you to put Lucia within touching distance of a car engine. She will ruin her dress. Further, young man, in that suit you are not to go within touching distance of it yourself. Have I now made myself clear?'

'Clear as a silver bell, Mama,' said Vicky.

'All right, we'll look at it later, Lucia,' said Paul. 'We can both get into something old and shabby. But I feel too busy to stand about until lunch, so I'll take you for a walk, if you like.'

'Oh, yes, I do like,' said Lucia.

'Lunch will be served soon,' said the baroness, 'so why don't all you young people go out together this afternoon?'

'Suits me,' said Paul.

'I'll come,' said Emma Jane.

'We all will,' said Vicky, 'I'm curious about—' She checked. 'Yes, let's all go.'

'Where's Anne?' asked James, particularly fond of his sister-in-law.

'She's out,' said the baron, 'but assured us she would be back for lunch.'

Chapter Five

It was a little before noon when Anne entered the foyer of the Opera Theatre. There were people around, some at the box office, some consulting the programme for the month, and some apparently simply dwelling on the imposing nature of the foyer and thinking of the wonders that lay beyond it. The atmosphere created by the theatre's history and tradition could excite one's imagination. Neither violent politics nor national crises could diminish its appeal. To Anne, it symbolized the splendour of Imperial Austria.

A German SS officer appeared. He surveyed the foyer as if the Party had been responsible for the creation of the Renaissance-inspired theatre. Anne experienced a little tremor. She was again wearing her cream-coloured raincoat and blue hat, thinking that perhaps whoever was to meet her here had received a description of her from Matthew Gibbs. The simplicity of the outfit was faultless, but because of the SS officer she wondered if she had made a mistake in wearing it again. However, she did not let any apprehension show as the SS officer glanced at her. Casually, she checked the time by her wristwatch. The man's glance lingered for a few moments, then he joined the queue at the box office.

At the front of the queue a tall man in a light grey coat and hat smiled and murmured thanks as he received an envelope containing tickets. He moved from the window, looked around, saw Anne and strolled up to her.

Lifting his hat, he said politely, 'You have something for me?'

That was what Herr Gibbs had told her to expect. Just that. All the same, she had thought it would be a little more dramatic. She looked up at the man. His smile was warm and reassuring. His features were weathered but handsome, his brown moustache faintly tinted with gold. A man exceedingly distinctive, she thought.

'Yes, mein Herr, I do have something for you, but I think that SS officer has been looking at me,' she said.

He laughed, very lightly, and just as lightly took her arm and led her from the theatre to the pavement.

'SS men are addicted to looking,' he said, 'but chiefly in cupboards and under the beds of people unfortunate enough to have upset them. They're very sensitive, poor devils, and take offence at the drop of a hat. But, occasionally, even a dedicated SS officer will look at a lady simply because she's worth more than a mere glance.'

Anne smiled.

'Thank you,' she said, 'and am I to give you the envelope now?'

'I think it will be perfectly safe to do so before we part company,' he said. People were passing, strolling, hurrying or stopping. The March day was bright, the Ring recapturing some of the colour stolen by winter. German army vehicles moved ponderously amid the traffic, and there was a suggestion in the fitful movements of some elderly people that the shadow of Hitler lay across the approach to the theatre. Vienna's initial exhilaration had gone, and the traumatic nature of the Anschluss was keeping many Viennese awake at night. The tall gentleman, however, appeared not to have suffered any sleeplessness himself. His eyes were quite clear, his smile unworried. 'Let me find you a taxi,' he said, 'and you may give me the envelope before you step into it. That, I think, will be more agreeable to you than handing it over here.'

'I confess to feeling I must be cautious,' said Anne.

'Let's walk,' he said, and they began to saunter, like two people of friendly acquaintance.

'Baroness – '

'You know who I am?'

'Yes, I know,' he said. 'It wasn't intended to make you a conspirator, to have you act as a courier and worry about how best to pass on a certain envelope. Do accept my friend's sincere apologies for landing you with – ' He smiled again. 'A hot potato.'

'Oh, but I'm enjoying my moment,' said Anne, 'and must tell you I'm madly curious.'

They stopped in their slow walk. He regarded her with interest. Anne felt an awareness of the fact that in his maturity he too must have known the long and golden pre-war summers, the summers that seemed to hold such fine promise for the future, with the premier countries of the world awakening to the need for more compassionate government. War and revolution had smashed that promise and brought years of misery to millions. This man had lived through all that, as she had.

'We are all curious about one thing or another, Baroness, but sometimes it's better to remain curious than to acquire knowledge. Knowledge isn't always beneficial. My friend will regret that his action has made you curious.'

'You may tell him I'm quite happy he was able to make use of my pocket,' said Anne, 'and as for being curious, isn't it true that curiosity was the incentive that led to the most beneficial discoveries of mankind? Allow me, please, the stimulation of being curious myself.'

'I'd never dream of depriving you, I'd only suggest it would be safer to remain curious and not informed.'

'But Herr Gibbs did inform me that what was in the envelope was very important,' said Anne.

'Is that so?'

'I pressed him, I'm afraid,' said Anne, the sunshine enhancing the clearness of her skin and the blue of her eyes. 'May I know who you are?'

'That's a fair question, I think. I'm John Kirby, from the United Kingdom.'

'I was sure you weren't German or Austrian, because you don't have a German or an Austrian way of speaking,' said Anne. 'My sister Sophie lives in your country. She's married to an Anglo-Scot, a lovely man.' Anne wanted to talk a little, especially as she felt she and John Kirby were a natural and innocuous part of the everyday scene. 'The rest of my family are thinking of moving to England. So am I.'

John Kirby, who knew every capital in Europe and had spent many years in Russia, said, 'Because Vienna is not what it was?'

'In my lifetime, it is never going to be what it was, or even close to what it was,' said Anne.

'You preferred the Vienna of the Habsburgs, Baroness?'

Anne, noting some uniformed Austrian Nazis a little way off, said, 'With all my heart, Herr Kirby. But that, of course, is because I lived a privileged existence.'

John Kirby thought of the close-guarded and privileged existence of the late Tsar's daughters, and how it had ended for all of them under a hail of bullets in a house in Ekaterinburg.

'Looking back, Baroness, can be painful for some of us,' he said.

'Not as painful as looking at the present,' said Anne.

'Baroness, if you and your family do decide to leave Austria, bear in mind that your borders are now being closely policed. Your new masters have their eyes on people they consider not entitled to leave.'

'Not entitled?' said Anne. 'No members of my

family have done anything to forfeit the right to travel freely abroad.'

'Accept my advice to take care, Baroness,' said Kirby. 'The National Socialist Party has a way of qualifying people's rights. Freedom, you know, is a casual thing to people who have it, a haunting thing to those who have lost it, and a strange dream to those who have never had it.'

'My brother's sister-in-law has a feeling her freedom is threatened unless she tells the Gestapo where a certain Jewish gentleman is living,' said Anne. She confided the details.

Kirby looked intensely interested.

'You're speaking of an artist called Mariella Amaraldi?' he said.

'Yes,' said Anne. 'Could you possibly know her?'

'My wife and I bought one of her canvases earlier this week,' said Kirby, and he too confided details. 'A charming lady and an excellent painter. If the Gestapo have their eyes on her, she needs a little protection. Now, let me call you a taxi.' He escorted her to the edge of the pavement. 'I hope, Baroness, we'll meet again, and in a less conspiratorial way. It's been a great pleasure to— Watch out!'

Two men came running, arms and legs moving fast, feet flying, bodies bruising the air as they raced for the pavement. Kirby took Anne by her right arm and pulled her clear. She saw the straining, sweating faces of the two men as they rushed by, desperate in their flight. Two cars turned in from the Opernring, accelerating noisily. They screamed and swerved through traffic. One came to a halt close to Anne and Kirby. Pedestrians stopped. Some slipped away hastily. From the car spilled uniformed Austrian SS men. They burst into pursuit of the running men. An officer alighted unhurriedly and stood to watch the chase that was scattering people to right and left, his hands smoothing his black gloves. He was tall, thin, dark and emaciated. The two running men turned a corner and disappeared, the SS men in full cry after them. The officer's eyes flickered and came to rest on Anne, only a few yards away.

Anne, looking into the face of Ludwig, her ex-husband, gave no sign that she was affected. She might have given him a look of contempt, but did not. She simply refused to acknowledge his presence. She knew him to be so twisted and embittered that he had come to see her as someone who intruded on his private darkness. And he knew that she had come to regard his moods as resulting from morbid self-pity. The rise of the Nazis had offered him an opportunity to find outlets for his hatred of people. And now that the Nazis were in power in Austria, he could look forward to years of persecuting all enemies of the Party and to settling scores with everyone who had offended him. His was the black uniform of the Austrian SS, now no different from the German SS. Overnight he had advanced from the rank of Sturmbannfuehrer (Major) to Standartenfuehrer (Colonel), and was as far removed from the easy-going man of 1914 as any henchman of the sadistic and odious Himmler.

There was, of course, mutual recognition. The cold eyes flickered again, then regarded her companion icily. The dark, lined face seemed to distort, and Anne knew what he would say of her to his colleagues, if he said anything at all.

'She's finished with her Jew. She's a cunning whore. She's found an Aryan lover.'

She did not flinch as he gave her a second glance. She looked through him. John Kirby noted her compressed mouth and her set expression. He moved forward, and it startled Anne to hear him address Ludwig.

'Trouble on the streets, Herr Standartenfuehrer?'

Icy eyes met enquiring grey.

'Only for those who can't keep out of it,' said Ludwig, then turned and re-entered the car. The SS man at the wheel drove off in the direction of the chase.

'A gentleman with many problems, Baroness,' said Kirby.

'Why did you speak to him?' asked Anne. 'Do you know him?'

'Happily, no,' said Kirby. 'He reminds me too much of Lenin's Bolshevik commissars, a deadly species.'

'You knew Russia during its revolutionary times?' said Anne.

'Yes,' he said, and was reflective for a moment. 'My wife is Russian.'

'Would you care to know that that SS officer was once my husband?'

A little frown appeared.

'A pity, Baroness, that he saw us together. A

man's ex-wife always holds some interest for him, even if only a hostile interest.'

'I assure you, Herr Kirby, he regards me as an anonymous nothing,' said Anne. Her thoughts quickening, she asked, 'Are you known to the secret police here?'

'I hope not, but their filing system is very extensive. Baroness, a taxi.' He had caught sight of one. He hailed it. It turned in their direction. 'May I say it's been a pleasure to meet you and talk to you? I understand now why Matthew Gibbs was so impressed.' The taxi pulled up. He opened the door, then offered a handshake. Anne put her hand into his and the envelope was transferred. 'Goodbye now,' he said, 'and I wish you peace and happiness.'

'Thank you,' said Anne. 'Goodbye.'

As she slid into the taxi, he murmured, 'Thank you for keeping such a cool head.' He closed the door and stood and watched as she was driven away, a woman of grace and elegance. There were such women still to be seen in Vienna, all belonging to a lost world in which they had existed as a privileged class. Today was the day of the politically privileged. But they had little idea of how to live and behave graciously. The privileged political class in Soviet Russia knew only how to exercise tyranny. Laughably and pathetically, they were more acceptable to liberals than old-world aristocrats like Baroness Anne. Silks and satins, coronets and courts, were out of favour in the seething capitals of disturbed European nations. Good manners had disappeared.

Kirby slipped his hand into his coat pocket, depositing the small envelope, and called a taxi for himself.

Early that afternoon, when Ludwig was back in his office, Voegler entered to deliver a report on his morning's work.

'I'm listening,' said Ludwig, stubbing out a cigarette. His men had failed to catch up with two running Jewish brothers this morning, and that, on top of his brief encounter with his ex-wife, was grating on him.

'Concerning the further interrogation of the young man, Walther Grasse, detained as a suspected contact of the Englishman Gibbs,' said Voegler. The interrogation had been thorough, the young man had howled a bit, but had come up with no information on the woman. No name, no address, no anything. He repeatedly swore he did not know her, had never seen her before, and all he had done was to justifiably accuse her of being an anti-Nazi because of her indifference to the arrival of the great Fuehrer. And all she had said to him was that she was not immune to events. However, he was able to give a correct description of her.

'Which was?' said Ludwig.

'To begin with, he estimated the woman was about thirty-seven,' said Voegler. Anne might at least have been pleased that the offensive youth had seen her as four years younger than she was. 'Good-looking, very fair, with blue eyes. Slender, and a little above medium height. Dressed in a cream-coloured raincoat and a dark blue hat.'

Ludwig's mouth tightened, and his eyes flickered.

'You are sure that's a correct description?' he said.

'I'm sure, Herr Colonel, that the interrogation was of a kind to guarantee correctness.'

'I believe you're also sure that despite his association with Staffler, the Englishman Gibbs is only a journalist and not an agent, yes?' said Ludwig.

'I repeat we have nothing on him,' said Voegler.

'Nevertheless, I'd like to see the file of photographs you have of British agents,' said Ludwig. 'Now, if you can manage it.'

Voegler effected the errand without pointing out he was not an office boy. SS Colonel Lundt-Hausen had the patronage of Seyss-Inquart, the new Chancellor of Austria, and Seyss-Inquart had the patronage of both Hitler and Himmler. Accordingly, it did not pay to cross Lundt-Hausen, never an even-tempered man and, at the moment, even more splenetic than usual.

Ludwig made a careful inspection of the file. There were no photographs identifiable with Matthew Gibbs, but he did come across two, one in profile, the other full face, of the man he knew he had seen this morning in company with Anne von Korvacs. Ludwig forgot his aching leg for the moment.

'This man,' he said, turning the file. Voegler took a look. 'You have his comprehensive personal file?'

'Yes,' said Voegler, and his photographic

memory went to work. 'Very experienced British agent. Clever, diligent, resourceful. Impressive record. Russia before and during the war. He was with the White Army during the Revolution, arriving in Ekaterinburg along with the Czech Legion just too late to save the Tsar and his family from execution. Subsequently, he married a Russian woman, and was active elsewhere. He has unusual flair. He became an intimate of the Tsar and his family, and it's fairly certain he had a love affair with the Grand Duchess Olga, the Tsar's eldest daughter.'

'An unusual flair indeed,' said Ludwig. 'What next is expected of him, that he'll become an intimate of the Fuehrer and have an affair with Goering's wife?'

Ignoring the sarcasm, Voegler said, 'No known activities during the last four years. He's—'

'No known activities?' said Ludwig. 'Is that because his unusual flair renders him invisible to our security services?'

'He's fifty-two,' said Voegler impassively, 'and probably retired from fieldwork. By the way, his views on the Soviet Central Committee are unprintable.'

'Due to the murder of his Grand Duchess?' said Ludwig, and lapsed into thought. The man, John Kirby, was here in Vienna, and Voegler did not know. It was something for the uniformed service to be ahead of the Gestapo. And it paid to keep ahead. He looked at the photographs again. Yes, that was the man he had seen with Anne, a woman of irritating pity and maddening patience. She had fashioned for herself the halo of a wife gently embracing martyrdom. She belonged, however, to the class that had pitched Austria into a horrifying war against the uncivilized peasant soldiers of Russia. She had sent him off to that war with a brave smile and sentimental cant, and she and her kind had allowed thousands of Austrian soldiers to rot and perish in unspeakable prisoner-of-war camps. And when he had limped back, she had posed as a loving and pitying wife, as a gentle nurse and patient angel.

He had come to hate Anne, and her family, and in the end to divorce her, implicating a Jewish friend of hers in the process. The damned woman knew the extent of his lies. So did the Jew. That was bitter gall, but how else could he have got rid of his white-winged albatross? The Jew had to be found and eliminated. As a Jew, of course, under the edict of the new order, not as a skeleton in the cupboard. And there was still Anne, who had looked through him this morning, the bitch.

So, she had been with John Kirby, a British agent of long standing.

Slender, very fair, with blue eyes and wearing a cream-coloured raincoat and dark blue hat.

So, she had also been close to another Englishman on the day of the Fuehrer's arrival, an Englishman who called himself a journalist and writer, and who had almost certainly received something from the traitor, Staffler.

'Herr Colonel, what is the reason for your interest in this British agent?' asked Voegler, not inclined to favour a situation that kept him standing about like a clerk.

He received a smile. It was not the smile of a comrade or friend. It was the smile of a wolf.

'My own reason,' said Ludwig. 'Voegler, where is the Jew, Josef Meister?'

'I'm arranging for the Italian woman, Mariella Amaraldi, to tell us later today,' said Voegler.

'I hope your arrangements will be effective,' said Ludwig. 'By the way, release the young man, Walther Grasse.'

'Release him?' said Voegler.

'You've arrested the wrong person.'

Chapter Six

It was terrible. Vicky and Paul looked on in-credulous and horrified. Lucia and Emma Jane, fortunately, were elsewhere, seeking a gift shop. Lucia wanted to buy a little present for Paul, without him knowing, of course. They were all to meet again later, in the gallery where Aunt Mariella was exhibiting paintings.

Vicky and Paul could not believe what was happening. Uniformed Nazis and young thugs had smashed the window of a shop and broken down the door. In front of a crowd of silent onlookers, they were dragging out the owner. Red streaked the afternoon sky, casting flushed light over this street off the Graben. Vicky and Paul knew the area well, and liked its atmos-phere, reminiscent for their parents of the charm of old Vienna. They had never imagined violence could intrude in such an awful and ugly way.

There was nothing charming at all about the smashed window and looting hands, or anything more sickening than the treatment of the shop owner. And it was totally unbelievable to see two State policemen turn their backs and walk away.

Vicky trembled, eyes enormous behind her glasses, and Paul was rigid with outrage. They were appalled by the hysteria of the thugs and the manner in which insults were screamed at their victim, middle-aged, black-bearded and be-spectacled. He had offended, apparently, not only by being a Jew, but by locking his shop door against them. With kicks and blows, they tumbled him into the gutter. His spectacles fell off and were crushed beneath a grinding jackboot. His mouth and nose were bleeding.

Some of the silent onlookers began to react. Vienna had not known the pogroms of Berlin, and several of its milling citizens did not like what was happening. A woman called out.

'Shame on you! Leave him alone!'

She was ignored, except by one uniformed Party member, who gave her a look, as if memor-izing her. The bruised and buffeted Jew came to his feet, staggering. Blood stained his beard. He was knocked down again.

A man shouted.

'Butchers! Hooligans! That's enough!'

Vicky felt Paul vibrating with anger beside her. She put a hand on his arm. She wanted to go, to fly from a scene that numbed the senses, but she stayed, and Paul stayed, both instinctively feeling that to run was to desert the weak and countenance brutality. Some of the men in the crowd would do something to help, surely.

A young man and a girl ran from the shop. They tried to break through the circle of vicious-ness, to get to the bearded man, their father. The girl begged the tormentors to show mercy, and her brother hit out. That earned him a savage blow in the face, and the struggling girl was struck in a way that sent her flying and falling.

'Dirty Jews! Filthy Jews!'

That was too much for some onlookers. Brutality was bringing shame on Vienna, even if a certain amount of anti-Semitism had reared its ugly head in the city from time to time. But this was intolerable and several men surged forward to strike a blow for the unfortunate. A tall young man in a navy blue sweater and grey trousers, in company with a beefy sympathizer, reached the dazed elderly victim and helped him to his feet. Momentarily, the thugs held off, gaping at an act of intercession made, by all that was un-believable, on behalf of a stinking Jew. The beefy man put an arm around him, other men formed a barrier to prevent the thugs snatching him back, and the tall young man brought the girl up from the ground. The thugs howled in fury, the uniformed Nazis shouted threats and warnings, and within seconds a brawling and dangerous melee began. Vicky and Paul were caught up in a seething crowd. The mistake the Austrian Nazis had made was in failing to orchestrate a suitable overture to their perform-ance. Their brothers in Berlin did these things so much better. Anti-Jewish propaganda went in advance of action, so that what was meted out to Jews was what the public thought they deserved.

Paul, becoming separated from Vicky, threshed around. He glimpsed her. A uniformed Nazi had her by her left wrist and was twisting her arm cruelly up over her back. Vicky was gasping in pain, her face white. Paul struggled to get at her. The tall young man materialized. People were scattering in retreat from the affray, spiriting the Jewish family away.

'Let the lady go, and take that, you pig,' said the young man, and kicked Vicky's assailant in the back of his right knee. He yelled, staggered and turned. The young man kicked him again, in his left knee, and then hit him hard. Down he went. Vicky's dislodged spectacles slipped off. A hand caught them. Screams, yells, blows and kicks punctuated the riot, and Vicky now had only a blurred picture of its ugliness.

'What's happening, what's happening?' she gasped in English.

'Never mind that,' said the young man, also in English, 'just run.'

'No, I can't – my brother – '

'Tell him to run too. Best thing at the moment.'

'My spectacles, please,' gasped Vicky. He gave them to her, she put them on and saw a milling fighting mob, but not a single policeman. She spotted Paul, struggling to get free of a red-faced, sweating thug. 'There, that's him, that's my brother.' She pointed.

The young man charged in and delivered another of his kicks. The thug yelled in pain. He let go of Paul. That was a mistake, for Paul and the young man jumped him together and downed him. He disappeared amid trampling feet and bruising bodies. Out came Paul and the young man.

'Run,' said the latter again. 'If the police do

condescend to break this up, you'll find they're biased in favour of the swastika.'

Sensibly then, Vicky and Paul ran, the young man with them. From the other end of the street, the police were beginning a tardy advance. Reaching the Graben, the young man stopped. Vicky and Paul pulled up.

'Oh, that was awful,' gasped Vicky. Her brown velvet blazer had lost a button, her white sweater was smudged and her pleated skirt was awry. She straightened it. She had a terrible feeling her stockings were laddered. Her little knitted pull-on hat was askew, her chestnut hair escaping in curling clusters beneath the rim. But her face was clean, if pale. The young man took an enchanted look at her. He saw big brown luminous eyes framed by the horn-rimmed spectacles. Vicky, quite naturally, removed them in a casual way, as if she didn't really need them. The young man looked again. Her colour came back and was tinted by slight pink. She saw clear blue eyes, a smile, and a young man healthily brown and athletic. She saw Sir Galahad. She smiled. 'On behalf of my brother Paul – that's him – I must thank you profusely, kind sir,' she said.

'I second that,' said Paul, 'and propose thanks on behalf of my sister Vicky.'

'You're welcome,' said the young man, brushed brown hair looking somewhat unbrushed.

Vicky, her customary poise surfacing, said, 'Are you a practised rescuer of people in distress?'

'Not very,' he said, and laughed. 'I'm much more practised at running.'

'Good thing we did run,' said Paul, brushing himself down. 'Listen, are you English?'

'I'm fifty-fifty. Well, English father, Russian mother.' The young man smiled. 'Very Russian. I'm Nicholas Kirby.'

'Nice to meet you,' said Paul. 'By the way, Vicky's famous, you know.'

'For what?' asked Nicholas, giving her another look.

'She walks on water,' said Paul. 'Well, she did once. Only she sank. Dad pulled her out. He asked her what she'd been doing. She said she was playing Jesus.'

'Please take very little notice of Paul, Mr Kirby,' said Vicky. 'At home, we mostly put him on a par with our potted plants. By the way, our family name is Fraser, and I'm actually Victoria Teresa.' Vicky liked her names. 'I was baptized, of course, in honour of the memory of Queen Victoria and after my maternal Austrian grandmother. Oh, yes, and our mother is Austrian and our father Anglo-Scottish. Do you think that a proud and splendid mixture, Mr Kirby?'

'I don't think I want to be called Mr Kirby,' said Nicholas. 'It makes me sound like my father, and I'm not quite as old as he is.'

'Well, I'm not as old as mine, either,' said Paul with a grin.

'One is never quite as old as one's parents, is one?' said Vicky. Reaction took over then, and she said quietly, 'Why are we talking like this? That was a terrible incident. That poor man. I wanted to cry for him, but was too angry. Imagine something as awful as that happening in

Vienna. Our mother will be dreadfully distressed. She was born here, and always says that before the war, Vienna was the most civilized and cultured city in all Europe. I'm not sure what she'll say about it now.'

'But things like that don't happen here every day, do they?' said Paul. 'D'you know if they do?' he asked Nicholas.

'I think there'll be complaints, probably from the police about what a noisy racket it was,' said Nicholas. 'I think they'll probably ask the Hitlerites here to organize their activities like they do in Germany. More efficiently.'

'I've got a horrid feeling you're right,' said Vicky. 'I mean, we've all heard things, haven't we?'

'Germans will tell you they're rumours,' said Nicholas, 'but they're not.'

'That poor man,' said Vicky again, distressed. 'I felt dreadful, because he didn't just look bruised and hurt, he looked terribly sad.'

'He was Jewish, did you realize that?' asked Nicholas.

'Yes,' said Vicky.

'You know, don't you,' said Nicholas, 'that the Jews represent a problem to the Nazis that Hitler says has got to be solved?'

'Have I heard about that?' Paul asked the question of himself more than of Nicholas. The fact was that in a world of cars and wireless sets, a fellow didn't rate politics high on his list of interests. Politics were for when you were about fifty. 'I honestly haven't read much about Hitler,' he said, 'but I know our parents didn't like him taking over Austria.'

'I think I must do some serious reading of newspapers,' said Vicky. 'I think I want to know a lot more concerning certain things one hears about but doesn't bother about.'

Nicholas, thinking the subject too depressing for this young lady and her brother after their ordeal, said, 'Enough of unpleasant things. Are you both recovered?'

'I feel a bit bruised, but that's all,' said Paul.

'I feel rescued in the nick of time,' said Vicky, and put her glasses back on. She gazed around. Everything seemed very normal, although there were a lot more uniforms to be seen than in previous years. They were all Nazi uniforms. 'I also feel for people who are a problem to Hitler.'

'I'd like a strong coffee,' said Nicholas. 'Would you two care to join me?'

'Not half,' said Paul. There were still forty minutes to go before they met Emma Jane and Lucia.

'Thank you, Mr Kirby,' said Vicky.

'Could you manage Nicholas instead of Mr Kirby?'

'Well, yes, if you really don't want to feel quite as old as your father,' said Vicky.

The coffee shop they chose was warm, cosy and typical of Vienna in its general appeal. There was a waiter with a round, balding head and a round, smiling face. He served them with the coffee and tempted them with a platter of delectable cream pastries. It was a temptation Paul could not resist. Vicky tried to, but failed. As for Nicholas, he took two.

'This sort of weakness is very enjoyable,' he

94

said, and the waiter beamed and looked at Vicky, who had taken her glasses off again.

'Very nice, yes?' he said in English.

'Yes, I think so too,' said Nicholas, responding in German, and the waiter departed happily.

'Did he mean me or my pastry?' asked Vicky.

'Good question,' said Nicholas.

'Well, I must decide he meant me,' said Vicky. 'After all, what girl wants to take second place to a pastry, even if it is delicious?'

'This is our first day in Vienna,' said Paul through a mouthful. 'We come every year at Easter to stay with our Austrian grandparents.'

'I'm here with my parents,' said Nicholas, 'my Russian mother and my English father.'

'Yes, you're Anglo-Russian, aren't you?' said Vicky. 'How fascinating. We're very polyglot ourselves, we're half Austrian, a quarter Scottish and a quarter English, as I mentioned. We're extremely nice, though. At least, I am.'

'I'm not going to argue,' smiled Nicholas.

'How kind,' said Vicky. 'I shall recount the story of your gallant charge to my family. Mama will be agog.'

'The way you'll tell it, they'll all fall about,' said Paul.

'No, they'll be shocked at first at such a dreadful happening,' said Vicky, 'but Mama will find wondrous consolation in the story of my rescue. She always says that the deeds of the brave cast a shining light over the dark wickedness of villains.'

'She sounds something like my own mother,' said Nicholas.

'Oh, there have to be our kind of mothers,' said Vicky, 'or there'd be no conversation at breakfast.' She was enjoying the civilized atmosphere of the cafe and the company of a new friend. 'Paul, d'you want to tell Mr Kirby – well, Nicholas – about how Mama was once rescued by Daddy against overwhelming odds?'

'Oh, that story about Bosnia and the brigand?' said Paul. 'Yes, all right. It was before—'

'Yes, before they were married,' said Vicky, 'when they were adventuring in the wild hills of primitive Bosnia. Well, it came about that Mama found herself in the frightening clutches of an enormous brigand, who she declared was almost as big as a mountain.'

'As large as that? Ye gods,' said Nicholas.

'Dad was desperate,' said Paul, 'so—'

'Yes,' said Vicky, 'he could visualize his beloved Sophie – that's our mother, his beloved Sophie – being carried off and lost to him for ever.'

'Very worrying,' said Nicholas.

'Worrying?' said Vicky. 'I should say it was. The brigand was like a huge mountain covered by a vast black forest. That was his enormous beard, you know. Our Aunt Anne, Mama's sister, will confirm everything I'm saying, because she was there too, and also in the brigand's clutches.'

'Two beautiful maidens in similar distress?' said Nicholas, greatly amused.

'Yes, utterly frightful, wasn't it?' said Vicky.

'However,' said Paul, 'Dad decided—'

'He decided it was do or die,' said Vicky, 'so he launched himself like a thunderbolt at the brigand, seized his legs and actually upended him. He crashed like a blasted oak tree—'

'A what?' asked Nicholas.

'An oak tree blasted by lightning,' said Vicky, 'and was utterly done for. Naturally, Mama fell madly in love with Daddy. Well, who wouldn't have? Mama wrote a poem about it. She called it "A Mountain Fell". It began—'

'Spare us,' said Paul.

Vicky smiled.

'It began, "In blood-red heat the fiery day,
Too hot for picnic parties,
From the fiery mountains drew
The giant Avriarches."'

'Avriarches?' said Nicholas.

'That was the brigand's name,' said Paul. 'He was a Greek. Did you like the way I told the story? I'm not often asked by Vicky to tell it. Well, she usually likes to tell it herself.'

'Fascinating,' said Nicholas, smiling at Vicky.

'Oh, I've been trying to be light-hearted,' she said, 'but I keep thinking of that poor man, bruised and bleeding, and the young man and the girl who tried to help him and were knocked down. I felt they were his son and daughter. It was terrible to see all the hate, and I was fiercely glad when some of the men went for the dreadful hooligans. I shall tell my parents how you led the charge, Nicholas. Oh, you must call one day and meet them, don't you think so, Paul?'

'Well, it's certain Dad will want to thank him,' said Paul.

'I'll call with pleasure,' said Nicholas, 'but play down the rescue stuff or your parents will think

I've come for a medal. It really wasn't very much, just a rush of blood to the head.'

'No, it was almost life and death,' said Vicky. 'Modesty is all very well, but you mustn't let it confuse my sense of deep gratitude.'

'You missed out undying,' grinned Paul.

'Mama will probably fall on your neck.' Vicky smiled eloquently at Nicholas. 'And you will probably fall in love with her, especially if she's wearing a hat. Mama is astoundingly beautiful when she's got a hat on. I've an awful feeling she's going to unintentionally deal my social life the most mortifying blows. Mr Kirby – Nicholas – are you laughing?'

'On my honour, no,' said Nicholas.

'I should hope not,' said Vicky, 'it's not amusing, you know. I shall never be able to keep a young man unless I hide him from Mama. My present young man, Clive Mortimer, met her when he had lunch with us on Boxing Day. It was a fatal error of mine to invite him when Mama was presiding.'

Paul choked on his last mouthful of coffee.

'Fatal?' he said.

'How fatal?' asked Nicholas.

'He hasn't looked at me since,' said Vicky. 'We meet and talk sometimes, but I'm only a kind of vague outline to him. He sent Mama flowers.'

'That was for the lunch,' said Paul.

'I have to brace myself for a very complicated future,' said Vicky. 'Is your future like that, Nicholas?'

Nicholas, whose father was sure it would be a miracle if Europe could avoid another war, regarded Vicky with a great deal of thought.

'My immediate future concerns a degree,' he said. He was nineteen, athletic and travelled. 'I'm at Bristol University, and I've a sister attending Badminton College.'

'Well, you're very brave,' said Vicky, then stiffened a little as two uniformed German soldiers entered the cafe. They stopped on their way to a table to deliberately look her over. She did what her mother would have done. She looked through them. They laughed, one said something to the other, and they both laughed again before moving on. Nicholas grimaced.

'They expect to inherit the earth,' he said.

'Paul,' said Vicky, 'I think we must go and meet Lucia and Emma Jane.'

'Yes, we'd better,' said Paul. He got up and shook hands with Nicholas. 'Thanks for everything,' he said.

Vicky came to her feet and so did Nicholas.

'Goodbye, Nicholas,' she said, 'we're enormously pleased to have met you.'

'If I'm to call and fall in love with your mother,' he said, 'could I have your address?'

Vicky smiled and gave it to him, and he memorized it.

'When will you come?' she asked. 'Not tomorrow. Mama's taking me shopping.'

'Thursday afternoon?' suggested Nicholas.

'At three thirty, say?' said Vicky. 'Then you can have afternoon tea with us.'

'Champion,' said Nicholas, and stayed to pay the bill while Vicky and Paul left to go to the Meister Gallery.

On the way, Paul said, 'Mum and Dad might not be in Thursday afternoon. You know how Mum likes to visit old friends and Dad likes to spend time at the factory with Uncle Carl.'

'Well, you and I will be able to receive our guest,' said Vicky.

'I might be in the garage with Lucia.'

'But Lucia will be on her way with Aunt Pia to visit her Italian grandmother,' said Vicky.

'Oh, so she will,' said Paul, 'I forgot.'

'Never mind, she'll be back in a few days,' said Vicky.

'But it's still not much good Nicholas coming to meet our parents if they're not going to be there,' said Paul.

'Oh, we can invite him again,' said Vicky casually.

Chapter Seven

Mariella suspected the coldly clinical hunter of Herr Meister would pay her another visit if he had failed to locate him. Her suspicions proved correct.

Attendances at the gallery had improved once Vienna's initial hysteria had died down. Some people were taking a new look at the situation, and some were calmer than others, calm enough to indulge an interest in Mariella's exhibition. A very kind middle-aged gentleman had spoken quietly to her today after buying one of her pictures, expressing admiration for her talents, and following that up with a gentle word of warning. It was a warning to the effect that as the gallery was owned by a Jewish gentleman, her exhibition might not last the week out.

'You mean, mein Herr, that it might be smashed up?'

'It is that kind of thing, Fräulein Amaraldi, that Austria has let herself in for.'

'Then Austria has inflicted a death wound on herself,' said Mariella.

The hunter, Voegler, arrived later, with three

hatchet-faced assistants. Some people might have questioned whether or not the ratio of four men to one woman was necessary. It was to Voegler. He knew Ludwig Lundt-Hausen badly wanted Josef Meister.

Mariella was now in the office with two henchmen and Voegler himself. Outside the closed door stood the third assistant to ensure that none of the visitors interrupted, and to tell enquirers that Fräulein Amaraldi was temporarily unavailable. Voegler was explaining the reason for his call.

'Since we consider it impossible that the Jew, Josef Meister, did not inform you where he was going, Fräulein, we have decided you must tell us. If you refuse, you will have an accident.'

'What kind of accident?' demanded Mariella.

'Facial, perhaps?' suggested Voegler. 'A broken nose, perhaps? Something that would spoil your looks?'

'You are disgusting,' said Mariella, 'but surely not as disgusting as that. Could any man be, any man who has a mother? See how you left this office the other day? Look at it.' She had tidied nothing up, although she had moved a few things out. 'That is bad enough. In any case, how can I tell you something I don't know? I repeat, I've no idea where Herr Meister is.'

'Fräulein, I'm not here to waste time,' said Voegler.

'Pigs,' said Mariella.

'Where is Meister?'

'I don't know!'

Voegler nodded, and one man, slipping behind

her, took hold of her arms and wrenched them up behind her back. The other man placed himself in front of her and scrutinized the perfection of her nose. Mariella shuddered at the thought of a blow that would break it and leave her disfigured.

'Quivers?' said Voegler. 'How touching. Don't scream, by the way, or the blow will be immediate.'

Mariella, outraged, hissed, 'You are animals, all of you!'

'Where is Meister?'

'My God, I have to tell you, don't I? But first, allow this man to release my arms.'

'No. First you'll tell us, Fräulein.'

'While this pig is hurting me?'

'Where is Meister?' Voegler, a calculating professional, had no intention of breaking her nose. He preferred psychology.

'If I tell you, will you promise to ensure my exhibition is not smashed up?' It was an attempt by Mariella to make him believe that the importance of her exhibition meant more to her than witholding the information he wanted.

'You aren't Jewish, Fräulein Amaraldi. Your exhibition will last its time, but the gallery, perhaps, will change its owner.'

'Very well,' said Mariella, 'there's a Meister shop in the Graben.'

'It's not a shop,' said Voegler, 'it's merely a rented closed-in window used to display some paintings.'

'Yes, with a notice informing potential buyers to contact Herr Meister here, at his gallery,' said Mariella. 'But behind the window is a room he uses to store various canvases. It's his little warehouse. The door at the side of the window will take you through, although it's bound to be locked. Herr Meister went there on the morning of the day you first called, and is staying there, in hiding. He comes out only at night. I didn't want to tell you, but since I don't wish to be brutalized, I'm forced to. May I now have my arms released?'

Voegler nodded again, and she was freed.

'Is there a key to the door at the side of the window?' asked Voegler.

'There must be,' said Mariella, 'but Herr Meister would have it, wouldn't he? I imagine that's no problem to you, however. I'm sure you have a way of opening a door without the use of a key. May I ask another favour, that you don't tell Herr Meister I've given him away?'

'It's our practice, Fräulein, not to disclose our sources of information except when absolutely necessary,' said Voegler. His strangely pleasant smile briefly appeared. 'That's all. For the moment.'

He was gone a minute later, with his men.

Mariella wondered if she had prepared the ground convincingly. A spare key to the door of the storeroom was kept in a drawer in Herr Meister's desk. She had gone to the Graben, taking with her tinned food, tea, coffee, two plates, some utensils, and the cup and saucer Herr Meister had left on his desk, stained with coffee grounds and bearing his fingerprints. She left another cup and saucer in place on the desk, making sure the cup contained coffee leavings too. Deliberately, she had made no attempt to clear up the mess Voegler had made. The replacement cup and saucer stood where the originals had.

On her way to the shop she bought a litre of milk, poured some of it away and left the rest, along with the tinned food, tea, coffee and other items on a table in the little storeroom. She handled everything with her gloves on, and she had hidden the key.

Voegler, of course, would have no trouble forcing an entry. She hoped that what he would find would convince him Herr Meister had been using the place as a hideout. Where he actually was, Mariella did not know, but she suspected he was attempting to leave the country, if he had not already succeeded in doing so.

When she came out of the office, after spending a few minutes reorientating herself, several visitors were in the gallery. With her nerves still a little on edge, she sat down at her desk. Almost at once someone approached and addressed her in a discreet murmur.

'Forgive my impertinence, Fräulein Amaraldi, but I think you've just had a visit from the Gestapo.'

Startled, Mariella looked up into the enquiring eyes of the golden-haired woman whose husband had purchased *English Cottage* for her.

'Frau Kirby?'

'Yes, we meet again, you see,' smiled Karita Kirby.

'Yes, I do see,' said Mariella. She glanced at the people absorbed in her canvases. 'Shall we talk in the office?'

'Willingly.'

In the office, Mariella said, 'How did you know about the Gestapo?'

'I was passing and saw them leave,' said Karita, elegant in a fur-trimmed blue coat and fur hat. Actually, her husband had asked her to pay a courtesy call on Fräulein Amaraldi and find out if she had any worries. He hadn't forgotten what Baroness Anne von Korvacs had told him, and he and Karita both felt disposed to help Mariella.

'How did you know they were Gestapo men?' asked Mariella.

'I have a nose, Fräulein, for the smell of Bolsheviks,' said Karita. 'Bolsheviks, Gestapo, they are all the same, they all have the same look, the same smell. Are you in trouble?'

Fascinated by this woman and affected by her obvious sympathy, Mariella told her what the visit had entailed, and what she had done in the way of laying a red herring. Karita laughed softly.

'Very good, Fräulein Amaraldi,' she said. 'I like you. We shall send you a protector.'

'A protector?' said Mariella.

'My husband and I wish to ensure that neither you nor the *English Cottage* come to any harm,' said Karita. 'Questions aren't necessary. Goodbye again for a little while.'

'But—'

'Not to worry,' smiled Karita, and left.

Amid her bewilderment, Mariella felt oddly reassured. Again she went back into the gallery and at once saw two young girls whom she knew. They came quickly towards her.

'Aunt Mariella!' Emma Jane was dramatic in her greeting. 'I'm ever so proud of you.'

'Are you?' Mariella smiled. 'Good, I think.' Her English was excellent, having profited from her visits to England. 'So, you have come again to Vienna, you and your family. And now, with Lucia, to look at my paintings?'

'Yes, I brought her,' said Lucia, and they all began to use German.

'Lucia, we brought each other,' insisted Emma Jane, 'you know we did.'

'It looks like that,' said Mariella.

'A man told us we would have to wait to see you,' said Lucia.

'Yes, I had some business to attend to in the office,' said Mariella, and then exchanged family news with the two girls. Lucia was a long-accepted family member.

Vicky and Paul arrived, and warm greetings and fraternal familiarities were the order of the moment. Vicky and Paul said nothing about the incident that had so shocked them, and Mariella said nothing about the Gestapo and Herr Meister. She conducted all of them around the gallery, smiling at the extravagance of Vicky's comments.

Voegler, having used a skeleton key to open the door beside the window display, found evidence in the storeroom that convinced him Meister the Jew was indeed using the place as a hideout.

'Don't touch anything,' he said sharply. 'Leave everything as it is. You two, Bauer and Lutz, take up surveillance until you're relieved this evening. If Meister appears, let him enter. He'll find nothing to make him suspicious. Go in, catch him off guard, arrest him and bring him immediately to headquarters.'

'Yes, Herr Kommissar.'

'An arrest, perhaps, will make up for the fact that Fräulein Amaraldi preferred opening her mouth to letting you break her nose, Lutz.'

'Very disappointing, Herr Kommissar, but I'll get over it,' said Lutz.

Voegler gave him a withering glance. He did not personally use violence. He did indeed prefer dialogue and subtlety, but when the tools of violence were to hand and no information was forthcoming, the orders of Lundt-Hausen took priority. In this instance, the final orders, correctly interpreted, meant only one thing. Smash her face in. If Voegler, like Himmler, would not do so himself, his men would, providing he gave the word.

'What if the Jew doesn't appear?' asked Bauer. 'What if he doesn't show up today, tomorrow or the day after? Do we go back to Fräulein Amaraldi and give Lutz another chance to change the shape of her face?'

'If she's told us the truth, she'll still be where we can find her,' said Voegler. 'If she's been lying, she'll already have disappeared. I'll look in at the gallery on my way back to headquarters.'

He did look in. Briefly. The Italian woman of Austrian citizenship was still there, conversing animatedly with some young people.

Baroness Pia von Korvacs, Mariella's sister and Carl's wife, returned home at five o'clock, following lunch and afternoon tea with a friend. She took a hot, luxuriating bath. Sophie and James and their children had arrived. Pia had seen their car on the forecourt. But she wished to present herself to them refreshed and changed.

Her pride was always close to the surface. It suffered agonies when she was told, after the birth of her son Franz, that she could have no more children. The adoption of Lucia had been a joyful consolation.

At thirty-eight, she was still very Italian in her vivid brunette looks and her volatile temperament. She could still experience jealousy if women looked speculatively at Carl, particularly young women. He was a war veteran of distinction. That alone excited some of them, never mind his popularity as a racing driver. The modern generation of females shocked Pia with their boldness and brashness.

She loved this grand house belonging to Carl's parents. The atmosphere of old and gracious Vienna, like some benevolent ghost, permeated every spacious room, and kept at bay all that the ageing baron and baroness disliked of the modern world. Even the proliferating evils of Nazism were kept out. There was no-one in the house who liked Hitler and his policies. Pia told Carl a year ago that the new order in some European countries didn't seem a great improvement on the overthrown old order, although she thought Mussolini had not done too badly for Italy. Carl in his dry way said the Italian dictator hadn't done half as well for Italy as for himself.

Her bath finished, she dressed, then sat at

her dressing table to apply delicate make-up. Carl entered the bedroom. He was home from the factory, lean-bodied like his brother-in-law James, and handsome in a tailored grey suit.

'So there you are, Pia,' he said.

'Yes, here I am,' she said, 'I've just had a bath.'

'With scented soap,' said Carl, and bent and kissed her temple.

'You're home a little early,' she said. 'Has something happened?'

'We had a visit today from two gentlemen belonging to one of the new ministries,' said Carl. 'They were quite impressed with our plant. I wasn't so impressed with them. However, I'm home a little early to see James and Sophie, and to talk to them. Anne's arranging for the talk to take place in her apartment, in half an hour. I think you'd better join us.'

'Is it about this suggestion to leave Austria and live in England?' asked Pia.

'Yes,' said Carl.

'It's crazy,' said Pia. 'There's Franz, we must think of him and his studies.' Their seventeen-year-old son was a student at a music academy in Salzburg.

'We must think of his future,' said Carl, 'and spend this weekend discussing everything with Anne, Sophie and James, and then with my parents.'

'No, no, you've forgotten Lucia and I are going to visit my mother tomorrow for a few days,' said Pia, 'and that Franz is joining the train at Salzburg.'

'I'll phone the academy this evening, and

tell Franz to make the journey on his own,' said Carl. 'You and Lucia can go after we've all come to a decision one way or the other about England.'

Pia stood up. Her admirable figure was sheathed in a creation of glossy peach that did a great deal for her vivid looks.

'I can't believe you're serious,' she said.

'Pia, the two officials who looked over the factory today advised the directorate at the end of their inspection that we're to receive financial help to re-equip the plant, so that by September we should be ready to begin the production of armoured cars.'

'Armoured cars?' Pia looked disbelieving.

'Yes, Pia,' said Carl soberly. 'Hitler, soon or late, is going to get his "living room" by going to war with one of his neighbours, or two of his neighbours, or even with all his neighbours. I don't want my family to be here when that happens.'

'Mother of God,' breathed Pia, 'not another war.'

'Austria is going to be swallowed up, Pia. Its head is already in the mouth of the Nazi wolf. So will you delay your visit to your mother while we decide what we should do, what would be best for all of us?'

Pia hesitated, then said, 'Yes, Carl. You must telephone Franz, and I will telephone Mama. I will make an excuse of some kind. Carl, we could consider going to Italy.'

'To Il Duce? Hitler's best friend?' Carl shook his head. 'I think not, Pia. Mussolini is Italy's warlord. Mariella is ready to leave with us, if we decide to, but not to Italy and Mussolini.'

'Mariella?' Pia's eyes flashed. 'You've seen her?'

'At her exhibition on Sunday, not in her bed, you goose,' said Carl.

'But sometimes I think I am having to compete with my own sister,' said Pia.

'For what?' asked Carl.

'For you.'

Carl laughed. Pia bridled.

'You're having to compete with your own imagination,' said Carl.

'Mariella is in love with you,' said Pia, 'and always has been. It's shameful you have never discouraged her from making eyes at you. She should be whipped.'

'That's rather hard on her,' said Carl, who was on familiar ground with his temperamental wife. 'Try a little talk.'

'A little talk?' Pia flounced about. 'No-one could have a little talk with my sister. It would last for ever.'

'Not a good way to go,' said Carl, shaking his head. 'If, when you arrived in the presence of our Heavenly Father, the two of you were still talking, His welcome speech might well fall on deaf ears.'

Pia stopped flouncing.

'That is very irreverent,' she said. A smile broke through, and she wrapped her arms around him. 'But also very funny.' He kissed her and, as usual then, all was forgiven and forgotten until the next time.

*   *   *

Sophie was aghast. The young people had returned from their outing to find her and James in the apartment that was their own. Vicky and Paul had recounted the incident that had so shocked them. Lucia and Emma Jane listened along with Sophie and James, their eyes wide open. Sophie simply did not want to believe that such a terrible thing could happen in Vienna, but Vicky, in giving a very sober account without any kind of light-heartedness, was all too convincing. So was Paul.

Sophie, in shock, looked at James. James was grim. Anne, entering, was immediately conscious that something was very wrong.

'What has happened?' she asked, and it was Paul who gave her the details. She was no less appalled than Sophie, but while Sophie still found belief difficult, Anne had no doubts. She remembered the hysterical adulation of thousands of Viennese for Hitler and his Storm-troopers. She remembered the fanaticism of the unpleasant youth, the jackboots pounding in pursuit of two desperate running men this morning, and the hatred Ludwig bore for Jews and the enemies of National Socialism. She was only surprised that a number of men had actually taken sturdy issue with the Jew-baiting hooligans. 'I've just been listening to the radio news,' she said. 'Among the reports was one to the effect that a troublesome family of Jews had provoked a riot near the Graben, and that the police were seeking to make arrests.'

'That's foul,' said Paul.

'It's a damned disgrace,' said James.

'It's disgusting,' said Sophie.

'And perhaps it's only the beginning,' said Anne.

'It's an abominable beginning,' said Sophie.

'But I wonder, Sophie, does it really surprise us?' said James.

'Surprise us? I'm close to fainting with horror,' said Sophie. 'Paul, how could you take Vicky into such a dreadful thing as a street riot?'

'Me take her?' said Paul. 'I couldn't take Vicky anywhere she didn't want to go. Actually, we were sucked in.'

'Well, I'm truly thankful that you and your sister managed to survive,' said Sophie.

Vicky, whose sober account had contained only a brief mention of a rescue act, said, 'Oh, for that you must most of all thank the young man who helped us.' Her addiction to theatrical descriptiveness made another recovery. 'He was truly heroic. He led the charge like King Henry at Agincourt, and other men followed. With guns to the right of them, guns to the left—'

'I think that was Balaclava, not Agincourt,' said James.

'Oh, for guns read hooligans, Dad,' said Paul, wanting, like Vicky, to lighten the atmosphere.

'All I know was that it was tremendously splendid,' said Vicky. 'Our King Arthur—'

'King Arthur?' said Anne.

'Oh, Vicky's off now, Aunt Anne,' said Emma Jane.

'Well, I was put in mind of gallant knights,' said Vicky. 'This one was the first to get to that poor, battered man, and then those dreadful hooligans were all fire and fury, and Paul and I were caught up in it. The young man charged to rescue us too, and bore us away on wings of blessed deliverance.'

Emma Jane suddenly let go a giggle. Sophie gave her a severe look.

'Well, I mean, Mama, wings of blessed deliverance,' said Emma Jane, 'that's a bit much, even for Vicky,'

'I fail to agree,' said Vicky, 'it's a very apt metaphor. Mama, Paul and I were overcome with gratitude, and not at all injured. He's just got a small bruise on his forehead, and I've got torn stockings. Well, a ladder, anyway.'

'Oh, Vicky, Vicky,' said Sophie.

'No, Vicky's emerged bravely,' said Anne, 'and so has Paul. It could easily have made them ill with shock.'

James regarded his son and elder daughter with new eyes. Damned if they hadn't come out of this with their chins high, Vicky with her sense of humour intact and Paul with his resilience uncracked. He let a little smile show.

'Proud of the pair of you,' he said.

'Oh, I'm in splendid fettle myself,' said Vicky. She looked at her father and made a little face. 'Yes, it was dreadful, and unbelievable too. But we all had some reviving coffee with cream pastries in a charming cafe. So please don't worry, Mama. Except,' she added soberly, 'about that poor Jewish family.'

'One will worry,' said Sophie, and thought about Josef Meister. She and James had been told by her parents that they were harbouring him.

'Nicholas was very concerned about everything,' said Vicky.

'Nicholas?' said James. 'Could that be the heroic young man?'

'That's him,' said Paul.

'A hero, how fascinating for Vicky,' said Lucia.

'In the cafe, he told us Jews were going to have a bad time,' said Vicky.

'He's probably right,' said James, thinking of Oswald Mosley and what his Blackshirts got up to in London's East End.

'Is he well informed on something that's a mystery to me?' asked Sophie. 'It's absurd. Why should people of a certain religion be given a bad time? Is it a warning that they must change their beliefs?'

'I think we both know it doesn't mean that, Sophie,' said James. 'I think our heads have got to come up out of the sand. Hitler's fostering gangs of damned dangerous maniacs.'

'Not in front of Lucia and Emma Jane, please,' said Sophie.

'Oh, we understand, Aunt Sophie,' said Lucia. 'Myself, I often hear Papa saying the same thing.'

'Mama, we're not really children, you know,' said Emma Jane. 'Not now, anyway, not after what happened to Vicky and Paul.'

'I object to unpleasant events making you all grow up too fast,' said Sophie. 'Vicky, who is this young man who has talked to you about the Jews?'

'Oh, you'll like him,' said Paul.

'I should like to thank him, yes,' said Sophie, 'but who is he?'

'His name's Nicholas Kirby,' said Paul.

'Kirby?' said Anne, startled. 'Kirby?'

'Oh, do you know him, Aunt Anne?' asked Vicky.

'No, I know no Nicholas Kirby,' said Anne. But she did know a John Kirby, an impressive man. The coincidence of the English surnames was remarkable. However, she had a secret to keep for the moment.

'He's English,' said Paul, 'but with a Russian mother.'

'Russian?' said Anne. John Kirby had said he had a Russian wife. Could Vicky and Paul have possibly met his son? 'You liked him, Vicky?'

'Oh, I'd say he was passably nice, in addition to being quite civilized,' said Vicky.

'I liked the tremendously heroic bit best,' said Emma Jane.

'Yes, how exciting for Vicky,' said Lucia.

'Paul thought we should ask him to call so that Mama could thank him for his bravery,' said Vicky. 'Oh, yes, and we told him of Daddy's bravery when he felled the giant brigand, Avriarches, many years ago, Aunt Anne. He was most modest about his own deed. Mama, he's calling at three thirty Thursday afternoon. He won't mind if you're wearing something old and comfortable. And no hat.'

'Something old and comfortable, and no hat?' said Sophie, classical in a costume of dove grey.

'Sort of motherly,' said Paul. 'Not too stunning.'

Anne laughed. Sophie didn't.

'Motherly?' she said in horror. 'What am I listening to?'

'Vicky and Paul, that's what,' said Emma Jane, 'and that's enough for anybody.'

Looking at her elegant Aunt Sophie, Lucia said, 'No, no, Vicky, you can't turn a swan into a pigeon.'

'Then I fear I'm doomed to live in the shade of Mama,' said Vicky.

'Such an absurd joke,' said Sophie. 'How can you make any jokes at all after such an alarming happening?'

'I'm only trying to wear a brave face, Mama,' said Vicky.

'Yes, darling, and we're really quite proud of it,' said Sophie, 'but no more jokes, if you please. I'm still very disturbed. Now, if all of you will go down and see Hanna, she will give you some refreshments to keep you going until dinner. We have to go with your Aunt Anne to her apartment and meet Aunt Pia and Uncle Carl. We have to talk together.'

'What about?' asked Paul.

'About all of us,' said James.

'And on Thursday we'll meet Mr Nicholas Kirby,' said Sophie.

Chapter Eight

Pia expressed genuine delight to see Sophie and James, even if she was envious of Sophie's slenderness. Carl's pleasure was just as genuine, but not quite as fulsome.

'Felicitations, Sophie,' he said. 'Welcome, James. You both look very healthy.'

'Healthy? Listen to the man,' said Pia, brilliant with colour. 'Sophie, how chic you are always, yes, always so much in the fashion. And you, James, you are getting more distinguished every year, and very attractive to women with wandering eyes, I am sure.'

'I don't recall any wandering my way,' said James.

'I intercepted them,' said Sophie, 'and they're all buried at the bottom of the garden.'

'Off with your heads,' said Anne, 'you're fiddling while Rome is burning.'

James said, 'Come over to England this summer, all of you.'

'That's a thought,' said Carl.

'Stay indefinitely,' said James.

'Yes,' said Sophie.

'We understand,' said Pia.

'It's something we're here to talk about,' said Anne, 'and something our old ones are thinking about.'

'I must tell Carl and Pia what happened to Vicky and Paul this afternoon,' said Sophie, and did so. Carl listened with compressed lips, Pia with her eyes huge.

'*Mamma mia*, is it possible?' she breathed.

'I said it was only the beginning,' observed Anne, 'and I say so again now.'

'Sophie,' said Carl, 'are you and James aware that Josef Meister is living in this house?'

'To put it frankly,' said James, 'we're aware he's in hiding here.'

'Mariella's exhibition has received a visit from a Gestapo man looking for Herr Meister,' said Carl.

'This is terrible,' said Pia.

'But we all surely know by now that Hitler's hatred of the Jews is paranoic,' said Carl.

'His followers hate everyone who isn't as fanatical as they are,' said Anne.

'Which is why we have to talk very seriously,' said Carl.

'Carl, pour some drinks, please,' said Anne, 'and then we will do that, we'll talk very seriously indeed.'

Later, when there was still some time to spare before dinner was taken with the baron and baroness, Anne called Lucia, Emma Jane, Paul and Vicky to her apartment, where Sophie let them know she wanted them to listen to a few things.

'Shall we line up?' asked Emma Jane.

'Line up?' said Lucia.

'Oh, Mama always insists we line up whenever she has something to say to us,' said Emma Jane. 'It's to prevent disorder.'

'You're excused on this occasion,' said James.

'I am only going to speak a few words myself,' said Sophie, 'and that is to ask you to listen carefully to your Uncle Carl.'

'Fire away, Uncle Carl,' said Paul, 'we're all ears.'

'Speak for yourself,' said Vicky.

'First,' said Carl, 'you and Mama won't be going to Oberstein tomorrow, Lucia. Your mama has things to do here. Franz will go, from Salzburg, then he'll come to Vienna next week. Now, during the weekend we have to talk to my parents, to help them decide if they would like to live in England.'

'England?' said Lucia, gaping.

'Yes, because of circumstances,' said Carl. 'We have to give them a few days to make the decision, we can't put pressure on them. We've made our own decision, and if your grandparents favour going along with it, we shall all make the journey together. If not, we shall have to do more thinking.'

'Papa, will we live with Aunt Sophie and Uncle James?' asked Lucia.

'In the interests of peaceful family relationships, that wouldn't be advisable,' said Carl. 'But we hope to find a house not too far from theirs, and your Aunt Anne and grandparents hope to find one too.'

'Oh, not too far will be nice,' said Lucia, 'I can help Paul take Uncle James's car to bits.'

'Not more than once a year, I hope,' said James.

'Not at any time,' said Sophie.

'Heavens,' said Pia, 'you will begin to think about being an engine driver, Lucia.'

'All I can say,' said Vicky, 'is that if everyone comes to live near us in England, I shall be enormously pleased.'

'Vicky's fond of being enormously this and that,' said Emma Jane.

'Aunt Anne,' said Vicky, 'it's all to do with political problems, isn't it?'

'Yes, my sweet,' said Anne, 'all to do with many problems.'

'We ran into one today,' said Vicky quietly.

On his drive to work the following morning, Carl called at Mariella's apartment. She opened the door to him, saw him and purred with pleasure. She was clad in a shimmering rose-pink negligee, and her dark hair was a morning tumble.

'Carl, how lovely, I'm only half dressed.'

'I don't need that kind of information,' said Carl, 'just a few quick words.'

She let him in and closed the door.

'But you'll have coffee, yes?' she said.

'A small cup,' said Carl, and followed her into her kitchen, a place splashed with colour. 'It's settled,' he said, as she poured coffee for both of them. He sat down to drink his. Mariella moved a chair to seat herself next to him. Light travelled in little rippling relays up and down her silk stockings. Carl took no notice. 'My parents needed no more time to think about it,' he said. 'We'll all be leaving next week. Thursday, we hope. Your passport's in order?'

'Yes, darling.'

'Just say yes. I'm too old for games. Get ready for the journey. Have your canvases packed and crated, and get them despatched to somewhere of your own choice in England.'

'I'm expected to be businesslike at this time in the morning, and with you here? That's ridiculous.' Mariella's hands performed a theatrical dance in the air. 'I'm not made of timetables and luggage labels.'

'Calm yourself,' said Carl. 'Get married.'

'In England?' said Mariella. 'To an Englishman? Well, they're all very civilized and polite, but have no idea how to make love.'

'You speak from experience during your time in England?' smiled Carl, rising from his chair.

'No, but it's true, isn't it?' said Mariella.

'How would I know?' said Carl. 'By the way, Vicky and Paul ran into a revolting case of Jew-baiting yesterday afternoon.'

'Did they?' Mariella became sober. 'But I saw them, and they said nothing to me.'

'Sparing your feelings, perhaps,' said Carl.

'My feelings were already raw,' said Mariella, 'I had the Gestapo at the gallery again yesterday, looking for Josef Meister. I spun them a story.'

'I can imagine,' said Carl, keeping to himself the fact that he knew where Herr Meister was. 'But what with that and the experience Vicky and

Paul suffered, you know now why you have to face up to timetables and luggage labels.'

'I'm glad we're going,' said Mariella, 'but I've loved my years here.'

'That's something to remember,' said Carl. 'I'll see myself out, so don't get up. I don't want your negligee to collapse.'

He departed, leaving Mariella softly laughing.

When she arrived at the gallery a little before nine, a man was waiting for her. In his early forties, he was wearing a brown cap with a soft peak, a dark brown suit and brogues gleaming with polish. He had broad shoulders, homely looks and thick-lashed blue eyes that, to Mariella, seemed too artful for her good. He lifted his cap and addressed her.

'Miss Amaraldi?'

'Excuse me?' said Mariella, glowing in a ruby-wine coat and matching beret.

'D'you speak English?'

'Yes.'

'Good-oh. My German limps a bit. Um, Colonel Kirby and his missus send their regards.'

'Kirby?' Mariella stared at the man. 'Do you mean Mr John Kirby?'

'Colonel that was, now retired. I'm Sergeant John Wainwright, also retired, but attached to the staff of the British Embassy, don't you see.'

'No, I do not see,' said Mariella. 'Why are you here, what is it you want?'

'Compliments of Mrs Kirby, marm,' said Sergeant Wainwright breezily, 'I'm here to see you and your exhibition don't get roughed up by various persons unfriendly.'

'It's absurd,' said Mariella, remembering Karita Kirby's bewildering remarks yesterday.

'Well, absurd it might be, marm, but on the other hand, it might not be,' said Sergeant Wainwright. 'Worrying times for all kinds of people, including the honest.'

'In English, I'm Miss Amaraldi,' said Mariella. 'What does marm mean?'

'Respect, marm.'

Mariella smiled.

'Are you a diplomat with the British Embassy?' she asked.

'Hardly that,' said Sergeant Wainwright. 'I do errands.'

'Perhaps we should talk in the gallery,' said Mariella, and used Herr Meister's keys to open up. Sergeant Wainwright followed her in. He glanced at the exhibits.

'I had two pictures once,' he said. 'Somebody laid thieving hands on them. Goodbye, pictures.'

'I'm sorry,' said Mariella. 'Excuse me, but did you say you do errands for the British Embassy?'

'You could say I'm an errand boy,' said Sergeant Wainwright, 'you could. But if I happened to get in a rough house with characters hostile, I do have what you call diplomatic immunity.'

'But what is your relationship with Mr and Mrs Kirby?' asked Mariella.

'Confidential,' said Sergeant Wainwright. 'Let's just say I do the occasional errand for him, and the occasional job. It's my pleasure, marm, to be at your service by request of him and his missus.

You go ahead, you do what you usually do, and I'll make myself at home doing nothing much except keeping my eyes open.'

'I am being informed I have a bodyguard?' said Mariella, not sure if her amusement wasn't greater than her disbelief.

'Let's say a friend, marm, a close friend.'

'How close?'

'Well, if you put this ring on,' said Sergeant Wainwright, 'we could say I'm your official sweetheart, don't you see.' A ring that looked like a diamond solitaire appeared in his hand.

Mariella burst into laughter.

'Very droll, Sergeant, yes. I cannot take you or Mrs Kirby seriously.'

'Understood,' said Sergeant Wainwright, 'but best to be on the safe side. Well, these are worrying times, didn't I say so? Let's put the ring on, shall we?' He took her hand and slipped the engagement ring on her finger. 'Look at that now, fits like a dream. Compliments of Mrs Kirby, of course.'

'I don't think all this is really necessary,' said Mariella. She smiled. 'But very well, I won't argue with a close friend.'

'Good-oh,' said Sergeant Wainwright, 'much obliged, marm. Argufying ladies embarrass me.'

'Silly me,' Anne murmured to herself.

She was in a department store, looking at umbrellas with a view to purchasing a strong one to cope with the rain of England, but had just realized the most sensible thing to do would be to wait until she got there. There was always a comprehensive selection of excellent ladies' umbrellas in any English store.

She turned away, and her elbow made accidental contact with a man's arm. She apologized at once. Hans Voegler, snatching time off from his duties to buy a new razor, looked at her. His eyes, clear and clinical, widened. He had never met her, but he had seen her once, in the court during the divorce case, which he had attended out of curiosity. It made him wonder what lay beneath her air of cool serenity, since Lundt-Hausen was obviously determined to rid himself of her. Was she a decadent woman, a promiscuous one? Had she actually slept with the third party, the Jew? If so, she was decadent beyond belief, for she looked as pure an Aryan as any woman in Vienna. Yet there was something about her that denied the grievous sin of adultery with a Jew. One could define it simply as the serenity of a woman who had no cause for shame. But for one reason or several, perhaps, Lundt-Hausen plainly hated her. There were, however, very few people the Standartenfuehrer liked.

For her part during these brief moments, Anne was aware of clear blue eyes with a hint of cold grey, eyes that were offensively inquisitive, although the man had the fine features and austere look of a university professor whose world was confined to lectures and the acquisition of knowledge. His discourteous stare, however, was an affront to her sensibilities, and he had made no acknowledgement of her apology. She turned again, abruptly, and walked away.

My God, thought Voegler as he watched her

go, what man in his right mind would discard such a woman unless she danced each night with Jews and the Devil?

Perhaps, if anyone danced with the Devil, it was Lundt-Hausen himself.

Matthew Gibbs, using a public booth, was talking on the phone with John Kirby.

'Have you had a print made of the negative?'

'I've an arrangement with a photographer I know for the use of his darkroom,' said Kirby. 'It's necessary, of course, to make the print myself.'

'I thought you'd have had it done by now,' said Gibbs.

'It's not always the best thing to be in a hurry,' said Kirby. 'It arouses curiosity among the kind of people one sometimes has to deal with. Do you still have the bloodhounds on your tail?'

'I'm damn sure I do, and I'm damn sure my apartment phone is still being tapped,' said Gibbs. 'Listen, John, you told me yesterday that the lady we've both come to know is arranging to leave for England with her family. She should leave quickly before someone begins to chew over the fact that for a short while she was next to me in that crowd. I wish to God I hadn't made use of her.'

'Stick to journalism in future,' said Kirby.

'That's it, be my best friend,' said Gibbs.

'Matthew, leave as soon as you get your passport back,' said Kirby. 'Take note they can't hold it indefinitely, not without showing good reason, and they don't have good reason or you'd be under arrest.'

'They know I was in Staffler's apartment and beside him when he lay dying,' said Gibbs.

'They also know that when they caught up with you, you had nothing on you relating to Staffler. It's not your problem he was on the run from Berlin, it's theirs. Make another protest through the British Embassy.'

'I mean to,' said Gibbs. 'I'll hang up now, I've just spotted the bloodhounds.'

'Good luck,' said Kirby.

Later that day, Ludwig, conferring with Voegler on the subject of a missing top secret document, touched on the fact that the woman in the crowd had been Baroness Anne von Korvacs. Voegler raised an eyebrow.

'Herr Colonel, your—'

'Baroness Anne von Korvacs,' said Ludwig, shutting off any attempt by Voegler to call her his ex-wife.

'She's the woman?' said Voegler.

'I know she is,' said Ludwig, shuffling papers. 'Bring her in tomorrow, along with Gibbs.'

Voegler, noted for his self-control and his ability to conduct any interrogation without raising his voice, actually stared at the head of Vienna's SD, the Security Service of the Austrian SS.

'Both of them? The baroness as well as the Englishman?'

'She was the subject of the altercation between Gibbs and the youth,' said Ludwig. 'But it was more than that, of course it was. She has to be the one who received something from Gibbs and subsequently passed it on to a man she met near the Opera Theatre.'

'You know this?' said Voegler.

'Yes,' said Ludwig curtly. 'So bring her in, and Gibbs. Tomorrow. I'm attending a meeting of SS heads today.'

Voegler was not sure then whether he was guilty of admiration or envy. Here was a man so dedicated to his work, to the elimination of all elements dangerous to the Greater German Reich, that he was prepared to have his ex-wife examined as a possible traitor. Such dedication was that of an incorruptible servant of the State.

Yes, one could be both admiring and envious. One could.

'Very well, Herr Colonel.'

'Your men can pick up Gibbs at any time?' said Ludwig.

'Our surveillance is constant,' said Voegler.

'Have them both here by not later than ten thirty tomorrow morning, then,' said Ludwig. 'What, by the way, has gone wrong with your search for Meister?'

Meister had not shown up.

'It's only a matter of time,' said Voegler. 'We shall find him.'

'But not in that storeroom, apparently,' said Ludwig. 'I hope your men didn't make their surveillance too obvious to the eyes of the Jew.'

'You're suggesting he spotted them?' said Voegler.

'Perhaps he was on his way back to the place when you actually made your entry,' said Ludwig.

'I accept that possibility,' said Voegler, 'but we'll find him.'

'I'm not prepared to countenance failure,' said Ludwig.

'I know nothing of failure,' said Voegler. 'It's forbidden to the Gestapo.'

James took a mid-morning cab to the car factory. The streets of Vienna seemed restless with the quick movements of people. That, perhaps, was because of proliferating uniforms, all symbolic of German or Austrian National Socialism. Their wearers were arbitrary representatives of power, whatever their rank, and probably the reason why some shops were shuttered.

Sophie, he knew, would dislike the atmosphere. She and Pia were taking Vicky and Emma Jane shopping. Paul and Lucia had put overalls on and were spending the morning tinkering with the engine of Pia's car. Lucia, if asked by Paul, would willingly help him take a Great War tank to pieces. James smiled to himself at the thought.

At the factory, he located Carl, and together they inspected the two new racing cars that were ready for the circuits of Europe.

'Magnificent,' said James.

'We don't know that for sure yet,' said Carl.

'Well, they look magnificent,' said James.

'There are still some finishing touches required to the two reserve models,' said Carl. 'But mainly, it's only the tuning that needs to be perfected on these, which will be done in the pits at Brooklands. In any event, I think they'll manage some practice laps there without losing their wheels.'

'I'll take your word, Carl. They're your children.'

'Your engines,' said Carl.

'Damned noisy ones,' said James.

Carl laughed.

'You still don't like internal combustion, James?'

'Infernal, I call it,' said James. 'I favour design and the look of a finished model. I like it looking pristine, dust-free and quite still. But the moment it's moving on a road, it's a menace and a noisy one.'

'Damned if I don't think you'd still prefer that old pony and trap you and Sophie liked so much,' said Carl. 'Come into my office and have a schnapps.'

In the office, they sat drinking the schnapps.

'The truck,' said James.

'I've put Hebert and Proust to work on it,' said Carl. 'One car will be cradled above the other, and there'll be boarded stays on each side.'

'Cupboards of a kind, I think we said.'

'We did say,' said Carl, 'but let's call them stays, needed to keep the cars in place. Screws, of course, not nails. Any ventilation holes we must do ourselves, or Hebert and Proust will ask questions. Now, how do we get Josef tucked in?'

'I've thought about that,' said James. 'Take a cab to the factory next Wednesday, and drive home in the truck. Back it in and leave it parked on your forecourt for the night. We can drill the holes then, and Josef can be smuggled in early in the morning, while it's still dark.'

'I'd say that sounds perfect,' said Carl, 'if I weren't opposed to using words that imply nothing can go wrong. Fate is a damned perverse witch.'

'We'll stick with keeping our fingers crossed,' said James.

'Is your assistant Boerker taking over from you, as he usually does when you're away?'

'Yes,' said Carl. 'At the moment, of course, he thinks the freighting job is merely to get the cars to Brooklands. He's not sure I know what I'm doing in arranging for the mechanics to travel independently, but he'll trust me in the long run. I'm not inclined to suggest to anyone I'm leaving for good. As things are, we know there's a possibility that a mass emigration of the von Korvacs family might provoke opposition from border Gauleiters, and any whispers of the move might mean opposition before we even leave. The Nazis can be bloody-minded about our kind of people.'

'Well, we'll prepare for that, Carl,' said James. 'You know, don't you, how delighted Sophie is about the move?'

'There's one aspect to consider,' said Carl. 'If Hitler launches another European war, we might find your country fighting Austrians again. That will mean internment for your Austrian relatives.'

James grimaced.

'Damn that,' he said, and regarded Carl sombrely. 'But on the other hand,' he said, 'better internment than a labour camp. From all I've heard, labour camps are to be strictly avoided.'

'At this time of the day,' said Carl, 'could you down another schnapps?'

'That's no problem,' said James.

Chapter Nine

Lunchtime.

'Where is that man?' Mariella asked herself. Sergeant Wainwright had an extraordinary way of making himself look absent, and she had had to conduct several eye searches in her endeavours to spot him. Each time he proved to be there, usually as a seeming member of a group of visitors, of which there were many this morning.

Catching sight of him, she beckoned. Detaching himself from a bunch of visitors, he came over.

'How's it going, marm?' he asked.

'I am not complaining,' said Mariella, 'I've sold three pictures so far. Do you wish to go out and have lunch somewhere?'

'Well, marm, I consider that a friendly offer, but it can't be done, no. Orders strictly forbid me to leave this picture palace until you leave yourself.'

'But what about your lunch?' asked Mariella.

'I've got a couple of bread rolls,' said Sergeant Wainwright, 'and a couple of spicy sausages,

135

which I'll partake of shortly. How about you and your lunch?'

'I don't eat lunch,' said Mariella, 'apart from coffee and a biscuit. I avoid food at midday.' She was always fighting the threat of putting on weight.

'Well, you're a fine figure of a woman, if I might say so,' said Sergeant Wainwright.

'I did not ask you to,' said Mariella coolly.

'Couldn't help volunteering the compliment, don't you see?' he said cheerfully.

'No, I don't see,' said Mariella, 'and I still think the situation is absurd.'

'Well, it can't do any harm for me to be here,' said Sergeant Wainwright.

'I will agree with that,' said Mariella, permitting herself a smile.

The gallery saw quite an exciting influx of visitors during the afternoon, which delighted Mariella. Interest really had picked up since the opening-day fiasco. Herr Meister, however, had not appeared, which was a relief to her. She was sure now that he had managed to get out of the country and to join his wife and children in London. There he might have to cope with winter fogs, but all year round it at least offered a sense of freedom to refugees from the Greater German Reich. People on the street, newspaper journalists and radio commentators could say what they liked about the Government. Cartoonists could mock the Prime Minister, the opposition could rail at ministers, and orators at Speakers' Corner by Hyde Park could curse and condemn every politician and every institution. And not a single policeman would knock on the door of a free-expressionist. It was like that in America too, a country alive with the most outgoing people in the world. It had the distinction of being called the Land of the Free. She would go there one day, perhaps, if only to feel as free as a bird.

The British, of course, were very reserved and awkwardly insular, but they cherished freedom and had the privilege at election times of turning out of office any party that threatened it. Austria had allowed that privilege to be taken away from its people.

Mariella kept giving thought to these factors because of her forthcoming move to England. She did not suppose she had seen the last of the man Voegler. He might be convinced that Herr Meister had used his storeroom as a hiding place, but a vain search for the gentle Jew would bring him back here again, she was sure. Yes, even if only to remind her that a tree was a tree.

Sergeant Wainwright remained unobtrusive. He had made no attempt at any time to place himself close to her and engage her in conversation, apart from the occasion when she had invited him. What an odd man he was. From her desk, she again beckoned. Seeing the gesture, he presented himself to her.

'At your service, marm,' he said briskly.

'Tell me,' she said, 'if Gestapo men arrive and accost me, where will you be?'

'Watching,' said Sergeant Wainwright.

'And if they attempt to drag me away?'

'Tricky,' said Sergeant Wainwright.

'Tricky?' said Mariella. 'What does that mean?'

'That I'll have to shout "Fire!", then take advantage of the confusion and cart you off to a safe location.'

'That is not a serious comment, is it?' said Mariella.

'Best I can think of at the moment,' said the imperturbable sergeant.

'Then I regret to say you're an idiot,' said Mariella. 'Do you think the Gestapo would allow you to play games with them?'

'Have to point out, marm, that my orders are to take care of you and the picture called *English Cottage*. Very attractive brushwork, I must say.'

'Well, you have looked at it a hundred times while attaching yourself to visitors,' said Mariella, 'but thank you.'

'All of a pleasure,' said Sergeant Wainwright, and returned to his unobtrusive but watchful role.

A lady entered the gallery ten minutes later and walked up to Mariella.

'Good afternoon, Fräulein Amaraldi.'

Mariella looked up. Brown eyes regarded her smilingly. Golden hair clustered below the narrow brim of a light brown hat. She was not young, but she looked extraordinarily vital.

'Frau Kirby? How nice to see you again.'

'Ah, we know each other now?' The soft accent was laden with music. At least, it was to Mariella, a woman of imagination.

'Yes, I think we do,' she smiled. 'There's a – ' She paused. ' – a gentleman here who says you and your husband have sent him for my protection.'

'Ah, yes,' murmured Karita Kirby. 'He has his ways of frustrating inquisitive enemies of people.'

'He has his ways of exasperating me,' said Mariella.

'You will come to like him,' said Karita. 'Now, about the picture.'

'You wish to take it away?' said Mariella.

'But no. Your exhibition does not close until Sunday, does it? I have come only to take another look at it and, if I may, to place this address label on the back.' From her handbag, Karita Kirby extracted a printed label of thin white pasteboard, with her name and address lettered in ink, and the reverse side gummed. 'It's a little precaution, yes, in case we forget to collect it, and to make sure of its destination. We are not always remembering everything when we are packing, and we are returning to England soon. May I stick the label on?'

'Please do, yes, you are welcome,' said Mariella.

'Most kind. Thank you.' Karita crossed to the picture. Visitors watched as she lifted it from the wall, placed it carefully face down over a padded chair, and applied the label. The gum adhered at once without being licked. She replaced the canvas, retreated a few paces and inspected it with an air of happy satisfaction. Some of the visitors, intrigued, came to inspect it with her. She turned, smiled at Mariella and made a little gesture of goodbye.

'You'll collect when?' called Mariella.

'Saturday, yes? Thank you, Fräulein.' Karita left without a glance at or a word to Sergeant Wainwright, who himself seemed not to have noticed her, but would take extra care of *English Cottage* from now on.

'John?'

'Yes?' said John Kirby into the phone.

'Matthew here. Public phone. My friends are outside, hoping to eavesdrop. Any luck?'

'Yes, I've made a print. Staffler was right when he told you it was one of Hitler's very special directives, and that its revelation would be a bombshell. The print is now destroyed.'

'Very wise, but remember the negative is mine,' said Matthew Gibbs. 'It's my pot of gold, secured at the risk of life and limb. Staffler wanted me to help him reach the Soviet Union. He'd broken free of Schuschnigg's secret police, and retrieved that envelope from a safe box.'

'What was he, a cupboard Marxist?' asked Kirby.

'He didn't say so.'

'Didn't need to, I suppose,' said Kirby. 'However, trust me to deliver the item safely to you in London, although I wouldn't guarantee an editor would be allowed to buy it from you for publication. In fact, I'd say no.'

'Hold on,' said Gibbs, 'someone's going to have to pay for it, either Fleet Street or the Government.'

'I'd say the Government,' said Kirby. 'Have you got your passport back?'

'No, damn it, not yet. But the embassy will

make further representations if it's not returned by Monday. Give me a résumé of the bombshell – no, never mind, the hounds have made a move.' Gibbs replaced the phone as the door of the booth was pulled open.

'Who were you speaking to?' asked a Gestapo man.

'My grandmother,' said Gibbs, and pushed past him and his colleague.

He returned to his apartment.

They followed him.

'Good afternoon,' said Nicholas Kirby, as Heinrich opened the front door to him. 'Is Fräulein Victoria Fraser at home? My name is Kirby, and I'm expected.'

'Please to enter, Herr Kirby,' said Heinrich. Nicholas stepped in and Heinrich took him up to the apartment occupied by the Fraser family. James opened the door and Heinrich announced the arrival of the visitor.

'So you're Nicholas,' said James. 'Come in. I'm Vicky's father, James Fraser.' He shook hands with the athletic young man, liking the look of him. Sophie appeared in the handsome lobby. 'And this is my wife. Sophie, here is Nicholas Kirby.'

'I am delighted to meet you, Mr Kirby,' said Sophie. 'You are, I believe, the saviour of my son and elder daughter.'

'I've a feeling exaggerations have been circulating,' said Nicholas.

'Adjectives,' said James, 'but I think the general picture broke through quite well.'

'Giving us cause to be very grateful to you,' said Sophie, looking almost queenly with her hair up to form a shining chestnut crown.

'It was all spur of the moment stuff,' said Nicholas, 'nothing more.'

'This way,' said James, and Nicholas entered the sitting room with Vicky's parents. Vicky was standing casually about, as if nothing much was going on this afternoon. Emma Jane was seated. Vicky's spectacles were off. 'Mr Nicholas Kirby,' announced James with a smile.

'Oh, hello,' said Emma Jane, 'you've come, then.'

'That's our younger daughter, Emma Jane,' said James.

'How d'you do, Emma Jane?' said Nicholas.

'Oh, very well considering I'm only third in line,' said Emma Jane. 'Vicky's over there.'

Vicky turned.

'Oh, hello,' she said, looking like a young man's dream of an Easter present in a yellow sweater and a pencil-slim skirt. Her developing figure was always on exceptionally good terms with a Hollywood-style sweater.

'Have you found any bruises?' smiled Nicholas.

Vicky advanced to shake hands with him, and to occupy centre stage.

'No, no bruises, just a laddered stocking,' she said. 'Have you met Mama?'

'Yes, and your father,' said Nicholas, at which point Anne came in, having told Sophie she would like to meet Vicky's saviour. James introduced the young man. Anne professed herself delighted. Nicholas declared himself enchanted.

Vicky groaned, as would any girl whose mother and aunt threatened to outshine her.

'Do sit down, Mr Kirby,' said Sophie, 'and I'll bring in the tea tray. You'll take tea?'

'Thanks, I will,' said Nicholas, and Sophie disappeared.

'Sit here, Mr Kirby,' said Emma Jane, indicating a chesterfield. Nicholas sat down, Emma Jane sat beside him, and Anne made a covert study of him. 'Well, I must say I'm bucked at meeting you,' said Emma Jane. 'Did you really snatch Vicky from the jaws of death?'

'I roundly deny it,' said Nicholas.

'Well, it sounded as if you did,' said Emma Jane.

'Let's see,' mused James, 'were the jaws of death mentioned in your account, Vicky?'

Vicky, still holding centre stage, thought for a moment, then said, 'If they weren't, I'm guilty of a grievous omission.'

'Jaws of death a grievous omission, oh Lordy,' said Emma Jane.

'I did mention to your parents, Vicky, that exaggerations have been flying about,' said Nicholas.

'I simply can't cope with such modesty,' said Vicky.

'Try sitting down,' said James, but Sophie reappeared with the tea tray and Vicky swooped to take it from her.

'I'll see to it, Mama,' she said. 'You sit down and relax. You must be tired out after such a long day.'

'I'm not,' said Sophie, 'I haven't had a long day.'

'All the same, do have a rest, Mama,' said Vicky, placing the tray on a table.

James smiled. So did Anne. Vicky was playing a chosen role, that was obvious. Sophie gave in to it and sat down.

'Vicky tells me you're at Bristol University, Mr Kirby,' she said.

'I am,' said Nicholas.

'And where is your home?'

'Richmond,' said Nicholas.

'Surrey or Yorkshire?' asked James.

'Surrey,' said Nicholas.

'That's not far from us,' said Emma Jane, 'we're at Shepperton.'

'Tea, Aunt Anne? Tea, Mama?' said Vicky, and served them. 'A biscuit?'

'No biscuit, thank you,' said Sophie, intrigued by her daughter's behaviour. Anne took one.

'Tea, Daddy?' said Vicky.

'And a biscuit, little mother,' said James.

Vicky brought a tin of Viennese biscuits to him. He took one, looking up into her myopic eyes. Vicky smiled, then served Emma Jane with tea and a biscuit.

'My, you do look grand in your new sweater, Vicky,' said Emma Jane.

'What, this old thing?' said Vicky. 'Tea, Mr Kirby?'

'Thanks,' said Nicholas.

'Sugar?'

'No sugar, Miss Fraser.'

'Bless us, aren't we formal?' said Emma Jane.

Vicky handed Nicholas his tea, then tempted him with the attractive contents of the tin.

'I'll have two, if I may,' said Nicholas.

'Please do,' said Vicky. The guest having been seen to, she took up her own cup and saucer and seated herself in a posture of upright grace. 'How is your dear mother, Mr Kirby?' she asked, at which James choked on a mouthful of biscuit and Sophie hid a smile. Anne let her own smile surface. 'Did you acquaint her and your father with the details of the awful riot? Were they dreadfully taken aback?'

'I told them, yes,' said Nicholas. 'They both survived the account and they're in excellent shape today.'

'I do hope those poor Jewish people have recovered,' said Vicky seriously, 'and that they've escaped.'

'We all hope so,' said Sophie.

'Aunt Anne, Mr Kirby's mother is Russian, you know,' said Vicky.

'Yes, so I heard,' said Anne, and smiled at Nicholas. 'What is she like?'

'Imaginative and melodramatic,' said Nicholas.

'Very Russian, you mean?' said James.

'There have been a few broken cups,' said Nicholas.

'Well, I never,' said Emma Jane, helping herself to another biscuit, 'she sounds just like Vicky, except Vicky hasn't started breaking cups yet. Still, I daresay she'll come to that. What do we do when that happens, Daddy?'

'We all duck,' said James.

'Best thing, I suppose,' said Emma Jane.

'I'm afraid I can't recognize the portrait,' said Vicky. 'More tea, Mama? It will buck you up.'

'Do I need bucking up?' asked Sophie.

'Not from where I'm sitting,' said James. 'Nicholas, I hear you're taking a holiday in Vienna with your parents,'

'I joined them here when my vacation began,' said Nicholas, and the conversation took a more general turn. Vicky, however, continued to be the centrepiece of the little gathering, addressing herself with flair to the responsibility of making the guest feel at home. The guest found it difficult to keep his face straight. Sophie and James encouraged him to talk about Bristol University, and his sister and parents. He referred to the university as stimulating, and to his sister as his best friend, although she was so brainy that she had few interests outside reference libraries. He did not say a great deal about the interests and activities of his parents, except to give the impression they travelled a lot and were of independent means. Anne asked, as casually as she could, what his father's name was. John, said Nicholas, and Anne was certain then that here was the son of the man to whom she had passed the envelope containing a negative.

Emma Jane and Vicky were very forthcoming about themselves and their own family, Vicky in splendid form. Sophie realized, as James did, that she had decided to convince Nicholas she was by far the most interesting young lady he had ever met.

Nicholas did not outstay his welcome. He declared, after an hour or so, that he must be going. He shook hands all round.

'Vicky will go down with you and see you out,' said Sophie, liking him.

'Yes, Mama, if you wish,' said Vicky.

'Mr Fraser,' said Nicholas, 'would you object if I called sometime tomorrow and took Vicky for a drive?'

'I've no objection at all,' said James, 'I'll leave it to Vicky.'

'How about it, Vicky?' asked Nicholas.

'Fortunately,' said Vicky, 'I've very few appointments for tomorrow.'

'I could pick you up at about ten fifteen, say,' said Nicholas.

'Well, I think that would be very nice,' said Vicky, and went down with him to see him out.

At the door, Nicholas said, 'Have you ever thought of addressing a seminar of young ladies on how to become socially popular?'

'Oh, I hardly consider myself sufficiently qualified for that sort of thing,' said Vicky.

'You'd be a knockout,' said Nicholas. 'See you tomorrow morning, then. By the way, I agree with you, your mother is astonishingly attractive. So is your Aunt Anne.'

'Yes, now you see why it is that at home or here in Vienna, I'm forced to live in the background,' said Vicky.

'Still, you're putting up a very good fight,' said Nicholas, and departed laughing.

My word, thought Vicky, that young man could be quite a challenge.

* * *

That evening, two men approached the door of Mariella's apartment. A third man materialized, apparently out of nowhere.

'Good evening, good evening, are you visiting Fräulein Amaraldi?' he asked in execrable German.

'Who the hell are you?' demanded Gestapo man Lutz.

'Her fiancé from England,' said Sergeant Wainwright, 'and who are you?'

'Secret State Police,' said the other man, Bauer. Gestapo. 'Clear off.'

'Speak English?' enquired Sergeant Wainwright.

'No,' said Lutz.

'Ah,' said Sergeant Wainwright, and in his terrible German let the men know he belonged to the British Embassy. He produced the relevant card. Bauer rolled his tongue about as if gathering spittle.

'Don't interfere,' said Lutz, and rang the bell.

Mariella answered. She was not surprised to see the Gestapo officer, but her eyebrows went up as she recognized Sergeant Wainwright.

'Is the Jew here?' asked Bauer.

'Don't be absurd,' said Mariella, and was immediately brushed aside as Lutz and Bauer forced their way in. Sergeant Wainwright entered with a show of good manners and an agreeable smile. 'My God,' Mariella whispered in English, 'did you bring them?'

'Now, now, marm, is that a nice question to ask of your sweetheart?' he murmured. 'Let's see what they're up to.' In he went, Mariella following. He located the intruders, and almost stood on their tails as they began a bruising search of every room and every possible hiding place. He said nothing, he watched them in silence, but with a notebook and pencil in his hands.

'What the hell is he up to?' growled Bauer.

'Eh?' said Sergeant Wainwright.

'He wants to know what you are doing,' said Mariella, a deep red silk jersey dress of tubular style doing its best to impart a slender look to her figure.

'I want to make sure you don't molest my fiancée in any way or help yourselves to her fur coats,' said Sergeant Wainwright in English to Bauer. 'As you see, I'll be taking notes.'

'What's that gabble all about?'

Mariella translated.

'Clear off!' shouted Lutz and Bauer in concert, glaring at Sergeant Wainwright.

'I'm staying,' said the object of their irritation, and he was at their backs as they resumed their search, a thorough one. He tried out his German again. 'If you knew Fräulein Amaraldi as well as I do, you'd know she might make use of a Jew's picture gallery, but never allow any Jew into her apartment.'

'Darling,' said Mariella, sensibly refusing to deny the innuendo, 'you speak German like a backward polar bear.' She made the comment in German.

But Lutz and Bauer had got the gist of Sergeant Wainwright's words, and looked as if it soured them, as if they would have preferred her to be a Jew-lover and accordingly fit for arrest and incarceration. They completed their search in sullen silence, finding neither Josef Meister nor anything relating to him, except a letter confirming the date of her exhibition. Lutz made one remark as they left.

'We'll find him.'

'Good luck,' said Sergeant Wainwright.

'You,' said Bauer, 'I don't like your face.'

'Can't be helped,' said Sergeant Wainwright, getting the meaning, 'it's something I was born with.'

Left alone with him, Mariella asked, 'How did you come to be with them?'

'Well, marm, while keeping your apartment under observation, as requested – '

'I made no request,' said Mariella.

'No, nor did you, bless your heart,' said Sergeant Wainwright. 'Beg to inform you it was made by Colonel Kirby and his missus. So, there I was, and along they came, the characters unfriendly, and as I was duty-bound to see no harm was done to you, I allowed myself to join them at your door and follow them in. I trust, marm, that their poking and ferreting about hasn't upset you.'

'I shall recover,' said Mariella. 'Thank you for being here. I'm sure I'd have been treated roughly had I been alone. Your credentials also helped.'

'Think nothing of it,' said Sergeant Wainwright. 'Pleasure to be of service, and as I don't think they'll come back, I'll say goodnight.'

'I'm happy to offer you coffee,' said Mariella.

'Kind of you, but there's a waitress I know, as pretty a piece of Austrian scenery as I ever saw,' said Sergeant Wainwright, 'and with a soft spot for me. She'll be coming off duty in ten minutes or so, and that'll give me time to meet her.'

'Off you go, then, Sergeant,' said Mariella.

'I'll report to you in the gallery tomorrow morning,' said Sergeant Wainwright. He touched his cap to her and left.

Ah, there's a man who was once a soldier and still is in speech and attitude, thought Mariella, and wished him luck with his waitress, his pretty piece of Austrian scenery.

Chapter Ten

The following morning, at ten minutes past nine, Anne's apartment doorbell rang. Answering it, she found herself confronted by two men, one in a belted black raincoat, the other in a dark blue overcoat. Heinrich was behind them, agitated at having been peremptorily shoved aside when attempting to observe formalities.

'Baroness Anne von Korvacs?' enquired the overcoated man, Hans Voegler, and Anne looked into the eyes that yesterday had scanned her so searchingly for a few brief seconds in a department store. There was not the slightest acknowledgement now of those moments, only an expression of polite enquiry.

Heinrich went for help.

'What is it you want?' asked Anne.

'To advise you you are under arrest,' said Voegler, 'and are required to come to head-quarters with us. You may, of course, put your hat and coat on. The morning is fresh.'

Paul appeared at Anne's elbow. He had had breakfast with her, to keep her company, Anne delighted to have him.

'You can't,' he gasped to Voegler.

'Who are you?' asked Voegler.

'He's my nephew,' said Anne. 'What are you charging me with?'

'Complicity—' Voegler was interrupted as Paul brushed by him, running on the same kind of errand as Heinrich, to get help. Voegler shrugged, advancing into the apartment with his assistant, a man called Schroeder. Anne was forced to retreat.

'Complicity?' she said.

'In a plot designed to endanger the security of the Greater German Reich,' said Voegler.

'Is that what I belong to now, the Greater German Reich?' said Anne.

'You share that good fortune with all Austrians,' said Voegler, 'although in your case we may prove a lack of enthusiasm.'

'The charge you spoke of is absurd,' said Anne, 'and you must know it is.'

'Do you want to put your hat and coat on, or come as you are?' asked Voegler, the quiet pitch of his voice making him sound a civilized and pleasant man. Further, he looked so. His assistant, however, looked what he was, a policeman who didn't encourage suspects to argue.

'What I want,' said Anne, 'is to know the exact nature of the charge. I've a right to know.'

'Ah, a right, yes,' said Voegler. 'Of course. We'll consider that at headquarters. You will come as you are, then?'

James strode in. Paul had alerted him.

'What's going on?' he asked.

'None of your business,' said Schroeder.

Sophie appeared. She rushed in.

'Anne, what's happening? Who are these men?'

'State Police,' said Voegler.

'I question that,' said James. 'The State Police are uniformed.'

'I should, of course, have said the Secret State Police.' Voegler made the correction in polite fashion.

'The Gestapo?' said James, and Sophie's mouth compressed.

'That is so,' said Voegler, 'and we're here to arrest Baroness Anne von Korvacs and to take her to headquarters. Your presence is not required. Nor yours,' he said to Sophie.

Sophie regarded him icily.

'Have you no manners?' she said. 'Or any sense of the absurd? Nothing is more absurd than to talk of arresting my sister.'

Running footsteps brought Carl to the scene. Heinrich had informed him of the arrival of the two men. He asked the same question as James had.

'What's going on?'

'Are we to expect the whole of Vienna to appear?' said Voegler. He looked at Anne. 'Who are these people?'

'My sister, my brother and my brother-in-law,' said Anne, wondering if someone knew Mr Gibbs had slipped that envelope into her pocket. That unpleasant youth, had he noticed?

'Are there aunts and uncles too, and cousins?' asked Voegler.

'Carl, these men are talking of arresting Anne and taking her to headquarters,' said Sophie.

'Which headquarters?' asked Carl.

'You are – ?' said Voegler.

'Her brother,' said Carl brusquely.

'Then let me inform you your sister is being taken to SS headquarters.'

Carl drew a sharp breath. James stiffened.

'That place houses the Security Service and the Gestapo,' said Carl.

'Both the SD and the Gestapo are interested in the activities of your sister,' said Voegler.

'Show me your authority,' said Carl.

'Stop wasting our time,' said Schroeder, but Voegler slipped a hand inside his coat and produced a wallet. He opened it. Carl, James and Sophie all looked. The Gestapo identity card was plain to see, naming the holder as Hans Voegler, Kommissar.

Sophie, anguished for her sister, saw James's expression of fury. She put a hand on his arm, and his arm was rigid. She was afraid he was going to strike Voegler.

'James – '

'Where's your warrant for the arrest of the baroness?' James shot the question at Voegler.

'A warrant is not necessary,' said Voegler, 'and I insist, Baroness, that you come at once.'

Anne, quite calm now, said, 'Wait a few moments more while I get my hat and coat.'

'I will allow you one minute,' said Voegler, and Anne went to her bedroom. Schroeder followed and waited outside the door.

James looked at Voegler and said, 'I'm damned if I'll accept you can arrest her without a warrant.'

'Where are you from?' asked Voegler, aware of an accent. 'You aren't German or Austrian.'

'I'm from the United Kingdom,' said James.

Carl, hoping it might carry some weight, said, 'His father is Sir William Fraser, owner of the Austro-Fraser car plant.'

'Very interesting,' said Voegler, 'but be so good as to tell him not to interfere in the affairs of the Greater German Reich.'

'Is it legal in the Greater German Reich to arrest people without a warrant?' asked Sophie.

'It's legal to arrest and detain any person suspected of conspiring against the State,' said Voegler.

'You suspect Baroness Anne of that?' said James. 'You're mad.'

'We shall see,' said Voegler. He was not supporting Lundt-Hausen's vindictiveness, merely the right of the State to interrogate any kind of suspect citizen, whoever he or she might be. Anne reappeared, her hat and coat on, Schroeder behind her, surly with impatience. Voegler, however, was not an impatient man. Nor was he ever inclined to push and hustle. He enjoyed a cat-and-mouse dialogue. 'You are ready, Baroness? Good. We will go, then.'

Anne remembered then that Nicholas Kirby was calling again this morning, to take Vicky out. Vicky at this moment was with Emma Jane and Lucia, all three girls having breakfasted with their grandparents.

'Sophie,' she said, 'when Nicholas arrives to collect Vicky, will you ask him to phone his father?' The request was motivated by instinct and hope. Contact could not be made with Matthew Gibbs, but it could with John Kirby, and instinct pointed her at him as a man who she was sure was more than a mere visitor to Vienna.

'His father?' said Sophie, distracted. 'Why?'

'Just ask him, please, to tell his father what is happening,' said Anne.

'Yes, yes, of course,' said Sophie, and embraced her sister.

'Come on, come on,' said Schroeder, and attempted to take Anne by her arm, but Carl pushed in to prevent that.

He squeezed her hand and said, 'It's a ghastly mistake, Anne. I'll go to Chancellor Seyss-Inquart himself.'

'Make an excuse to Mama and Papa for my absence,' said Anne.

Carl pressed her hand again, and James touched her shoulder reassuringly as Voegler and Schroeder took her away.

John Kirby, with his wife Karita, arrived at the house on the Salesianergasse twenty minutes after receiving a phone call from their son Nicholas to the effect that Baroness Anne von Korvacs, having been arrested by the Gestapo, had asked for the call to be made. John Kirby said he would come at once, and would be grateful if the family took no action until he had spoken to them.

Lucia and Emma Jane were out with their grandparents, these four people having been kept ignorant of the crisis. Nicholas introduced his parents to Pia, Carl, Sophie, James, Vicky and

Paul. Pia, Sophie and Vicky were in shock, James and Carl tight-lipped. Paul was disbelieving.

Carl said to John Kirby, 'Is it possible you know my sister Anne, and that she thinks you can help her?'

'Yes, I do know her,' said Kirby. 'That is, I met her. Once. On Tuesday.' He paused. Sophie regarded him in anxious hope. He seemed encouragingly calm. So did his Russian wife, even if Nicholas had said she sometimes broke cups. 'She was seen with me.'

'Why should that be a reason for arresting her?' asked James.

'It's a little complicated,' said Kirby.

'Oh, yes, only a little?' said Pia scathingly. 'There is nothing little about being arrested by Himmler's police.'

'It means the Bolshevik wolves have a lamb in their larder,' said Karita.

'Bolshevik wolves?' said Sophie.

'They are all Bolsheviks, Hitler, Himmler and all the others,' said Karita. 'They are no different from Lenin, Trotsky and Stalin, they all exist on hate for those who do not think as they do.' She smiled. 'But a larder can be robbed,' she murmured.

Vicky, Pia and Sophie all flung questions at her together, and Karita put up her hands as if to ward off the barrage.

'This won't do,' said James, 'let's calm down.'

'Calm down?' said Sophie. 'Who can calm down?'

'I think Mr Kirby has more to say,' said Carl.

Kirby said, 'I believe the Gestapo arrested

Baroness Anne on the orders of SS Standarten-fuehrer Lundt-Hausen.'

The bombshell had a shattering effect.

'God Almighty, Ludwig?' said Carl.

'It was her former husband who saw us together near the Opera Theatre,' said Kirby.

'But why should that have made the swine order her arrest?' asked Carl. 'He doesn't know you, does he?'

'A man who visibly hates his former wife as much as he does can summon up hate for any man seen in company with her,' said Kirby, who had no intention of telling the real story. In any case, disclosure would involve these people, and burden them with information that would put them at risk just as Matthew Gibbs had put Baroness Anne at risk by slipping the envelope into her raincoat pocket. Was that known to the Gestapo, was it that which had given her ex-husband a reason to arrest her, or was there another reason? Kirby knew he had been seen with Anne by Lundt-Hausen himself. Had malice and suspicion led the man to inspect files and photographs of known agents? If so, the man might be thinking about Kirby's arrest, too. As it was, the detention of Baroness Anne could be blamed on himself and Matthew Gibbs.

'Would you please say something, Mr Kirby?' begged Sophie.

'Your sister's arrest could simply be put down to a malicious impulse on the part of her ex-husband to have her investigated,' said Kirby. 'As Karita, my wife, pointed out, Himmler's men are no better than Leninist Bolsheviks. They believe instinctively that all men and women should be investigated. It's possible that in time Himmler will even order the investigation of Hitler. Baroness Anne, in my opinion, is almost certainly the victim of personal spite. I saw how her ex-husband looked at her, and because she was with me, a stranger to him, I imagine I was immediately suspect myself.' He looked at Carl. 'You know this man, Baron. Are you able to confirm he does have an intense dislike of your sister?'

'We can all confirm it,' said Sophie.

'He was sick,' said Pia, 'sick like a man who had lost his soul to the Devil.'

'The Devil must be fought tooth and nail,' said Karita. 'To lose anything to him is to open the gates of hell for oneself.'

'Hang on,' said James, 'why didn't he order your arrest too, Mr Kirby, since you feel he might have suspected you of plotting anti-Nazi politics with Anne?'

'He could make an attempt to,' said Kirby, 'but I have diplomatic immunity while in Austria.'

'Mr Kirby,' said Carl, 'exactly how did you come to meet Anne?'

'I bumped into her at the Opera Theatre,' said Kirby. 'One has to apologize for that kind of thing, and usually that's the beginning and end of it. But Baroness Anne and I began to talk, and we continued our conversation in the street. That was when the Standartenfuehrer saw us.'

'The who?' said Vicky.

'It's the SS equivalent of colonel,' said Carl, 'and the man who was once your Uncle Ludwig now holds that rank in the SD. That's the Security Service, all part of the SS.'

Vicky, excessively worried about her Aunt Anne, made a face. Nicholas felt for her and the whole family.

'When he came face to face with Baroness Anne,' continued Kirby, 'he said nothing to her, nothing at all.' Kirby thought again of the moment. 'He simply looked. I thought his expression vicious.'

'He is vicious,' said James. 'If he lost his soul for good, it was when he accused Anne at the divorce hearing of committing adultery with a Jewish friend. Look, you asked us through Nicholas to take no action until you'd spoken to us. So far you've only told us why you think Anne was arrested. Carl intends to see Chancellor Seyss-Inquart as soon as possible. Can you improve on that?'

'Let me first suggest,' said Kirby, 'that Lundt-Hausen will attempt to pin something on the baroness, to frame her on a charge that will put her out of sight and sound. In a concentration camp. He hasn't had her arrested simply to frighten her. Can anyone tell me why he obviously hates her so much?'

'Yes,' said Carl. 'He hates her because Anne is a normal and healthy woman, because she was a caring and patient wife, and because he came back from the war with a lame leg, a twisted mind and, in my opinion, a condition of impotence. Anne, of course, knew he lied in the divorce court, and Josef Meister, the Jewish friend, also knew. Ludwig knows that they know, and it's my belief he can't tolerate that. The Gestapo went after Josef Meister soon after Hitler arrived in Vienna, and came for Anne this morning. When they find Josef, they'll murder him.'

'Now I fully understand,' said Kirby. 'Would you say that Ludwig Lundt-Hausen's hatred of Baroness Anne and the Jewish gentleman is greater than his love of the SS and the power his uniform gives him?'

Carl gave the question considerable thought before replying.

'No, I don't think it is,' he said. 'His uniform helps him nurture his hatreds and his fanaticism. It's his life, the only thing he cares about.'

Kirby smiled.

'That's something,' he said. 'You can arrange to see Seyss-Inquart, if you like. Do you know him? Is he a friend, or an acquaintance?'

'I've no friends or acquaintances in the Austrian National Socialist Party,' said Carl, 'but I do have friends who may be able to arrange for me to see Seyss-Inquart.'

'A butcher,' said Karita. 'Who would go to a butcher to save a lamb?'

'Well, one can appeal to an advocate of the Devil, but I wouldn't fancy his chances,' said Kirby. He addressed Carl. 'Let my wife and me first try to free your sister for you.'

'Do you have the means?' asked Carl.

'Possibly,' said Kirby.

'You are saying that you and Mrs Kirby can find a way of freeing Anne?' said Sophie.

'But yes,' said Karita, 'that is why we have come to talk to you.'

'I'm astonished,' said Vicky, 'but in a desperately hopeful way.'

'In the event of success,' said Kirby, 'the baroness will have to disappear out of the country, and quickly.'

'If you can get her out of the hands of the Gestapo,' said James, 'we'll take care of the disappearing act.'

'Baroness Anne mentioned to me that those of you who live here are all thinking of moving to England,' said Kirby.

'You must have had quite a conversation with her,' said Carl. 'Yes, it's true, we are moving to England.'

'Then can we now talk about that?' asked Karita.

'Yes, oh, yes,' said Sophie earnestly, 'let's talk so that we can make the impossible sound possible. And let us have coffee.'

'Most kind,' smiled Karita.

'Perhaps you could say something over coffee,' said Vicky to Nicholas. 'You haven't spoken a single word so far.'

'It hasn't been necessary,' said Nicholas.

'Your father is a fascinating man,' whispered Vicky.

'Yes, I live in his shadow, in the background,' said Nicholas, and that represented the first light moment of the morning for Vicky.

Lucia and Emma Jane, together with their grandparents, were back from their outing and present when coffee was served. Introduced to Nicholas's parents and put into the picture, they were appalled to know Anne had been arrested. Carl assured them, however, that there was a hope of freeing her.

To Nicholas and his parents, Carl and James then outlined their plan of departure, a plan that had to take into account the inclusion of Josef Meister, wanted by the Gestapo. John Kirby expressed doubts. A party of fourteen people? No, far too unwieldy and noticeable. Would they allow him to propose an alternative?

'Try us,' said James.

'First,' said Kirby to Carl, 'don't have your son Franz come to Vienna. Let him stay where he is in the Italian Tyrol. Who is your wife's sister, by the way?'

'An artist, Mariella Amaraldi,' said Carl, and Karita smiled.

'Arrange for her and your wife and daughter, and your parents, to join your son,' said Kirby. 'They're probably all of no consequence to Ludwig or the Gestapo.'

'I wouldn't be too sure of that myself, especially if Ludwig is forced to give Anne her freedom,' said James.

'You've made a point,' said Kirby. 'However, the train should carry them across the border without incident if their passports aren't suspect, and once across they'll be able to reach England without difficulty. Italy is a Fascist dictatorship, but nowhere near as repressive as Nazi Germany.'

'We are all family,' said Sophie, 'and don't really wish to be divided.'

'Fourteen people are too many in one party,' insisted Kirby.

'My husband is more often right than wrong,' said Karita, 'and for me that is sometimes not what I like, living with a man who is nearly always right. However, I like it now, his belief that fourteen of you are too many.'

'I'd suggest, in fact, that all the young people take the train to Italy, along with Baroness Pia and her sister, and your parents,' said Kirby to Carl, 'and that the adults alone make themselves responsible for the safety of Baroness Anne and Josef Meister.' Josef Meister was presently living in the basement of the house and keeping out of the way.

Carl looked at his ageing parents.

'I think you two should go with Pia and Mariella to Italy,' he said.

'Your mother and I will be guided by whatever you all think best,' said the baron.

'Perhaps,' said the baroness, 'we can look after the children.'

'What children?' asked Paul. 'Anyway, Dad, I'll be happy to go with Lucia and Aunt Pia.' For which concession he received a happy smile from Lucia.

'Well, I'd better be with Lucia and Paul,' said Emma Jane, 'there ought to be one sensible young person present.'

James looked at Sophie. She was up in arms immediately.

'No, never,' she said. 'I shall stay with you and Carl and Vicky.' Under no circumstances would she let James out of her sight. He always adventured recklessly. He had done so before the war and during the war. She needed to keep an eye on him now. The children would go their own way when they were married. She was not going to risk being left without a husband.

'Sophie,' said James, 'I—'

'Please don't argue,' said Sophie.

'I am always against allowing husbands to argue,' said Karita.

'I can confirm that,' said Kirby. 'Now, exactly what has been decided?'

'Yes, what?' said Vicky. 'I wish to say that I myself am not going anywhere unless Aunt Anne is with us.'

'But arrangements must be settled,' said Karita, 'and everyone must know exactly what the arrangements are.'

It was agreed there and then that Pia and Mariella would go with Lucia, Paul and Emma Jane, and that the baron and baroness would accompany them. They would all join Franz at the home of Pia's mother in the Italian Tyrol. They would take the train on Monday, thus allowing three days to do all that was necessary prior to leaving Vienna for good.

James and Carl, bringing their previously planned departure date forward, would leave with Sophie and Vicky on Tuesday morning, providing Anne was free and could go with them. They would also take Josef Meister. Carl was to drive the truck containing the two racing cars, Vicky up in the cabin with him to keep him company. James would drive his large Fraser limousine, with Sophie beside him. Anne and Josef Meister would be in the truck. Carl and James knew the framework for stabilizing the cars could be used to conceal Anne as well as Josef.

Anne was still a question mark, of course. Her place in the scheme of things depended on whether she was released or not, or, as Kirby implied, forcibly freed. He would give no details on how this might be done.

It was certain, however, that James and Carl would not leave without her. Pia and the others, once they were at her mother's home, were to wait until contact was made.

After the Kirbys had left, everyone worried about how Anne was being treated.

'How long before the Gestapo and this devil's man Ludwig Lundt-Hausen come looking for you?' asked Karita, as she and her husband walked from the taxi to their rooms above a shop in Hoher Market.

'I think Lundt-Hausen will have checked files for a photograph of me,' said Kirby. 'I think he may have done that after seeing me with Baroness Anne. Matthew is certain no-one saw him slip the envelope into her pocket, but he can't know whether or not her nearness to him at the time wasn't noticed and thought about. She may have been under suspicion before she was seen with me, and perhaps Lundt-Hausen put two and two together. Well. we shall have to do what we can to help her. This afternoon I'll call on the Inkwell.'

'Can we trust him?' asked Karita. The Inkwell was the pseudonym of a recommended forger.

'I can trust the go-between,' said Kirby. 'What

we want, of course, will be expensive, since we must have it by Monday at the latest.'

They let themselves into the apartment. The rooms were very comfortable, and the amenities included a telephone.

'Nicholas seems very attached to the girl called Vicky,' said Karita. Nicholas had stayed to keep Vicky company and to have lunch with her and her family. 'One wonders if we will see anything of him for the rest of the day.'

'That's an interesting thought, not a worry,' said Kirby.

'Ah, perhaps you are right,' said Karita, 'the girl is sweet. This afternoon, while you do what you must, and there's so much for both of us to do over the weekend, I'll go to the gallery and collect the picture. Fräulein Amaraldi won't mind if I collect today, I'm sure. I'm also sure I should like to put a bomb under the bed of Baroness Anne's former husband.' Born and raised in the Crimea, and active for the Whites during the Russian Revolution, Karita was on familiar terms with bombs. 'Be careful of that man, by the way.'

'Lundt-Hausen?' said Kirby.

'I have told you, he sounds like a Bolshevik commissar,' said Karita. 'All such men are fiends from hell, torturers of people and enemies of God. This man will have no mercy on you if you make a mistake. Then I will have to kill him. Then they will hang me. Do you want that to happen?'

'Not exactly,' said Kirby.

'I want us to live until we are both old and have

168

nothing to do except sit in the sunshine together,' said Karita.

'A pleasant thought, little Russian wife and mother,' said Kirby. 'But you're the one who'll have to be careful.'

Karita, whisking eggs, smiled.

'I have eaten Bolshevik commissars for breakfast,' she said, 'and will eat this Austrian one. For supper, I think.'

Chapter Eleven

It was an unpleasant fact that on arrival at SS headquarters, Anne received a push from Schroeder that impelled her into the vestibule. Much to her surprise, Voegler spoke cuttingly to his underling.

'It's true, then, is it, Schroeder, that you have no manners?'

Schroeder shrugged. Kommissar Voegler fancied himself as a cut above the honest rank and file. It was all talk with him when conducting an interrogation. Talk, talk, talk, when one blow would have brought an answer.

It was Voegler who conducted the interrogation of Baroness Anne and Matthew Gibbs in Lundt-Hausen's office. Schroeder looked silently on. Ludwig stood at the window, his back to the scene, his eyes scanning the street below. Gibbs, who had been brought in earlier than Anne, sat at the desk with her, Voegler seated opposite them.

'I'm afraid, Baroness, circumstances are against you,' he said. 'You've been seen in company with Herr Gibbs, suspected of espionage activities, and with a man known to be a British agent.'

'I do not know any British agents, whatever that may mean,' said Anne, 'and you have not seen me in company with Herr Gibbs.'

'Come, Baroness, come, come,' said Voegler, shaking his head gently, 'he's sitting next to you and is as close to you now as you were to him on a certain day.'

'What day was that?' asked Anne.

'A day glorious in the history of Germanic Austria,' said Voegler, 'a day when Vienna witnessed the arrival of the Fuehrer.'

Schroeder opened his mouth.

'Heil Hitler,' he said.

Gibbs had a feeling that all Nazis, from Hitler downwards, were mad. He was silent, but his mind was fixed on the probable necessity of lying his head off to protect Baroness Anne.

'Baroness,' said Voegler, 'you were next to Herr Gibbs in the crowd. You spoke together.'

'You have told me this gentleman is Herr Gibbs,' said Anne, acutely conscious of Ludwig's presence, 'and I must tell you that if he was indeed standing next to me, it was by accident. I must also tell you I spoke with no-one except an abrasive young man.'

'You say so?' enquired Voegler gently. He did not want his civilized front to be outdone by this woman's serenity.

'I do.'

'We'll see, shall we?' said Voegler, eyes reflecting quiet confidence. He nodded at Schroeder. 'Fetch Walther Grasse.'

Schroeder rose, and made a rapid exit. Ludwig remained silent, gloved hands behind his back, clasping a short black stick, his eyes still watching the street. Voegler regarded the suspects in a detached way. Schroeder returned in company with a youth whom Anne and Gibbs both recognized. Gibbs said a few swear words to himself. He was suffering pangs of conscience on Anne's account. Her calm demeanour sharpened the pangs. It was a consolation, albeit an uncomfortable one, to be with her in an office that was as austere as Kommissar Voegler and as cold as the uniformed SD officer at the window. God Almighty, what kind of a man was he to have his ex-wife brought here by the Gestapo?

'Good morning, Herr Grasse,' said Voegler to the patently nervous youth. 'Tell me, is there anyone here you've seen before?'

Walther Grasse, looking at Anne and Gibbs, said, 'Yes, that woman. Yes, and that man. You arrested him and me last—'

'When did you see him, and the woman?'

'Just after the Fuehrer had passed by.' Walther Grasse glanced at the stiff back of the silent SD officer. 'Heil Hitler,' he said, nervousness uppermost. He had been beaten and bruised during his detention.

'Where were they when you saw them?'

'I saw her first, next to me, Herr Kommissar, and I'd noticed she wasn't very enthusiastic. Far from it. So I reprimanded her and told her she must be a Communist or Jewess or some such. Well, I ask you, Herr Kommissar, who wouldn't have been suspicious of her?' The youth was

172

gabbling in his eagerness to prove himself a good Nazi. 'All she said was that she wasn't unaffected by events, which could have meant anything, and then he – that man – pushed in between us. He'd been standing on the other side of her. He insulted me, accusing me of indecent behaviour.'

'Had you noticed them in conversation?' asked Voegler.

'Yes,' said Walther Grasse, knowing that was the required answer.

'That's a lie,' said Anne.

'Two of a kind they were,' said the youth, 'thick as thieves.'

'That's another lie,' said Anne.

'Pathetic,' said Gibbs. 'Look at him. He's so pitiful he couldn't even look his own mother in the face.'

'And what about yours, eh?' Walther Grasse seethed. 'I bet you don't even know who she is.'

'Young pig, I'm on exceptionally good terms with her, and my father,' said Gibbs.

'He sounds like a Jew,' said Walther Grasse to Voegler, 'so does she.'

Voegler's smile was lightly sarcastic.

'Herr Grasse, we value your opinions, of course,' he said, 'but you can leave now and we'll try to manage without them.' He nodded at Schroeder again. 'See the young gentleman out.' Schroeder took him away, and Voegler glanced at Anne. 'Well now,' he said, 'I think we've established that you and Herr Gibbs know each other and spoke together on the occasion in question.'

'I had never seen this gentleman before,' said Anne, 'and we did not speak together. Is that specimen of indifferent young manhood supposed to be your witness? How laughable.'

Ignoring that, Voegler said, 'Further, you can't deny you had a meeting with the British agent on Tuesday morning. You were very definitely seen, and you know you were. You are a go-between, Baroness, and as such could be charged with treason.'

'You are so fixed in your mind that you seem incapable of listening,' said Anne. 'It is simply not acceptable for you to say this is so or that is so, as if this or that is the truth. Your desire to believe yourself does not turn assumptions into facts, but is merely an example of wishful thinking. I find it very annoying.'

The gloved hands clasping the stick tightened in a spasm of temper. Voegler, however, remained equable. At least, that was how he seemed.

'Well, Baroness,' he said, 'instead of this or that, let's deal with facts and circumstances. It's an undeniable fact that you were seen with Herr Gibbs, that he accused the witness of insulting you, and that you were subsequently noticed in company with another Englishman. Both are suspected of espionage, and these facts and circumstances make you suspect too. I consider that a reasonable assumption, although whether it's the truth or not, we don't yet know. I suggest you have a role as a go-between.'

'You may suggest the moon is square, if you like,' said Anne, 'but it would not be true.'

'Stop harassing this lady,' said Gibbs.

Voegler, who had ignored him so far, said, 'You are not yet required to speak, Herr Gibbs. Baroness, be so good as to turn out your handbag.'

'Very well,' said Anne, not a woman who carried secrets in any of her handbags. She turned this one out on the desk without fuss. Voegler acknowledged her compliance with a smile that seemed friendly, then made a prolonged examination of the items. They were all conventional and innocuous, but he had not expected them to be otherwise. It was simply another way of getting on the nerves of a suspect.

Schroeder, who believed in the kind of methods that would shorten an interrogation, looked irritable. Ludwig remained at the window, stiff and unmoving, and although Anne was conscious of his dark brooding figure, she exhibited no sign that his presence affected her.

Voegler flipped through her diary. That too was innocuous, and the only entry for last Tuesday referred to the expected arrival of Sophie and James.

'Damn it,' said Gibbs, 'you're chasing shadows, and you know it.'

'Did you speak, Herr Gibbs?' asked Voegler in a quite pleasant way. 'Ah, yes, I think you did. Tell me, what is your opinion of Baroness Anne von Korvacs?'

'I know nothing about her, except for the obvious fact that she's a lady of grace and dignity,' said Gibbs. 'I think so now, and I thought so when that young oaf was trying to intimidate her on the day that was so glorious for Austria. One could not fault her.' Ludwig did move then. He turned sharply, his face savage of expression beneath his peaked cap. He glared at Gibbs, who said, 'She is neither an acquaintance nor an associate of mine, can't you get that into your thick heads?'

'Shut him up!' That came in a hiss from Ludwig, who gestured with his stick. Voegler, who would have preferred to provoke Gibbs into the kind of angry harangue that would give him away, sighed.

It was Schroeder who did what was necessary. He struck Gibbs across his mouth.

Anne bit her lip. She caught sight of Voegler's expression. It was one of regret. He glanced at her, and their eyes met. Hers showed distaste for the violence, and his reflected agreement.

Gibbs, dabbing at a split lip with his handkerchief, said, 'I'll advise His Majesty's Britannic Government that Austrian interrogation leaves a lot to be desired.'

'Shut up,' said Schroeder.

Ludwig had his back to them again.

'Baroness,' said Voegler, 'would you swear on oath that you did not accept anything of any kind from Herr Gibbs?'

Anne did not take long to decide how to answer.

'I swear I have never accepted any item of any kind from this gentleman,' she said. It was true enough to satisfy her conscience. Receiving under the relevant circumstances was not the same as acceptance. One did not literally accept what was foisted unknown on one's person.

'What, then, did you give the man you were seen with near the Opera Theatre?' asked Voegler.

'Why should I give anything to a man I did not know?' countered Anne.

'How strange, Baroness, that on this occasion you were seen with a man you did not know, and, two days previously, with another man you also did not know,' said Voegler, and mused on the fact. 'Even stranger, both men are engaged in espionage.'

'Not true,' said Gibbs, 'I'm an accredited journalist and biographer, and challenge you to produce any proof that shows me to be otherwise.'

'We have proof that you had meetings with a traitor, a man called Staffler,' said Voegler.

'A notorious character, I agree,' said Gibbs, 'and as a journalist I was naturally interested in getting his story. You can prove nothing else, and you know it.'

'Let me see,' murmured Voegler, 'I presume the baroness had a reason for meeting the other man, a known British agent. What was the reason, Baroness?'

'Accidental meetings don't need a reason,' said Anne.

'We're now speaking of accidental meetings?' said Voegler, looking quite pacific.

'They form the basis of some new friendships and many romantic novels,' said Anne.

'Ah, so?' Voegler smiled. 'I don't read romantic novels myself, I'm too involved with the harsh realities of life.'

'I'm not responsible for your choice of occupations,' said Anne.

'It was accidental, was it, for you to be seen in close company with two men, both of whom are suspected of acting contrary to the security of the Third Reich?' said Voegler.

'I would call it one of life's strange coincidences,' said Anne.

'Would you?' said Voegler, quite happy to spend all day in an attempt to wear her down. There was something very stimulating in crossing swords with this remarkably serene woman. It occurred to him that, providing the interrogation was on these enjoyable lines throughout, he would not mind if she was guilty or innocent. He smiled to himself. Colonel Lundt-Hausen would be outraged if her guilt could not be shown to be a fact. 'Pardon my scepticism, Baroness.'

'Oh, we all suffer doubts that prove unjustified,' said Anne, 'and must pardon each other on these lamentable occasions.'

Ludwig's teeth grated.

Schroeder thought Kommissar Voegler irritatingly indulgent of this aristocratic female. One could even suppose he liked her.

'Baroness,' said Voegler, smiling again, 'do you admire your country's enemies more than the ideals of National Socialism?'

'How can any of us admire our country's enemies?' asked Anne.

'Traitors do!' shouted Schroeder, and Voegler looked pained. Gibbs held his peace only with an effort.

'I have never been a traitor to Austria, nor ever will,' said Anne.

'Well, do you admire Herr Gibbs?' asked Voegler.

'I know nothing about Herr Gibbs, except that he's sitting next to me.'

'Do you admire the man you met near the Opera Theatre?'

'You mean the man I was seen with? I liked his friendliness, but for all I know he may have other characteristics that render him far from admirable.'

'A correct assumption, Baroness. His record as a British agent includes murder of patriots.' Voegler did not mention they were Lenin's Bolsheviks. 'Did he refer to that during his meeting with you?'

'Oh, dear, you really are tiresome,' said Anne.

'So sorry,' murmured Voegler, 'but I must ask my questions. However, I shall understand if you lose your temper.'

'I'm not in the habit of losing my temper,' said Anne, and Ludwig's teeth grated again.

Gibbs spoke.

'I'm afraid, Baroness, that in some extraordinary way, these people seem to think we're plotting to blow up Vienna.'

'It isn't your fault, Herr Gibbs, that they suspect even a red salmon of having Communist affiliations,' said Anne.

Ludwig spoke, but without turning round.

'Remove that damned Englishman for the time being,' he said.

Schroeder made a bruising business of getting Gibbs out of the office and into a bleak waiting room, with two men to keep an eye on him. That left Anne alone with the inquisitors.

'You still insist you don't know Herr Gibbs as a friend or associate?' said Voegler.

'Yes, I do insist,' said Anne. 'Further, if some people make a habit of lying, I do not.' Again Ludwig's gloved hands tightened around his stick, and Schroeder growled disparagingly. 'Let me make it quite clear that on the day glorious in the history of Austria, Herr Gibbs, whom I repeat I did not know nor had ever met, made a chivalrous gesture in saving me from the unpleasantness of the young man who lied to you a little while ago. Herr Gibbs left after delivering his rebuke, but at no time did he have any conversation with me.'

Voegler, wondering what Lundt-Hausen was making of his ex-wife's calm demeanour and composed responses, said, 'We'll leave Herr Gibbs for the moment, and refer to the other Englishman. What is his name?'

'His name?' Anne was beginning to feel the pressures of the sustained questioning, and Ludwig's silence and rigid back did not help. She could sense his hatred. She had a great longing to be among kind and civilized people. 'How should I know his name?'

'Of course you know,' said Voegler. 'Also, where does he live?'

'Is this the man you say is a known British agent?' asked Anne.

'That's the man, Baroness.'

'This has been absurd from the beginning,' said Anne. 'It's even more absurd now. How can any man be a known British agent living in Vienna if your files give you neither his name nor his address? I'm expected to know what you don't?'

Voegler's appreciation of that response was almost readable. A love-hate relationship was being born.

'That, Baroness, is as specious an answer as any woman could devise,' he said. A smile of malice split Ludwig's tight mouth. 'I did not say we don't know the man's name. It's John Kirby.' Voegler had had to be informed of Kirby's presence in Vienna.

'The name is supposed to be familiar to me?' said Anne.

'You were with him on Tuesday, that is a witnessed fact. Come, Baroness, the fact incriminates you, confess it.'

Anne remembered an incident.

'Tuesday morning was lovely, and I was out walking,' she said. 'Near the Opera Theatre I was almost knocked over by two running men. Had it not been for the quick assistance of a gentleman, I should have fallen heavily. He was kindness itself in his concern for me. We watched as some SS men took up the chase from a car.' Anne paused, then added calmly, 'My former husband also arrived and seemed in charge of the pursuit.' Ludwig's gloved hands almost snapped his stick. 'The gentleman was still with me, and we were discussing, naturally, what was going on. He asked my ex-husband what it was all about. We parted soon afterwards. If he's a British agent, he did not tell me so, and he spoke excellent German. I really would like to be released now, for I've told you all I know.'

'It's a treadmill, this kind of interview, isn't it, Baroness?' said Voegler pleasantly. 'But it has to be done. Where was it John Kirby told you he lived?'

'He didn't tell me,' said Anne.

It went on like that for another ten minutes, without Ludwig saying a word or removing himself from the window. Anne fought uneasiness and every question. Voegler played cat-and-mouse but without reducing the mouse. Damned if she wasn't worth every subtlety, every moment of his time. What did the conclusion matter when she was unfailingly stimulating to his mind? However, he suddenly and abruptly had her taken to the waiting room. And, at a mutter from Lundt-Hausen, he ordered Matthew Gibbs to be brought back.

Gibbs was not this time asked to sit down, but he did so all the same. Anne's ex-husband, he noted, had turned to watch his entry.

'So sorry to have made you wait, Herr Gibbs,' said Voegler, 'but I've time now to put a few questions to you.'

Eyeing him in exasperation, Gibbs said, 'Why don't you stop trying to make something out of nothing? I'm a journalist and writer, presently gathering material for a biography of Freud. I'm not an espionage agent.'

'Do you admit knowing a man called John Kirby?'

'Who?'

'John Kirby.'

'I know of him. He's had stories written about him in newspapers and magazines.'

'What kind of stories?'

'About his adventures in Russia before the Great War, during the war and during the Revolution. I'll tell you something that should please you. He hates Russian Communists.'

'He told you that?'

'He said so in a newspaper article.'

'You know, of course, that he's presently in Vienna,' said Voegler.

'That's a fact, is it?' Gibbs assumed a look of professional interest. 'I'd like to interview him.'

'Of course,' said Voegler. 'Where is he living?'

'I'd like you to tell me,' said Gibbs.

'Herr Kommissar, give me ten minutes with this bag of English horse dung,' said Schroeder.

'Schroeder, are you trying to give the Gestapo a bad name?' asked Voegler.

'He's already done that,' said Gibbs. 'Jesus Christ, how much longer and how many more times are you going to subject me to the same questions?'

'I suppose we're hoping for some different answers,' said Voegler, 'I suppose we're hoping for the truth.'

'Damn it,' said Gibbs, 'you've examined me repeatedly, and without allowing me the services of a lawyer. You've impounded my passport and had me followed daily. Either you return my passport or specifically charge me, or my embassy will make representations to the British government. I'll answer no more questions, not unless I'm formally charged, with a lawyer present. As for the baroness, kindly tell me what's happened to her.'

'She's being held for further questioning,' said Voegler.

'Well, as I've told you,' said Gibbs, 'I hardly know the lady, but my impression of her is that if she's guilty of treason, I'm the King of Siam. If there's a conspiracy at all, I'd say it's against her.'

Ludwig looked wolfish. Schroeder scowled. Voegler examined his fingernails, which were quite clean.

'What makes you say that, Herr Gibbs?' he asked slyly. 'May we be told?'

'Release him,' said Ludwig.

'Herr Colonel?' said Voegler.

'Release him.' Ludwig spoke brusquely. 'Give him back his passport.'

Voegler unlocked a drawer in the desk, took out a British passport and passed it to Gibbs.

'Thank you,' said Gibbs. 'If you'd now consent to releasing the baroness, I could escort her home.'

'H'm,' said Voegler, and considered the offer. 'Would it be out of your way? Where does she live?'

Seeing through that, Gibbs said, 'I've no idea, I didn't arrest her. You did.'

'Voegler, get him out of here,' rasped Ludwig.

It was Schroeder who escorted Gibbs out of the building.

'A morning of failure, Herr Kommissar?' suggested Ludwig bitingly.

'Not in my book,' said Voegler. 'An interesting one, I thought. Gibbs is guilty, of course, and Baroness Anne could, I think, be brought to tears and a confession. Or a final denial,' he added blandly.

'Kirby's the man,' said Ludwig, 'he's the one in possession of what we want. Put a new watch on Gibbs. He's a second-rater, an amateur with the bit between his teeth, and he'll lead us to Kirby sooner or later. Place the baroness in solitary detention. Leave her there for twenty-four hours, and don't communicate with her until you question her again tomorrow. You don't believe that fairy story of hers, do you? That Kirby saved her from being knocked over? Get the real story from her one way or another. Meanwhile, regarding Kirby's location, have some enquiries made of taxi drivers.'

'We're already at work on that,' said Voegler.

'Keep at it,' said Ludwig. 'We may not be able to wait for Gibbs to lead us to him. I tell you, Kirby's the man. That woman passed the document on to him.'

'The baroness?' said Voegler.

'Yes, of course she damned well did. Find him. The document must be retrieved. A certain person insists.'

'Which certain person?' asked Voegler.

'Himmler,' said Ludwig. 'And it's time you also found Meister, that damned Jew.'

Since all Jews were damned, thought Voegler, did one matter that much more than another?

One did to Lundt-Hausen.

His hatred of Meister was obviously on a par with his hatred of his former wife.

There's more in such hatred than meets the eye, thought Voegler.

Chapter Twelve

Gibbs made a phone call from a public booth. A woman answered. In German.

'Yes, who is this, please?'

'Karita? Matthew here. Speak English.'

'Ah, Matthew my scribbling friend, what do you want? We've been out, now we are in, and soon we go out again. Meanwhile, we are having a late lunch.'

'You're lucky. I've had no lunch at all. Tell John the Gestapo have pulled in the baroness.'

'Baroness Anne?' said Karita. 'That is stale news. But don't worry. Go and find some lunch while we finish ours.'

'Never mind your lunch. Let me speak to John, frivolous woman.'

He heard Karita laugh softly. Something was on. She was always like that when excitement was hovering.

'He's here,' she said, and Kirby came on the line. Gibbs recounted the morning's events. Kirby in turn recounted some parts of his conversation with Anne's relatives.

'Well, that's a fine kettle of fish,' said Gibbs.

'You've surfaced now, and with a vengeance. I hope it won't make things worse for Baroness Anne. She's heroic. Her ex-husband hates her, and you and I have put her where she is. How the devil can she join the family exodus from Vienna unless she's released?'

'Karita will effect her release,' said Kirby, 'providing I can obtain the necessary leverage.'

'Karita can get her out of the hands of the Gestapo? Is Karita as crazy as that? Are both of you?'

'Karita's looking forward to it,' said Kirby. 'To her, every SD and Gestapo official is the equivalent of a Bolshevik commissar.'

'I know she hated Lenin's butchers,' said Gibbs, 'but the Bolsheviks are history now, aren't they? The Soviet hierarchy, the Central Committee in Moscow, is packed with venerable Communist Party members.'

'Old Bolsheviks, my friend, so don't argue that with Karita, or she'll split your head,' said Kirby. 'They're all Bolshevik assassins to her, hiding under the label of Communism. D'you mind if I finish my lunch now? You keep your head down. That is, stay out of the way and leave things to us.'

'You and your damned lunch,' said Gibbs. 'There's a very courageous woman being persecuted by—'

'Yes, I know, by her ex-husband. Well, put your trust in Karita. Phone again later, on Sunday, say.'

'Wait a moment,' said Gibbs, 'I want to know how—' The phone went dead.

He shrugged and left the booth. He was tailed all the way back to his apartment without realizing it. He thought Voegler had called off the dogs, that it was Baroness Anne they wanted most of all. Further, the new dogs were better trained.

'Vicky?' said Nicholas. He was taking an afternoon walk with her along the Salesianergasse, and she was visibly unhappy.

'I'm sorry, I know I'm a misery,' she said, 'but Aunt Anne, I can't bear to think of her in the hands of the police, those Nazi police.'

'The Austrian Gestapo,' said Nicholas.

'Awful,' said Vicky.

'Well, let's try looking on the bright side,' said Nicholas. 'My father doesn't make idle promises, and he knows his way about the diplomatic corridors.'

'What does that mean?' asked Vicky.

'Well, let's put it like this,' said Nicholas. 'Your Aunt Anne is in at the moment, in at the deep end. With luck, she'll soon be out.'

'You're speaking in riddles,' said Vicky. 'Oh, it's all so unbelievable. How could anyone arrest such a sweet person as Aunt Anne?'

'Someone with enough spite?' suggested Nicholas.

'You mean the man who used to be our Uncle Ludwig? He's disgusting. Oh, I'll just have to put all my hopes in your parents. They seemed so self-assured.'

'Yes, leave it to them, Vicky,' said Nicholas.

*   *   *

The gallery was very well attended on this cold crisp afternoon. Mariella was delighted at the number of visitors and the purchases that had been made, although on her mind was the fact that she had any amount of work to do in regard to her departure from Austria. Sergeant Wainwright was present, but hadn't spoken to her or been anywhere near her. He existed in what she thought was an anonymous way, which she supposed was the best way. But managing to catch his eye, she called him over.

'What is the matter with you?' she asked.

'Hello, do I look ill?' he queried.

'You look disgustingly fit,' she said. 'I meant, why are you sulking?'

'Beg to differ, marm, I'm my usual sociable self,' he said.

'I'm pleased to hear it,' said Mariella, 'since I've been wondering if I had fleas.'

'Perish the thought,' said Sergeant Wainwright, 'there's not a single sign that you're flea-bitten. I never saw a healthier-looking woman. My compliments, in fact, on your looks, and a reminder that I don't go in for sulking about. The word is watchful, which allows me to be ready to jump on persons harmful. Permission to carry on, marm?'

Mariella wanted to laugh. The man was taking himself seriously in an absurd way.

'Permission?' she said, keeping her face straight. 'Yes, of course. Please to carry on, Sergeant Wainwright.'

* * *

Karita Kirby arrived mid-afternoon, in a white fur hat and a black waisted coat with a Cossack-style skirt. She sauntered around while waiting for Mariella to finish talking to a group of visitors, and had a cheerful word or two with Sergeant Wainwright, whom she and Kirby had known for many years. Mariella, spotting her eventually, came over.

'Frau Kirby?'

Karita smiled. She looked strikingly Russian. Mariella, in glossy red, looked a glowing full-bodied Italian.

'You have a splendid way of dressing, Fräulein Amaraldi,' said Karita.

'Oh, I'm addicted to wild colours,' said Mariella. 'Have you come to collect your picture today, then?'

'Do you mind my taking it now?' asked Karita. 'You see, we have advanced our leaving date.'

'You're very welcome to take it now,' said Mariella. 'Thank you for allowing it to stay. It's been much admired.'

'Ah,' said Karita, 'then perhaps it is worth much more than we paid for it.'

Mariella laughed.

'I'm not complaining,' she said. 'Shall I wrap it for you?'

'How kind,' said Karita.

Mariella spread a large sheet of brown paper over her table, crossed the floor, took the canvas down under the eyes of interested visitors and carried it to the table. She placed it face down on the paper. The address label was secure in its adhesion to the back of the frame, and Mariella

191

made a quick and efficient job of the wrapping, tying it with string.

'There,' she said.

'Thank you,' said Karita. Knowing Mariella was the sister-in-law of Baron Carl von Korvacs, she murmured, 'My dear Fräulein, are you aware that Baroness Anne von Korvacs was arrested by the Gestapo at her home early this morning?'

Mariella's colouring receded. She turned white.

'No, no, it can't be true.'

'I met your relatives this morning, with my husband,' said Karita. 'I am so sorry to upset you in this way, but it is right you should know, I think.'

'Mother of God,' whispered Mariella. 'Anne? But she's so sweet, so kind. Carl will be devastated. Oh, I must go, I must see them all.'

'Yes.' Karita was gentle. She had many moods, and could leap easily from one to another. 'If you wish, I will look after the gallery and the paintings, and stand in for you. I have an hour to spare.'

'Thank you, thank you.' Mariella snatched up her hat and coat and ran. Sergeant Wainwright, at a gesture from Karita, did not follow.

'Carl!' Mariella burst into the apartment the moment Carl opened the door to her. 'Is it true, that Anne's been arrested?'

'Yes, it's true.' Carl was grim, his blue eyes steely. 'Who told you?'

'A woman. Frau Kirby. She and her husband bought one of my paintings. She said they had

192

seen you this morning. Carl, what has Anne done? Why have they arrested her?'

'For being a danger to the security of the Greater German Reich, so they said.'

'The Gestapo said?' queried Mariella, anguished.

'We believe Ludwig is responsible,' said Carl. 'You know how much he hates Anne, and the rest of the family.'

'He's a mad dog,' breathed Mariella, 'and should be shot like one. What is being done, Carl, what is being done?'

'I've been trying for hours to arrange to see Seyss-Inquart,' said Carl. Kirby had suggested not to do so yet, but Carl felt he needed insurance against Kirby's possible failure to deliver Anne. 'However, I'm being told he's too busy at the moment to give interviews to people who belong to my class and not the Party.'

'Carl, you'll get nothing in the way of help from Seyss-Inquart,' said Mariella, 'he's Hitler's performing dog.'

'I'm willing to go to Hitler himself to save Anne,' said Carl. 'I've been to SS headquarters, to the SD and Gestapo departments there, but I've been refused permission to see her. James wanted to go, to see Ludwig, but Sophie dissuaded him. It seems James was ready to tear the place down. Sophie said he'd get himself shot and that she'd let him go only over her dead body.'

'Carl, oh my God, I can't believe this,' said Mariella.

'I think we can all believe anything of Ludwig,' said Carl.

*　　*　　*

Two men entered the gallery. They wore black raincoats and dark trilby hats. Karita recognized them at once for what they were. They walked through the salon to the office, taking no notice of the visitors or of Karita, who was sitting at the table. They opened the door of the office and looked in. It was empty. They turned and studied the visitors, then looked at Karita. They walked towards her. She rose and walked to meet them.

'You have not closed that door,' she said.

'What door?' asked one man.

'The door you have just opened,' said Karita. 'Where are your manners?'

'Close the door for Her Highness,' said the man to his colleague, who did as requested. He came back silently, to regard Karita with searching eyes.

'Who are you?' he asked.

'A lady,' said Karita. That evoked nothing but blank stares. 'I am a naturalized British subject, and must tell you that in Britain gentlemen usually take their hats off when addressing a lady.'

'So?' Members of the Gestapo all had an in-built or readily acquired facility for absorbing verbal punishment. 'Your name?'

Karita smiled, and there was a suggestion of bright steel surfacing.

'Ah, you are Bulgarian?' she said.

'What?'

'I am Bulgarian,' said Karita. 'That is, I was. Now I am British. But in Bulgaria, I've known many policemen without manners. They stop

194

one and ask, "Your name?" Why are names so important to police of that kind? Do we not have faces and eyes? Do you not know eyes are more important than names? It is our eyes that hold our secrets, and our innocence or our guilt, not our names. Look into my eyes. They will tell you far more than my name will.'

If they had looked into her eyes, they would have seen the bright steel. As it was, they looked only at her person.

'All the same, tell us your name. You are not Mariella Amaraldi, in charge here.'

'Did I say I was? I am in charge only for a while.' Karita's accent had lost its softness. It was edged with glass. 'Fräulein Amaraldi is out at the moment. My name? Ah, yes, Constanza Helene Franklyn. Lady Franklyn. My husband is Sir William Charles Franklyn, Commander of the British Empire.'

'Your identity papers?' They were interested in her because here she was, temporarily in charge of the Meister Gallery, and obviously a friend of Mariella Amaraldi, who was suspected by Colonel Lundt-Hausen of knowing the whereabouts of Josef Meister the Jew, who had apparently given up hiding in his storeroom.

'Papers? Papers?' said Karita. 'What do you mean, papers? The British do not carry papers. Who are you that you ask such an absurd question of a visitor to your country? No-one in Britain, not the highest in the land, will stop you and ask you for any papers.'

'You have your passport?'

'Of course.' Karita had a forged passport in

her handbag, lately acquired as a precautionary factor. She made no attempt to produce it. 'Why do you ask about it?'

'We're security police.'

'Yes?' Karita was icy. These were the new Bolsheviks, the Bolsheviks of Germany and Austria, born with a whip in their hands. 'Yes?'

'Where's Fräulein Amaraldi?'

'Out,' said Karita. 'I have already told you.' People, curious, were gathering. 'Perhaps she is meeting a gentleman friend. Or visiting the tombs of Austrian emperors. Or perhaps she is breathing in air. Who knows?'

'Where's Josef Meister?'

'What is the matter with you?' Karita now looked ready to lose her temper. 'Do you think I have come to Vienna to be asked questions about people I have never met? In a moment, I shall go to the office and telephone my husband, who will then telephone the British Embassy. First, I wish to have your own names. What are your names?'

A young man smiled. A girl even giggled. Voegler's men, unsure of their ground now, except that they knew Hitler favoured a sympathetic foreign press, eyed Karita with their first flicker of uncertainty.

But they tried once more.

'Do you know Josef Meister, who owns this gallery?'

'I told you, I've never met him,' said Karita. 'Is there no limit to your impertinence?'

They looked at the listening visitors.

'Does anyone here know Josef Meister?'

'I don't, no.'

'No, nor I.'

There was a general falling-back, a shuffling retreat. Listening to men of the Gestapo questioning the woman in the white fur hat was interesting, even absorbing, but they were totally disinclined to invite questions of themselves. Most did not stop retreating. Most left the gallery. Sergeant Wainwright was not one of them. He had a smile on his face. He knew Karita Kirby. She would not need his help.

'Time to go,' said one man to the other, and they brushed past Karita and made their way into the street. 'A crazy woman, that one.'

'Ach, a crazy Bulgarian woman with a touch of the insufferable English about her, what a cow. What I'd like to know is where's the Amaraldi deviant?'

'Deviant?'

'That's what Voegler calls her. He said she paints a tree to look like something else.'

'Where's the Jew, that's more to the point. It's the Jew who's wanted, not the Italian deviant.'

Among the few people who remained in the gallery was an elderly gentleman who not only bought a painting, but complimented Karita on her way of dealing with unmannerly policemen.

Karita, enchanted to receive payment on Mariella's behalf, said, 'Oh, it's a matter of wishing people to observe civilized courtesies, mein Herr. If they had taken their hats off, I should not have been quite so vexed with them.'

*   *   *

Mariella returned to the gallery.

'I have sold a picture for you,' said Karita.

'Excuse me?' Mariella was too distracted to take that in.

'You are unhappy?' said Karita gently.

'Yes. I can't bear to think of Anne in the hands of the Gestapo.'

'It is more correct to say she is in the hands of the man who was once her husband, isn't it?' said Karita. 'But Ludwig Lundt-Hausen will let her go.'

'How can you know that?' asked Mariella, with the gallery almost empty.

'He's a Bolshevik,' said Karita.

'A Bolshevik?'

'All men who worship the State and despise people are Bolsheviks,' said Karita. 'Lenin worshipped the State and despised everything except cold logic. While his wife's mother lay dying in a bed on the other side of a room he was using, he wrote a pamphlet on social systems. When his wife returned from an errand of mercy and asked him how her mother was, he said, "Dead, probably." And she was, but he did not stop writing. He was a monster, but not of fire and passion. No, of ice and ink. Hitler is a Bolshevik. He despises the whole world except Prussia. His Gauleiters are all Bolshevik commissars. A Bolshevik is a person whose chief liking is for eliminating people. Children too. Stalin has eliminated millions of men, women and children. Hitler will do the same. Men like Ludwig Lundt-Hausen will help him. But, like all commissars, however much power he has, he will always want more. He could not tolerate losing any of the power he has now. Therefore, he has a weakness. Therefore, because of this weakness, he will have to let Baroness Anne go.'

'I don't understand,' said Mariella.

'It's only important, if you love Baroness Anne, to pray for her,' said Karita. 'Look, there is the cheque for the picture I sold for you.'

'Sold? Oh, thank you.'

'I must go now. Goodbye, Fräulein Amaraldi.'

'You are a very confusing woman,' said Mariella, 'but I can't help liking you. Thank you many times for looking after the gallery.'

'Ah, a moment,' said Karita. 'Two men came, looking for a gentleman called Josef Meister.'

'Two men?' said Mariella.

'Bolsheviks,' said Karita, and smiled and left, taking the wrapped picture, *English Cottage*, with her.

Mariella beckoned Sergeant Wainwright. He approached like a man happy with events.

'Frau Kirby is a remarkable woman, yes?' she said.

'Well, some women are remarkable, marm, some not so remarkable, and most need to be watched or they'll have the shirt off a man's back and every hair off his chest.'

'How dare you abuse my sex, you swine?'

'Just a comment in passing,' said Sergeant Wainwright, 'and nothing personal.'

'Ah,' said Mariella, 'I know. Your waitress has had the shirt off your back.'

'Not yet, but she will if I don't keep my distance from her itchy fingers.'

'You're safe in my company,' said Mariella.

'It's questionable, marm, if any man is safe in any woman's company.'

'How would you like your face smacked?' asked Mariella.

'No more, I daresay, than you'd like your bottom smacked.'

'*Mama mia*, what an English pig you are.'

'Very good, marm, will that be all?'

'Isn't that enough?'

'It'll do to be going on with,' said Sergeant Wainwright.

Chapter Thirteen

The following day, after twenty-four hours in isolation, Anne had to face up to further questioning. Ludwig was not present, for which she was thankful. Voegler, with Schroeder again sitting in, assured her, much to her disgust, that Colonel Lundt-Hausen had her interests at heart and was, indeed, distressed at the predicament in which she had placed herself. Anne said nothing to that, although Voegler delivered his assurance kindly and earnestly, even if it was no more believable to him than to Anne. She looked at him and there was a brief eye-to-eye confrontation before she glanced away.

Voegler's manner changed then, and he resumed his interrogation in sternly accusing fashion. It was disgraceful, he said, that a woman of her background could be capable of assisting enemies of her country. What was the reason?

'Come along, answer up.'

'Herr Voegler—'

'Kommissar Voegler.'

'Herr Kommissar, how can I give a reason for

something of which I'm innocent? The offence exists only in your mind.'

'Don't be impertinent. You've associated with foreign agents, the enemies of your country, and you must explain why.'

'Since I haven't done so, no explanation is necessary.' Anne did not, in any case, consider enemies of the Nazis to be enemies of Austria.

'Understand this, Baroness, I'm not a fool.'

'Who has said you were? I haven't. Has my ex-husband?'

Voegler might have said there were times when her ex-husband swore everyone in Vienna was a fool except himself. What he did say was that Anne's impertinence astounded him.

'Have her strip-searched for her secrets, Herr Kommissar,' said Schroeder roughly.

Voegler cast him a dismissive look, but said to Anne, 'It may come to that, and unless I'm present myself to protect you, God knows what might happen to you. Some of our policewomen are strange creatures.'

'Is that an attempt to frighten me?' asked Anne.

'You should be frightened. You can be executed for treason. Earn yourself a temperate sentence, or even a pardon, by confessing. That will save time and my temper. Do you see what a rage you're putting me in?'

'I see nothing of the kind,' said Anne, 'I see only a policeman with no soul in his eyes.'

The clear orbs darkened as Voegler experienced a definite surge of hate. But a spasm of total admiration trod on its heels. What command she had of the riposte, surely either the natural weapon of the innocent or the forged weapon of the guilty. Could anyone believe that the minutes she had spent with Kirby had come about because he had saved her from being knocked over? But there she was, as cool and serene as a saint, a woman found guilty of adultery with a Jew. Yet what woman married to Lundt-Hausen wouldn't happily fall into the arms of the first man who stepped into her boudoir? But a Jew? This woman? If so, her serenity was a pose, the mask of a whore.

In contempt of such women, Voegler attacked her with icy shafts. The man Gibbs was her lover, of course. That was why he had abused the youth. She should be ashamed, a woman of her age allowing a man twenty years younger to take her to bed.

Anne flushed.

'How old do you think I am, Herr Kommissar?' she asked, with Schroeder grinning.

'Fifty?'

'I am forty-one, as you know very well from my details.'

'It's your own fault if your way of life makes you look fifty. Is Kirby your lover too?'

'No man is my—'

'You're renowned, aren't you, for jumping into bed with all kinds of men, even Jews?'

'Herr Kommissar, you are disgusting.'

He had cracked her poise at last. She was very flushed, her eyes hot, her voice angry. A smile touched his face and mellowed his austere features. He spoke pleasantly.

'I'm used to hard names.'

'However,' she said, as if he had not spoken at all, 'what else can be expected of a man who has no soul and is lost to God? But of course, I'm sure you're happy enough supping with Satan.' The crack had closed. Her poise restored, she regarded him like a woman curious about what had crawled into the light from beneath an upturned stone. He wanted, incredibly, to shout his applause at the superb way she had turned the tables. Instead, he chose to begin at the beginning again, to refer to the events on the day of Hitler's triumphant return to Vienna.

Back to clinical perseverance, he asked questions he had asked before, determined to wear her down. The contest had to provide a winner, and he felt extraordinary pleasure in continuing to cross swords with her, for she would not give way.

Anne made no mistakes in her answers, which never varied from those she had given before. In enduring eighteen dark and bitter years with Ludwig she had acquired a great fund of resilience, and an ability to cope with every kind of mental stress and acidulous examination.

She conceded nothing to Voegler all morning, although he gave her no rest, nor called for any refreshment, nor prevented Schroeder from occasionally shouting at her.

'I hope, Baroness,' he said at the end of the morning, 'that we shan't have to use other methods in order to extract the truth from you.'

'If I'm to suffer beatings and broken bones,'

said Anne, 'I shall probably say whatever you want me to, but such may still not be the truth.'

'A signature to a written confession will make it true in law,' said Voegler.

'Yes, the law of the jungle, not of a civilized society,' said Anne.

Voegler shook his head at her.

'It's regrettable to make things difficult for yourself, you foolish woman,' he said, 'and tiresome to make them difficult for me as well.'

'How very sad things are for both of us,' said Anne, and was taken back to her cell by the scowling, growling Schroeder, who, on returning to the interview room, complained that they were getting nowhere fast with the haughty bitch.

'Haughty?' said Voegler. 'I've seen no signs of haughtiness.'

'It's there right enough, Herr Kommissar.'

'Cool calculated defiance, Schroeder, is not haughtiness.'

'It's a curse and it's turning the interrogation into a circus act, if I might say so,' said Schroeder.

'Well, you have said so, but I fear you have no imagination, and are learning nothing about psychology as applied to interrogation.' Voegler became caustic. 'What,' he said, 'would be the point of beating this woman to death?'

'She slept with a Jew, didn't she?'

Voegler, beginning to entertain doubts about that, said, 'She did not dispute it during the divorce hearing. So this afternoon, we'll concentrate on the credibility of a suspect who maintains a look of purity but can allow a Jew to bed her. Oh, and give instructions that she's not permitted to wash.'

'Herr Kommissar?' said Schroeder. 'Ah, I see,' he said, 'that is psychology.' And he grinned hugely.

The night was dark and cold. Two large SS men came out of one of Vienna's handsomer and more exclusive apartment blocks. They entered a car and drove away.

'That, I understand, is the usual routine,' said Kirby. He stood with Karita inside the entrance to another block on the other side of the street. 'He arrives home with a bodyguard of three, and two leave about fifteen minutes later. So it's now.'

'Now?' murmured Karita. 'Before the third man leaves?'

'Haven't I told you he's Lundt-Hausen's batman and personal bodyguard?'

'No,' said Karita. 'You gather information and don't always tell me all of it. But never mind, what does it matter that there is still one man with him? Three would have been difficult, one is no problem.'

'Don't crow too soon, little chicken.'

'Cocks crow, chickens do not,' said Karita, looking at lighted windows.

'Well, don't lay a cracked egg,' said Kirby. 'I'll come up when—'

'You will not. It is agreed. He is not to see you, to know you are involved, or you will never get out of the country.'

'Take care,' said Kirby.

'Of course,' said Karita. She flitted across the street and disappeared into the well-lit block.

Fredric Huber, a square-faced Stormtrooper and servant to Ludwig, answered a ring at the apartment door. His formidable bulk almost filled the doorway. Karita smiled.

'I wish to see Colonel Lundt-Hausen, if you please.'

'He sees no-one without an appointment.'

'He'll see me.' Karita's smile was sweet and confident. 'Tell him I have something to say to him about Baroness Anne von Korvacs, something he will be happy to hear.'

'We'll see about that,' said Huber, massive in his black uniform. 'What's your name?'

'If you are going to be difficult, I shall go away,' said Karita. 'If I give you my name, you will throw it about. I know you people. You like to cause trouble. Do you think I want my friends to hear I've been informing on the baroness? By the way, does Colonel Lundt-Hausen pay for information?'

Huber looked hard at her.

'Wait there,' he said, and closed the door on her. Karita waited. The handsome four-storeyed building breathed with the sounds of life. Huber reappeared after an interval of three minutes. 'Enter,' he said. He stood aside, but his bulk was still something of an obstacle. Karita slipped by. 'Wait,' he said. He closed the door. Karita stood still in the square lobby of the apartment, and Huber began to search her for possible weapons. His hands passed with slow deliberation up and down her body and legs.

'I do not like that,' said Karita. Dressed in a black velour hat and a black coat with a fur collar, over a fine woollen dress, the coat and dress moved under the prying hands. 'No, I do not like that at all.'

'Well, you'll have to put up with it,' said Huber. 'Communists, Jews and dissidents get strange ideas if they can lay their hands on a gun or a knife. You might be one such. D'you think we're idiots?' He completed his search by lifting the front of her coat, dress and slip to inspect the tops of her stockings, convenient sheaths for a knife or dagger. Nor was his inspection cursory. Her thighs looked splendid.

'You are a pig,' said Karita, brown eyes burning.

Huber let her garments fall into place.

'You say too much,' he growled. 'As to your name, if you want paying for your information, you'll have to make a written statement and sign it, understand? Open your handbag.' Karita opened it. He took it from her, searched it and gave it back to her. 'Right, in you go.' He opened a door and Karita entered the living room, which looked comfortable but had little character. Huber closed the door and stood with his back to it. Ludwig, standing near a radiator, regarded the visitor out of dark smudged eyes. He put in very long hours. In the way of a dedicated hunter of the State's enemies, he did not like to vacate his office while there was still work to do. Nor did he like delegating his authority. Underlings were ambitious.

His leg a curse, he spoke, curtly.

'What are you offering?'

'Information, Herr Colonel,' said Karita, and he noted an accent softly foreign.

'Are you Hungarian?' He moved towards her, his limp perceptible. Karita knew about his leg. Carl had spoken of it to her and her husband.

'I am Greek,' she said.

'What are you doing in Vienna?'

'Living with a gentleman,' said Karita truthfully.

'You know Baroness Anne von Korvacs?'

'Yes,' said Karita.

'I know her very well myself,' said Ludwig, his thin face lined. 'I don't know you. Nor have I ever seen you with her.'

'That is not my fault. Or yours. You can't be expected to be everywhere at once.' Karita eyed him disapprovingly. 'Am I to sit down or to be kept standing? Are there no manners in Vienna these days? Your servant has none at all. He examined my legs and underwear.'

'I wasn't aware manners were to play a part in this meeting,' said Ludwig bitingly. 'I thought it was to do with paid information. But if you want to sit down, do so.'

'How kind,' said Karita, and chose an armchair that allowed her to face both men. She took off her high-crowned velour hat and placed it on her lap. In an entirely feminine gesture, she fluffed her golden hair. Its abundance sprang to life. 'The information, yes, I am sure you'll find it worth paying for. My gentleman and I like to live well, and we are a little short of money at the moment.'

'If you think you'll be paid a fortune,' said Ludwig, 'let me tell you you won't.' All the same, and despite his damned leg and his need for a good night's sleep, he was interested in this woman and what she had to offer on his sanctimonious ex-wife. She was no brash girl, she looked a woman of sophisticated maturity, intelligent enough to know it would be dangerous to offer him rubbish and make a fool of him. Voegler had got nothing out of Anne, yesterday or today, and his men had drawn blanks in their search for John Kirby. Berlin was getting impatient, Himmler fretful. Heads would roll if Vienna got nowhere. Ludwig did not intend to lose his own head, not when he could arrange for Voegler to be shown up as incompetent. 'Go ahead, let's see what the information is worth,' he said.

Huber looked on from the door. Karita smiled.

'Herr Colonel, I shall ask only for enough to pay our rent,' she said, and lifted her hat as if to put it back on. But she replaced it on her lap. 'There now,' she said, 'what do you think of this?' And Ludwig looked down at the black snout of a silencer fitted to a squat revolver. Huber moved fast, tugging his own revolver free. Karita shot him, in his right thigh, the bullet exploding from the silencer with no more sound than that of a cough. Huber collapsed, his gun falling on the carpet, his hands clutching his thigh. 'There, you pig,' said Karita, 'you looked at my legs. Tie him up,' she said to Ludwig, 'and put him where he won't be able to hear us.'

'You bitch, you've just signed your own death

warrant,' hissed Ludwig, expression vicious, fury communicating violent stabs of pain to his leg.

Huber, bleeding and groaning, attempted to get to his feet, but collapsed again.

'Tie the pig up,' said Karita, revolver steady in her hand and pointed at Ludwig.

'I'll be damned if I will,' he snarled. 'I'll give you some advice instead. Get out and start running.'

'Bolshevik,' said Karita, eyes on fire, 'do as I tell you or I'll shoot you too. In your leg. Your right leg. Twice. You will never be able to stand up straight again. And to walk, you'll need crutches. Ah, that will be something to see, a Nazi Bolshevik on crutches. Tie that man up and put him somewhere. It will be better for you not to have him hear our conversation. What is he groaning about? Can't he stand a little pain? He's ready to inflict pain on others, isn't he? So he should be able to stand a small amount himself.'

Ludwig looked into the eyes showing above the unmoving revolver. They were a strange mixture of fire and ice.

'I repeat, you've just signed your own death warrant,' he said.

'Give me your gun – yes, and his,' said Karita, 'then use his belt to strap his legs, and his tie to bind his wrists.'

Ludwig loosened his holster flap, drew his revolver and leaned as if to toss it into her lap. Karita, reading him, pistol-whipped his weapon and struck it from his hand.

'Damn you,' said Ludwig.

'Bolshevik,' said Karita, 'throw me the pig's gun.'

Ludwig picked up Huber's revolver and threw it savagely. Karita, on her feet, let it strike the skirt of her coat. She gave him a warning look.

'Bolshevik?' said Ludwig. 'You're out of your mind.'

'There's no difference between Stalin's men and Hitler's men, they are all like Lenin's Bolsheviks,' said Karita.

'What the hell does a Greek bitch know about Lenin's Bolsheviks?' asked Ludwig, watching the black silencer, his leg an outrage.

'I know enough,' said Karita, who could have told him that Lenin's Bolsheviks had murdered her Crimean parents. 'Now do as I say.'

Ludwig, his mouth shut like a trap to prevent spittle ejecting, silently trussed Huber's legs and wrists with the groaning man's own belt and tie, then began to pull him by his ankles towards the bedroom door.

'Herr Colonel, for God's sake!' Huber yelled with pain.

'Take him by his arms, then,' said Karita, 'or the weakling will faint.'

'He needs a doctor, damn you,' said Ludwig, 'or he'll bleed to death.'

'Is that a joke?' said Karita. 'I'm not here to listen to jokes. Move him.'

Ludwig stooped, put his hands under Huber's armpits from behind and dragged him into the bedroom, Karita following. Huber groaned, his face white. Karita gestured and Ludwig returned to the living room. Karita closed the bedroom door.

'What now, bitch?' asked Ludwig. The woman knew about his leg, knew how easily she could reduce him to a hopeless cripple. Therefore, she did know Anne. It would have been like that suffering saint of an ex-wife to tell the tale of his wound. His face, etched by sharp bone, grew harsh.

Karita said, 'You will telephone your headquarters and ask them to release the baroness.'

'They won't do that, not through a telephone order.'

'Perhaps you are right,' said Karita. 'So, ask them to bring her here.'

'No,' said Ludwig.

'Either you will have the baroness brought here,' said Karita, 'or your Bolshevik Party membership card will be sent to Himmler. Not to Seyss-Inquart, a friend of yours, but to Himmler.'

'Bolshevik Party?' Ludwig glared at her. She was quite still, her hair a golden halo, her expression fixed and pitiless. She had fought the Bolsheviks with her husband and a band of White guerillas. She had known the murderous excesses of the commissars, their implementation of the Red Terror, their slaughter of the Imperial family. If Ludwig hated his former wife in the senseless way of the self-pitying, Karita Kirby had an incurable hatred of the Soviet Union's Central Committee and all that Stalin, Lenin's successor, stood for. In Hitler, she saw a German Stalin. 'Membership card of the Bolshevik Party?' said Ludwig. 'You're mad.'

'Dated February 12 1918,' said Karita, 'three days after Lenin signed the treaty of Brest-Litovsk, when the Bolsheviks announced they were at peace with Germany, and many German and Austrian prisoners of war were encouraged to support the Red Revolution. Some became members of the Party, including you. Ah, perhaps you will say you are a lapsed member. But what will that matter to Himmler?'

'You're a lunatic,' said Ludwig, watching her, weighing her up. 'Bolsheviks, Bolsheviks? You're raving. Communists, yes, I'll allow they're a species that need expunging, but – '

'Communists, Nazis, Fascists – all Bolsheviks,' said Karita, 'all enemies of the people, all happy and willing to murder each other, as well as the innocent. You are a Bolshevik. Look.' She stooped swiftly and drew from the top of her fur-trimmed left boot a card that looked old and faded. 'Look.' She held it up. Ludwig peered and squinted. It was a membership card of what had once been known as the Bolshevik Party after its separation from the Mensheviks. Ludwig saw his name in faded black ink, and the signature of the secretary, J. Stalin. Savagely, he lunged in an attempt to snatch it. The card eluded him, and the toe of a boot thudded into his left leg. It made him stagger and gasp. He glared again.

'A damned forgery,' he spat.

'You would say that, of course you would.' Karita's smile was mocking. 'What Nazi would not? You will repeat it a thousand times when your own security police come to arrest you. You will be screaming it while they are pulling out your fingernails. Pulling out fingernails is a cultural activity of Nazi Bolsheviks, of course. However, finally, when you can stand no more of what they'll be doing to you, you will confess what they wish you to confess, and beg them to believe you made a foolish mistake while you were still a prisoner of war. Perhaps they will spare your life and put you to work in a labour camp, where you will find strength through joy.'

Her even voice, delivering every word sweetly and mockingly, had Ludwig in a sudden sweat. He sat heavily down. He was quite aware the card was a forgery, but he was also aware that the reactions of Himmler to a sight of it would be as this relentless woman had spelled out. Himmler gave no man the benefit of a doubt.

'You think I'll turn the baroness over to you in exchange for that stupid forgery?'

'You may call it a forgery,' said Karita. 'I do not. Nor will others. So yes, you must release the baroness to me or this card will arrive in Himmler's office.'

'I'll tell you this,' said Ludwig. 'The moment you leave here with her, begin counting the hours you have left. I'll make the call now.'

Karita's eyes never left him as he telephoned headquarters. He ordered the baroness to be brought at once to his apartment. Requested to repeat the order, he did so, then replaced the phone. He waited. Karita waited, covering him. It came, the call back from headquarters to check the order. He confirmed.

'Good,' said Karita, and ripped the telephone lead from the wall socket.

'That won't help you,' said Ludwig savagely.

'Ah, I see.' Karita smiled and nodded. 'But of course. Once you have the card, you will feel free to come after me, yes?'

'I assure you, you won't get very far with the prisoner,' said Ludwig. 'The bargain is restricted to the exchange. It does not include allowing you or her the freedom of Austria once you leave this apartment together.'

'I might have asked for that concession,' said Karita, 'and you might have given it, but you would not have meant it. So I asked only for the baroness, although the card is priceless. It's worth your life.'

'It's a damned fake, I tell you!'

'Is it? Now, when the baroness arrives, send the escorts back to headquarters with orders to return for her in two hours. I shall be outside. Somewhere outside. So I shall see them arrive and see them go. Then I will come in again, take the baroness off your hands and tell you where the card is.'

'Then shoot me?' said Ludwig.

'Have I said I would? I have not. Vienna would be a better place without you and your kind, but that is not part of the bargain. Now, be so good as to lock your bodyguard in and then give me the key.'

Ludwig, mind working feverishly, did not argue. He complied. Karita pocketed the key, and he noted the fact that not once had she put herself at a disadvantage. Her ugly revolver had remained a permanent threat, and his damned leg had felt painfully vulnerable.

'I'll come after you, I promise you that,' he said.

'Of course,' said Karita, 'but perhaps the baroness is a good runner. Wait for my return, Kommissar, and be kind to her. When I ring, let her answer the door. By herself.'

The moment she was gone, carrying the SS revolvers in her hat, Ludwig went to his bureau, opened a drawer and took out the pistol he always kept there. Downstairs, Karita showed herself at the entrance to the building. From his place of concealment opposite, Kirby saw her. He stepped out, looked up and down the lamplit street, noted it was clear and went across to join his wife. They retreated from the hall, and with the concierge absent, put themselves out of view. Karita handed her husband the two SS revolvers, which he put into his coat pockets. She replaced her hat. He kissed her nose.

'I am excited,' she whispered, 'and kissing my nose might not be enough for me later.'

'Be your age, little chicken,' murmured Kirby. 'How did things go?'

'As we planned. The card has frightened him to death.'

'The Inkwell is a master.'

'I have told Lundt-Hausen that Baroness Anne is to open the door to me.'

'By God, you have, have you?'

'You think he is going to try something?'

'He's bound to,' said Kirby.

'Yes. He's full of bitter bile and can't wait to blow my head off. However, he won't kill me, not until he has the card.'

They said no more. They waited. They did not have to wait long. They heard a car pull up outside the block. Seconds later they heard footsteps in the hall, some light, some solid, followed by the sound of feet ascending the stairs. No-one spoke, and Karita and Kirby naturally kept their peace. They continued to wait and to listen.

Within a minute footsteps sounded again, the solid footsteps. Two men were descending the stairs. One spoke.

'It's my guess he's going to pass the time torturing her into confession by getting Huber to rape her.'

'Shut up, you fool,' said the second man.

They reached the hall and left the building. A few minutes later the car fired into life and swished away. Kirby came out of the block and watched its lights disappear. It might come back. Ludwig Lundt-Hausen might have told the men to circle a few blocks and then return.

In the apartment, Anne faced her former husband. She was pale but still unbowed. She had felt threatened from the moment of her arrest, and every question relating to espionage had confirmed her fears. But she had given neither Matthew Gibbs nor John Kirby away. Nor had she done so badly for herself, basing her responses on the fact that she knew Voegler had no proof. He and Ludwig were relying entirely on breaking her down. She suspected part of that process was in the fact that although she had been allowed to eat, she had not been allowed any change of clothing, nor from this afternoon any access to a handbasin. Everything she was wearing felt stale, and so did her body itself.

'Why am I here?' she asked.

'Because I sent for you,' said Ludwig sourly.

'Why?'

His expression showed his pathological dislike of her. She had been his cross, intolerable to bear, and she had heard him lying in the divorce court.

'Why? A friend of yours is due any moment. When the doorbell rings, go and answer it.'

'I'm to go and open the door?' said Anne.

'You are to do just that and nothing more,' said Ludwig, and added a curt rider, one that would persuade her to give no trouble. 'Or your chances of going free will vanish. That's all I wish to say to you.'

'May I at least ask a small favour of you?'

'What favour?' It was truly bitter bile to him, the fact that he could not meet her eyes.

'Please don't come to the funeral you're pre-paring for me,' said Anne, showing just what she thought of his implication that he was going to arrange her release.

And what did he mean by saying a friend of hers was due any moment? What friend?

She had a sudden feeling it might be John Kirby.

Ludwig examined the corridor and the land-ing in a little while, first warning Anne again not to move until the doorbell rang.

Chapter Fourteen

Karita rang the bell. It was answered after a few moments by a fair slender woman in a hat and coat.

'Ah, Baroness Anne von Korvacs, I believe,' smiled Karita.

'Yes, I—' Anne stopped, eyes widening.

'Go in, Greek bitch,' said Ludwig, having arrived silently at Karita's back from a concealment, and she felt the snout of a pistol against her spine.

'Is this what was agreed?' she asked, moving forward. Anne retreated and Ludwig closed the door with the heel of his left boot.

'Go in, both of you,' he said, and Karita winced as the Luger pistol dug viciously into her back. She followed Anne into the living room. Ludwig placed his left hand on her shoulder and spun her round to face him, and she stared at the Luger, and then up into his dark, savagely triumphant face.

'Really, you have no manners at all,' she said, and delivered a lightning-fast kick. The toe of her left boot connected violently with the shin of his suffering leg. He staggered. The dark blood ran from his face, leaving it a dirty white, and a sharp hiss of agony escaped from between his clenched teeth. His right arm flailed, the Luger executing uncontrolled parabolae, such was his pain. Karita pushed him. He reeled backwards and fell heavily, crashing on the carpeted floor.

Anne stared down at him out of dilated eyes, and then at the woman, a complete stranger to her. Karita pounced like a tigress, her booted foot coming down on Ludwig's right hand, grinding it into the carpet. The pistol slipped from his tortured fingers. Karita picked it up. Ludwig lay on his back, his body racked with convulsions, his drained face distorted by spasms of excruciating pain, his mouth a closed, clenched trap. His eyes seemed a glittering red as they fastened on the woman who had delivered the crippling kick.

'Ah, you see?' said Karita. 'Not all Greeks are idiots. Did you think I would expect you to do exactly as I asked?'

'Damn you for an everlasting bitch!' hissed Ludwig, his leg a thing of white-hot torment, his thoughts livid about what he would do one day to this she-cat.

Anne was finding it difficult to draw breath. Not so Karita. She looked down at Ludwig and spoke with no effort at all.

'We made a bargain,' she said. 'You broke it. That is the trouble with Nazis, Fascists and Communists. One cannot trust any of them. It's bad enough, Baroness, that they have no manners. It's worse that they have no honour, that for the good of their stone-eyed gods they would cheat their own mothers.'

'Dear Lord, what is happening here?' begged Anne.

'Only the result of a man trying to cheat me,' said Karita, watching the grounded, writhing Ludwig. 'But there it is, Baroness, one can never do honest business with these people. This one, a Nazi, agreed to exchange you for a certain card. This one.' She extracted it from her coat pocket, showed it to Ludwig, then put it back. 'Naturally, being what he is, he broke his word. Now you and I must go. He has probably asked the men who brought you to come back in ten minutes or so.'

'Yes, yes,' said Anne, keeping her eyes off the pain-tortured Ludwig, 'but – '

'As your friend, I beg you to come with me, and quickly,' said Karita. She took something else from her coat pocket and dropped it beside Ludwig. It was a little white packet containing a headache powder. 'There, when you are able to get up, you can release your groaning servant and do something for him.' She crossed to the door with Anne, who looked back at the still prostrate Ludwig.

'But his leg – '

'It's only hurting,' said Karita, 'and he's only grinding his teeth because it will not allow him to run after us. Come now.'

Anne drew a breath, shook off her agitation but not her bewilderment, and left the apartment with this strange woman. They hurried down the stairs, Anne's back feeling cold, as if Ludwig's glittering eyes were following her.

They ran into the street. A car, parked at a discreet distance, moved forward at once, then pulled up. Karita opened the back door, and she and Anne scrambled in. The car was away almost before the door had been closed.

'Good evening, Baroness,' said Kirby from the driving seat. He spoke in English. 'How are you feeling?'

'Mr Kirby?' Anne was incredulous. 'It's you?'

'Yes, and next to you is my wife Karita,' said Kirby. 'But keep down. You too, Karita.'

The two women huddled low on the back seat.

'Will someone please tell me what is happening?' asked Anne, as the car was driven unhurriedly through the street.

'Your family was worried about you,' said Kirby, 'so Karita and I thought something should be done to get you out of the hands of the Security Police. We can't take you back to your home, I'm afraid. It'll be searched before the night's out. Ah, here are the hounds returning already, I fancy, and probably with orders to execute you, Karita. Stay down.'

A car, travelling fast on the other side of the street, rushed past them. Kirby, recognizing it, kept his own car going at a modest speed.

'Such excitement,' murmured Karita, 'and I am delighted to meet you, Baroness.'

'You are amazing,' breathed Anne, 'but I thought you were Russian. Your husband said you were.'

'I am,' said Karita. 'I am also English. By adoption.'

'But you spoke to my ex-husband as if you were Greek,' said Anne.

'Yes, so confusing, of course,' said Karita, 'but sometimes one should confuse an opponent. Ivan is known to the security police, so – '

'Ivan?'

'My husband. The daughters of the Tsar called him that. It is what I often call him myself. As I was saying, because he is known to the security police, I would be known too, as his Russian wife. So this evening I am Greek. You understand?'

'I am amazed, bewildered and grateful,' said Anne.

The night lights of Vienna danced as the car entered a street of shops. Kirby pulled up.

'I must use that public phone box,' he said. 'Stay down, Baroness, while I call your family.' He slipped from the car and entered the booth. He got through to Carl.

'Kirby here, my friend. We have your sister Anne, and as agreed, we're taking her to our apartment.'

'God in heaven,' breathed Carl, 'you actually have her?'

'Yes, believe me. I'm calling to warn you to prepare yourselves for a visit from the Gestapo. They may not expect to find your sister there, but I think your house is the first place they'll check.'

'We're ready,' said Carl, 'although we've been living more in hope than certainty. Josef Meister is out of the way.'

'Good. You'll be able to phone your sister later, if you wish.'

'Your number?' said Carl.

Kirby gave it, but said, 'Memorize it, don't write it down. I'll be in touch with you regarding the journey.'

'How can we thank you?' asked Carl. 'What can I say?'

'Just goodbye for the moment,' said Kirby, and rang off. Back in the car, he noted Karita and Anne were keeping themselves out of sight. Resuming the drive, he said, 'Your brother sent his love, Baroness. He'll phone you later and talk to you.'

'Thank you, thank you,' whispered Anne, overwhelmed.

'There were no real problems, Karita?' said Kirby, joining busy night traffic. The sudden rise to power of the National Socialist Party made Vienna seem a busier and brasher city, the lights brighter, the bustle and glitter a deceptive facade that hid the inner darkness of Nazi totalitarianism. A symbolic demonstration of its power caught the eye as a small convoy of two military cars and a truck appeared, going at speed and roaring by. The truck was full of Stormtroopers. Kirby suspected a round-up of Jews was in the making.

'Problems?' said Karita, who felt, as Anne did, that conversation would be easier if they could unfold themselves and sit upright. 'Only minor ones. I had to shoot the bodyguard.'

'I hope you didn't kill him,' said Kirby. 'That would put the cat among the pigeons with a vengeance.'

'No, no,' said Karita, 'I wounded him, that's all. He drew his gun. Also, he looked at my legs.'

'He did what?' said Kirby.

'Inspected my stockings to see if they concealed a cannon,' said Karita. 'Ah, Baroness, Nazi Bolsheviks are all pigs, with no respect for anyone, not even for a wife and mother. Were your stockings inspected?'

'Heavens, no,' said Anne, and managed a faint smile, her bowed head close to Karita's. 'But why do you call them Bolsheviks?'

'Oh, I have told a thousand people that Hitler's Nazis are no different from Lenin's bloodthirsty commissars,' said Karita.

'You are a remarkable woman,' said Anne.

'No, no, I am quite ordinary,' said Karita. 'Ivan will tell you so.'

'Only at the risk of having my head knocked off,' said Kirby, driving entirely without haste to avoid attracting attention.

'I was born in a Crimean village,' said Karita, 'and met Ivan when I was a servant in the household of a Russian princess. Such a wild one she was, and in love with Ivan. Ah, you should have known him then, so young and handsome. Of course, he is old now, as you can see. I am much younger myself, and therefore object to Nazi Bolsheviks looking at my legs.'

Anne, beginning to feel light-headed at the wonder of deliverance, allowed herself the luxury of a laugh.

'Mr Kirby, your remarkable wife is also very entertaining,' she said.

'Russian wives are unique, Baroness,' said Kirby. 'At least, mine is.'

He entered a narrow street and pulled up outside the rear of the shop over which he and Karita had their apartment. Within a few minutes, Anne was safely installed there and begging to be allowed a bath. Karita, adrenalin still high, prepared a meal for her while she soaked herself in hot water.

'It's wonderful, isn't it?' said Sophie, eyes shining, and Vicky thought her mother quite radiant with blessed relief.

'The day's not over yet,' said Carl. They were waiting for the expected arrival of the Gestapo. Lucia, Emma Jane and Paul were in bed. Baron Ernst, the venerable patriarch, had been the first to point out that at this late hour, the younger ones should be in bed. If they were up, if everyone was up, it would look as if something unusual was keeping the whole family out of their beds. It would look, in fact, as if everyone knew Anne had been freed.

'But God has been very good to us,' said Pia, who had played the dutiful sister by phoning the news to Mariella.

'With the help of Herr Kirby and his wife,' said Baroness Teresa.

'Yes, how could they have managed such a magnificent rescue act?' said Sophie. 'It has stopped James committing murder.'

'It's cooled me down at least,' said James.

'One must forgive him his thoughts of assassination, Mama,' said Vicky, much more herself.

'After all, he is the family provider and the one who has to get out of bed if you think there's a burglar in the house. I have a feeling Nicholas would be very exemplary in dealing with burglars.'

'Ah, that is something to consider in a young man, an exemplary way of dealing with burglars,' smiled Baroness Teresa.

'In considering him as a possible prospect?' ventured James.

'Nicholas is a fine young man,' said Baroness Teresa, 'and such a welcome change from the aggressive kind so prevalent in Vienna these days.'

'Grandmama,' said Vicky, 'I have only known Nicholas for a few days.'

'A few days is a long time for some young people,' smiled Pia.

'Do you think so, Aunt Pia?' said Vicky, looking large-eyed in her spectacles. Nicholas had been with her most of the day, but had left immediately after hearing that his parents had freed Anne. He did not want to be in the house if the Gestapo did turn up, not when his name was Kirby.

'Yes, I do think so, Vicky,' said Pia.

'Dear me,' said Vicky.

'It's occurred to me,' said Carl, 'that it might be wise if we retired to our own apartments.' They were all in his parents' drawing room at the moment.

'I agree,' said James. 'We don't want to be caught having a family conference. We should be nursing our worries about Anne in our own rooms.'

'Are we all sure we can face up to questions?' asked Carl.

Everyone declared themselves ready, and they split up.

Ten minutes later, the Gestapo did arrive in the shape of Voegler and three assistants. With them were a dozen uniformed SS men. Voegler was experiencing mixed reactions. He almost envied Colonel Lundt-Hausen his single emotion of murderous fury. He himself was suffering unusual frustration at having been robbed of such a challenging suspect, while at the same time hoping she would lead her ex-husband the very devil of a dance before her recapture. Also, he felt at times that he wanted to laugh aloud at the hysteria she had aroused in headquarters by her escape, apparently with the connivance of a Greek woman. What, he wondered, was happening to him? Only a short while before he was called out to the emergency, his long-widowed mother, with whom he lived, had told him he'd begun to talk to himself like a man in muttering dotage. She was an outspoken woman, his mother, once a star of Vienna's famous opera company and now a danger to herself in that she thought little of National Socialist ideals.

Well, he had a job to do on Baroness Anne's relatives, and would do it. First, he compelled the families to assemble in the ground-floor drawing room. He said nothing as in turn they arrived, but he looked into the face of each person, searching for signs of ignorance or knowledge of Baroness Anne's escape. Every face seemed to wear an expression of defiance or affront.

Lucia, Emma Jane and Paul were in their dressing gowns, having been dragged out of their beds. The servants, Hanna and Heinrich, also had to attend. Heinrich, perhaps, was the sternest and most aloof figure present. With his mutton chop whiskers he was not unlike the late lamented Emperor Franz Josef, permanently aloof.

Voegler conducted the examination, while the SS detachment combed the handsome house, turning over every room. Voegler's three hard-eyed assistants moved about, peering into faces. In between Voegler's questions, they threw questions of their own.

Voegler's questions were put quietly, so that he seemed a man detached from the noisiness of the searching SS and the intimidating aggressiveness of his assistants. He seemed austere but human, except for the threat of his accusing eyes. His purpose, of course, was to find out if anyone present knew what had taken place in Ludwig's apartment or had any knowledge of the woman responsible. He did not say what had taken place, nor did he specifically say that Anne had escaped. He waited for an involuntary comment or impulsive answer that would tell him they knew she was free. James called his bluff, however.

'Something's obvious,' he said.

'Tell me about it,' said Voegler.

'You've lost Baroness Anne,' said James.

'Have I said we have?' asked Voegler.

'You've lost her,' said James, 'she's slipped you.'

'Of course,' said Carl, 'that's why this house is being invaded.'

'And why there's so much banging and stamping going on upstairs,' said Sophie.

'Oh, I don't mind it myself,' said Pia, 'not if it means James is right.'

'If he is right, it will be nothing for any of you to feel happy about,' said Voegler. 'The Third Reich doesn't hand out boxes of chocolates to the relatives of suspected traitors.'

One of his assistants shouted a question.

'You,' he bawled into the face of the elderly baron, 'where is your daughter?'

That question, thought Voegler, confirms what these people only suspected. I'll have the idiot shot for it.

'I have two daughters,' said the baron. 'One is here. The other was arrested yesterday. I find that outrageous.'

'Old one,' said Voegler, 'you haven't looked outraged. Or even worried. Why, I wonder? Obviously, because you already knew of the escape.'

'I was not brought up to show tears to strangers,' said the baron.

'But your wife, old one, she's been known to cry, perhaps, being a woman,' said Voegler. 'She hasn't been crying in my sight, despite knowing of her daughter's arrest as a suspected traitor. Why is that? Most mothers would be weeping.'

Baroness Teresa spoke up.

'I am upset, yes,' she said, 'but since no-one can make me believe in anything but my daughter's innocence, why should I weep?'

'Don't you weep for the innocent, then?' shouted another assistant.

'Must these men of yours bawl and roar?' asked James of Voegler.

'Yes, is roaring necessary?' asked Sophie.

'It is making me angry,' said Pia.

'It's the enthusiasm they have for serving the Greater German Reich,' said Voegler. 'Tell me,' he said to the baron, 'from whom did you learn the happy news?'

'If you mean my daughter Anne is truly free,' said the baron, 'you brought the news yourself by making it obvious.'

'You are a duplicitous breed,' said Voegler. 'Who are you?' he asked Emma Jane, looking young and girlish in her nightie and dressing gown.

'I am Emma Jane Fraser, and the lady who was being shouted at is my grandmama.' Emma Jane sounded quite calm.

'I'm sorry, of course, if that has upset her,' said Voegler. 'Tell me, has the woman with golden hair been here lately?' Ludwig had given a very exact description of Karita. He would have been here himself, but was receiving treatment for his inflamed and suffering leg.

'No, not lately,' said Emma Jane, and felt Paul's hand around hers.

'Ah, so?' said Voegler softly, and Sophie held her breath.

'She's been away,' said Emma Jane.

'Has she?' Voegler moved closer to the girl. 'She stays here sometimes?'

'She lives here,' said Emma Jane, 'she's my

232

Aunt Anne, and if she has escaped you, I am glad. Well, you wouldn't expect me to be sorry, would you?'

'And why do you say her hair is golden?' asked Voegler.

'She didn't say so, you did,' said Vicky, and Voegler turned to regard this new challenge. Vicky's short-sighted eyes saw him as quite a handsome if stern-looking man. She thought he ought to be on stage doing Shakespeare's *Henry V*, not working for the Gestapo.

'Did I say so?' he asked.

'Anyway, it is golden,' said Emma Jane.

'I'd say yellow myself,' said Voegler. That was a provocation, and he knew it.

'Yellow? Yellow?' Emma Jane was indignant. 'Hay is yellow. Aunt Anne doesn't have hair like hay.'

'Leave her alone!' burst Paul. James put a hand on his shoulder and pressed. Emma Jane was doing very well.

'Speak when you're spoken to, boy,' said one man. 'Speak now.' He raised his voice. 'Where is your Aunt Anne, eh, where is she?'

'How do I know?' said Paul. 'I didn't arrest her, you did. I wasn't in charge of her, you were.'

'I was thinking of some other woman,' said Voegler.

'You're a puzzle to me,' said Carl.

'How long is this questioning going on?' asked Sophie.

'I might ask how long these young people are to be kept from their beds,' said James.

'Let me see,' said Voegler to Sophie, 'you are

233

Frau Fraser and that gentleman is your English husband. Yes.' He regarded them with new interest, a slight smile on his face as he made a particular survey of Sophie. Sophie burned, feeling he was undressing her. He wasn't. The only woman he would have liked to undress had rejected him as a lover as soon as he joined Austria's National Socialist Party.

He noted Sophie's brown eyes, quick and expressive. How would she look with her dark hair covered by a golden wig? Not unlike the woman Ludwig Lundt-Hausen had described? And her sinewy-looking husband? A waiting accomplice who had helped her spirit Baroness Anne away?

'I object to this,' said Sophie.

'Of course you do,' said Voegler, and spoke to James. 'Herr Fraser, where were you and your wife between eight and nine o'clock this evening?'

Vicky stiffened, but Sophie lost none of her composure and James was not in the least discomfited.

'My wife was here, worrying about her sister and making phone calls to your headquarters,' he said. 'You'll find that easy to check. I was at the Austro-Fraser works, with my brother-in-law.' He nodded at Carl. 'We have two racing cars needing to be finished in a hurry. We spoke to some of the night-shift workers, and arrived back here about thirty minutes ago. I'm a British national, as you know, and request you don't make farcical assumptions about my wife.'

'Or you'll go to the British Embassy, of

course,' said Voegler, and was reminded of a man who had definitely complained to the embassy. Matthew Gibbs. Had he played the part of an accomplice? The swine had a facile way of slipping surveillance.

'What makes you so determined to get hold of my sister again?' asked Carl. 'You obviously haven't been able to charge her. Are you working to the orders of her one-time husband?'

'I don't answer questions,' said Voegler, 'I ask them.'

'Don't speak to my papa like that,' said Lucia. 'He races cars and people admire him.'

One of Voegler's men had a change of expression.

'Carl von Korvacs, yes, of course,' he said, and nodded. It was almost an agreeable nod. It could not be disputed that a record-breaking racing driver, well known to the public, was of greater credit to the Reich than degenerate artists or radical writers.

'I want to know,' said Voegler, 'if any of you can tell me something about a Greek woman with golden hair, a friend to Baroness Anne. I beg you won't all speak at once. On the other hand, silence isn't recommended.' He looked at young Lucia. 'I don't want to go away and to come back with orders to arrest your aunt's parents, the old ones.'

'What, because they're old?' Lucia's indignation leapfrogged her apprehension. 'Well, I don't think that's right, I don't think anyone should be arrested just because they're old.'

'Young lady, people of any age can be arrested

for withholding information necessary to the security of the State,' said Voegler.

'I'm sure I don't know what you mean,' said Lucia.

'I think you and everyone else here know what I mean.'

'Leave Lucia alone,' said Paul, 'she's only a girl.'

'Tell me about the Greek woman,' said Voegler, 'yes, and about other friends of Baroness Anne.'

'If anyone here knows a Greek woman, it's news to me,' said Carl, 'and my sister's friends are all family friends. Are we to give you potted histories?'

'He'll arrest them all,' said Pia, her blood hot. 'What is Vienna coming to, yes, what is it coming to? No-one said when the Fuehrer arrived that we would have people bursting into our homes asking questions no-one understands, and arresting my innocent sister-in-law. No-one said the Fuehrer would want young girls bullied. It's disgraceful.'

'Ah, someone is upset, someone has a tongue,' said Voegler. 'Perhaps you can tell us about the Greek woman?'

'How can I tell you anything about someone I don't know?' Pia waved her hands about furiously. Carl smiled. Pia could be alarming when she was in an Italian temper. 'Am I an idiot that I am asked such a question?'

'This Greek woman, what's her name?' One of the men shot the question at Hanna, who had said not a word so far but had visibly quivered with indignation throughout.

'This family has nothing to do with Greeks,' she said. 'We have never, no, never, had to go looking for friends who run restaurants and lend money. Isn't that so, Heinrich?'

'His Excellency the Baron has nothing against Greeks,' said Heinrich, upright and stiff, 'but I don't recall ever admitting any into this house.'

Sophie glanced at James. He gave her an understanding look, knowing what she was thinking, that it had to be Kirby's golden-haired Russian wife Voegler was talking about. In some way, and for some reason, Karita had passed herself off as Greek.

Voegler could get nothing out of any of them concerning the woman who had shot the body-guard, temporarily crippled Lundt-Hausen himself, and made off with the baroness. But he did get two impressions, first that the Greek woman really was unknown to them, and second, that the whole lot of them would need to have their arms and legs broken before they would say anything to incriminate Baroness Anne or any of her friends.

The officer in charge of the SS detachment finally appeared to report that the exhaustive search of the house had been negative. Voegler reflected, then addressed Carl.

'I should be sorry, in view of your popularity, to have to return here with orders to arrest your parents.'

'With a view to persuading my sister to place herself back in custody?' said Carl. 'If you made that kind of foolish mistake, I'd be very sorry myself. For you.'

Voegler smiled. He preferred to encounter strength of character. Some people, the moment the first really sharp question was put to them, became such miserable wretches that they howled with fear. Of course, that often meant someone like Schroeder was doing a little painful arm-twisting.

'As I've said to other people, the Gestapo are forbidden to make mistakes,' he said, and left with his men and the SS detachment. He might have been furious or seething with new frustration, but wasn't. Colonel Lundt-Hausen was the man at war with the von Korvacs family. Let the fury and frustration be his. What I shall feel myself, he thought, if Baroness Anne isn't caught, is great disappointment at not being able to cross swords with her again. On the other hand, if we catch neither her nor Kirby, I shall probably be put on trial for the kind of incompetence detrimental to the security of the Greater German Reich. Damn Baroness Anne for escaping, and damn twice over the woman who helped her.

'Carl?' said Pia, coming from her dressing room into the bedroom.

'Yes?' said Carl, showing himself at the bathroom door, toothbrush in his hand. He was in his pyjamas, Pia in a black silk nightdress that revealed her shapely curves.

'The Gestapo won't really arrest your parents, will they, if they can't find Anne?'

'Not between now and tomorrow morning, I hope,' said Carl.

'I think I'm beginning to hate the power of Hitler's police,' said Pia. 'I'll be glad to leave tomorrow with Lucia and the others, although I wish you were coming too. But I do understand, you and James must look after Anne and Josef Meister. Neither of them could risk travelling by train. The police will be searching every train leaving Vienna, and the road journey would be too hard on your parents. Anne really was all right when you spoke to her on the phone a little while ago?'

'A little light-headed about her escape and a little delirious about what seems to have been an amazing performance by Karita Kirby,' said Carl. 'Otherwise quite herself.'

'We are all so relieved,' said Pia, slipping into bed. 'Oh, by the way, Sophie said she'll find Mariella a husband in England. An Englishman of the severe and masterful kind.'

'If Sophie said so, then Mariella's doomed,' said Carl.

'Good,' said Pia.

Carl smiled. Mariella wouldn't take kindly to the prospect, since she was sure an English husband would be better at walking his dog than pleasuring his wife.

'James?' whispered Sophie.

'Uh?' murmured James.

'Are you awake?'

'No, sound asleep.'

'Of course you aren't,' said Sophie, 'turn round and talk to me.'

'At this time of night?' said James.

'What difference does that make? Really, men have no souls. How can you sleep when I can't? Aren't you excited about Anne being free? Aren't you in wonder at what John Kirby and his wife have done for us? And praying that Pia and the others will have a safe journey to Italy? Talk to me.'

In this mood, Sophie had to be humoured. James turned. She snuggled up.

'I hope we're doing the right thing, letting young Emma Jane go with Pia and the others,' he said.

'It's the right thing for all of them, especially Mama and Papa,' said Sophie. 'Paul will do his share of looking after Emma Jane and Lucia. He's a tower of strength. Yes, it's better they're all going by train. We mustn't fuss like old hens.'

'I'm an old hen?' queried James.

'Yes, you are, over your daughters,' said Sophie. 'But I'm longing for Mama and Papa to discover the freedom of living in Britain. No Gestapo, no jackboots, only homely bobbies on bicycles. That's a precious thing, you know, homely bobbies on bicycles. Our children have a treasured heritage. We must protect it for them and never let it be spoiled.'

'God save the King and all that?' said James.

'Oh, you people,' said Sophie, 'you take it all for granted, you even make jokes about it. I want to tell you something.'

'Which is?' said James.

'That although I will always love my kind of Austria,' said Sophie, 'I know I'm going to be so very glad to get home.'

*   *   *

'Anne's asleep?' said Kirby, climbing into bed.

'Peacefully asleep,' said Karita, 'and so is Nicholas. That young man is beginning to feel his shoes.'

'I think you mean his feet.'

'It's all the same,' said Karita. 'You have noticed how devoted he is to his new friends?'

'Is that to do with feeling his feet?'

'Of course,' said Karita, undressing. 'He is telling himself he's now a grown man.'

'He's not far short,' said Kirby.

'I thought the girl Vicky fascinating,' said Karita, inserting herself sinuously into a negligee.

'Yes, I thought Vicky was the main object of his devotion.'

'She is mesmerizing him,' said Karita. 'Ivan, such an exciting day it's been. We have robbed the wolves.'

'It's time we gave up this kind of life,' said Kirby, 'and went in for garden games.'

'No, no, you would be bored,' said Karita, 'although it's true I know games that would set the garden on fire. But such things are not for every day. God is right, marriage is first for the creation of children. Catching fire is only for now and again, and should not be spoiled by familiarity.'

'That is so, is it, little chicken?' said Kirby.

'I think I'm on fire now, because of robbing the Nazi beasts of the field,' said Karita. 'So I'm going to the bathroom to clean my teeth and put on some scent instead of a nightie. Then I'm coming to bed.'

'Scent instead of a nightie?' said Kirby. 'Will that work for me at my age, fiery primrose of the Crimea?'

'Old English Eskimo, we must fight our years,' said Karita. 'Vienna is asleep and I have closed my mind to the present. I am a virgin again, and shall give in to being overcome and seduced.'

'You'll be lucky,' said Kirby.

'But you must seduce me,' said Karita, 'I'm on fire.'

'Very well,' said Kirby, 'go and put your scent on, and then we'll see if my fire extinguisher works.'

Chapter Fifteen

Kirby was up early the following morning, mingling with hurrying workers on his way to see the Inkwell, master forger. He collected six passports, paid for them and returned to his apartment. From there, Nicholas took the passports to the house on the Salesianergasse. He stayed only long enough to hand them to Carl.

Later, Pia and Emma Jane left for the station with forged Austrian passports that identified them as mother and daughter. James and Carl were watching the avenue from a window on the second floor, checking whether or not the house was under surveillance. There were no signs that it was.

In another twenty minutes the baron left, with a forged passport identifying him as an English gentleman of independent means. And ten minutes later the baroness left, in company with Paul and Lucia. Their passports showed Paul and Lucia as English brother and sister, the baroness as their English grandmother.

All six were to travel in this way, not as a single party. Goodbyes had been said in the house. As expected, the main Vienna station was alive with police. State police, uniformed security police, and plain-clothes officers of the Gestapo. It had been like that since the annexation, for Jews, dissidents and other enemies of the State had been trying to leave from the moment of Hitler's proclamation. This morning the Gestapo in particular were especially watchful. Descriptions of Baroness Anne von Korvacs and a golden-haired Greek woman had been circulated, together with a rider that these two women, if seen, might be in company with a man. All three were to be arrested.

Pia and Emma Jane boarded the train without incident. So did Baron Ernst von Korvacs, and so did Baroness Teresa, Lucia and Paul. They were not Jewish, nor did they relate in any way to the three people especially wanted by Ludwig Lundt-Hausen.

Mariella was due to travel the next day, Sunday, after her exhibition had closed.

The train left on time.

Although Mariella had dramatic events and a new future on her mind, she was looking forward to a swarm of visitors on this, the last day of her exhibition. Sergeant Wainwright arrived well ahead of the first.

'Hello there, have you got everything ready for tomorrow?' he asked in breezy fashion.

'What do you know about tomorrow?' enquired Mariella.

'Well, I know we're catching the mid-morning train to Italy.'

'We?'

'Yes, you and me, marm.' He lowered his voice in case the canvas-hung walls had ears. 'Fine piece of work last night, did you hear?'

'I heard, but it's not to be talked about,' said Mariella. 'And what makes you think you and I are catching the train together?'

'Orders,' said Sergeant Wainwright.

'Orders?'

'That's correct. I'll pick you up in a taxi at ten.'

'*Mama mia*, what a boozy man you are,' said Mariella.

'I think you mean bossy.'

'Yes, that is it, bossy. I have heard all sergeants are bossy. And have you heard I don't take orders?'

'Can't be helped, marm, there it is, Colonel Kirby and his missus are looking after your welfare with a bit of modest help from me.'

'Ah, so?' said Mariella. 'There is something modest about you, is there, yes?'

'One of my virtues,' said Sergeant Wainwright. 'Now, we'll be a married couple when we board the train. I'll escort you back to your apartment after you've rung the curtain down here. I've got a new passport, except it doesn't look new, and I need a photograph of you to stick in, and that's best done inside your four walls. Well, I'll have to make sure your photograph doesn't look as if it's just been taken. I'm talking about a married couple's passport. Understood?' Mariella fumed. 'Good. Pop along to the studio round the corner from here sometime this morning, and get them to take a passport photograph of you on the spot. I've got a ginger wig you can wear, as—'

'Stop!' Mariella was breathing hard, and Sergeant Wainwright noted with interest the rise and fall of her bosom. 'Married couple? A passport photograph? Ginger wig? Ginger? I refuse, yes, refuse.'

'Now, marm, you know I don't like argufying women, and it would be more than my head's worth to let Mrs Kirby know you downed me. She'd hit me with a chopper. Besides, two can travel more sociably than one, and my personal orders are to see you safely to the door of your mother's home in the Italian Rivol.'

'Tyrol, you fool. And do you think—'

'Tyrol, is it?' said Sergeant Wainwright. 'Never been there myself, but I'll still land you on your mother's doorstep well out of the way of characters contrary, rely on it.'

'I'm speechless,' said Mariella.

'Never knew any woman as badly off as that,' said Sergeant Wainwright. 'They invented talk, didn't they?'

'Listen to me, you crazy man—'

'Here we are, let's see if it fits you while we're still alone,' said Sergeant Wainwright, and placed a valise on the little table serving as a desk. He opened it up and took out an auburn wig.

'That is not ginger,' said Mariella.

'Nearly,' said Sergeant Wainwright, shaking it, 'and a fair one wouldn't do, not with your dark lashes, which I admire. There we are, then.' With Mariella fighting hysteria, he pulled the wig down over her hair, then viewed the result. 'A bit

246

lopsided,' he said, 'and some of your hair needs tucking up. Look, there's a mirror in the office. Use that to help you straighten it out and to find out if it fits to your pleasure.'

'Pleasure? Pleasure? If you don't go away,' said Mariella, pulling the wig off, 'I think I shall kill you.'

'Now, marm, that won't do, not when you consider what happened last night and the ruddy Gestapo swarming all over Vienna and likely to drop in here to find out if you know anything about where the sister-in-law of your sister might be holed up. Best to make sure we're fully prepared for a smart getaway with you looking conveniently different in that ginger wig.'

Mariella picked up a long cardboard tube used for protecting rolled-up canvases, and hit him with it.

'Idiot! Fool!'

'I think I can hear the first visitors arriving,' said Sergeant Wainwright.

Mariella rushed into the office. A grin touched his homely face. She'd taken the wig with her.

Karita had risen with a smile. She and her husband, after his return from Inkwell the forger, went out together, Karita wearing a drab coat, a woollen hat pulled down to cover her hair, and a pair of plain-glass spectacles. Kirby wore an old brown raincoat and a black French beret. They used last night's hired car to get them to the industrial area of the city.

Anne, finally succumbing to physical and mental exhaustion, had fallen asleep the moment her head touched the pillow last night. Nicholas did not wake her, not until ten o'clock, when he took rolls and coffee to her. She came dreamily awake, gazed wonderingly at him, then smiled and sat up. A rose-pink nightie, loaned by Karita, did its best to remain in situ as a strap slipped from a bare shoulder. Anne adjusted it.

'Good morning,' said Nicholas, 'care for some breakfast?'

'Nicholas, how nice,' she said, taking the tray, 'and I had such a fine sleep.'

'You did, it's ten o'clock,' said Nicholas, wondering what kind of a man her ex-husband was to have divorced such an enchanting woman. 'But there's no hurry, so take your time. My parents are out for the morning.'

'Your mother is a remarkable lady,' said Anne, sipping coffee.

'You're worth a mention or two yourself, Baroness.'

'Thank you,' said Anne, 'you're all so kind, and I'm very very grateful.'

'You're more than welcome,' said Nicholas, and left her to her simple breakfast.

At eleven she was talking to him in the living room, and discovering him to be a young man of intelligence and good humour, and quite mature for his age. He let her know that when he had graduated he hoped to enter the export and import business. He said this with a smile.

The phone rang. He answered it, then turned to Anne.

'Someone would like to talk to you,' he said. 'Mr Matthew Gibbs.'

'Yes?' said Anne, and took the phone. 'Mr Gibbs?'

'Good morning and thank God,' said Gibbs. 'If I had any idea of becoming an atheist, I've kicked that into bits now. I was given details of events by marble-eyed Voegler himself, when he came to my apartment late last night and tried to link me to your escape. Fortunately, I was able to prove I was dining in a restaurant at the time. Well, there you are, safe and sound, I hope. How are you?'

'Splendid,' said Anne, 'and how are you?'

'Far better than I have been,' said Gibbs. 'When they released me but not you, that was the beginning of the worst time of my life. It's near to rapture to know you're free of the wolf pack. How much more questioning did you have to suffer?'

'Enough to make me doubt my endurance,' said Anne.

'The species is even deadlier than I thought,' said Gibbs. 'If I hadn't been a foreign national, I'm damned sure I'd be in bits and pieces by now. The outside world has no real idea of what's going on in this great Germanic paradise, and most nations don't want to know. Have you heard that the American airman Charles Lindbergh is one of Hitler's most ardent fans?'

'Then you must go to America and write the truth about Hitler,' said Anne. Close to the window, the gap between net curtains gave her a view of the street. It was instinctive now, to look and to watch.

'Well, I've slipped some new bloodhounds for

good this time, I hope, and if my luck holds, I'll be in Switzerland by tomorrow,' said Gibbs. 'I want to say it's been a privilege knowing you, but a burning arrow to have placed you at risk in the way I did. You were magnificent in your duel with Voegler. He's a wolf, that one, but strange. Before he left me alone last night, he said he didn't doubt I'd be seeing you again, and when I did I was to give you his compliments and his hope you'd give him and his team a good run for their money—'

'Mr Gibbs, forgive me,' said Anne, who was still watching the street, 'but I must ring off – goodbye and good luck.'

'Is something happening?' asked Gibbs.

'Nothing for you to worry about,' said Anne, and put the phone down. She spoke to Nicholas. 'There's a man walking up and down on the far side of the street. I know him. He belongs to the Gestapo. He was in the office where I was being questioned yesterday, and was with the Gestapo Kommissar, Voegler, when I was arrested.'

'I think we've found him, Herr Kommissar,' said Rudolf Fleischer of the Gestapo. He was calling from a public telephone.

'Who?' asked Voegler.

'Kirby.'

'Where?'

'A cab driver informed me he took a man answering Kirby's description to a shop in the Hoher Market yesterday. There's an apartment above the shop. I was also informed Kirby had a woman with him.'

'His wife?'

'The cab driver couldn't say. He took more notice of Kirby, who hired him, paid him and gave him a generous tip. Schroeder is watching the shop and the entrance to the apartment. He'll follow if Kirby comes out.'

'There'll be a rear exit,' said Voegler. 'You go back and watch that. Do nothing unless Kirby comes out. The woman may be with him. Under no circumstances are you to alert him. Nor, if he comes out, with or without the woman, are you to lose him. I want to know where he goes. Inform Schroeder of my instructions. I'll be there in twenty minutes. Wait, did you get a description of the woman from the cab driver?'

'A very attractive blonde,' said Fleischer.

'Interesting.' Kirby and a blonde woman, a woman who might be a golden blonde. 'Make a note to keep your eyes open for the baroness. She may be there too, although I don't think she'll show herself, not in broad daylight. Make no arrests, not yet.'

'That's fine,' said Nicholas, who had acted at speed. Anne's head was covered with a scarf and she was wearing his raincoat. It reached to her feet and drooped shapelessly on her body. That and the scarf gave her a dowdy look. 'I'll take you down to the shop. You can enter it from the passage. We know Herr Brummenger, the shopkeeper. He's a friend of ours and doesn't like the Nazis. Buy some groceries. Here's a carrier bag to put them in. You've got some money?'

'Yes, in my purse,' said Anne. 'You have my handbag.'

'Yes, it's too smart for you at this exact moment,' said Nicholas. 'It's in this valise, which I'm taking with me. When you leave the shop, go to the Marzin Platz. Wait at the corner, where my parents will pick us up.' Nicholas had rushed a call through to Carl's office at the factory. His parents were there. 'Ready, Baroness? Good, let's go down.'

They went down. He opened the back door to the shop and Anne went in. He closed the door, bounded back up the stairs and carried down two large bundles of feminine apparel and other items. He had swept the place clear of all his mother's things, packing some in two valises. The rest made up the bundles. He placed these in a capacious and empty rice bin in the shop's storeroom, hefted up a large sack of rice and poured most of the contents in until the bundles were covered and the bin full. Herr Brummenger looked in.

'Finished, my young friend?'

'All done,' said Nicholas, and up he went again. He collected the valises and left by the rear exit. There were shop delivery vans in the narrow street, two of them in the process of being loaded. He sauntered. A man turned into the street, a man in a black raincoat and trilby hat, the mufti of a member of the Gestapo. Nicholas carried on at a sauntering pace. Fleischer, walking briskly, passed him without a glance, and Nicholas thanked his lucky stars he had left the apartment just in time, before the man turned into the street. When he reached the corner, he glanced back. The representative of the omnipotent Gestapo was standing on the far side of the street, watching the rear door of the shop. Nicholas went on.

Schroeder, sour-veined – he suffered from an acid stomach – was maintaining his surveillance of the shop in the Hoher Market. An entrance at the side of the shop led to the apartment above. People went into the shop and came out of it. Groceries, groceries. Life was more a thing of groceries than anything else. When one came to know that, one realized what a stupid existence people led. Were there any people who did not go into a grocery shop several times a week? Look at them now, going into the shop and coming out of it, concerned only with stocking their larders.

But at least there was activity here. His colleague, Fleischer, who had returned from phoning Voegler ten minutes ago with all kinds of instructions and half-baked suppositions, would find little to interest him while watching the rear of the shop. Boredom was dangerous. It gradually took the sharpness from one's mind.

Schroeder strolled, up and down, up and down. The shop door opened again and a boy went in. Doing an errand for someone's stomach, probably. Two women came out. One was nondescript, the second a boring sight in a scarf and a sloppy raincoat, a bulging bag of groceries clutched to her chest. She peered about as if she thought someone was going to snatch the bag. Groceries, groceries. She ought to have his stomach. That would take her mind off food for a change. She stood there yapping to the nondescript female. Yapping, nodding and peering.

There she goes, shuffling along with her coffee and sausage, no doubt, and her flour and tinned herrings –

Tinned herrings. Oily tinned herrings. His stomach turned over, and his heartburn was sickly and bitter. He chewed an anti-acid tablet, and strolled up and down, stopping occasionally ostensibly to interest himself in a guidebook he was carrying.

When Anne arrived at Marzin Platz, Nicholas was there, the valises resting on the pavement. Anne smiled as she joined him, and he took the laden carrier bag from her.

'What have you bought, half the shop?' he asked.

'I thought the more I bought, the more genuine I would look,' said Anne.

'Baroness, I like you,' said Nicholas.

'As I am now, a terrible sight?' smiled Anne.

'As you are at any time,' said Nicholas.

'Perhaps we can all meet in England sometimes,' said Anne.

'That shouldn't be difficult— Hello, here they are.'

A black Opel saloon car slipped out of the traffic and pulled up at the kerbside. Nicholas opened the back door and Anne got in. He then stowed the large valises and the carrier bag in the boot. Following that, he joined Anne on the back seat. The car moved off, Kirby at the wheel,

Karita beside him. He turned left to make for the Stubenring, the traffic flowing.

'So sorry to move you so quickly, Baroness,' he said.

'Please, I understand perfectly,' said Anne, 'and Nicholas was splendid.'

'The credit's all yours for spotting the place was being watched,' said Nicholas. 'It seems they're onto you, Dad. You look like a French onion-seller, by the way. Mother, you look frightful.'

'Good,' said Karita, spectacles perched on the tip of her nose, woollen hat fully covering her hair.

'No trouble, Nick?' said Kirby.

'Not as far as I know,' said Nicholas, and described the precautions he and Anne had taken, and the fact that the shop was now being watched from the rear as well. He also mentioned that Herr Brummenger had agreed to co-operate, even to the extent of informing any enquirer that Frau Kirby had returned to England two days ago.

'Well done, Nick,' said Kirby, going along patiently with the traffic. 'And how did you get on, Baroness?'

'Oh, I bought my groceries,' said Anne, 'and managed to get into conversation with a lady so that we left the shop together like old friends. The Gestapo man was still keeping watch, but didn't follow me.'

'There's only one thing to worry about,' said Kirby. 'That he might come to realize that although he saw you leave the shop, he didn't see you go in. I wonder when Voegler will turn the apartment over? Nick, I'll drop you off near the Salesianergasse, and you can let Vicky and her mother know of the latest development. Tell them not to worry. If they'll have you, stay there all day, and we'll see you this evening. I'll take the baroness to the car factory, where her brother and James Fraser will be able to look after her and your mother for a while. I'll get rid of this beret and raincoat, and go back to the apartment.'

Anne, alarmed, said, 'Mr Kirby, I beg you, no. They'll arrest you.'

'They'll question me, of course,' said Kirby, 'but officially I'm in Vienna only as an observer of the political situation. My credentials emanate from our Foreign Office. But it won't do to look as if I've left in a hurry. And I know what to say now about the occasion when you and I bumped into each other at the Opera Theatre.'

'Mr Kirby, I dislike you taking such risks,' said Anne.

'Please not to worry, Baroness,' said Karita. 'Ivan will only have to deal with people who are still infants compared to Lenin's secret police. If I could not rely on Ivan to get the better of them, I would divorce him and marry Sir Piers Fitzgerald, a man of many gifts and many riches who is madly in love with me.'

'And so on and so on,' said Nicholas.

Anne, thinking of the envelope and the negative it contained, said, 'Mr Kirby, is there something else you're doing besides observing the political situation?'

'You're thinking of Matthew Gibbs, a friend of

our family?' said Kirby. 'I did run into him. That complicated things a little.' Gibbs, in fact, had originally contacted him concerning a defecting member of the Nazi hierarchy in Berlin. His meeting with the man in Vienna promised to be interesting enough for Kirby to take a hand. Then trouble began with the arrival of the Gestapo at the defector's hideout. 'The matter's settled now. Between myself and Matthew at least.'

'Nicholas, keep out of trouble,' said Karita, as Kirby began to slow down.

'Oh, well, you know how it is,' said Nicholas, 'united we stand, divided we fall.'

'Ah,' said Karita, 'you would try to fly, would you, dearest boy, when you haven't yet learned to walk? You are still wet behind your eyeballs.'

'Ears, Mother, ears,' said Nicholas, as his father brought the car to a stop.

'What is the difference, eyeballs or ears?' said Karita. 'It is all the same.'

Nicholas was laughing as he got out of the car.

Later, on his way back to the apartment, Kirby stopped at Sacher's Hotel and, with the kind permission of the proprietor, whom he knew, made a long-distance phone call to Paris. His contacts were international.

Schroeder came to a sudden stop as a thought disturbed him. Groceries, groceries. He had let the rabbit-like routine of people take the edge off his concentration. That woman, the one who had been clutching a bulging carrier bag to her bosom, could he remember her entering the shop? The other one, the nondescript woman, he could remember her. He darted across the street, shouldering his way in and out of shoppers, and ran to the corner. Hopeless. She had turned there several long minutes ago, and could be anywhere now. He hurried to the shop, went in, found the proprietor and asked him about the woman in a shapeless raincoat, with a scarf over her head. No, the proprietor did not know who she was, he had never seen her before.

Leaving the shop, Schroeder decided to say nothing to Kommissar Voegler. Better to write the woman off as a shuffling, peering nonentity.

Voegler arrived then, in a car, with three assistants.

Chapter Sixteen

The long train, with its two mighty engines, was heading for Salzburg and the Italian border. To the south lay the beauty and grandeur of the Styrian Alps. Paul and Lucia were in the corridor, where they could talk freely. Grandmother Teresa von Korvacs, in a corner seat of the compartment, was watching the green countryside of her beloved Austria. She was dreaming of the years that had gone, the years of the Empire, when Vienna had been the pre-eminent city of Europe and its cultural heart.

'Of course, I'm not sure which school I'll go to in England,' said Lucia, 'but I know Franz will want to attend a college of music.'

'Could be a bit boring,' said Paul. 'Well, I'm not sure if they play cricket at music colleges. Rotten hard luck if they don't.'

'Franz doesn't play cricket, you silly,' said Lucia, 'no-one does in Austria. In any case, Franz is devoted to his violin. He's very talented. Mama says a genius, yes.'

'I like Harry Roy and his band myself,' said

Paul. 'Wait till you hear him play "Tiger Rag" on his radio programme.'

'Oh, I'm sure I'll like what you like,' said Lucia, 'and I like your parents very much. Your mother is so elegant, isn't she? Mama worries about putting on weight, you know.'

'She looks fine and healthy to me,' said Paul. He turned to check on his maternal grand-mother. Baroness Teresa caught his eye and smiled reassuringly. Paul smiled back. 'Look, Lucia,' he said, 'if the police come on the train at the border and examine everybody, you be read-ing one of the magazines and act as if that's all you're interested in. Grandmama will be OK, she'll know how to act like a haughty old English lady. I'll have a word with Aunt Pia and Emma Jane when we go for lunch, and I'll make sure Granddad is keeping his end up. It's not as if the police will be specially looking for us, but Dad said to be on our guard and not to let our real names slip out.'

'Isn't it awful that we have to be on our guard?' said Lucia.

'It's because we're all relatives of Aunt Anne,' said Paul. 'But we'll be all right, Lucia, and I'll give you a kiss once we're over the border.'

'Oh, we can be kissing cousins, then?' said Lucia.

'Well, the Pope hasn't told us no,' said Paul with a grin.

'Mein Herr?' said Heinrich on opening the door to Nicholas.

'Good morning, Heinrich,' said Nicholas, 'do

you think I might see Baroness Sophie – Frau Fraser?'

'Please enter,' said Heinrich, and took the athletic young man up to the apartment on the second floor. Heinrich and Hanna knew what was afoot, and although they were sad that everyone was going to England, there was a promise to re-employ them there when the families were settled. Until then they were to look after the house.

Sophie let Nicholas in. She and Vicky were packing. There was a great deal of stuff to be transported, and there were cases and trunks in every apartment, some fully laden and others to be filled. Heinrich and Hanna were to take care of the latter, and to arrange for the carriers to collect everything in due course.

'Nicholas, how nice to see you,' said Sophie.

'Mutual, I assure you, Mrs Fraser,' said Nicholas. 'I come bearing news.'

'Not bad news, I hope,' said Sophie.

'No, of course not,' said Nicholas, and told her simply that circumstances had made it advisable to transfer Baroness Anne into the care of her brother and Mr Fraser, and that she would be securely tucked away at the factory by now. 'They'll bring her here tonight.'

'I'm so glad,' said Sophie. 'Thank you, Nicholas.'

Vicky entered the living room. Wearing her glasses, her face was a little flushed, her hair a little awry. Packing was a hot and tedious business.

'Who— Oh, it's you, Nicholas.'

'Hello, Vicky.'

'What d'you mean by doing this to me?' demanded Vicky.

'Doing what to you?' asked Nicholas.

'Arriving without prior warning,' said Vicky, 'and catching me in an unpresentable condition. That's a black mark, I can tell you.'

'You don't look unpresentable,' said Nicholas.

'Yes, I do, I look like a ragbag,' said Vicky.

'This is very tragic,' smiled Sophie.

'Nothing can be done about it now,' said Vicky, 'and since the gentleman is here we might as well ask him to stay to lunch.'

'Thanks,' said Nicholas.

'Perhaps you could also help with the packing,' said Vicky.

'Pleasure,' said Nicholas.

'How nice,' said Sophie, 'tragedy over.'

'The discomfiture remains,' said Vicky. 'Mama, I actually came in to ask you if you realize that having bought two new hats here, your hats all together now outnumber your hatboxes. Shall I throw some away?'

'Hats may be given away,' said Sophie, 'but never thrown. Especially my hats. Perhaps Hanna would like one or two. I'll see to them.'

'Oh, very good, Mama,' said Vicky. 'Come along, then, Nicholas. That's if you don't mind helping a ragbag with the packing.'

'I'll take my jacket off, loosen my tie and slip my braces,' said Nicholas. 'Then we'll look like two ragbags together. Will that help your discomfiture?'

'Mama, did you ever hear such a terrible joke?' said Vicky.

'I've heard even more terrible ones from your father,' said Sophie, 'and have survived them all.'

'Well, I'll do my best to survive this one,' said Vicky. 'Come along, Nicholas.'

'I'm right behind you,' said Nicholas, and followed her out.

Sophie smiled. How lovely to be young.

'Clear the shop,' called Voegler from the landing of the apartment that had been found empty except for masculine clothes and accessories. His men emptied the shop of its customers, and he came down to talk to the shopkeeper, a stout man of fifty, who thought to see in the fine-featured Gestapo Kommissar an inquisitor more humane than his hatchet-faced assistants. He was not to know that Voegler had a reputation for reducing a suspect to grovelling misery without laying a finger on him. Voegler cherished his preference for non-violent methods, which had earned him commendations when he was attached for two years to one of Himmler's departments in Berlin. But for once his willingness to use patience to secure a result, either in the matter of tracking down a suspect or conducting an interrogation, was wearing thin. Foremost in his mind was not the Jew, Josef Meister, or Gibbs or Kirby, but Baroness Anne von Korvacs, a damned provocation who was also a fascinating opponent. The Jew had still not been found, and Gibbs, with his passport back, had managed to slip surveillance and disappear while visiting the Vienna Press Club. As for the Baroness Anne, even Himmler, a man fortunate enough to have no tiresome emotions, would have torn his hair at her disappearance. And Colonel Lundt-Hausen was, of course, in the foulest of tempers. 'Your name?' Voegler addressed the shopkeeper.

'Brummenger, Huego Brummenger. Mein Herr, what—'

'Kommissar. Who's been using the apartment?'

Huego Brummenger, a man whose rosy exterior and placid expression hid a violent dislike of the National Socialist Party and its thuggery, answered without hesitation.

'An English gentleman and his wife. Yes, and his son. They're nice people, polite and charming.'

'Do I want to know what their manners are like?' said Voegler. 'Did I ask to know?'

'It costs nothing to say so, Herr Kommissar.'

'So, they're polite and charming,' said Voegler. He lifted the lid of a tin of wafer biscuits. He took one and ate it. 'Is that by way of a character reference or your excuse for being taken in by them?'

'How taken in, Herr Kommissar?'

'Duped into not informing on them,' said Voegler.

'I don't understand,' said Brummenger. 'Why should I feel I had to inform on them?'

'We'll find that out.' Voegler ate another biscuit. 'You know their names, of course.'

'Yes. Kirby. But they aren't my tenants. The shop and apartment are leased by Frau Wirth, a widow who has made an excellent place of the apartment, and who relies on the rents—'

'You're a good citizen, Herr Brummenger,' said Voegler, 'plainly willing to advance all kinds of facts and information.'

'I'm a Party member, mein Herr,' said Brummenger, who with his wife believed in fighting the enemy from within. 'I had the honour on the day the Fuehrer arrived of presenting the SS Standarte 89 with a scroll of honour on behalf—'

'What a fine citizen you are, Herr Brummenger, and a fine shopkeeper too, although these biscuits could be crisper.' Voegler ate another. 'I'm pleased to meet such a friendly Party member. Mind you, Caesar was assassinated by his best friends.'

'I'm not amused by that remark,' said Brummenger.

'No, why should you be?' said Voegler. 'The murder of a man by his best friends is hardly funny. Now, give me a description of Frau Kirby.'

'About forty, mein Herr, but most attractive, with pale gold hair and brown eyes.' Brummenger was not making the mistake of giving a description that might quickly become a proven lie. 'A little above medium height. She left two days ago to go back to England.'

'You are mistaken,' said Voegler sharply.

'No, Herr Kommissar, she said goodbye to me on Thursday morning before leaving to catch her train,' said Brummenger, forthcoming but not obsequious. 'She said – I'm sorry, but she said Vienna had become an unhappy city and that – ' Brummenger hesitated.

'Yes?' Voegler's eyes took on a hard polished look.

'That she preferred to be home in England, where she had some gardening to do.'

Schroeder, Fleischer and the other men looked at the shopkeeper as if his idiocy was outstanding.

'Herr Brummenger,' said Voegler, 'did you personally accompany her to the station?'

'That isn't a serious question, is it?' said Brummenger.

'What else? Ask yourself, if you didn't see her board the train, how can you be sure she actually caught it?'

'Mein Herr, she said she was going, she said goodbye, and there were customers in the shop who must have heard her. I'm sorry, but I can't see why I should have puzzled myself about whether she actually caught the train or not. Is she in trouble? In all honesty, I found her a charming woman.'

Voegler ate yet another biscuit.

'Kirby's Russian wife, of course,' he murmured through crumbs. 'Not English, and not Greek.'

One of his men, rummaging around, entered the storeroom and looked it over. He lifted the lid of a large rice bin. It brimmed with pearly-white grains. He replaced the lid.

Brummenger said to Voegler, 'Is there anything else I can help you with, Herr Kommissar?'

'What time did you leave your shop last night?'

'I closed at six and left a few minutes later.'

'Who was in the apartment at that time?'

'I can't say.' Brummenger looked a trifle upset. 'This questioning is all very well, but you must know I don't go up to look at Frau Wirth's tenants each time I leave the shop.'

The back door, left open by the man who had just returned from the storeroom, opened wider at that moment, and Kirby looked in.

'Herr Brummenger,' he said, 'someone's been in the apartment— Oh, apologies for interrupting. So sorry.'

'Herr Kirby?' said Voegler.

'Yes?' said Kirby.

'I'd like to talk to you.'

'Who are you?' asked Kirby, and Voegler produced his card for inspection. 'Secret police?' said Kirby. 'What can I do for you, Kommissar Voegler?'

'First, where is your wife?'

'On her way to England by now,' said Kirby. 'She left on Thursday.'

'Did she?' Voegler eyed his man thoughtfully. 'You speak excellent German, Herr Kirby.'

'How's your English?' said Kirby.

'So-so.' Voegler shrugged. 'Shall we go up to the apartment?'

'That will allow Herr Brummenger to reopen his shop,' said Kirby, and went up. Voegler followed hard on his heels, and behind him trod Schroeder and Fleischer, Schroeder's irritated stomach noisy.

In the living room, Voegler said, 'We have an accurate description of your wife, Herr Kirby. It corresponds with that of a woman who committed a criminal assault on Colonel Lundt-Hausen, shot his servant and escaped with a lady being held for questioning concerning espionage.'

'Heavens, all that?' said Kirby. 'When was this?'

'Last night.'

'Quite a performance for any woman,' said Kirby. 'But it can't have been my wife. I'll allow she's versatile, but I don't think her arm is long enough to reach from Paris to Vienna.'

'Paris?' enquired Voegler.

'Yes, she intended to spend two days in Paris before going on to Dover this morning.'

'Why?'

'Why?' Kirby smiled. 'Paris, Herr Kommissar, is irresistible to women like my wife.'

'So I believe, but I'd like to talk to her.'

'Unfortunately,' said Kirby, 'I can't produce her.'

'What hotel did she use in Paris?'

'Hotel D'Orsay.'

'I'll use your telephone,' said Voegler. 'With your permission, of course.'

'It's there,' said Kirby.

Voegler first asked the operator to let him have the number of the hotel, then booked the call, replaced the receiver and waited.

'Herr Kirby, what is the reason for your visit to Vienna?'

'Ah, yes,' said Kirby, grey eyes mild. 'I'm an accredited representative of my government, and I'm here as an observer of historical and political events. It's been extremely interesting. My son is with me. As a university student reading history, he's found it fascinating.'

'Be so good as to turn out your pockets,' said Voegler.

'Well, you seem to have turned everything else out very thoroughly up here,' said Kirby, and emptied his pockets, placing the contents on a table. 'You're risking an official protest.'

Voegler looked at Fleischer.

'Search him.'

Fleischer ran his hands over the Englishman's long frame, satisfied himself that all pockets contained nothing more, and nodded. Voegler inspected what lay on the table. He did not expect to find that which was worrying Berlin. His men had made a minute but unrewarding examination of every possible hiding place in the apartment. His own examination of the items on the table was cursory, except for the wallet. In that, he did find a document, folded. He opened it up.

'That,' said Kirby, 'is from your Chancellor's Foreign Ministry. You'll note I'm to be assisted, not hindered.'

Voegler threw the document down and emptied the wallet. There was nothing of any consequence. He had never known any investigation to be confounded by so many negatives as this one, or give him such an obsessive interest in one particular suspect.

'Herr Kirby, we know about you. Your record is impressive. But you are being tiresome. You took possession of a certain document from Baroness Anne von Korvacs. Where is it?'

'Kommissar Voegler, is that a hopeful question or a suggestive allegation?' asked Kirby.

'It's a suggestion you've been abusing your terms of reference,' said Voegler.

The telephone rang. He picked it up. The operator announced he was connected.

'Hello? Hello? This is the Hotel D'Orsay.' It was a Frenchwoman's voice. Apart from a tiny intermittent crackle, the line was good.

'Reception, if you please,' said Voegler in passable French.

'A moment, m'sieur.' A click, and then a man's voice.

'Reception.'

'Good,' said Voegler in a pleasant tone. 'I'm trying to locate a lady, Madame Kirby. Is she there?'

The clerk, well primed by the manager, said, 'I regret, m'sieur, she is not.'

'She has not been staying there?'

'I mean, m'sieur, that she has left.'

'When?'

'This morning, m'sieur.'

'Thank you.' Voegler replaced the phone and looked at Kirby. 'I'm not convinced.'

'Of what?' asked Kirby.

'Of your wife's absence from Vienna last night and that you know nothing about the assault on Colonel Lundt-Hausen,' said Voegler. 'Nor do I believe you did not receive a document from Baroness Anne von Korvacs when you met her near the Opera Theatre last Tuesday.'

'Met her?' said Kirby. 'I saw a lady in danger of being knocked head over heels by two running men, and was able to pull her out of the way. Naturally, we then talked a little. An SD officer appeared, and the lady informed me he was her ex-husband. You can make what you like of the incident, but assumptions aren't enough. You know that, and so do I. I'm being very tolerant of your questioning, and you know that too.'

Voegler felt negatives were cheating him, that he had nothing that would allow him to be positive, nothing on this man and his wife, or on Gibbs, except circumstantial factors. And since they were foreign nationals, he could not simply fling them into a cell and leave them to Schroeder. He was, however, certain that they and the baroness were accomplices. But along with that certainty was an uncomfortable feeling that the document was now approaching London, by way of Kirby's wife. Yes, that could have been the reason why she left. Not a single item of feminine clothing had been found in the apartment. Lundt-Hausen's temper would explode. Well, thought Voegler, damned if I'll give a pfennig for that, I've got frustrations of my own.

The woman last night was possibly a Greek, after all. A golden-haired Greek? No, one with a wig. The Baroness's sister? No, Lundt-Hausen would have known her, despite any kind of wig.

'Herr Kirby, if I were to believe your story about Baroness Anne, I'd count myself a simpleton.'

'Yours is the privilege,' said Kirby.

'You are probably thinking of following your wife home,' said Voegler. 'I must tell you you are not to leave without a permit signed by Colonel Lundt-Hausen. Further, you are to present yourself at SS headquarters at two tomorrow afternoon.'

'If that's an order, you'll first have to get it authorized by your Chancellor or your Foreign Ministry,' said Kirby.

'You're misinformed,' said Voegler, 'our authority is Berlin. Our Foreign Ministry is merely a department of Berlin's.'

'It won't do, Herr Voegler,' said Kirby, 'it won't do for you, your Chancellor or His Majesty's Government. And it won't do for me. That is something else you must know.'

'Two o'clock tomorrow afternoon, Herr Kirby. That is official. Colonel Lundt-Hausen will be available to meet you.'

'One can hardly wait,' said Kirby in English.

He was to be busy for the rest of the day.

Voegler, about to enter his car, turned to Schroeder.

'You and Fleischer go and pick up the old man. And his wife.'

'The baron and baroness?' said Schroeder.

'The old man and his old woman,' said Voegler. 'If nothing else comes our way today, we'll at least end up with hostages that might force their daughter out of hiding.'

Schroeder had no qualms. Fleischer had reservations. The senior baron and baroness were not unknown. The son, Baron Carl, a racing driver, was idolized by the whole of Austria and much of Germany. Would the arrest of the old ones serve the cause of National Socialism or merely the whims of Colonel Lundt-Hausen? Baroness Anne might be a mote in his particular eye, but the British agent, Kirby, was bound to be a larger mote in Himmler's eye. He was the one who had the document, or knew where it was. That was the opinion of everyone at headquarters.

'This is what you definitely want, Herr Kommissar, the arrest of the old ones?' he asked.

Voegler showed a brief smile. He was quite willing to help Lundt-Hausen cook his own goose by allowing him to let his personal spite put him on the wrong course.

'I have my orders, Fleischer. You and Schroeder have yours. Arrest the old baron and his wife.'

Chapter Seventeen

Schroeder and Fleischer came up against an unflappable Sophie, an even more composed woman than her elusive sister.

'You may search the house from top to bottom, if you wish,' she said, 'but it will do you no good. My parents, as I've already told you, have gone to England. Do you think, after your threats to arrest them simply because my sister is their daughter, that they would wait for that to happen? I am ashamed that Austria could become such an unhappy place for people who have loved it so much.'

Schroeder, whose stomach was giving him a bad day, regarded her in scowling suspicion. Fleischer was more inclined to believe she made sense. The old ones had taken fright and run. Very sensible. Not that he cared much for their kind.

'When did they leave?' he asked.

'Early this morning,' said Sophie. Only she and Vicky, together with Hanna and Heinrich, were in the house. Nicholas had made himself scarce in the garden, and Josef Meister was securely hidden in the garage. 'One could say they might be anywhere in Switzerland by now.' One could say that, of course.

'It's an offence to leave the country without permission,' growled Schroeder.

'You're speaking of people suspected of crimes?' said Sophie.

'And of the parents of your sister,' said Schroeder.

'Who can see justice in that?' said Sophie.

'Come on,' said Fleischer to Schroeder, 'there's work to do.'

They left. Back at headquarters, they found Voegler was out. He was hunting Josef Meister, having received a report that the Jew had been seen in the vicinity of a synagogue not far from the cathedral. Schroeder and Fleischer began making telephone calls to border-control posts of the railways.

Afternoon, and the gallery was crowded. Mariella was spending a culturally satisfying time discussing her techniques with visitors whose interest was of a knowledgeable kind. Sergeant Wainwright was studying one exhibit with a critical eye.

'Can I help you, mein Herr?' she asked, as if he were a visitor too.

'Speak English?' responded the sergeant.

'Yes.'

'Good-oh,' said Sergeant Wainwright. 'This picture of a church – '

'St Stephen's Cathedral,' said Mariella.

'Not bad,' said Sergeant Wainwright, 'not bad at all.'

'I see. What is wrong with it, then?'

'The dome looks as if it's made of marzipan in different colours.'

'Those colours are always there during fine autumn afternoons,' said Mariella.

'You sure?' said Sergeant Wainwright.

'Positive.'

'Good brushwork, I'll say that much.'

'Patronizing beast,' whispered Mariella, 'I shall kick your leg off in a moment.'

'Don't do that yet,' murmured Sergeant Wainwright, 'just note the enemy's arrived.'

The enemy, Bauer and Lutz of the Gestapo, walked straight up to her.

'You,' said Bauer, 'you're wanted.'

'Excuse me?' said Mariella.

'Fräulein Amaraldi,' said Lutz, 'you're to present yourself at SS headquarters at two thirty tomorrow afternoon. If you're wise, you'll bring the Jew with you.'

'How can I bring—'

'You're being given twenty-four hours to either bring him or lead us to him,' said Bauer, and he and Lutz left.

Mariella, with people eyeing her in curiosity, moved to her desk and sat down. Sergeant Wainwright seated himself on a visitors' bench and used a pencil to make an entry in a notebook. He removed the page and folded it. A little later, when Mariella was again in conversation with people, he slipped the note unseen into her hand. She was able to read it when she repaired to her table once more.

'We were wondering, weren't we, if or when

276

they'd come after you again. We're in luck, we know now you'll have until two thirty tomorrow, and we'll be well gone by then. Don't throw this note away, eat it, that's always the best thing.'

The man was a clown, but she was beginning to feel he wasn't actually a liability.

The train was at a standstill at the Italian border. The Austrian border police were swarming through compartments, looking into faces and inspecting passports. Because of telephone calls from Vienna, trains at all border crossings were being searched for an elderly couple, Baron Ernst von Korvacs and his wife. It was possible that their daughter, Baroness Anne, a fair woman, might be in company with them. All three were to be taken off the train and detained.

Pia and Emma Jane were ready to produce their forged passports, Pia's being in the name of Gretel Else Weber, Austrian citizen of Vienna, Emma Jane's in the name of Helene Gretel, her daughter. A policeman, entering the compartment, made a quick survey of its occupants. Passports were offered for inspection. He ignored them, and after his survey he brushed them aside and left.

In another compartment, Paul and Lucia chatted in casual fashion, indifferent to the presence of a policeman. Looking for an elderly couple possibly in company with a fair woman, his survey alighted on Baroness Teresa, seated with a boy and girl. Paul, noting this, said in English, 'Have you got your passport, Grandma? The policeman's looking at you.'

'Oh, my,' said Baroness Teresa, and other passengers eyed her as she produced it. The policeman took it and examined it, a British passport in the name of Mary Caroline Dickens.

'English?'

'Yes, of course she is,' said Paul, 'she's our grandmother.'

'Here's my passport,' said Lucia bravely.

'Not necessary, not necessary,' said the policeman and left.

Paul breathed a sigh of relief. Five minutes later, however, he was alarmed to see his grandfather, the baron, passing by in company with two policemen. He jumped up, slid back the door and went after them.

'Mr Woodley, Mr Woodley,' he said as he caught them up, 'fancy seeing you. What are you doing here?'

The baron, a worried man, nevertheless caught on at once.

'Heavens, it's young William Dickens, yes, it is.' His English was good, if stilted. The accent was not recognizable to the policemen. They stared in curiosity at Paul.

'I can't believe it's you, Mr Woodley,' said Paul, 'what a small world.'

'What is this, what is this?' asked one policeman.

'Do you speak English?' asked Paul.

'A little.'

'Why is Mr Woodley going with you?' asked Paul.

'It is not your business.'

'But he's our neighbour.'

'Neighbour?'

'Yes, he lives near us in London,' said Paul.

'You know him?'

'Yes, he's a family friend,' said Paul. 'A widower.'

'What? Widower? Say his name, please.'

'I've said it. Mr Woodley, Mr John Woodley.'

The passport, which had been confiscated on the reasonable grounds that its owner could easily fit the description of one Baron Ernst von Korvacs, was reinspected. Yes, that was the name, John Woodley. John Alexander Woodley, of St Albans Grove, Kensington, London.

The baron now came under very acute inspection. There were doubts then. For one thing, he was travelling alone. For another, here was this fine-looking English boy claiming him as a neighbour and friend.

'It is Mr Woodley, *ja?*'

'Of course,' said the baron, 'I have told you.'

'He's not done anything, has he?' said Paul.

'Speak his address, please.'

'It's St Albans Grove, Kensington. That's in London.' Paul fought to be as natural as possible, although his heart was thumping. 'We live in Cottesmere Gardens. That's the next street.'

'What?'

'The next street,' said Paul. The train engines hissed steam.

'Passport, please, passport.' A hand gestured, and Paul handed his passport over. The policeman checked it, then eyed the baron, whose nerves were enduring an uncomfortable time. In

279

brusque German the policeman asked, 'Do you know this young man?'

'I am sorry?' said the baron, intelligently staying with his English.

'His name?' This in heavy English.

'Yes. William Dickens. A nice boy.'

The policeman looked at his colleague.

'There's no wife,' he said.

'Or daughter.'

'They left the train at Salzburg, perhaps.'

'With the daughter?'

'It's possible. This man is English, you think? He and the boy obviously know each other.'

Paul, catching only a little of the whispered dialogue, said brightly to his grandfather, 'Where are you going, Mr Woodley?'

'Rome, William,' said the baron with a smile.

'Your passport, mein Herr.' The baron's passport was returned to him, and Paul received his too. 'Our apologies.'

'Excuse me?' said Paul, for German had been spoken.

'OK, OK,' said the policeman, and moved on with his colleague, leaving Paul and the baron giddy with relief.

'Where's your travelling case, Grandpa?' whispered Paul.

'I left it on the rack, I disowned it,' murmured the baron, and smiled again.

Ten minutes later, the train crossed the border into Italy. Feeling wonderfully free, Emma Jane, Lucia and Paul all met in the corridor, where Paul recounted, in discreet whispers, the tale of the two policemen and Mr John Woodley of

Kensington. Lucia was overcome with admiration. Emma Jane was more prosaic.

'Well, fancy that,' she said.

Evening darkness arrived. The packing had been finished. In the large ground-floor kitchen, Hanna and Heinrich were preparing dinner. Josef Meister was back in the basement, where he had been existing fairly comfortably. It had never occurred to Voegler or Ludwig that the von Korvacs family had taken him in.

Nicholas had been a great help, delighting Sophie by the cheerful way he had performed every kind of useful task. Vicky, while acknowledging the value of his assistance, wasn't at all sure she approved of his growing compatibility with her mother.

Eventually, she spoke to her.

'Mama, really,' she said.

'Really what, darling?' said Sophie.

'All this familiarity between you and Nicholas.'

'Familiarity?' said Sophie.

'Yes, he's beginning to make eyes at you,' said Vicky. 'Can't you wear something that will make you look old and wretched?'

'Must I?' said Sophie.

'Yes, something like a tatty old shawl and cracked boots,' said Vicky. 'I don't wish to live with the shame of being cut out by my own mother.'

'Oh, dear, it's like that, is it?' said Sophie.

'I must point out, Mama, that at my age I'm entitled to have a young man to myself,' said Vicky.

'Very well, darling, I'll do everything I can to look old and wretched,' said Sophie.

'Well, I wish you would sometimes,' said Vicky.

'However, don't take him too seriously, darling,' said Sophie. 'He mentioned to me, when he was speaking of Bristol University, that he has a friend there, a young lady undergraduate.'

'Oh?' said Vicky.

'Well, you're both of an age to have many friends,' said Sophie.

'I see,' said Vicky, and went to find Nicholas. He was sitting on a trunk that was overflowing, using his weight to close the lid. 'You've deceived me,' she said.

'Have I?' said Nicholas.

'Yes, you've made up to me without disclosing the fact that you have a young lady at the university.'

'Well, she's a close friend, I admit,' said Nicholas, 'but so are you now, Vicky.'

'I have no desire to be one more of your close friends,' said Vicky. 'I consider myself no more than one of your acquaintances. If there's anything I seriously object to, it's a young man worming his way into my good graces when he already has a girlfriend.'

'But a girlfriend isn't necessarily a fixture, Vicky, unless a fellow's serious about her,' said Nicholas.

'I know what that means,' said Vicky, 'it means you're the type to play the field. Did you actually suffer a moment of conscience? Was that what made you confess your liaison to my mother?'

'Liaison?' said Nicholas.

'I despise you,' said Vicky.

'All is over between us, Vicky?' Nicholas attempted a light-hearted comment.

'Do you have a girlfriend at university or not?' demanded Vicky.

'Well, yes, but – '

'No more need be said. I feel you've made an idiot of me. We shall say goodbye to each other later on.'

'Now look, Vicky, I expect you go about with other fellows, don't you?' said Nicholas.

'Kindly refrain from speaking to me,' said Vicky, and walked out.

Nor would she come down from her high horse.

There was an unused office, reached by an outside iron staircase, in the upper section of a warehouse adjacent the main plant of the Austro-Fraser car works, from where it could not be seen. The blank side wall of the plant faced it. It contained an old electric fire, a table and chairs, and facilities for making coffee. Anne and Karita were in occupation, and conveniently out of the way of prying eyes. Over a period of several hours they had come to know each other well, and Karita had related a fund of reminiscences about Russia and the doomed Imperial family, as well as the horrors of the Revolution, when the Bolsheviks and the Whites between them had spilt rivers of blood far deeper and wider than had ever been known, even under Ivan the Terrible. Karita asserted that Ivan the Terrible was a novice compared to Lenin the ice-cold monster and his successor, Stalin the butcher.

'My own Ivan – '

'Your husband,' said Anne.

'Yes.' Karita's smile was very reminiscent. 'He was like a crazy man when he found the Bolsheviks had taken the Imperial family to Ekaterinburg. He was in love with Grand Duchess Olga, the Tsar's eldest daughter, and Olga, poor Olga, could not take her eyes off him during the days when life was sweeter for her. He and I advanced with the White Army and the Czech Legion on Ekaterinburg, and together we took off the heads of a thousand Bolsheviks.'

'A thousand?' said Anne, gazing in wonder at this captivating woman who could be so tigerish and deadly.

'Who can truly say how many?' Karita gestured. 'But they rolled like red turnips. Ah, how sad that we were too late. The Ekaterinburg Soviet murdered them all. Ivan was terribly upset. Fortunately, I was there to make him realize I was much more exciting than Olga. We made love, and left Russia to go to England and marry. It was very necessary by then, you understand. Nicholas was born only four months after our wedding.'

'Karita, you have lived such an exciting life,' said Anne. 'Mine has only been difficult, shall we say. I'm still waiting for excitement to begin.'

'But it has begun,' said Karita, 'you have known the excitement of challenging Himmler's police and escaping them. Now, while you are still young – '

'I'm not still young,' said Anne.

'You are still attractive enough to be exciting to a man,' said Karita. 'You must choose one who is truly a man, the kind who will laugh at you when you throw things at him.'

'Must a woman throw things, Karita?'

'Of course,' said Karita. 'That is how a man will know you are a real woman and not a footstool. It will provoke him to make love to you while you are still spitting and scratching. Ah, that is one of the best ways to enjoy love.'

'But I couldn't behave like that, spitting and scratching,' said Anne.

'You must learn,' said Karita, 'then you will never be boring to a new husband.'

Someone knocked on the door. Anne stiffened, and Karita rose as swiftly as a panther. The door opened and James appeared.

'Hello,' he said.

'Here is a man able to fight Himmler's wolves,' said Karita.

'Years ago he fought frightful Bosnian bandits,' said Anne.

'Give all credit to Karita for downing Ludwig,' said James. 'What could we have done without her?'

'Very little,' said Karita, and James laughed.

'Everything's arranged,' he said. 'Anne, I think you know a truck containing two racing cars will be leaving tomorrow.'

'Yes, I do know,' said Anne.

'I'll be driving my car, with Sophie and Vicky,' said James. 'The truck and car will rendezvous with Karita and John, and their son Nicholas, by

Esterhazy Park. John's returned his hired car and rented another, a strong reliable model. He'll lead the way.'

'Everyone is going to England, everyone?' said Anne.

'Before Vienna gets too hot for all of us,' said James. 'By the way, the weather forecast is for a clear day tomorrow.'

'That is so?' said Anne. 'Well, we need the weather to be kind to us since we'll be motoring.'

'It'll be clear but cold,' said James. 'Warm clothes must be worn.'

Karita laughed.

'There's more to talk about than the weather and what clothes must be worn,' she said. She and Anne knew the Gestapo were now hunting Anne's parents. Carl, having received a phone call from Sophie about this new development, had passed the news on. 'Let us have some hot tea,' she said.

'You and Anne help yourselves,' said James, 'and I'll be back in about an hour, when it'll be time to move. You've got tea here?'

'Oh, we have a huge bag of groceries,' smiled Anne.

At the house, Sophie received a phone call from Pia to say everyone had reached Italy safely, and that the children had behaved splendidly.

Paul, standing by, objected to the reference to children.

'So do I,' said Lucia.

'Who is saying what?' asked Sophie.

'Oh, two young grown-ups here are muttering about their advanced years,' said Pia.

'I understand,' said Sophie, 'our love to all of them.'

Ludwig was just back from another protracted round-up of dissidents and certain members of newly proscribed opposition parties. Such a task should have given him enjoyment and satisfaction, but his leg was in a damnable state and there were people he wanted in the cells far more than dissidents. It obsessed him, his need to get his hands on Josef Meister and Anne. Further, he was just as obsessed with cornering the bitch of a woman who had outwitted him and crippled him for long painful hours. In addition, he wanted proof of the espionage activities of Matthew Gibbs and John Kirby. Accordingly, he received Voegler's account of certain events with grinding ill temper.

'So what are you telling me? That the dirty Jew is still at large, the baroness is thumbing her nose at us, her parents have escaped us, that you've nothing on Kirby and still nothing on Gibbs, and that Kirby's wife has an alibi for last night?'

'Kirby and Gibbs are British, and need to be caught red-handed,' said Voegler. 'Kirby is a professional who knows his trade. He also knows his rights as an accredited representative of his government at the moment. To nail him we need him to incriminate himself. Unfortunately, I've a suspicion his wife took the document to England with her.'

'You're convinced she's there, are you? Think, man,' said Ludwig impatiently. 'She told the shopkeeper she was returning to England. She made a point of doing so in front of customers. She created a picture of departure. She fooled the shopkeeper, and she hoped, through him, to fool us.'

'Some women, Herr Colonel, do have the ability to fool better men than shopkeepers,' said Voegler. 'We have to acknowledge it and live with it.'

'What the hell are you talking about?' shouted Ludwig.

'I'm suggesting our intellect isn't unassailable, even by women,' said Voegler.

Ludwig, containing himself, said pointedly, 'Do you have any particular women in mind?'

You might well ask, thought Voegler, and I might well tell you that your ex-wife is the most impressive of such women. But I won't, of course.

'Such particular women are those who succeed in outwitting us,' he said.

'Outwitting be damned,' said Ludwig. 'What you're talking about is your gullibility. That isn't your usual style, is it? Concentrate on the obvious, that the baroness was the go-between used by Gibbs and Kirby, and that Kirby's wife has to be the damned woman who wormed herself into my apartment.'

'Do we accept the obvious as facts, Herr Colonel, or are they still assumptions?'

'Kirby used his wife, of course he damned well did,' said Ludwig. 'He had to get the baroness free, he owed it to her. Find his wife, find her. I want roadblocks and railway stations manned all night. If Kirby is still in Vienna—'

'He's been ordered to present himself here at two tomorrow afternoon,' said Voegler.

'So you've already said, and I tell you, if he's still in Vienna, then so is his wife. And the baroness is probably with them. We'll comb the city tomorrow with your men and mine, and hope to land Meister in the net as well, with the help of the fat Amaraldi woman after Schroeder's had half an hour with her.'

'Fat?' said Voegler, austere countenance masking a contempt for Lundt-Hausen's personal hatreds. 'I'd call her handsome of figure myself. Herr Colonel, there's other business that still needs our attention.'

'Damn other business,' said Ludwig. 'This has got priority and you know it.'

'If you say so,' said Voegler.

He was home late and had to listen to his crotchety mother telling him that if she'd known he was going to end up in Germany's secret police, she'd have drowned him at birth.

'Austria's police,' he said.

'Don't fool yourself,' said Frau Voegler.

'Police work suits my talents,' he said.

'Your kind of police work will bring you to a bad end, and what good will your talents be then, eh?'

'For the sake of the National Socialist Party—'

'A pox on it,' said Frau Voegler.

*　　*　　*

In the darkness, Karita was driven away from the factory by Kirby, while James assisted Anne into the back of the truck. Carl was at the wheel.

'Good girl,' said James.

'Girl?' said Anne. 'Is that to flatter me or to help steady my pulse rate?'

'My own's going at a gallop,' said James.

'We both need the help of Providence,' said Anne.

James smiled and closed the rear doors. He gave the word to Carl, and Carl set the truck in motion. James followed in his limousine. The journey to the Salesianergasse was encouragingly uneventful, and at the house Carl backed the truck up to the front door. Moments later, Anne, hidden by the looming bulk of the vehicle, was out and flitting silently into the house. James and Carl entered, and the door closed.

Nicholas said goodbye at ten. Carl had informed him his father would be waiting for him in a car at the corner of the Bayerngasse. Nicholas shook hands all round. Vicky, of course, allowed him only a brief touch of her fingers. Sophie said he must come and see them in their home at Shepperton.

'We'll see him before then,' said James.

'Will we?' said Sophie. 'When?'

'Tomorrow, probably,' said James.

Vicky looked disgusted at the prospect.

Chapter Eighteen

At eight the following morning, Carl drove the truck out of the forecourt. Behind him came James in his Fraser limousine, Sophie beside him, Vicky in the back.

AUSTRO-FRASER RACING CARS was boldly emblazoned on each side of the truck. The name caught the eyes of work-going people, and was at once associated with Baron Carl von Korvacs, a veteran of the circuits and wholly admired.

Vicky, cosy in a black fur hat and a cherry-red coat, noted that some people looked at the truck with interest.

'If they knew it was actually Uncle Carl who was driving, they'd want him to stop and give them his autograph,' she said. 'I really wouldn't have minded sharing the cabin with him and basking in his fame.'

'I know you wouldn't,' said James, 'but let's keep to Carl's change of plan.'

They all knew Carl was taking by far the greater risk. If the truck was stopped and searched, he might be in deep trouble. That would depend on the nature of the search. He had insisted that James must keep going if the truck was compelled to stop. Vicky must be in the car, therefore. He himself had a certain immunity from Nazi ill will because of his popularity as Austria's foremost racing driver.

He handled the truck with the care of a man needing to avoid either accident or incident. The weather forecast had proved correct, the morning being clear, cold and crisp. Opposite Esterhazy Park a dark blue Opel slipped out of the Kopernikgasse, threaded itself smoothly into the traffic and motored along a little in advance of the truck.

Vicky, wearing her spectacles, said, 'Well, I'm blessed, it's happened.'

'What has?' asked Sophie, full of nervous excitement.

'I've just seen Mr Kirby junior,' said Vicky, 'he's in that car that pushed in.'

'Yes, that's the Kirbys' car,' said James. 'He and his parents are going to lead the way.'

'Are they?' said Vicky. 'Why?'

'So that we'll have some forward eyes,' said James. 'We're the rearguard, the Kirbys are the vanguard.'

'All the way?' said Vicky.

'Yes, all the way,' said Sophie.

'I'm thrilled, of course,' said Vicky.

The little convoy moved steadily on with the western flow of traffic. In Vienna, Ludwig had reached his desk. At the rear of headquarters, men of the SD and Gestapo were climbing into the cars or trucks that would help them comb the city.

'Herr Kommissar,' said Ludwig the moment Voegler entered his office, 'Berlin's losing patience.'

Voegler was close to losing his own patience, remarkably long-suffering though it was. He was certain the missing document was now out of the country, and would have liked Lundt-Hausen to help himself to the embarrassment of telling Berlin so.

'Berlin is always anxious for quick results,' he said.

'I reminded myself this morning that the Jew and Baroness Anne are friends,' said Ludwig. Voegler noted he did not mention an adulterous relationship. 'So first of all, send two men to arrest her sister, Baroness Sophie, the wife of the man Fraser.'

'On what charge, Herr Colonel?' asked Voegler.

'Complicity, of course.'

'She's the wife of a British subject,' said Voegler.

'Arrest her,' said Ludwig. 'Interrogate her. On the whereabouts of her sister and Meister. And her parents.' Voegler's fine mouth tightened. Here was a man holding an office of power who chose not to come face to face himself with members of the family he hated so much. Others had to do his work. 'As soon as she's here, bring in Kirby and Gibbs.'

'Herr Colonel, aren't we in danger of going against the Fuehrer's directive concerning the maintenance of harmonious relations with countries of the West? The arrest of the wife of a British national, and the arrest of—'

'The responsibility is mine, if that's what is worrying you,' said Ludwig.

I must get that in writing, thought Voegler.

He sent two men to arrest the wife of James Fraser.

The men returned to report that the von Korvacs's residence was empty except for two servants, who told them everyone had left to go to England. To protect Hanna and Heinrich from harassment, Carl had instructed them, in the event of enquiries, to give the required information and to stress that the journey related to the launching of the new racing cars on the Brooklands circuit in England.

Voegler reported to Ludwig, whose reaction was to look as if a canker was consuming his soul.

'Gone? All of them? To watch some car race?'

'So we're meant to believe,' said Voegler.

'Does that take in the baron and baroness too?'

'If you remember, the old couple left for Italy yesterday,' said Voegler.

'And weren't picked up at the border? Damnation,' breathed Ludwig, 'what kind of organization are we running that we're letting these people slip through our fingers, that we can't find the Jew or any proof of the illegal activities of Gibbs and Kirby?'

'Regarding the Jew, can I remind you the woman Amaraldi is to report here this afternoon?' said Voegler. 'It's your own idea that she can be made to tell us where Meister is.'

'She's the sister-in-law of Baron Carl,' said

Ludwig, 'and knows the Jew as well as all that damned family does.'

'She's an artist,' said Voegler. 'Of a decadent kind,' he added. 'She has a strange idea of what a tree looks like. My idea—' He stopped on the sudden realization that his attitude towards painters was governed by the ideals of National Socialism, which was not the same thing as making up one's own mind. Not for the first time lately, he asked himself what the hell was happening to him. National Socialism, now breathing new life into a tired and riven Austria, was too necessary to be questioned.

Ludwig massaged a knee joint.

'They're running,' he said. 'Are you thinking what I'm thinking?'

'Yes, that the Jew is running with them,' said Voegler.

'The Jew?' said Ludwig sourly. 'Yes, he may be. Yes. But I meant the Baroness Anne.'

Yes, you would, of course, thought Voegler, quite willing to go after any woman suspected of treason, but not if she was merely the object of a personal hatred.

'The Baroness Anne, yes, that might be possible,' he said.

'Might be?' said Ludwig, his teeth grinding. 'What's the matter with you, Herr Kommissar? Would they all have gone, all of them, leaving her to fend for herself, wherever she is? Not that damned collection of stuck-up reactionaries. There's also Kirby's wife to consider. I know what everything points to, that they're all in it together, Gibbs as well, and Kirby's behind it all.'

Ludwig rose. 'We'll take two cars,' he said, 'with two of your men and six of mine. Let's call first on the servants.'

The driver of a truck that had left the Austro-Fraser works at eight o'clock pulled up at a tavern some way out of Vienna. At this precise moment, Ludwig was confronting Hanna and Heinrich and asking his first question.

'What transport was used by your employers when they left this morning?'

'Transport, Herr Standartenfuehrer?' said Heinrich, stiffly polite. He could neither forget nor forgive what Count Ludwig Lundt-Hausen had done to Baroness Anne over a number of years.

'Don't play the innocent with me, you old fool. What cars did they take?'

'Herr Fraser took his English limousine, and there was also a works truck,' said Heinrich, with Hanna looking on mutinously.

'A works truck and a single car?' Ludwig fixed Heinrich with an icy stare. 'I'm to believe some of these people are travelling to England in a truck, the rest in the car?'

Since he had not been asked to state how many people were involved, and since he correctly assumed Ludwig had all of them in mind except the elderly baron and baroness, and Baroness Anne, Heinrich said, 'I assure you, Herr Standartenfuehrer, they went only in the car and the truck.'

'I think he's telling the truth,' said Voegler. 'The route?' he enquired of Heinrich.

'They did not tell me their route,' said Heinrich, 'but Herr Fraser and Baron Carl have made the journey many times, and I've heard them talk of places they've been through. Munich and Rheims and Calais.'

'The most direct route,' said Ludwig. 'Did you hear them talk of places this time?'

'I assure you, no,' said Heinrich. Carl had told him to answer up, and he was doing so, although only in the way he thought best. 'I assumed they would take the direct route as usual.'

'You, did you hear them mention any place names?' asked Ludwig of Hanna.

'I'm always too busy to stand about waiting to listen to talk that doesn't concern me,' said Hanna, bridling.

'I know you well enough to know you listen to everything,' said Ludwig brutally. 'You,' he said to Heinrich, 'tell me about Josef Meister, the friend of Baroness Anne. How many times has he been here since the Fuehrer entered Vienna?'

'I've not answered the door to him for two or three months,' said Heinrich.

'You're lying.'

'I protest,' said Heinrich proudly. 'You know I don't tell lies.'

'Who were in the car?' asked Ludwig.

'While I didn't stand at the door to watch them go,' said Heinrich, 'I believe it was Herr Fraser, Baroness Sophie and their elder daughter.'

'And the rest were in the truck?' said Ludwig.

'Including the Baroness Anne, perhaps?' suggested Voegler.

'As you know, mein Herr—'

'I am Kommissar Voegler.'

'As you know, Herr Kommissar,' said Heinrich, 'Baroness Anne was arrested on Friday.'

'And as you damned well know, she has since escaped us,' said Ludwig.

'Then where she is now, Herr Count, I can't tell you,' said Heinrich. Nor could he. He did not know where the truck was on its journey. 'I can only tell you the car and the truck left at eight this morning.'

'And I can only tell you my husband does not lie,' said Hanna.

'You two are as pompous as your employers, and the Reich would miss neither of you,' said Ludwig. He and Voegler left. They entered their waiting car, in the front of which were Schroeder and Fleischer. Ludwig was seething. He still had nothing to offer Berlin. His pathological hatred of Anne and her family, together with his contempt for his own country, affected him like a festering wound for which there was no salve. Those servile lackeys, the idiots, had been useless as informants. Carl would be leading the wholesale exit of the family. Yes, he'd be in the truck, perhaps driven by one of his mechanics, and he might choose any route except the usual one. If he was to pick up Anne, Meister and the Kirbys somewhere, he would avoid Germany. The racing cars were only a blind. Switzerland was far more likely than Germany, for once there they'd be safe. 'Salzburg and the Swiss border,' he said to Fleischer at the wheel, 'but stop at the first public telephone.'

'Wait,' said Voegler, 'we may be chasing shadows.'

'The whole damned bunch are on the run together,' said Ludwig. 'Get going, man,' he said to Fleischer.

'Very good, Herr Colonel,' said Fleischer.

The car shot forward, followed by the one carrying six uniformed SD men.

Voegler's expression denoted disbelief. Lundt-Hausen seemed to have forgotten his order for Vienna to be combed, and that the operation was now under way without him. His conclusion that the men and the women he most wanted for interrogation were already out of Vienna made nonsense of the sweep.

A taxi stood waiting outside Mariella's apartment. Out she came, Sergeant Wainwright with her, he carrying her large suitcase and his valise. They boarded the taxi and away it went to the railway station.

An attractive hat crowned Mariella's auburn wig.

They said nothing to each other except to comment in English on the brightness of the morning.

At the station, Security Police examined their faces and inspected their joint passport. It was in the names of Mr Percival Dixon and Mrs Brigid Dixon. He was shown to have been born in Blackheath, London, she in Innsbruck, Austria. The passport photographs were a good likeness, hers given a little treatment by him to undermine its new look. The inspection was formal, not probing. The Security Police were looking for Gibbs, Kirby, Mrs Kirby and Baroness Anne von Korvacs, and neither of these passengers answered given descriptions of any of the wanted.

The passport was handed back, and one policeman said to Mariella, 'What's it like, then, being married to an Englishman?'

'Hell on earth,' said Mariella, and both policemen roared with laughter.

They had a reserved compartment to themselves on the train. Sergeant Wainwright had arranged it at substantial cost to his funds.

'I hope the journey will be comfortable and without trouble,' said Mariella.

'There might be a small amount of hell on earth,' said Sergeant Wainwright.

'You understood what was said?'

'Just about,' said Sergeant Wainwright.

'You should speak German more if you want to understand it better,' observed Mariella. 'I only said what I knew those policemen wished to hear.'

'Saucy, though,' said Sergeant Wainwright, 'and gave me a bad name.'

'Are you a married man?' asked Mariella.

'Not yet,' said Sergeant Wainwright.

'You mean you are engaged to someone?'

'Not yet,' said Sergeant Wainwright.

'But you will be? I'm happy for you. Who is she?'

'No idea.' Sergeant Wainwright settled himself into the window seat opposite Mariella.

'Ah, I see,' she said. 'You like women but won't marry any of them.'

'All I can say, marm, is that it hasn't happened yet. You're my only wife so far, and that's only what the passport says. Still, to make it look right, if any nosy Gestapo characters look in on us, I'll cuddle up with you.'

'Ah, you would like that, would you?' said Mariella.

'They won't be looking for a happy married couple.'

'They won't find one, either,' said Mariella. 'Your orders don't command you to make love to me, do they?'

'Well, no, marm, not on a train.'

'I would smack your face if you tried to,' said Mariella.

'Very right and proper,' said Sergeant Wainwright. People were moving through the corridor, the standing train gently issuing steam. 'Anyway, don't you worry. I've got my orders to hand you over safe and sound to your mother, which will be done.'

'Hand me over?' said Mariella. 'Am I a parcel, then?'

'Not you,' said Sergeant Wainwright, 'you're a fine-looking woman top to bottom, and—'

'Stop,' said Mariella.

'Begging your pardon, marm?'

'Top to bottom?' said Mariella. 'How dare you?'

'You're talking about your derrière?'

'No, you are.'

'Figure of speech,' said Sergeant Wainwright cheerfully. 'Anyway, it's safe and sound, marm. You're sitting on it.' Mariella seized her handbag, leaned forward, swung it by its strap, and hit him with it. 'Well, I hope we both feel better now,' he said.

Mariella collapsed into laughter.

The door slid back and two uniformed State policemen showed themselves.

'Excuse, but your papers, please,' said one.

'No papers, my husband is English,' said Mariella.

'Ah, so, you are his wife?' Two pairs of keen eyes surveyed her.

'Of course.'

'Passport, please.'

Sergeant Wainwright produced the joint passport, and it was examined with official thoroughness.

'It has already been inspected, by police at the platform gate,' said Mariella.

No comment. The State policemen continued their examination, studying the photographs and checking resemblance.

'Good,' said one eventually, and the passport was handed back. A little smile appeared on the face of the other man, and he whispered to his colleague, who shrugged but also smiled. 'Our apologies for troubling you,' he said, and they left. The door slid to.

'What were they grinning about?' asked Sergeant Wainwright.

'For the same reason as the Security men,' said Mariella. 'What it was like for me to be married to an Englishman.'

'What would you have said this time?'

'That I was wishing to go home to my mother,' said Mariella.

'I'll get you there,' said Sergeant Wainwright.

Some fifty miles west of Vienna, the little convoy passed through Melk with other traffic. Kirby, at the wheel of the Opel, had led the way out of Vienna by a very minor road to avoid what he suspected was certain, a checkpoint on every exit of importance. He entered the main road six miles beyond the city.

A little way out of Melk, however, a notice announced a traffic check.

'On our account, I wonder?' said Nicholas.

'We'll soon see,' said Kirby.

Ahead, two State policemen were signalling some vehicles to pull up in a lay-by and allowing others to pass. Highways officials were questioning drivers of the halted vehicles. The Opel was directed to pull over, and so was the truck. The limousine, driven by James, was waved on.

Kirby, his engine still running, wound his window down at the approach of an official.

'Good morning, mein Herr,' said the official, 'our apologies for interrupting your journey, but a traffic census is being conducted. Would you mind telling me if you're travelling on business or pleasure?'

'On pleasure,' said Kirby, 'we're visitors.'

'Thank you.' The official made a note. 'My compliments. May I know where you have come from and where you are going?'

'To Salzburg from Vienna,' said Kirby.

'Thank you. You have – yes, two passengers? Thank you. Please proceed, mein Herr.'

Kirby drove away. A second official, talking to Carl, requested information on what he was carrying and to where.

'Two Austro-Fraser racing cars, to England via Calais,' said Carl, peaked cap pulled low down.

'Ah, yes, Austro-Fraser. How often do you make such a journey for your company?'

'Only when it's necessary to transport similar models to England, say once a year.'

'Thank you, mein Herr. Please carry on.'

James had come to a halt in another lay-by a mile further on. Kirby and Carl pulled in ahead of him. Kirby got out and spoke to Carl.

'Anyone following us will be able to pick up information at that census point,' he said.

'We'll keep our fingers crossed that they'll let Gottlieb's truck through without specifically noting it,' said Carl.

In the limousine, Vicky asked, 'What are Uncle Carl and Mr Kirby talking about?'

'Nothing worrying, I'd say,' said James, 'or Mr Kirby would be talking to us as well.'

Horns blaring, the two Nazi cars raced along, each flying its pennant. Ludwig had telephoned the SS command post in Salzburg to arrange for the truck and the limousine to be stopped at a checkpoint east of the city. Tearing out of Melk, the two cars overtook others in a headlong rush.

'Slow down,' said Ludwig, 'there's a traffic census ahead. Stop when you reach it.' Fleischer slowed, pulled over and stopped. The second car pulled in behind. A State policeman came to attention on sighting the pennants. A highways official approached. Ludwig lowered his window. 'What vehicles have you been stopping?' he asked.

The official, noting his uniform and rank, became careful.

'Just two or three at a time and at random, Herr Colonel,' he said.

'Have you stopped a truck from the Austro-Fraser car plant?'

The official thought. He called a colleague and spoke to him. His colleague said yes.

'The driver informed me his destination was England, via the ferry from Calais.'

'Describe him,' said Ludwig. The official did his best. His best didn't seem very satisfactory. 'You call that a description?' said Ludwig. 'That he was wearing a coat and cap, and looked over forty?'

'Herr Colonel, it's difficult to notice faces when one is writing down answers.'

'He had eyes, I presume?'

'Ah.' The official remembered then. The reference had unlocked his crowded mind. 'Blue eyes, very blue.'

Carl, thought Ludwig.

'What time was it when you stopped him?' he asked.

The official referred to his notepad, turning pages.

'Ten ten,' he said.

An hour and twenty minutes ahead, thought Ludwig.

'Did you notice an English car, a Fraser limousine, in company with the truck?'

'I'm afraid I did not, Herr Colonel.'

'I share the fear that you didn't,' said Ludwig, and wound up his window. 'Go,' he said to Fleischer.

Voegler murmured, 'Very blue eyes. Good. An hour and twenty minutes ago. Good. We've made up time on them.'

But was it good? Should he, as a loyal Gestapo Kommissar, act in concert with an SD officer who was pursuing a personal vendetta? The original objective, the recapture of a stolen document, had apparently taken second place to the vendetta. Perhaps, in any case, it was no longer pertinent. Perhaps the document was now in London.

That Kirby's wife would have been the one to take it there, Voegler didn't doubt. Schroeder would complain that if Baroness Anne von Korvacs had been subjected to a more forceful interrogation at the beginning, success would have replaced failure.

Schroeder had no manners. Which, thought Voegler, makes me ask myself what would be wrong with the Gestapo acquiring a reputation for good manners? My answer has to be that it's more effective to be feared than liked.

Chapter Nineteen

Between Linz and Wels, Kirby, who had been motoring a quarter of a mile in advance of the truck, turned off the Salzburg road to drive for a mile to the Reisende Inn, which lay hospitably in wait for travellers to Gmunden and Bad Ischl. The truck and limousine reached the inn a minute after Kirby's arrival. Progress had been good, with only one brief hold-up, at the traffic-census point. In a little over four hours they had covered a hundred miles.

The truck and both cars parked behind the inn, shutting themselves off from the road and the eyes of customers. The cars' occupants got out and stretched their limbs, breathing in clear air as intoxicating as chilled sparkling wine. Carl climbed down from the truck, and James opened the rear doors. The Austro-Fraser Comets, painted in the Austrian racing colour, were in their fixed positions, one strongly racked and bedded above the other, four feet from the doors. They were closely cradled by what looked like stout pinewood boxes, six feet high and two feet wide. Luggage trunks stood on the floor.

James climbed in, removed two screws from the side of one upright box, and opened it on concealed hinges. Anne, sitting on a makeshift padded seat at the far end of the box, stood up and came out. She smiled at James.

'Have you suffered?' he asked, while Carl went to work on the door of the other box.

'Only from a little claustrophobia,' said Anne.

'Hello up there,' said Nicholas, waiting to help her down. She leaned, put her hands on his shoulders and he swung her lightly to the ground. 'Happy to see you,' he said. In a dark brown fur coat and hat, with her eyes bright, she was a denial of her age.

'I need a few repairs,' she said, and looked up at Josef Meister, released by Carl from the other box. 'How did you find the travelling, Josef?'

'Shall a man blessed with good friends burden them with complaints?' he said. 'And at a moment when they've brought him to an inn?'

Nicholas approached Vicky. She eyed his advance discouragingly.

'Hello, Vicky, are you—'

'No, I'm not,' said Vicky, 'and shall be taking refreshments with my parents. We are all to sit as independent parties, and not all together, in any case.'

'We'll have a talk later, perhaps,' said Nicholas.

'Don't count on it, you beastly Casanova,' said Vicky.

They were nine in all, James, Sophie and Vicky, Anne, Carl and Josef, and the Kirbys. They occupied three separate tables. There were other diners, mostly young people on their way to ski resorts.

A quick lunch was taken, and as soon as Carl had finished his, he asked the proprietor if he might use his telephone. The proprietor took him to it. He returned a few minutes later, at which point the bills were paid and each little party left in turn.

At the truck, Carl said, 'I phoned Heinrich. Ludwig's been to the house, asking questions about our departure and our route. Heinrich told him he didn't know, but assumed it would be our usual one.'

'Did he tell Ludwig exactly who had departed?' asked James.

'That exact question wasn't asked,' said Carl. 'Heinrich thinks Ludwig assumed all of us, apart from my parents. Incidentally, prior to Ludwig's arrival at the house, the Gestapo called to arrest you, Sophie. God knows on what charge. Heinrich wasn't informed.'

'Damn that,' said James.

'I'm not thrilled, either,' said Sophie. 'I wonder if Mariella is safely aboard her train with her escort?'

'I shall say much to Sergeant Wainwright if she isn't,' said Karita.

'Let's move off,' said Kirby.

'It won't do, standing and talking,' said Karita, who had received an embrace and grateful thanks from Sophie for her incredible success in freeing Anne.

'First,' said Kirby, 'I suggest you and yours change to the Opel, James, and lead the way,

309

while we use your limousine, which is known. The Opel isn't. In the event of trouble, you won't be stopped.'

'You'll manage?' said James.

'Of course,' said Karita.

So James drove the Opel away, Sophie and Vicky with him. Carl followed in the truck, with Josef Meister and Anne boxed in again, and Kirby brought up the rear in the limousine.

A mile away on the road to Salzburg, the second Austro-Fraser car-carrying truck thundered by. Behind it was a car containing mechanics. Behind them, at a distance of eighteen miles, were the two Nazi cars. Ludwig had stopped in Enna, where he was able to commandeer the use of two police motorcycles. Ridden by two of his SD men, the machines roared away. The cars followed at speed.

James motored purposefully without putting too much distance between himself and Carl. The sunlight was crisp and sharp, the vista one of increasing grandeur, a grandeur with a magnificent irrelevance to the political darkness that had overtaken a mesmerized Austria. Sophie was quiet, glancing at James from time to time. His five o'clock shadow accentuated the grim set of his jaw. James hated men who made war on women, any kind of war. She put a hand on his knee and gently pressed. He glanced at her.

'We'll do it, James, we'll get home,' she said. She smiled. 'Rule Britannia, don't you know.'

'Good for you, Mama,' said Vicky, 'it's always nice to know you're one of us.'

Sophie, having known the Empire of Franz Josef and the fall of the Habsburgs, had willingly given her allegiance to the British Empire on marrying James. The pomp and ceremony of an established monarchy, and pride in traditions, uplifted her. She considered the Socialist republics of Europe dull, dreary and miserably political.

Carl had the truck going at a steady speed of forty, Kirby fifty yards behind in the limousine. Two miles from Lambach, the powerful motorcycles, despatched by Ludwig and eating up the road at sixty-five, had the truck in sight. It was on its own save for the limousine. The SD riders accelerated, roared past the limousine and headed for the truck.

'Ah,' smiled Karita, noting the uniforms, 'the Bolsheviks have arrived.'

'SD men,' said Nicholas from the back.

'If you would sometimes listen to me,' said Karita, 'you would know there is no difference.' She reached under her seat and drew out an old, polished and well-loved Enfield rifle, one she had acquired in Russia during the war and used with devastating effect during the Revolution.

'Holy Moses,' said Nicholas, 'are you serious, Mother?'

'She's serious,' said Kirby, watching events ahead. 'Don't get her excited or she'll start brandishing it.'

They saw the motorcyclists cutting in front of the truck and waving it down. Carl slowed. One man turned his machine to face the truck, and Carl came to a stop. The other man waved down the limousine. In the distance, James, using his mirror, noted what was happening.

'They've been stopped,' he said.

'Oh, my God,' said Sophie.

'We'll go on a little way and wait,' said James.

'But can't we help?' asked Vicky, distressed.

'Not yet,' said James. 'We wait. That's the agreed procedure.'

With the truck at a standstill, Kirby brought the limousine to a stop behind it. The SD men propped their machines and looked up at Carl. He wound the window down.

'What's this all about?' he asked.

'Your name?' said one SD man.

'Carl von Korvacs.'

'You're under arrest. Get down.'

'You're joking,' said Carl.

'Get down.' A Luger intruded into the dialogue. A car coming the other way passed by, its driver turning curious eyes on the scene, but letting discretion take him on in a hurry.

Carl climbed down.

'I think you're making a mistake,' he said to the man with the Luger, who gestured with it.

'Open up,' he said. His comrade shouted and beckoned, ordering the limousine to draw up closer, and Kirby let the car roll forward until it was three yards from the truck. He switched off the engine and got out. Carl was opening the truck doors.

'Your name?' said the second SD man to Kirby.

'Jones,' said Kirby.

'You're a liar and you're under arrest. Get back in your car.'

The truck doors swung open, revealing the two Comets, one mounted above the other, and both braced and cradled by the box-like stays. The SD man with the Luger surveyed the racing cars and the luggage trunks.

'I'm taking these cars to the Brooklands racing circuit in England,' said Carl, 'and you're wasting my time.'

'Clear it.'

'Excuse me?' said Carl, deceptively enquiring.

'Get inside. Shift everything out.'

'Everything?' said Carl. 'The cars as well?'

'All the luggage, not the cars, you fool.'

The other man was holding open the door of the limousine, gesturing to Kirby to get back in. Karita emerged from the other side of the car, a striking picture in her fur hat and coat.

'Excuse, please?' she said, and the man found himself looking down the shining barrel of the Enfield. His colleague whipped round. Carl struck. His gloved hand, balled, smashed the Luger free. It clattered to the ground. Kirby took a quick glance up and down the road. Clear. The SD man, cursing the pain of a broken finger, dived for his fallen pistol. Carl kicked it away. Kirby downed the bending man with a heavy chop to the back of his neck. The other man, defying the menace of Karita's rifle, went for his own Luger. Karita threw the rifle like a javelin. It struck his chest, and he gasped with pain. Kirby struck again, and the man dropped senseless over his colleague.

Nicholas shot out of the car to help pull

the unconscious men behind the side of the truck.

'Jesus,' he said, 'I'm all for disabling the enemy, but it's a bit violent.'

'Darling boy,' said Karita, 'for the sake of the nice people of the world you must be prepared to blow off the heads of a few of the other kind.'

'Mother, you're disgraceful,' said Nicholas.

'Move the motorcycles,' said Karita, 'I can hear cars in the distance.'

When the cars passed the drivers saw three men and a woman chatting and laughing beside the truck, and there was no sign of any motorbikes. The machines had been lifted and thrown over the hedge. And when the truck and the limousine moved off several minutes later, there was no sign either of the SD men.

Carl, seeing the stationary Opel in the distance, gave a little toot.

'Daddy, they're coming,' said Vicky.

'With an OK signal,' said James.

'Prayers are sometimes answered,' said Sophie.

The truck came on at speed, and Carl gave two toots, a signal that he was going to pass James and take the lead. James let him go by. The limousine was close behind. James waited, then pulled out and took up the rear position.

Carl drove into Lambach and the two cars followed him as he left the Salzburg route and turned north towards the German border and the road to Munich. After a mile, however, he turned again, taking a rural road to a village. He came to a stop in a lane with woods on either side, and out of sight of the road. The cars pulled up behind him, the time just after one thirty.

The two trussed and gagged SD men were brought out of the truck and dumped in the adjacent wood. They were left there, struggling to free themselves. James went back into the lead, and the convoy returned to the road that would take them to the German border. But they turned south and re-entered Lambach, where they ignored the road to Salzburg and continued south to pick up the route for Bad Ischl. The going from now on would be full of laborious climbs, but in using the main road for as long as they had, their progress had been excellent.

The day was still fine, but the temperature was already dropping and the mountains were sharply outlined.

Later that afternoon, the sun was a glowing red ball poised on Alpine ridges. A short distance east of Salzburg, an Austro-Fraser truck approached a roadblock manned by a detachment of SS. The truck was waved down, together with the car immediately behind it. The drivers pulled over and brought their vehicles to a halt. The truck driver, Martin Gottlieb, wound down his window. Beside him, his assistant peered.

'What's this for?' asked Gottlieb.

'Climb down. And the other man.'

The two men climbed down, and four mechanics were ordered out of the car.

'You're all under arrest,' said an SS officer,

an Obersturmfuehrer (lieutenant). 'Which of you is Josef Meister? And where are the women?'

'What, what?' Gottlieb was bewildered.

'You, your name.'

'Gottlieb, Martin Gottlieb. Herr Lieutenant, what—'

'Gottlieb? Gottlieb?' The SS officer's expression plainly told the truck driver he was a liar. 'We'll see about that. First, open up your truck.'

The perplexed driver opened the rear doors, disclosing nothing more than freight consistent with his responsibilities, two brand new Austro-Fraser racers, reserves to those in Carl's truck. The perplexity spread during the next five minutes, for all six men were subjected to a barrage of aggressive questions entirely meaningless to them. A certain amount of physical harassment was also introduced. The Austrian SS were taking on the same sense of power as their German counterparts.

Gottlieb finally broke through the barrage in a loud and angry voice.

'I'm not Baron Carl von Korvacs. Do I look as if I am, or speak as if I am? What do I know of where he is, where his family is, where his sister is or who Josef Meister is? And I've never heard of an Englishman called Kirby, or his wife, either. All I know is that Baron Carl is taking two other Comets to England, and we're taking these. This man here is my relief driver, and these other men are mechanics who'll service the cars. That's what we always do, bring our own mechanics. It's not good enough, Herr Lieutenant, to keep calling me a liar. I've got my papers, I've got my works documents and freight documents, and I don't see why you and your men should be abusing us and pushing us about.'

The SS officer glared at him. A Stormtrooper jumped down from the truck, and another finished an inspection of the cars.

'Nothing, Herr Lieutenant,' they reported.

It was the lieutenant's turn to suffer perplexity. He had been instructed to stop the truck and an accompanying English Fraser limousine, and any other vehicle patently part of the convoy. He was to arrest Baron Carl von Korvacs and all other persons in the vehicles. He was to pay special care to the apprehension of a Baroness Anne von Korvacs, a Jew by the name of Meister, and possibly an English couple, Herr Kirby and his wife, a woman with golden hair. But no such persons were present. And there had been no limousine. What they had rounded up was a group of men who looked like respectable workers. There were no women and no young people.

The SS lieutenant, conscious that he belonged to Himmler's elite, objected violently to the humiliation of feeling confused.

'Watch your damned tongue,' he shouted at Gottlieb, 'this whole thing is as suspicious as hell, and so are you!'

'I tell you, I don't understand,' said Gottlieb.

'I don't like it, you hear, you dumcluck? I don't like it that you people aren't what you're expected to be.'

Gottlieb, burly, and not given to letting his

honesty be browbeaten, said, 'I can't see the sense of that. We're what we are and always have been, since birth, the sons of our fathers. You've seen our papers. What more d'you want? Herr Lieutenant, allow us to go on our way.'

'That can't be permitted. You'll have to wait here until our superior arrives.'

They had to wait. When Ludwig did arrive and was put in the picture by the SS officer, he turned in a cold fury to the Austro-Fraser men.

'Explain, damn you,' he said.

Since they did not know what they were required to explain, Gottlieb said, 'Herr Colonel, all we're doing is taking these two cars to—'

'Your truck, man, from where have you driven it?'

'From our works in Vienna. We left at eight this morning.'

'From your works?' said Ludwig, gloved hands tight around his stick, leg hurting. Voegler stood by with his expression reflecting nothing of his current dislikes. If anything, he actually seemed amused. 'Not from the von Korvacs's house on the Salesianergasse?' ground Ludwig.

'No, Herr Colonel. His Excellency, Baron Carl—'

'He's nobody's damned Excellency.'

'We pay him that honour,' said Gottlieb. 'He himself in another truck is taking the first-choice Comets to England. We are taking the reserve two.'

'Which route?'

'We're going through Germany and France to—'

318

'Not your route, you fool. Baron Carl's.'

'Ah,' said Gottlieb, feeling a sudden reluctance to impart the information. 'Ah, let me—'

'Which route?' shouted Ludwig, and Gottlieb, thinking of his wife and children, answered up.

'I believe he was documented for Switzerland, France and St Malo.'

'Where the hell is he, then?'

'Somewhere on this road, Herr Colonel.'

'We haven't passed him,' said Ludwig, dark and sour, 'and he hasn't reached this roadblock. If he has and you've let him through,' he said to the SS officer, 'God help you.'

'No Austro-Fraser truck has passed, I assure you,' said the lieutenant. 'Nor has an English Fraser limousine.'

'Then damn everyone,' said Ludwig furiously, and Voegler looked at the pale blue sky like a man detached from all violent emotions.

A motorcyclist from SS headquarters in Salzburg came roaring up. He informed the lieutenant that a telephone call had been received from a Stormtrooper acting under the orders of Colonel Lundt-Hausen of Vienna. He was referred to the presence of the colonel himself. Ludwig then demanded details. The messenger gave them. They concerned the two men who had caught up with the truck driven by Baron Carl, and the subsequent events that culminated in their being bound and gagged, and dumped, without their machines, in woods close to the road leading north from Lambach to the Munich route. They had managed to free themselves and find a house with a phone.

They wished it to be known it looked as if the truck and limousine were on the way to Munich.

'Munich, you idiot?' hissed Ludwig. 'Never!'

'I suggest we retain our preference for Innsbruck, the Arlsberg Pass and Switzerland,' said Voegler, his calmness very welcome to all concerned. 'The works driver has confirmed this preference, and I recommend we leave here at once.'

Without a word, Ludwig got back into his car. The SS lieutenant approached.

'Herr Colonel, this truck, these men – '

'They're no damned use to me,' said Ludwig. 'Let them go.'

Voegler slipped in beside him and they spent a few moments studying their map.

'There,' said Voegler, pointing. 'Lambach. From there, Salzburg can be bypassed. They never reached this roadblock because they turned south at Lambach, after dumping those men some way along the north exit to the Munich road. But Munich is a red herring.'

'Agreed,' said Ludwig. 'And we know now, from the Stormtrooper's phoned report, that Kirby and his wife and son are in the limousine. So where is the Fraser family, and Carl's family? Where are Meister and Baroness Anne? And Gibbs too? Voegler, they're in the truck. You saw the amount of spare room in the truck here. So, it's Innsbruck and Switzerland.' He called the SS lieutenant. 'Go back to your headquarters. Telephone Innsbruck. Arrange for them to set up a roadblock there. Immediately. And to keep it manned all night and all tomorrow, if necessary.'

'Very good, Herr Colonel. Heil Hitler.'

'Heil Hitler,' said Ludwig. 'Go,' he said to his driver.

The two cars careered away. The Austro-Fraser men resumed their journey.

Chapter Twenty

The truck and the limousine finally caught up with the Opel on the winding climb half a mile from Gmunden. The mountains were beginning to turn purple in the red light of the descending sun, and the afternoon was frosty.

James stopped. The truck and the limousine pulled up behind him. He got out, made a quick walk to the truck, and Carl gave him a résumé of the incident involving the SS motorcyclists.

'Good God,' said James.

'Karita Kirby is a Cossack,' said Carl.

'Well, I'm damned glad she's on our side,' said James. 'Look here, let's give Anne and Josef a break. They could safely ride in the cars on this stretch to Bad Ischl.'

'Right,' said Carl, 'but be quick. We're more noticeable when we're lingering.'

A car passed, full of skiers. They were singing, their skis lashed to the roof rack. James opened up the truck and climbed in. It was the work of only a minute to bring Anne and Meister out of hiding.

'Ride in the cars,' he said.

'James darling, that will be bliss,' said Anne.

Josef Meister joined the Kirbys in the limousine, and Anne slipped in beside Vicky in the Opel. Vicky hugged her.

'What kept you, Aunt Anne?'

'How should I know?' smiled Anne. 'I've been travelling in the dark.'

'James, what did Carl say?' asked Sophie.

'I'll tell you as we go along,' said James.

The convoy began to move again. Snow lay frozen on every high slope, its whiteness flushed with rosy light.

From Salzburg, the two chasing cars, flying their pennants, raced along the main road to Innsbruck. Ludwig fidgeted with the map.

'Do you have doubts?' asked Voegler.

'No, thoughts about the options they've got,' said Ludwig. 'If they're bypassing Salzburg via Ischl, when they reach Bruck they can turn south again and head for Switzerland through the north of Italy.'

'It's a hard slow grind from Bruck,' said Voegler.

'Carl von Korvacs knows the Tyrolean regions like the back of his hand,' said Ludwig. 'He commanded a mountain unit during the last year of the war. I can't leave him free to exercise the Bruck option. We'll turn south at Lofer and go to Bruck, where your two men can pick up another car and go on to Innsbruck, to check at the roadblock there. You and I will take my men with us to Bruck. I've a feeling now about our quarry using Italy as a gateway to Switzerland.'

'Wherever and whatever, they'll be stopped at any of our border controls,' said Voegler. He knew the pursuit was enraging Lundt-Hausen. He himself was finding it an enjoyable challenge, a contest fashioned by the wit and ingenuity of the hunted and the relentless perseverance of the hunters. His one personal wish was based on a hope that Baroness Anne was with the quarry. It was obsessive, his need to come face to face with her again. He knew it, and chastised himself for what was a weakness. One enemy of National Socialism was no more important than all others, theoretically. But what others had her serenity, her cool challenging wit, her resolution?

'I want to get them before they reach any of our border controls,' said Ludwig.

'We're mainly concerned, of course, with retrieving the document,' said Voegler drily.

'What?' said Ludwig. 'Yes, of course, the document. Yes.'

'Then I think Frau Kirby is our chief prey,' said Voegler.

'She'll be with them, not in England,' said Ludwig, and his mouth tightened and clamped. 'She's also my particular prey.'

In Bad Ischl, Carl drove the truck into what had once been the spacious carriage yard of the Hotel Franz Josef. He parked it deep in black shadow. Evening had arrived, and the streets and avenues of the charming town glowed with lamplight. It was still mainly a summer resort, but its warm springs and saline baths could be enjoyed all year round by visitors. However, since there were not too many at the moment, the manager of the hotel was delighted to accommodate a party of nine. The grandeur of the foyer and the general splendour of the hotel offered a magnificent welcome to the travellers, all of whom were thinking of a hot bath, an enjoyable dinner and a restful night.

James and Sophie opted for a suite, so did Kirby and Karita. Anne shared a room with Vicky, Josef Meister shared another with Nicholas, and Carl had the luxury of a room to himself. Cases and trunks were brought up by the hotel staff, for of all things a civilized change of clothes was the first necessity after a bath. That, at least, was how the ladies looked at it. Tea and coffee were requested to be sent up, and arrived on huge silver trays.

'I'm not sure exactly why we're staying over-night,' said Anne to Vicky.

'Oh, don't you know?' said Vicky. 'Our deep-thinking menfolk feel the enemy will be floundering about all night on the road to Munich, and that will give us the chance of resting here until morning.'

'I hope they're right,' said Anne.

'Well, we have to put our trust in them,' said Vicky, 'they're all we've got.'

Karita, in a black satin slip, sat at the dressing table in a gilded bedroom, viewing herself critically in the mirror. She had just taken a bath. Kirby came in. He had been into the town.

'So?' she said.

'I've arranged the hire of another car and other matters,' said Kirby.

'Good.'

'A pity about the two SS men,' said Kirby, 'but apart from that, things haven't gone too badly.'

'The monster won't give up, of course,' said Karita.

'Lundt-Hausen?' said Kirby. 'No, nor his Gestapo associates. You'd be disappointed if they did.'

'It's exciting to lead them a dance,' said Karita, and frowned at her reflection. Well preserved at forty-six, she thought she could detect the birth of lines at the corners of her eyes. How distressing still to feel so vital and yet to see the signs of the years that had run away from her. 'And you yourself would hate it to become boring.'

'I'm frequently in favour of the boredom of retirement,' said Kirby.

'I am to believe that?' Karita shook her head. 'However, our new friends are worth the adventure. Nicholas is fascinated by that delicious girl Vicky, you know. Myself, my looks have gone.' She glanced at her husband. He was preparing to take a bath himself. 'What is there left for me to live for?'

'Dinner?' suggested Kirby.

'Ivan, you have lifted me out of despair. Dinner, yes. Hurry up with your bath, I am starving.'

'What do you think, James?' asked Sophie, a towelling turban around her head. She had taken her bath and was dressing. 'Are we making a mistake in staying here for the night?'

'In these regions, Sophie, once you've lost daylight you come off the road, whether you're chasing or being chased,' said James, a bath towel draping him from the waist down. 'You hole up, enjoy some rest and wait for morning. Unless you're either an idiot or a fanatic.'

'Ludwig's a fanatic,' said Sophie.

'So we could wish for him to rush around all night and break his neck?' said James. 'He won't, of course.'

'Should we have thought about going by train?' asked Sophie.

'There'll be police aboard every train out of Vienna, Sophie, and we couldn't have risked it, especially as we'd have had Anne and Meister with us.'

'Well, we'll see what tomorrow brings,' said Sophie.

'Bad luck to Ludwig, I hope,' said James, and went to his bath.

Vicky answered a knock on her room door later. Nicholas smiled at her.

'Good evening, Miss Fraser,' he said, 'and can I say you look a treat?'

Vicky, in a Cambridge blue dress, with loose, semi-transparent sleeves, her mouth delicately touched with Sunset Silk lipstick, new and fashionable, said, 'Excuse me?' Her spectacles in her hand, she put them on, and her eyes became clear and all-seeing. 'Oh, yes, it's the younger Mr Kirby. To what do I owe the displeasure of your appearance at my door at a time when I'm alone?'

'Yes, your Aunt Anne informed me you were still here,' said Nicholas, 'so I thought I'd escort you down to the Imperial Room, where cocktails, aperitifs and other heady drinks are being served before dinner. The others are already two aperitifs ahead of us.'

'Well, as I can't see anyone else around, I'll have to make do with you,' said Vicky, 'but don't commit the mistake of thinking you can add me to your collection of unfortunate women.'

'Er – women?' said Nicholas,

'I may be shy and retiring, with no conversation to speak of,' said Vicky, 'but I can recognize a philanderer a mile off.'

'Pleased to hear it,' said Nicholas. 'Every young lady ought to have that kind of gift, it would save all of you eloping to Gretna Green with shockers.'

'We are not amused,' said Vicky, picking up her little evening bag.

'Sorry about that, Queen Victoria,' said Nicholas. 'Ready? Come along, then, woman.'

'We are still not amused,' said Vicky, but she wanted to giggle, just the same.

Subsequently, they all enjoyed an excellent dinner, during which the conversation excluded anything relating to the SD and the Gestapo.

Ludwig had indeed chosen not to rush around all night. He, Voegler, and their men, put up at a hotel in Bruck after discovering there was no sign whatever that the quarry had reached this little town. Ludwig went to bed grinding his teeth once more. Voegler laid his head philosophically on his pillow. What had eluded them today would appear in their sights tomorrow. Perhaps.

Not unexpectedly, he dreamt of Baroness Anne. He dreamt she was laughing at him for his inability to reduce her. Another woman was there, his mother. Her money had seen him through university after his academic father had died, although she said these days that she had thrown it away on a son who was a disgrace to her. In the dream she was laughing at him too. In contempt for his National Socialist ideals.

It was not the kind of dream he liked. When he awoke, it made him more resolved than ever to catch and reduce the quarry.

Chapter Twenty-one

Carl and the others were at breakfast by seven the next morning. At seven twenty, the night porter, still on duty, came to inform Kirby that two men wished to see him. Accompanied by Carl and James, Kirby made his way to the foyer, where the callers were waiting.

'Herr Kirby?' said one.

'Are you from Hofmeyers Transportation Services?' asked Kirby.

'We are, mein Herr.'

Kirby asked them to follow him, and he led the way out of the hotel to the car park at the rear, Carl and James in attendance.

'Ah,' said one man, seeing the truck and limousine.

'Your firm has undertaken to deliver these vehicles to the Greber International Delivery Services in Lienz,' said Carl.

'Correct, mein Herr. We are the drivers.'

'You're ready to leave now?' said Kirby.

'That's why we're here.'

'Good. We ourselves have to catch the morning

train to Bolzano, but didn't want to leave before seeing you.'

'Yes, mein Herr, and we understand payment for the required services is to be made in advance.' The man produced an invoice. Kirby inspected it and paid, adding an extra banknote for a tip. 'Thank you, mein Herr.'

'The keys,' said Carl, and handed over both sets. Along with James and Kirby, he watched the truck and the limousine being driven out of the park.

'Two more red herrings,' said James.

'Shall we get going?' said Carl. 'We've a long journey in front of us, and it'll be mid-afternoon before we arrive. James, if you'll settle the bill, I'll hurry the others up.'

While settling up, James told the reception clerk that they were leaving all their luggage in their rooms, and that a carrier would collect the trunks for despatch to England. The carrier would be calling today. Could the hotel see that the trunks were brought down?

'With pleasure, Herr Fraser,' said the clerk, accepting a generous tip.

'Let's see, we're catching the eight fifteen train for connections to Bolzano,' said James. 'Is your hotel transport available to take us to the station?'

'Of course, mein Herr.'

Carrying only hand luggage, they were driven to the station in good time for the train. They milled around a little, and as soon as the hotel bus had departed, they walked to some parked cars, among which was Kirby's Opel and a newly hired black Mercedes-Benz saloon.

'Who is sitting with whom?' asked Anne, who had not let pursuit by Ludwig spoil her sense of freedom.

Kirby, in charge of the Opel, took Karita, Anne, and Josef Meister as passengers. James, who was to drive the Mercedes-Benz, took Sophie, Vicky, Nicholas and Carl as company.

'Are you responsible for this arrangement?' Vicky delivered the question directly into Nicholas's left ear.

'No, but I'll enjoy being with you in the back seat,' said Nicholas.

'Your enjoyment will be very limited,' said Vicky.

The cars moved off, Kirby's Opel leading.

The day was another bright and crisp one, the air glittering in the sharp sunshine. Anne wondered where Ludwig was. She hoped he was scouring the roads to the Swiss border.

Ludwig was doing no such thing. He had slept badly and his mood was sour. With Voegler, who seemed irritatingly immune to frustrations and setbacks, he was intending to drive to Bad Ischl. His mind was not on Switzerland or Germany, it was on Italy. He was convinced the quarry had left the main road to Salzburg yesterday and headed for Bad Ischl, which pointed at anywhere other than Switzerland. At least it did in Ludwig's mind. Here in Bruck, the roadblock had been manned since yesterday afternoon, an enterprise barren of results. It strengthened Ludwig's feeling the quarry were heading south, not west. But what he didn't like at the moment was the time it would take to reach Bad Ischl.

'Damn it,' he said to Voegler, 'I'll phone the Bad Ischl police before we make our move.'

'I recommend that,' said Voegler.

'You're a great help,' said Ludwig sourly. He made the call, received a promise of assistance, and said he would wait for them to call him back.

The Opel and Mercedes were well on their way to Radstadt, a town midway between Bad Ischl and Bruck, when two policemen arrived at the Hotel Franz Josef. They were making enquiries at all hotels, and the Franz Josef represented their third. The manager answered all questions as a good citizen should, but with the natural concern of a man who did not want the reputation of his hotel to suffer a blemish. He allowed the policemen to call Colonel Lundt-Hausen in Bruck.

Five minutes later, Ludwig and Voegler, with their second car following, were on their way to Stainach, a railway junction south-east of Bad Ischl. It was there that the quarry would have to change for a connection to Bolzano in Italy, and Ludwig left instructions for the Bruck police to phone Stainach and arrange for their arrest.

'Voegler, would you believe this? Would you believe the swines have had the audacity to transfer themselves to a train?'

'Have they?' murmured Voegler.

'By God,' said Ludwig, 'I wasn't so wrong in my conviction that Carl would opt for the Italian Tyrol.'

'Your intuition, Herr Colonel, may have served

you remarkably well,' said Voegler. Yes, it may have, he thought. On the other hand, it may not make the quarry jump into our arms.

The route to Stainach would take the hunters through Radstadt. It was some time before they reached a point three miles from the latter. Approaching was a large truck. As they passed it, Ludwig drew a breath, his driver glanced over, and Voegler smiled. Following the truck was a limousine.

'God damn it, turn back, get after that truck and car,' Ludwig shouted at his driver, who pulled up, made a three-point reverse turn and set off in chase. The other car, containing five of Ludwig's men, followed suit.

'It seems the audacious swines aren't on a train, after all,' murmured Voegler.

'Is that something to smile about?' hissed Ludwig.

'Am I smiling?' asked Voegler. 'If I am, it's because it seems we're about to apprehend everyone we want in that truck and car.'

The driver sounded his horn repeatedly as he caught up with the limousine and overtook it. He raced ahead of the truck, put himself in front of it, and the other car closed up on the limousine. Limousine and truck came to a stop. From the Nazi cars emerged the hunters, eight men in all. One could have said there was already a question mark in Voegler's expression, for he'd noted that the driver of the limousine was its sole occupant.

Ludwig, uniform the symbol of awesome authority to citizens who had ordinary standing, strode to the truck, ignoring the protest of his suffering leg. Voegler approached the limousine and pulled the driver's door open.

'Mein Herr, kindly get out,' he said.

The driver, an employee of Hofmeyers Transportation Services of Bad Ischl, looked uncertainly at the slender man in a black hat and a belted dark grey overcoat. There seemed nothing threatening in his countenance, that of a professor, perhaps, but the nearness of armed uniformed Security Police resolved his uncertainty and he emerged from the limousine. At the same time his colleague, shouted at by the SD officer, climbed down from the truck. Voegler brought the two men together, and Ludwig's dark eyes, livid with sudden new suspicions, scanned the faces of both.

'Who the hell are you?' he rasped.

'Not quite what we expected,' murmured Voegler.

'You – ' Ludwig, skin tight over his cheekbones, dug one man with his stick. 'You – what are you doing with this truck, and you, from where did you get that English car?' The other man received a poke.

The flustered and intimidated men explained that their firm had contracted to deliver the vehicles to an international transport firm in Lienz. Ludwig looked as if he considered the contractors' employees could do him a favour by hanging themselves. But at least, in giving all the information they could, they repeated something the hotel manager had told the Bad Ischl police, that the people concerned with the transportation deal were going by train to Bolzano. The man called Kirby had said so.

It occurred then to Voegler that this particular piece of information had been offered too readily by the quarry.

Ludwig ordered the truck to be opened up. It disclosed nothing but the two racing cars, one cradled above the other, between upright timber boxes, open-ended. Voegler climbed up and inspected the boxes. James and Carl had removed the doors and also makeshift seats. Voegler discovered marks left by hinges.

'They were up here, Herr Standartenfuehrer,' he said, 'Baroness Anne and the Jew. Both these compartments had doors fixed to them.' Voegler climbed down. 'Ingenious.'

Ludwig looked at the two men and made a dismissive gesture. Relieved, they got back into the vehicles, although they could not move until the leading Nazi car did. So they sat and waited. Ludwig walked to his car with Voegler.

'Well?' said Ludwig. 'Are they now definitely on their way to Bolzano by train?'

'If I were any one of them,' said Voegler, 'I'd feel trapped on a train. Do you like the fact that they let it be known they were catching one, and that they were openly driven to the station by the hotel bus?'

'No, I'm damned if I do,' said Ludwig. 'But one way or another, I'm still convinced they're heading for Italy. We'll make a phone call in Radstadt.'

*   *   *

In the Alpine town of Radstadt, the Opel and the Mercedes were parked outside a shop that specialized in the sale of skiing equipment and ski wear. Kirby and Carl, already clad in outfits just purchased, were fixing newly bought roof racks to the cars. Out came Josef Meister and Nicholas, carrying new skis. Inside the shop, Anne, Sophie, Karita and Vicky were making their selections of boots, trousers, sweaters, lined windcheaters and woollen pull-on hats. James was trying to hurry them up. All the men were fitted out. Anne, having decided, carried her selection to the fitting room.

'Come on, Sophie,' said James.

'James, am I to look like an Alpine tramp?' protested Sophie.

'Five more minutes, that's all,' said James.

Carl and the other men re-entered the shop, and a general hurry-up was sounded.

'Barbarians,' muttered Karita.

Anne emerged, looking colourful and fully ready for the slopes. She took her discarded clothes out to the car. Along the street came two cars flying Nazi pennants. Anne looked up as they passed. From the back seat of the first car, Kommissar Voegler was eye to eye with her for a brief second. Anne went rigid. Voegler made not the slightest sign of recognition, but Anne stood rooted and in frozen certainty that the cars would stop and disgorge their Nazi occupants. But they went on, disappearing as they turned a corner. Incredulous, Anne unfroze as James came out carrying a case containing Sophie's discarded clothes.

'James, oh, my God,' she said, 'they're here.'

'The enemy?' said James, looking up and down the street.

'Two cars – they passed only a minute ago – that way.' Anne pointed.

'You're certain?'

'I saw Voegler in the first car, I saw him, James, and I was sure he saw me, but both cars went on.'

'If they went on, he couldn't have seen you, Anne, but all the same it's time to move, and quickly.'

He dashed back into the shop and little screams ensued from the fitting room.

'Arrest him, someone,' demanded Karita in lacy black lingerie.

'We'll all be for the drop if you girls aren't kitted up in one minute flat,' said James. 'The enemy's in town, so move.'

'I don't think the train bluff worked,' said Vicky.

They were all out of the shop in a miraculously short time, everyone dressed for skiing, woollen hats covering every head. Ski boots, however, were stowed in the boots of the cars. Eighteen new skis, with sticks, were lashed to the roof racks. There were no novices among the party, and Josef Meister had assured Carl at the beginning that at fifty-seven his age would not be a problem.

They drove out of Radstadt, eyes alert, and picked up speed once they were clear. They ignored the road that led to Bruck and the Swiss border, and motored directly south to Spittal, some fifty-five miles from Radstadt, and twenty miles from the Italian border as the crow flies. But in this region of the Alps, even the crows had a hard time.

The road was stiff with gradients varying from one in eight to one in five, but as long as the weather remained fine and traffic was light, they anticipated they could average twenty miles an hour. Both cars were well engined for Alpine roads, and that they were in Alpine country was breathtakingly evident. Every vista was a magnificent panorama of white ridges, snowy peaks, fir-encrusted slopes and great chasms. The sunlight was sharp, and the glitter of snow required the use of sunglasses.

James led in the Mercedes. In the event of trouble, Kirby and Karita preferred at this stage to be given the extra seconds of time that might be denied to the leading car. During those extra seconds, one or the other would work out what was to be done to save the situation for all. It was what each expected of the other.

James drove with typical determination and skill, quite sure Kirby would maintain contact. There was very little traffic. Most Easter visitors were already at their ski resorts. He overtook the occasional vehicle that threatened to hold him up, using his gears to obtain the necessary power.

In the Opel, Karita said, 'Heavens, we are being led by a fearless madman.'

'Oh, James and Carl have both been madmen in their time,' said Anne.

'Good,' said Karita, 'we can't afford to dawdle.' Kirby overtook a car in the wake of James. The driver of the overtaken car jumped in his seat. 'There, Ivan is just as mad, you see.'

'Yes, I do see,' smiled Anne.

'I do not,' said Josef Meister, 'my eyes are closed and I'm praying.'

'Prayers will do us no harm in any event,' said Anne.

'Years ago,' said Karita, 'I offered up a thousand prayers, but the Bolsheviks still murdered the Tsar and his family. Such people are all godless.'

The cars climbed into the dizzy heights of the Alpine road.

At the police station in Radstadt, Ludwig and Voegler were both making phone calls. Voegler spoke to Salzburg and Innsbruck. Neither had anything to report. Ludwig spoke to the station-master at Stainach and ordered him to have the Bolzano train stopped before it reached the Italian border, and that no passengers were to leave until the police arrived and made a check. Bolzano was in the heart of the Tyrolean region that Carl had known during the mountain war against Italy. When it belonged to Austria, the town had been known as Bozen.

Ludwig also spoke to the police in Bad Ischl, asking them to make enquiries of any firms that hired out cars. Then he talked to the manager of the Hotel Franz Josef. The manager, his ears assailed by the acid rasp of an SD colonel, was able to inform him that subsequent to earlier police enquiries one of his staff, cycling to work, had seen the English and Austrian people driving away from the railway station in two cars, a dark blue Opel and a black Mercedes-Benz, at about ten minutes past eight.

Ludwig knew then he need not wait for the Bad Ischl police to call him back. He conferred with Voegler, their map spread out on the desk of the station superintendent. Ludwig advanced various guesses as to the road route taken by the quarry. Voegler nodded, murmured, and suggested they had better stick to one guess. His expression was unreadable. Ludwig's was venomous, and Voegler saw him as a man who was allowing his hatreds to sabotage his responsibilities. Instead of interrogating the woman who had crippled him and robbed him of Baroness Anne, he was likely to murder her as soon as he laid hands on her.

'Look.' Ludwig used his index finger on the map. 'Consider the road from Bad Ischl, and consider their actions. What have they been doing, damn them? They've been pointing us west to Switzerland first, then south-west to Bozen in Italy by their mention of taking a train. But look at the route directly south. It will take them via Spittal to Thorl on the Italian border.'

'That guess is as good as any,' said Voegler.

Ludwig shot an irritable glance at the Gestapo Kommissar.

'You're advancing no suggestions yourself?'

'I suggest an immediate police alert is required,' said Voegler.

Ludwig spoke to the superintendent, who assured him he would at once alert the police at Spittal. Ludwig then requested the despatch of two police motorcyclists to comb the road for a dark blue Opel and a black Mercedes-Benz

341

saloon. He himself and Kommissar Voegler would be following with their men. If the cars were spotted, no contact was to be made, and nothing was to be done to make the occupants of the cars suspect they were being tailed. The motorcyclists were to ride back and report. Was that understood?

It was.

Ludwig and Voegler left. Their cars sped through Radstadt.

'I now believe their destination was always Italy,' said Ludwig. 'That was where the old baron and his wife went.'

'And who, I wonder, went with them?' asked Voegler.

'What?'

'We're now in pursuit of two cars,' said Voegler. 'Two. Ten people at the most.'

'Their sons and daughters, they went with the old couple, yes, of course they did,' said Ludwig. The cars, racing out of Radstadt, were passed by two police motorcyclists. 'Well, that's the better for us, it allows us to deal only with the adults.'

Yes, thought Voegler, and to shoot them all, perhaps. He himself would never have wanted to forgo the satisfying exercise of interrogation.

Where, he wondered, was Baroness Anne now?

Not very far away.

Chapter Twenty-two

To their right, the heights of the Turkenwand
soared to kiss the blue sky, and the steepness of
the road reduced the Mercedes and Opel to a
low-geared ascent. They were fifteen miles out of
Radstadt, and it was not the Alpine vistas that
kept conversation to a minimum, but thoughts of
where the hunters were. Vicky, sitting between
Nicholas and her Uncle Carl in the Mercedes,
thought, well, both are proven heroes, but I still
object to Nicholas making up to me when he
already has a girlfriend at university.

The cars continued to climb.

It was Kirby who saw the approach of police
motorcyclists. Making one of his regular checks
in the mirror, he glimpsed them about seventy
yards to his rear. They vanished as he followed
the Mercedes around one more bend. They reappeared, and were closer. He took the next
bend in the wake of the Mercedes. The motorcyclists disappeared again. Kirby flashed his
headlights. Three times. James acknowledged
the warning signal with a brief pressure on
his footbrake. The brake lights glowed for an

instant, and the Mercedes powered on. A small van, making heavy weather of the ascent, seemed to fall back on the hard-driven Mercedes. James swung wide to overtake. An approaching car, making the descent in low gear, pulled over to the very rim of the precipitous drop as the Mercedes, overtaking the van, squeezed through the gap. The car driver punched his horn and shook his fist. The Opel came up, surging in pursuit of the Mercedes, and the outraged motorist, his car at a standstill above the giddy drop, gave Kirby a ferocious blast.

'Poor man, a rearing ant would turn his hair white, one imagines,' said Karita. 'Ivan, is there a crisis?'

Kirby, examining his mirror, said, 'Two police motorcyclists.'

'Ah, that's a crisis,' said Karita.

Josef Meister turned his head and looked through the rear window. He glimpsed the little van, chugging up, but no motorcyclists.

'I don't see them, Mr Kirby,' he said.

'No, they've disappeared,' said Kirby, 'but not, I think, because they've sailed over the edge. I suspect, in fact, that your ex-husband, Anne, has come to an intelligent conclusion. Well, he was always going to be able to pick up information. We sold him some on a plate. The rest couldn't be helped.'

'We're found out?' said Anne. 'The Gestapo man did recognize me, you think?'

'Very odd if he did,' said Kirby, 'since he didn't stop.'

'Ah, well,' said Karita, 'it's one thing to find us

out, it's another to catch us. If we are caught, I shall divorce Ivan. I did not marry him to have him deliver me into the arms of Hitler's black-shirts.'

'Chatter on, little Russian chicken,' said Kirby, now thinking about the possibility of roadblocks.

James, powering on, was rousing moments of alarm in some of his passengers.

'I protest,' said Sophie.

'No problems,' said James.

'There will be if we finish up at the bottom of the Alps,' said Sophie. Knowing her husband capable of shaking hands with the Devil in an emergency, she added, 'Something has happened.'

'Yes,' said Carl from the back, 'we've had a warning signal from John, which means James is in no position to hang about.'

'Oh, well, that's different,' said Vicky, 'so drive on, Daddy, be like David, mighty son of Saul.'

'Was David the son of Saul?' asked Nicholas, watching the way every bend seemed to rush up to the surging car.

'Really,' said Vicky, 'is this the time to start an argument about biblical lineage? Oh, my goodness.' She slid helplessly against Nicholas as the Mercedes slewed fast round a bend.

'Good going, James,' said Carl.

'I think I'm going to scream,' said Sophie, but she didn't.

It was a long hard grind up to the summit, and then the road began the welcome descent towards the small town of Tweng. James made the run at a controlled speed, using gears in the main to slew round corners, the Opel still following.

'If the warning meant someone's on our tail, they won't have to look very far for a phone,' said Carl. 'They're common on these roads. That could mean we've got to look out for a roadblock in the very near future.'

'Thank you for those cheerful words, Carl,' said Sophie. 'That, and James's driving, put me on the very edge of my seat.'

'Idiots who take up more than their fair share of the road can't expect to be indulged for ever,' said James, and continued to drive as fast as possible down the winding incline. The Opel stayed in contact. Vicky quivered from time to time as great canyons yawned at them and empty space beckoned hungrily.

Ludwig, Voegler and the six SS men were at a halt. The police motorcyclists were giving their report, to the effect that they had seen the Opel and Mercedes travelling together, and that at this moment they could be assumed to be about ten kilometres from Tweng. Both cars had skis lashed to roof racks.

'Skis?' said Ludwig, his leg tender.

'That is correct, Herr Colonel.'

'What can one say, except that they've chosen excellent weather?' murmured Voegler.

'I'm to take that remark seriously?' ground Ludwig.

'We can both take it, I think, that they mean to ski their way across the border,' said Voegler.

'If that's their intention, they'll fail,' said Ludwig, and instructed one policeman to find a roadside phone, contact his colleagues at Tweng, and also at St Michael, some distance on from Tweng. Roadblocks were to be set up in both places, the second as insurance against failure of the first. The other policeman was to re-establish contact with the quarry as fast as possible, as insurance against losing them. His colleague was to catch up with him as soon as he had made his phone calls. In the event of an unexpected happening, one man was to ride back and report.

The motorcyclists roared away, and the pennanted cars resumed their own pursuit, Ludwig instructing his driver to use his horn whenever it became necessary to clear the way ahead. The painful tenderness of his leg had mercifully gone. His blood was quick. Anticipation of a triumphant kind was an antidote.

The Mercedes and the Opel rushed into Tweng. Pretty and picturesque, it received them, swallowed them and then disgorged them, as if it found them unpalatable. They raced on, climbing and descending, the icy heights majestic and the deep valleys swamped with light.

Only two minutes after passing through Tweng, the police there moved to set up a roadblock. In distant St Michael and in Spittal, further on, the police were taking similar action. The road, route 99, was a little kinder for the hunted, and they made good time, traffic still being light. They were in advance of their calculations. James motored purposefully towards Althofen, which lay in advance of St Michael.

He thought about Kirby's warning signal. Kirby hadn't repeated it, but had followed James fast through all the hazards, as if in agreement with his hurry.

Sophie and the others were fairly quiet. Nerves that had been close to the surface since they left yesterday morning were still on edge. They all looked as if they were on a skiing holiday, travelling to a resort, but there were no songs, no high spirits, just the occasional little byplay of words. Sophie put a hand on James's knee and squeezed it, as if she knew he was debating with himself.

He asked her to look at the map, to let him know about any detours out of Althofen. She made a quick survey and told him a left turn would take them south by routes 96 and 95, although it would mean an extra twelve miles.

'You're thinking of coming off this road, James?' asked Carl.

'I'm thinking we should spare a few moments to stop and talk to the others,' said James. 'I'd like to know exactly why Kirby flashed us.'

'Pull in as soon as it's convenient,' said Carl.

'Good idea,' said Vicky. 'Even only ten seconds at a standstill might settle my stomach a little. How is your stomach, Mr Kirby?' she asked Nicholas.

'Under siege, Miss Fraser,' said Nicholas, 'but battling away.'

Entering a straight stretch, James wound his window down and signalled he was going to stop. He pulled over and came to a halt. The Opel drew up behind him. He and Carl got out, and Kirby opened his window. He anticipated James's question.

'I flashed you to let you know we'd been spotted. Two police motorcyclists came up on us, took a look and then disappeared. We have to assume they went back to report our position, probably to Anne's unfriendly ex-husband.'

'We can expect a roadblock or a police trap any moment,' said Carl.

'I'm suggesting a detour at Althofen,' said James, and Kirby consulted his map.

'That'll do, James,' he said. 'Take it and we'll follow.'

'Go, go,' called Karita, 'please to stop standing about.'

'Women are sweet creatures,' said Carl.

They were away again within seconds, driving fast for Althofen and route 96.

It was, however, this brief halt that enabled the police motorcyclists to pick them up again at a moment when a few seconds might have made all the difference. James had taken the left turn in Althofen. Kirby, twenty yards behind, glanced in his mirror just as he was about to make the turn himself. He caught a glimpse of the machines. They had not been there half a minute ago. They were there now. He made the turn, knowing they would have recognized the Opel, if only because of the roof rack and skis. He accelerated to catch up with the Mercedes, flashing his lights and then indicating he was going to overtake. James pulled over, slowed, and wound down his window. With the Opel travelling alongside the Mercedes, Karita called through her open window.

'Police, James, police. You go, but not too fast. We will see to them and then catch up.'

The Opel dropped back and James motored on.

'But Aunt Anne and Herr Meister,' breathed Vicky, 'they're –'

'Trust the scourge of Bolsheviks,' said Carl.

'Who? What?' Vicky was quivering.

'My Russian mother,' said Nicholas.

Kirby drove unhurriedly. He again glimpsed the motorcyclists. They disappeared when he rounded a bend. They reappeared, keeping their distance. There was no other traffic at all. Kirby accelerated, driving fast for a tight corner. He slowed as he took it, then accelerated again, like a man determined to get away. But he came to a sudden stop that tumbled his passengers about. Karita, ready for it, however, was out of the car in a flash, and out came Carl as well. He made a back for her Enfield rifle. She brought the butt hard into her shoulder and sighted. The motor-cyclists appeared in quick, noisy chase. Both policemen saw the stationary Opel and checked. Karita fired, jerked the bolt back and rammed home a second cartridge. She fired again. She had brought down charging Red cavalry and running Red infantry with her Enfield, and two slowing motorcycles presented targets she would never miss. The first bullet burst the front tyre of one bike, and the second crippled the other. Both motorcycles crashed with their riders. Karita and Carl leapt back into the Opel, and Kirby motored fast to catch up with the Mercedes.

The bruised policemen picked themselves up and righted their machines. Both bikes were out of action. Leaving them on the verge, they began to run back to Althofen.

Ludwig's mood was black, his lined and almost fleshless face suffering contortions. The road-block at Tweng had yielded nothing.

'You damned dawdling incompetents,' he shouted at the police manning the block, 'you were too late!'

'Herr Colonel, there are only two of us – '

'Two too many! I'll have you both shot!'

Now the Nazi cars were racing for Althofen, and Ludwig's mouth was full of spittle. Here, thought Voegler, is a man going off his head. His enemies are his own, not those of National Socialism. I ask myself now, what is National Socialism? My eccentric, perverse mother, who is always living her days of greatness, tells me it's a bellowing, bruising creature born of a bellowing lunatic. Should I allow her to call Hitler a lunatic? I've warned her that one day the wrong kind of person will hear her. What is the wrong kind of person? All those in my department. Schroeder, Fleischer, Lutz, Bauer, all of them. Any of them would consider it his duty to denounce my cranky old mother. That reminds me, where is the woman whose art is not of a kind Hitler would approve? Did she report to headquarters as ordered? If so, in view of my absence, have they locked her up to await my return? If so, they can let her go, for

Josef Meister is undoubtedly with the Baroness Anne and her brother Carl, and they are slipping us at every turn. The excitement of the chase is in my veins. There is no excitement for Lundt-Hausen. Frustration and fury are wrecking him. Do I care? Not in the least. Would I care if Baroness Anne escaped me? Hans Voegler, that's a harder question to answer.

'Herr Colonel—'

'Herr Kommissar, shut up.'

Althofen was in sight, and the two police motorcyclists were waiting for them, flagging them down. Ludwig had a look of fixed rage on his face as he listened to them. Barely able to conceal their own rage, they rushed into their accounts of what a woman and her rifle had done to their motorcycles. It was their duty to report this criminal assault to their headquarters in Radstadt.

'Idiots!' hissed Ludwig. 'You were ordered to keep them in sight, not to ride on the Opel's back. Go to the police station here, contact the SS Commandant in Spittal and tell him to do me the favour of having mountain troops available, together with a spotter plane.'

'A spotter plane, Herr Colonel?'

'That,' said Voegler with a faint smile, 'is a machine that flies and carries an observer. Isn't the type known to you?'

'Yes, Herr Kommissar, of course.'

'If the roadblock at St Michael stops them,' said Ludwig, 'I'll phone from there and cancel the arrangements.'

'St Michael?' queried Voegler. 'But according

to these officers, the cars are now on route 96. They've cut out St Michael.'

'Christ,' said Ludwig, 'I'm beginning to slip.'

'Is it surprising when they're leaving banana skins behind them?' said Voegler.

'Where the hell are you getting these jokes from?' rasped Ludwig. 'Let's get after the swines. Now. You two – make that phone call to Spittal.'

'At once, Herr Colonel.'

The Nazi cars shot away and turned left in new pursuit of the quarry. They were far far behind them.

Route 96 took the Mercedes and Opel in wandering, twisting fashion into the wild and rugged splendour of the Gurktaler Alps.

Vicky told herself she was beginning to prefer the hills and dales of the English Lake District. One never got dizzy there, nor did one have to pray.

Sophie, studying the map again, said, 'We need not go through Spittal, James. See, Carl.' She handed the map to Carl. He studied it in his turn.

'Right,' he said.

'Good,' said Vicky, 'I've a feeling of dislike for Spittal.'

'Women's intuition?' smiled Nicholas.

'Yes, it's a gift men are born without, poor things,' said Vicky.

'Well, if we take your gift into account, Vicky,' said James, 'and let your mother use her own gift for pointing me in the right direction, we may eventually arrive at our front door. Sophie, take the map and point us.'

'Yes, my lord, of course,' said Sophie, and patted his knee.

The two cars climbed and descended, climbed and descended, snaked around hairpin bends and forged on. Far behind them were the relentless hunters, Voegler immersed in his thoughts, Ludwig immersed in a vicious desire for revenge.

The afternoon sun became warmer and the sharp light mellowed.

Chapter Twenty-three

St Francis was a small town in the Italian Tyrol.
Before 1918 brought the Austrian Empire
crashing down, the region had been part of
that Empire, and St Francis bore the name
of Oberstein. It was there that Pia and Mariella's
mother lived, and it was in her handsome,
commodious house that the elderly Baron
and Baroness von Korvacs were now staying.
So were Pia and her children, Lucia and
Franz, together with Paul, Emma Jane and
Mariella. As promised, Sergeant Wainwright,
with the help of a forged passport and an
auburn wig that turned the lady into a different
person, had brought Mariella safely home to
her mother. Accommodation had been found
for him in the attic room, and he professed
himself privileged to be under such a warm
roof.

He was outside the house now, looking over
the snow-covered garden and the view of the
little town's rooftops. In the distance rose the
peaks of the Tyrol.

Mariella appeared.

'I'm going for a walk,' she said, and Sergeant Wainwright turned.

'A walk?'

'There's no need for you to come.'

'No, not now you're safe,' he said. 'Off you go, then, marm. Enjoy yourself.'

'I shall probably call on an old friend.'

'He'll be pleased to see you, I daresay, you being a fine figure of a woman.'

'I've heard you say that several times,' said Mariella, 'and don't wish to hear it again.'

'Well, in my book, it ought to be said. Any woman with a fine figure ought to be complimented on same from time to time.'

'Shut up,' said Mariella. 'It's a lovely afternoon and everyone is out walking except Mama.'

'I'll ask her if she'd mind letting me make a pot of tea,' said Sergeant Wainwright.

'God, what a silly man you are,' said Mariella crossly. 'I'm going for my walk.' She flounced away. She flounced back after ten seconds. 'Are you coming or not?'

'I thought a pot of tea—'

'Take that.' Mariella scooped up a handful of snow, balled it and flung it at him. It struck his face and smothered it in white. His nose and eyes peeped through.

'Ruddy hell, who did that?' he asked.

Mariella burst into laughter.

It was one way of letting him know a lady, even a temperamental artist, didn't expect to go walking by herself.

Ten minutes later they left the house together to walk to the centre of St Francis, Mariella wrapped in a warm fur-trimmed coat and a fur hat. She took deep breaths of the mountain air.

'There, this is better than a pot of tea, yes?' she said.

Sergeant Wainwright, wearing cap, jacket, trousers and a brown woollen Alpine jersey, bought that morning, said, 'So-so.'

'Ah, that is like you, to think more of tea than walking with me.'

'I didn't say that.'

'It was what you meant, you swine.'

'Nothing of the kind.'

'How would you like more snow in your face?'

'Well, I daresay a regular barrage of snowballs could improve it.'

'Improve what?'

'My face,' said Sergeant Wainwright, and laughed.

'You would like a better one?' Mariella gathered up a large handful of snow from a window sill. 'Come here.'

'I'm warning you, marm, that if you chuck that lot at me – '

Mariella, spirits high, threw it. It smothered his left shoulder. A cheerful smile split his mouth and his teeth gleamed in the sunlight.

'Oh, well, rotten shots don't count,' he said.

A man on the other side of the street stopped, stared and hared across, boots crushing thin melting ice. He was large, paunchy and ruddy-faced.

He burst into excited Italian.

'Mariella! You beautiful one. All these years! Where have you been?'

Mariella blinked. He swept her into his arms and planted a resounding kiss on her mouth.

'I think I'm in the way,' said Sergeant Wainwright, and strolled off.

Mariella struggled in the arms of the robust Italian bear whom she remembered as one Nicole Bertolini, an admirer years ago.

'Clown! Scoundrel! Let me go!' She flung the words in Italian.

'But once we were in love, my darling.'

'You were, I wasn't. Get away, do you hear?' Mariella shouted then, in English. 'Sergeant Wainwright, come back, you swine!'

'Ah, that man is your new lover?' said Bertolini. 'I'll kill him.'

Mariella wrestled free.

'Kill him, you fat pig?' she said. 'He would eat you for breakfast. Sergeant Wainwright!'

Nicole made another adoring grab at her. He missed. She kicked him, and he hopped in anguish on one leg, his brief re-entry into her life already at an end. Mariella swept away in pursuit of Sergeant Wainwright. He was waiting for her. She rushed up to him, fur hat askew, colour high.

'You coward, you snake – ah, a fine protector you are, I don't think.'

'I thought he was the old friend you were going to see,' said Sergeant Wainwright.

'Miserable worm, he's an ape, and so are you. For letting him assault me, I would hit you with a hammer if I had one.'

'Well, let's go to the town square and have some tea at one of the cafes, and afterwards we'll see if we can buy a hammer,' said Sergeant Wainwright. 'Will that do?'

Mariella burst into laughter again.

'Yes, that will do,' she said, 'but I shall have coffee, and the hammer must be a large one.'

'Come on, then,' said Sergeant Wainwright, and they began walking again. 'When d'you expect the others to arrive?'

That was the burning question troubling everyone concerned.

'No-one knows exactly,' said Mariella, 'but by not later than tomorrow, we hope.'

'They'll get here sooner or later,' said Sergeant Wainwright, 'Colonel Kirby and his missus will make sure of that.'

'Karita Kirby?'

'That's the lady.'

'Are you in love with her?'

'Who wouldn't be?' said Sergeant Wainwright.

'Then you're stupid,' said Mariella. As I am myself, she thought, for being in love with Carl. 'You should have your own wife and family.'

'I never seemed to get round to it, and come to that, you don't have a husband and family yourself.'

'I have my painting.'

'Can't go to bed with a picture,' said Sergeant Wainwright. 'Well, you could, I suppose, but I don't know what would come of it except a lot of—'

'Don't say it, you rat.'

'Well, marm—'

'Stop calling me that silly name.'

'I'm under orders to address you with respect.'

'Ah, do you say so?' Mariella sniffed scornfully. 'Is it respect to tell me to go to bed with a picture? Give me your arm.'

The little descent to the square was slippery underfoot. Sergeant Wainwright gave her his arm, but then her feet ran away from her and he flung his other arm around her just in time to prevent a fall.

'Steady there,' he said.

'What are you doing?'

'Keeping you on your feet.'

'Ah, you will kiss me next, yes, and with people looking.'

'With respect, marm – '

'Let me go.'

He did so. She took his arm again and they walked into the sunlit colourful square that seemed set amid a vista of Tyrolean peaks. The old bandstand still stood, and around the square people were sitting at the tables outside cafes.

There Mariella had coffee, Sergeant Wainwright had a pot of tea, and they talked, discussed and quarrelled. Mariella thoroughly enjoyed herself, so much so that anxious thoughts of Carl and the others took a more optimistic turn.

It was mid-afternoon by the time the Mercedes and Opel reached St Stefan, five miles north of the Italian border. From there they made another detour, taking a very minor mountain road that came to an end a mile from the border. Facing them were the heights of Osternigg, soaring to over six thousand feet. This territory was Carl's choice. He knew it well, and he also knew there was a way through the lower slopes west of Osternigg. It was going to be difficult and hazardous, but it could be done, and once his parents had agreed to go with the younger ones by train to Italy, he and the others had opted for this method of escape.

They parked the cars at the road's end. Limitless slopes and ridges were brilliant white, the temperature still rising. Snow looked soft and moist. They stood to survey through their sunglasses what was ahead of them, Carl pointing the way down to a long, irregular valley, bounded by slopes dense with snow-dappled firs.

Flasks of coffee, purchased in St Stefan, were drunk with fortifying brandy, and bread and cheese hungrily consumed. Then skis, sticks and boots were unloaded. Discarded clothes were abandoned. Ski boots were pulled on and tightly laced, Josef Meister deft and calm.

'Don't go swanning off,' said Nicholas to Vicky. 'Stick with me for safety's sake.'

'Don't make me laugh,' said Vicky, 'no girl is safe with you. If you were a sailor, I suppose you'd have one in every port. Would you like to tighten my laces for me?'

'Enchanted,' said Nicholas, and applied himself. 'What lovely feet.'

'My feet happen to be hidden in my boots,' said Vicky, seated on a car fender.

'My intuition tells me—'

'What rot,' said Vicky. 'I told you before, men don't have intuition.'

'All right,' said Nicholas, 'let's say I like the size of your boots.'

Carl had a coiled rope. The other men took charge of small valises containing the personal items belonging to the ladies. They strapped the valises to their backs. Karita had her rifle slung. James went down on one knee to help Sophie fix her skis. She smiled down at him.

'We're running again,' she said, reminding him of the time in 1914 when they had made a long and exhausting run from assassins and brigands in the mountains of Bosnia.

'Well, we have the edge on the wolves this time,' said James.

'Don't do anything crazy,' said Sophie.

'Stay close,' said James.

'I will. Nicholas is keeping an eye on Vicky.'

'He can't help himself,' said James. 'Vicky's mesmerizing him.'

'Yes,' said Sophie, 'and isn't she pleased with herself?'

'Ivan,' said Karita to her husband, 'there is nothing like doing Bolsheviks up, is there?'

'Down,' said Kirby. The sun was on his face, tinting the gold of his moustache, his eyes unreadable behind his sunglasses. 'Doing them down.'

'Down or up,' said Karita, a picture in her white woollen hat and dark blue windcheater, 'what is the difference?'

'None to you, little Crimean hen,' smiled Kirby, 'but remember your age.'

'My age?' Karita quivered. 'My age? I have no age.'

'Only last night, you said—'

'How would you like me to blow your head off?'

'Not very much,' said Kirby, 'I don't carry spares.'

'Is everyone ready?' called Carl. 'No-one has forgotten anything?'

The ladies made quick searches of their minds. Anne's mental search was broken by an image of Ludwig's dark hostile gaze, followed immediately by the clear clinical eyes of Kommissar Voegler, the eyes that had briefly met hers outside the shop in Radstadt. Had he actually not recognized her?

James and Nicholas took a last look inside the cars. Nothing had been forgotten.

'Let's away,' said Vicky, clip-on sunshields worn over her spectacles.

'Go, Carl, go,' said Karita, and he led the way down through a sloping, snow-covered meadow. It was a descent which Vicky thought represented a plunge into the unknown. One after the other they came sailing down over the lip. Their skis rasped over snow, sticks biting into it. The top layer of snow was softer than Carl had hoped for, the rising temperature of the April day threatening a partial but clogging thaw. But the slope took them down fast, knees and bodies bent and skis running well. The run widened and behind Carl they manoeuvred to pair up, Anne with Josef Meister, Vicky with Nicholas, James with Sophie, and last, Karita with Kirby.

They skirted the first outbreak of firs and swept down to the floor of a glacial valley, its frozen surface packed with hard snow that powdered under their scurfing skis. Here the shadows were huge and cold, and the air stung their faces. Scarves wrapped around their chins and mouths kept any chill from searing their lungs. Despite knowing they were in flight from Nazi pursuers, the forward run of skis induced exhilaration.

Carl led them through the valley and out of it, and they used their sticks to help them climb rising ground. I am astonished at myself, thought Josef Meister, I feel as vigorous as a young man. I also feel sad that Austrian and German people now worship the Devil.

At his elbow, Anne spoke through her scarf.

'On we go, Josef.'

'We are the happy children of God, eh?'

'Are you happy, Josef?'

'Should I not be when I am blessed with such fine friends?'

'Friendship is a mutual blessing, and let's save our breath now,' said Anne, face glowing above her scarf. One did need to talk little when one was trudging upwards and air seemed to become thin so quickly. Some stretches were steeper than others. Skis plodded, sticks propelled, and each one of them felt insignificant in the vast landscape of white, and of green so dark that sunglasses turned it black.

They were like crawling ants moving over this huge canvas of white, every vista dominated by soaring walls of ice. In the distance rose the rugged peaks and ridges of the formidable barrier separating Italy from Austria. Some six miles or so to the east lay the official frontier crossing at Thorl. That would only take them into the waiting arms of Nazi border guards.

What Carl was heading for was an accessible gap well to the west of the heights of Osternigg.

They were progressing now by means of ascents and descents, ascents prevailing, heading for the gap that would take them into Italy, where Mussolini, a declared friend and ally of Hitler, ruled like a man whose dictatorial power gave some of his people the impression he was greater than the Fuehrer of Germany. In reality he was jealous of Hitler's meteoric rise, and very capable of turning a deaf ear to any request for co-operation in the matter of returning German or Austrian refugees whom the Gestapo classed as criminals. Jewish refugees were seen as the worst criminals, but so far none had been returned by Italian authorities, who had never persecuted any of their own Jews.

It did not occur to Josef Meister that the Gestapo had friends in the Italian secret police, or that the hunters might contact such friends.

'It's not that I don't like music,' said Paul. He was back from his walk with Lucia and the others. Mariella and Sergeant Wainwright were still out. 'In fact, I used to like it a lot.'

'Yes, so did I,' said Lucia. From the drawing room came the sounds of a violin accompanying a piano, the violin played by Franz, Lucia's brother, the piano by Emma Jane. 'Well, I still do,' said Lucia, but apologetically. She was sitting with Paul on the wide window seat in the living room.

'What I mean is that there's pleasure in moderation,' said Paul.

'Yes, I know, but Franz does have to practise a lot,' said Lucia in sisterly loyalty.

'I wouldn't mind so much if my ears weren't beginning to hurt,' said Paul. 'The rest of me is fine.'

'I could get you some cotton wool, if you like,' offered Lucia.

'Thanks, Lucy, but if the phone rings I'd like to be able to hear it,' said Paul.

'I wonder when we'll hear from them?' said Lucia.

'Not later than tonight or tomorrow morning, I should think,' said Paul.

'I'm a little worried, though,' said Lucia, 'aren't you?'

'They'll be all right,' said Paul, 'they'll phone from somewhere as soon as they can.' He glanced out of the window. He frowned.

'Is something wrong?' asked Lucia.

'I'm not sure, except that's the third time I've seen that man since we've been sitting here,' said Paul. 'Look.'

Lucia followed his gaze and saw a man in a dark coat and hat strolling on the other side of the street.

'What do you think he's doing?' she asked.

'He's having a walk up and down,' said Paul, 'but what for, I'd like to know. Listen.' The music had stopped. 'Oh, good,' he said.

'Oh, dear,' said Lucia a moment later.

It had started again.

Chapter Twenty-four

A light biplane appeared, riding the sky on silvery wings above peaks and valleys. It seemed to float, to swing gently from side to side on currents of rising air, its delicate motions at variance with the buzzing noise of its engine. It dropped and drifted towards the pass at Thorl, then circled and flew back.

The skiers heard it. They were gliding over level ground, making for one more ascent, banks of fir on either side. Carl was still leading the way, Josef Meister and Anne close behind him, the others following. Kirby and Karita were still the watchful rearguard. High above, the snow clung thickly to shelves and ridges, its surface wet. The afternoon sun spread light and warmth, the temperature climbing above freezing. The biplane hovered over the nine moving people, slipped away in a sideways drift, and then began to circle lazily. The observer was transmitting messages.

The skiers, reaching the ascent, came to a halt. They grouped and looked up at the plane.

'Can I believe Ludwig's sent that plane to search for us?' asked Sophie.

'We can all believe it,' said Carl, 'it's staying with us.'

'If it's true,' said Josef, 'they're even hungrier for us than I thought.'

Karita glanced at Kirby. They both knew the hunters were hungriest for what was now a film negative. The defector, Staffler, had scrapped the document after photographing it in Vienna. Well, the negative was now on its way by carrier to an address in England. It was carefully sealed inside an address label of thin cardboard, the label firmly adhering to the back of a framed painting of a cottage.

'We go on, don't we?' said Anne.

They were all glowing, all physically and mentally stimulated by the exercise that, although enforced, could not be divorced from the sheer magic of Austria's Alpine regions.

Vicky, looking up at the plane, said, 'I'm not actually too worried, but I'm also not too pleased, and I know that buzzing engine is going to irritate me soon.'

'We are holding a meeting?' said Karita, little loops of golden hair escaping from beneath her woollen hat. 'Meetings can be very pleasant, but now? No, no, not now, I think.'

'Well, another hour's work will see us through,' said Carl, 'and as there's no point in turning back, let's get moving again.'

Yes, before the wolves appear, thought Anne. The plane was calling them up, she was sure.

They went on, trudging up the ascent, skis

leaving lines that marked the yielding snow, which was becoming sticky in places. Carl glanced upwards, a little disturbed by the climbing temperature, the weight of snow on slopes and ridges, and the vibrating noise of the circling plane. He had known the sound of a single gun to bring an avalanche into being. Avalanches had been commonplace during the mountain war Austria had fought with Italy from 1914 to 1918.

The parachutes snaked and opened, and a dozen Austrian SS paratroopers under the command of Colonel Lundt-Hausen drifted downwards, the clumsy-looking transport plane flying on. Ludwig had spent time training in Germany. Since joining the SS, he had fiercely opposed any idea that his damaged leg limited his physical capabilities. Parachute drops could cause him the devil of a pain, but his leg endured, and, at forty-two, he was never disposed to let younger men claim they could do what he could not. He had always been a jealous guard of his status from the time of his first promotion.

He landed in cushioning snow, rolling over in free-limbed fashion, and his parachute tugged, quivered and sank. Pain shot through his damned leg, but only for a second or so. The Stormtroopers, mountain-trained, came down fast, and each man rolled as he hit the snow. Parachutes jerked, stuttered and collapsed. A large pack containing skis, sticks and rifles thudded softly.

Ludwig, helmeted, was on his feet, freeing himself of his harness. The men gathered and bundled the parachutes, and opened up the pack. The transport plane lumbered on, and the light plane came winging in low. The noisy engines of both planes radiated vibrations and caused thawing surface snow to tremble. The light machine touched down on the level ground over which the quarry had passed a short while ago. Snow sprayed from beneath its landing wheels. It ran on, slowing down, and when it was almost at a stop something was thrown from it, and a man jumped out, bending his knees as he hit the ground and tumbled forward. The plane turned, picked up speed, taxied fast and took off again.

Kommissar Hans Voegler picked himself up, brushed snow from his windcheater and adjusted his woollen pull-on hat. He retrieved the ejected bundle, a pair of skis with sticks, roped together. He walked up to Ludwig, who eyed him with more interest than usual.

'I had my doubts you could or would land as you did, Herr Kommissar.'

'I said I would.' Voegler, wearing a borrowed fur-lined leather jacket, looked as if he was on very agreeable terms with himself. 'At the last moment, I wasn't sure if I could. But I did. I've an appointment to keep, I hope, with – ' He paused. 'With the Greek woman, perhaps.'

'Russian,' said Ludwig bitterly. 'Kirby's wife. Where are the swines now?'

'Not too far,' said Voegler. The plane was aloft. It circled, then took up a course pointing due south. 'That way,' said Voegler with a smile, and fixed his skis.

'Why have you been so damned pleased with yourself all day?' asked Ludwig.

'I dislike being miserable except under impossible circumstances,' said Voegler, and glanced upwards at high ridges. Patterns of iridescent light travelled over sloping white surfaces, like sun-tipped ripples on shining lakes, and from an angled ridge a thousand feet up a mass of snow slid slowly over the lip and spilled. Gently it piled itself on the thickly covered slopes below the ridge. It quivered, sighed and subsided.

Ludwig was ready, his men were ready, and Voegler was waiting. Everyone was wearing sun goggles, regulation Alpine issue. Ludwig tested his leg by bearing down on the fixed ski. The snow cushioned the pressure. He gestured and moved forward, with Voegler. The Alpine troops followed. Ludwig wore a fixed smile, his teeth a thin line of white in his dark face. If it was the last thing he did, he would eliminate the woman who had called herself a Greek, but who he was certain was Kirby's Russian wife.

The hunt was on again.

Another ascent, another climb. Carl, however, had known what he was doing in his choice of routes. No climb had been too arduous, and shortness of breath was more troublesome than weariness of limb. Over the ascent, they let their skis take them forward, four couples following Carl towards a wall of icy stone that reared starkly free of snow.

Karita noted the endurance of Anne, Sophie and Vicky, and of Josef Meister too. If any people were worth saving from Himmler's wolves, these were. No-one was yet complaining of exhaustion. Anne, Sophie and Vicky, all excellent on skis, were still moving well. Carl was almost effortless, James strong in his propulsion, and Nicholas had the undiminishing vigour of a young man. Josef Meister moved economically.

Carl stopped, and everyone came up with him. They found themselves looking at a gap in the wall of stone. Carl explained it would take them to a ledge no more than three feet wide. Beyond the ledge, unseen from this point, was a plateau leading to an unmarked border crossing.

'It's our only way through,' he said.

'The ledge, then,' said Kirby.

'No other option means we go,' said Anne.

They released their skis and strapped them, with sticks, to their backs. They retained one stick each for support when negotiating the curving ledge.

'My God,' said James suddenly, 'they're on our tail.'

They all looked back. The hunters were visible against the snow below the final ascent. They were figures that seemed to be moving slowly. It was a deceptive impression, and they knew it.

'Go,' said Kirby, and it was Carl, their leader, who entered the gap first. Kirby brought up the rear.

From the distance and from out of the clear air came a shout. It reached the ear faintly but distinctly.

'Halt! Halt!'

A rifle cracked and the bullet, ascending,

smacked into the wall of stone. Chips showered above their heads.

'Ah, there's a Bolshevik for you,' said Karita, 'not minding whether he kills the innocent or the guilty.'

Carl's boots scraped slippery stone as he climbed through the gap to the ledge, stick in his left hand, rock face against his right shoulder. He turned, held out his stick, Anne took hold of it and used it to lever herself up onto the ledge. They edged along. Up came Josef Meister, then Vicky, given a helpful lift by Nicholas, who followed her. Up came the others, and all formed a crocodile that snaked around the curving ledge, sticks used to steady themselves.

The light was dim. Below them the rocky ground began to fall away until a dark fearsome drop leapt at every eye. Within minutes they were hanging in space, shoulders pressed to the wall on their right. Urgency was an impelling force, but the narrowness of the ledge was the governing factor and they moved slowly and carefully. Mouths expelled noisy breath above scarves pulled down. Carl, judging the hazards ahead, passed warnings that travelled back to Kirby at the rear. Each watched the one in front, ready to act if feet slipped.

Anne, behind Carl, took comfort from the sureness of his step, slow though it was. Her heart was hammering, and while the rest of her body was hot from exertion, her spine felt cold, much as if Ludwig was close behind them. Was he there, among the hunters? And was Kommissar Voegler there too? He had conducted his interrogation in the strangest way, never losing his temper or raising his voice, and she had even thought once or twice that those clear eyes of his had been anything but hostile or accusing. Why was a man with such fine eyes and such a fine face committed to the ugly despotism of the Nazis and the Gestapo?

Her nailed boots trod the slippery ledge cautiously, and her heart continued to hammer. No-one spoke for a while, all concentrating on careful forward movement above the dizzying gulf.

It was shoulder contact with the stone wall that alone kept Sophie from feeling she was walking a tightrope in a dark cavernous void. The one consoling thought was that they could not be seen by the enemy. But where were the enemy? How close? To have avoided them so far was wonderful. To be caught when the border was now so reachable would be ghastly.

Carl eased his way around a sharp corner.

'Take great care here,' he said, and they all edged round inch by inch.

'All right, Sophie?' whispered James behind her.

'I'm only terrified,' she said.

'I share your feelings.'

'Vicky, you're a marvel,' murmured Nicholas, escaping breath steaming towards the back of her head.

'What a time to start a conversation,' gasped Vicky. But anything that took her mind off the frightening drop was acceptable.

Carl reached a point where the ledge narrowed

to two feet. He turned to face the wall, calling a warning. Below them, the void was a thing of yawning enormity, and they all turned to face the wall, to press against it and to edge along in crabwise fashion. The time was nearing five o'clock, and the sun had moved from its high point to sink westwards. Suddenly they were out in the open and they felt warmth on their backs, warmth that induced the rise of perspiration. Painfully they progressed, booted feet searching for the hazards communicated by Carl. So intense was their concentration and so noisy their breathing that they did not hear the plane that was circling overhead.

Nicholas's left foot slipped. He dragged it back in time.

'Clumsy,' he muttered.

'Don't play games, young man,' called Karita.

'Not in the mood, Mother.'

The ledge widened to a heavenly four feet, and before them rose a lengthy plateau of snow-covered ice five hundred yards wide. Carl reached the end of the ledge. A little below it was a series of ridges forming a steep incline of stepping stones, but thick with ice. Carl slipped the coiled rope free, wound the end around his waist and tied it. There was now room to move on the ledge, and James and Nicholas made their way forward to take hold of the rope. James wound it once around a jutting bulwark of stone, and he and Nicholas held it firmly as Carl began to let himself down. The rope stretched and tightened, creaking around the bulwark. Carl descended slowly, facing the incline of stone, the

rope being played out, his boots digging and
scraping as he negotiated each icy step. When he
reached the bottom, he looked up.

'Make fast,' he said, 'then let the ladies come
down.'

'I don't feel like a lady,' said Vicky, 'I feel like
a coward.'

With Carl down below, the rope stretching
tautly upwards to its anchor, Anne followed,
gloved hands gripping what she considered to
be her lifeline, feet planted against the ridged
stone. One by one they all descended. Kirby, last,
threw down the ski sticks, knotted the rope and
used his pocket knife to cut deeply into its under-
side just below the clove hitch.

'Will it hold you?' called Carl.

'Just about,' said Kirby, and down he went.
The rope, taking his weight, whispered harshly at
the point of the cut.

At that moment they all heard the sounds of
the hunters well forward on the ledge. Something else also attacked their ears, the buzzing
engine of the plane. With not a second to
lose, they strapped on their skis. The light was
blinding, the dipping sun a burning gold, the
snow-covered plateau a moist dazzling brilliance.
Behind them and above them, shelving walls and
great ridges, thickly plastered with snow, reached
upwards to the sky. At the far end of the plateau,
massed firs banked high.

'The border,' said Carl, pointing. 'Let's get to
it.'

They all went, skis rushing. Kirby felt admiration for the women who, after two full days of

existing on their nerves, were now being stretched to the limits of their strength, courage and resolution. He also felt a familiar surge of anger towards political animals who in their fanaticism played God. Such men always avoided having to witness the inhuman consequences of their ordinances. Lenin had never come within a hundred miles of watching his Bolsheviks burying people alive. He knew it happened. By remaining detached from it, he remained unaffected.

The snow was soft on top, denying the skis a free run, and the going was harder work than previously. Above them the plane swooped and danced, the loud vibrations of its engine creating echoes that ran into each other. Snow, softer by the minute, quivered to expanding reverberations. Carl looked up. He saw the plane and he scanned the high slopes. He had witnessed the many wartime avalanches in these regions, and conditions now needed only a physical disturbance to set one off.

The first of the SS mountain troops burst through into the unhindered light.

'There they are, there they go!' shouted one man.

'And look, there's their rope.'

'Down you go, men!' shouted the SS officer.

Down they went, fast, using the rope.

Ludwig appeared. He gave no sign that his sense of balance was disturbed, that his leg was a swine. He had felt close to disaster on this ledge. Relief flooded him at finding there was now room to move, and triumph leapt to add exultation to relief as he saw the moving figures on the plateau. The plane dipped its wings as if the pilot had seen him and wanted him to know the watching brief would continue.

Voegler arrived. The moment he saw the fugitives, he glanced at Ludwig, taking note of his expression. Visibly, it was gloating. Just as visibly, it changed. Voegler knew why. The plateau, at least half a mile long, was the gateway to the border with Italy, and the quarry were too far ahead to be caught. Once through that stretch of firs they would be in Italy, and Lundt-Hausen had suddenly realized they had every chance of escaping him unless alerted Italian collaborators took them into custody.

Ludwig turned to the SS officer, who was about to join his men down below.

'Herr Colonel?'

'Those damned criminals have got to be turned back. Fire a warning volley.' Ludwig issued the order demandingly, urgently, and the SS officer cupped his mouth. His voice boomed through the clear air.

'Halt! Halt!'

The quarry kept moving. The Stormtroopers were unslinging rifles.

'Halt! Halt, or we fire!'

The quarry took no notice. They went on, skis channelling the snow, sticks propelling. The rifles, sighted, aimed to discharge a volley over their heads. The order was rapped out. Gloved fingers squeezed triggers, and the sound that was born of the collective discharge was like ice explosively cracking. Vicky and Sophie shuddered at the perceptible whine of bullets above their heads. Anne instinctively ducked at the sound, which turned into a series of vibrating echoes. Her left ski dug itself into thick snow, pulled her up and made her keel over. Nicholas rushed to her, dropped his sticks and helped her up. The others checked.

'I'm not hurt,' she gasped. 'Go on, everyone, go on.'

Within seconds they were all moving again.

'Halt!' The bellowing voice boomed.

'Shout, shout, roar, roar, they have no manners, any of them,' grumbled Karita to herself.

'Halt!'

Carl silently swore at the increasing wet softness of clogging snow.

Ludwig swore out loud at the infuriating refusal of the quarry to give him what his dark soul most wanted – Kirby's wife, Meister the Jew, and Anne. In a few more minutes they would have reached the border, and he knew the chances of catching them here were lessening every minute. To hell with letting them go. He would still go after them while the light held.

Voegler, eyes straining in an attempt to pick out Anne, heard the SS officer, now down with his men, telling them to get ready to fire again.

'It won't bring them back,' he said to Ludwig.

'It might bring one or two of them down,' said Ludwig ferociously.

'I object to the possibility of killing any of the innocent,' said Voegler.

'Are you mad?' shouted Ludwig. 'They're all

guilty.' He shouted again, this time at the SS officer. 'Fire!'

'Herr Colonel, under these conditions – '

'Fire! That's an order! Repeat fire!'

The SS officer issued the order to his men.

'Fire! Repeat fire!'

The explosive crack of the first volley savaged the air, and was followed by another. The reverberations were like faint rolls of thunder. Bullets whistled over heads or kicked up snow at the feet of the skiing quarry. The ubiquitous plane's engine roared as it zoomed upwards, and the roar attacked the sensitive white walls. Snow trembled on mountain slopes. High above the ledge on which stood Ludwig and Voegler, thawing layers of snow shivered and shook. Sighing and whispering, they unfolded and broke. Running white ripples disturbed the clinging carpets on shelving ridges. The slow movement of weighty masses began to split the frozen inner layers.

Carl heard sounds similar to the crack of whips. He turned his head and his experienced eyes detected movements on the slopes above the ledge. Ragged patterns of dark lines appeared on the vast wall of white as the frozen layers burst apart and tore free. Vibrations travelled the length of the plateau.

Carl shouted.

'Move, move! Avalanche!'

The dreaded word leapt at every ear. Instinctively, they all took a look over their shoulders as they propelled themselves forward. They saw, in horror, the movements of tumbling masses of snow amid what seemed like rising clouds of white steam. They knew what would happen. The breaking banks would pressurize and dislodge layer after layer. The movements would quicken by reason of mighty weight and the laws of gravity, and great oceans of snow and ice would plunge all the way down, gathering volume and speed, and rush in spreading, smothering violence over the plateau. It would come at them like a foaming, steaming tidal wave of monstrous proportions.

'Oh, my God,' gasped Sophie.

'Go, go!' shouted Carl. 'Vicky, Anne! Go, go! Josef, Karita, for God's sake, go!'

Every nerve and sinew went to work.

On the ledge, Voegler said in an extraordinarily calm voice, 'Herr Colonel, do you realize we are listening to the formation of an avalanche caused by the rifle fire?'

'Christ Almighty,' hissed Ludwig, 'do you have to give me that kind of news? We're going after them— Oh, my God.'

The first fall came from the overhanging ridges, like a ragged curtain of white and grey. Down below, the SS men, touched by the falling curtain, yelled and scrambled for the dangling rope. They threw themselves at it as snow and lumps of ice began to shower them. The fall increased, accelerated, ice striking helmets. Ludwig stared down with his lips drawn back and his teeth clenched. Voegler moved fast, sat down and slid his feet over the edge, offering his long legs as purchase for the man scrambling upwards. The fall became thunderous as great masses of snow shut off the view of the plateau. There were two men, three men, scrambling, climbing and pulling on the rope.

It snapped and broke and the men hurtled backwards down the angled incline. Voegler could not believe his eyes, for as they fell on top of their comrades snow and ice began to bury the struggling, shouting screaming men. The roaring curtain that hid the plateau did not hide the frightful nightmare of men being buried and carried away by the forward impetus of the avalanche. Some visible arms and legs were cartwheeling.

For the fugitives, the same threat of extinction was in being. At their backs, the wall of disintegrating white exploded, and thousands of tons of snow and ice burst forth. Down came the vast, tumbling masses, down came the great ocean of white and grey, the noise a thunderous roar. Snow leapt and spewed from ridges and was sucked in by what fell past it. A huge booming sound paralysed the ears of the fugitives as the avalanche struck the plateau. The billowing white ocean began to roll, gathering weight and impetus. The great curtain in front of Ludwig and Voegler was suffocatingly close, and Voegler thought its malevolence would draw him off his feet and suck him into its deadly embrace. God Almighty, those mountain troops, buried in seconds. Stunned, devastated, his imagination conjured up pictures of Baroness Anne and her companions being overwhelmed.

Over the plateau, the avalanche was rolling and pounding, issuing huge clouds of powdered snow. Carl was shouting to keep everyone going. They were fighting to beat the great surging flood of snow and ice. Kirby, casting another look back, saw the rushing advance of the monstrous tidal wave, forty feet high at the distant stone wall and shelving to six feet at its spreading rim. Its speed was frightening.

The avalanche curved inwards on its left, as if intent on outflanking the straining skiers. The rim of the spilling, rushing snow flood swept at Kirby and Karita. They turned then, and he thrust her behind him. He faced the coming assault. The turbulent snow, levelling out, swamped their legs. The following mass hit them as he bent his body to meet it, to drive into it and stay on his feet. But as it struck it lifted him and Karita, and they fell into the surging white rollers. It swept them along.

The foaming blanket was thinning over the flat surface of the plateau, but it trapped Anne by her legs, whirled around her, sucked at her and brought her down. It overtook Carl and Meister, then Sophie and James, trapping them waist-high.

The curtain had vanished in front of the ledge, leaving a hill of snow and ice up to the ledge itself. The spewing clouds of powdered snow were settling. Staring at the plateau, Ludwig and Voegler saw the distant rim of the avalanche reaching the desperate figures of their quarry.

'It's finishing,' said Ludwig, his voice cracked and hoarse, 'it's finishing. They'll escape.'

'Jesus Christ,' said Voegler bitterly, 'does it matter now?'

'Damn you, it matters even more now! They're indirectly responsible for the deaths of those mountain troops!'

'That might be disputed,' said Voegler, still staring at the distant scene of spreading snow and just one tiny struggling figure. 'But it's not something I want to argue about at this moment, except to say your command to fire had to be obeyed.'

'What the hell's got into you? Look there.' Ludwig pointed to the hill of ice and snow that began its descent from the ledge. 'We can use that to get at them, to find out who has survived.'

'I'm willing to do that.' Voegler, in fact, was already fixing his skis. He thought there was a chance of digging some of them out, since they'd all been caught when the tide was ebbing. His movements became urgent.

Ludwig, obsessed, forgot the curse of his suffering leg and blanked out the deaths of the SS mountain troops.

The plane had gone, the pilot intent on alerting rescue teams.

Chapter Twenty-five

Nicholas alone had escaped the flood of ice and snow, the flood that had torn Vicky from his side. Kirby and Karita were buried, Anne had been carried far to one side of the plateau before being swallowed. Carl, Sophie, James and Meister had all been knocked off their feet to become partly submerged. Vicky, bowled over and whirled about, now lay with her head and arms visible. Nicholas trod snow frantically to get to her. Vicky shouted.

'I'm all right! Go to your parents! Over there, over there!'

She and Nicholas had both seen Kirby and Karita disappear in the billowing mass.

Nicholas was aware that Carl, Sophie, James and Josef Meister were in no immediate danger. The avalanche was at a standstill, its surface quivering and settling. Vicky, drawing breath, her body covered but not sinking, yelled at him again.

'Dig them out, dig them out!'

'Oh, Christ,' breathed Nicholas, appalled that Anne was no more visible than his parents were. But because he knew where those two had disappeared, he had no option but to go to them first.

Karita was on her back, Kirby on top of her, astride her, their skis gone, the snow threatening to completely smother them. At the moment, miraculously, it formed a tiny cavern around them, and Kirby was using his shoulders and back to keep the weighty roof from collapsing and robbing them completely of air.

'Ivan?' It was a sigh.

'Don't talk, don't.'

'My hand is on a stick.'

'Yes, use it, then.'

Karita turned the stick. They were buried in a dark hole, with perhaps just enough air to keep them alive for five minutes. She thrust upwards, the point of the stick passing Kirby's left shoulder and digging into the roof of snow. Slowly she pushed. If she could get it through, if she could make the stick show above the surface, then someone might see it. But who? If the others had all been smothered, where was help to come from?

She pushed, slowly, carefully, praying the snow would not break and fall, and that its depth was not greater than the length of the stick.

Carl and James, bruised bodies breaking free, struggled over the rim of snow to help Sophie and Josef Meister. They heard Nicholas shout.

'My parents! They're buried! Over here!'

'Dig!' shouted James, forehead bleeding from a jagged cut. 'We'll be there in a moment! My God, where's Anne?'

Anne came to. She lay on her back, a thick blanket of snow and ice covering her, her scarf an untidy mass of wool over her mouth, a freakish result of what the avalanche had done to her in rolling her over and over. It was now keeping the snow from smothering her mouth and robbing her entirely of breath. For a little while, it would provide air. For a little while. She moved her legs and tried to bring them up in an effort to dislodge the wet, muffling blanket, and she thrust her hands and wrists upwards into it. How thick was it? Could her hands break the surface? She pushed. The snow seemed to thicken around her hands and wrists. Her hammering heart was a violence, her wish to stay alive a thing of desperation. She kicked, pushed and struggled, knowing she had only minimal time left.

The blanket suddenly opened up. Digging hands shovelled and the opening widened.

Ludwig, on his knees, looked down into her eyes, the blue eyes that for years had pitied him and pried into his soul until in the end she had said, 'How sorry I am for you. There is nothing there. You have no soul.'

Who could live with a woman who acted as if she had made herself his conscience?

Anne, body bruised, mind numb, stared up into the dark, lined face of the man who had relentlessly hunted her. His smile was animal-like in the way it drew his lips back and showed his teeth.

'My dear Anne,' he said softly, 'so there you are.' Other hands shovelled more snow aside, and the head and shoulders of another man appeared. She saw the clear eyes and ascetic countenance of Kommissar Voegler. 'You remember Hans Voegler, my love? He led me here, he was sure that this was where the avalanche took you. Now, what are we to do with you?'

'Baroness?' said Voegler gently, and gave her his hand. She took it and painfully sat up. Her numbed mind began to work. The others, where were Carl and Sophie and the others? She did not know it, but on the other side of the plateau, four hundred yards away, Carl, Josef Meister, Vicky and Nicholas were surrounding the spot marking the disappearance of the Kirbys, and all were successfully digging. Nicholas a while ago had seen the point of a stick slowly come up through the snow, and that had marked the exact spot for digging. The Kirbys were now partly uncovered. 'Baroness, are you unhurt?' Voegler's voice was concerned. Concerned? He was concerned?

'Where – where is Sophie – where – '

'Get her up,' said Ludwig, and came to his feet.

'Give her time,' said Voegler.

'Leave her, then,' said Ludwig, 'standing or sitting, her time is up. She has associated with criminals.'

Voegler lifted his head. His eyes took in the incredible. Lundt-Hausen had drawn his revolver, and Voegler saw him release the safety catch. He was going to shoot the woman he had been married to for years? He was. Deliberately, he took aim at Anne's head. Voegler was up in a flash. His gloved hand delivered a furious chop to the side of Ludwig's neck. Ludwig fell like a man pole-axed.

Anne, body aching and mind incredulous, gasped, 'Herr Voegler?'

'Did you think, Baroness, I would ever permit a man like that to kill a woman like you?' said the Gestapo Kommissar.

'I don't understand.'

'Perhaps I might say I don't understand, either,' said Voegler, 'but I do, I understand very well. I mean I understand myself. As to your friends and relatives, all seem to be alive. Only the rim of the avalanche caught them and you.'

Anne struggled to draw breath, to comprehend.

'Herr Voegler, did you see me when you passed me in Radstadt?'

'Baroness, you are not a woman a man could easily miss seeing.'

'Then why didn't you stop?' she asked.

'Perhaps one day I'll write to you and tell you why,' said Voegler. 'Here come your sister and her husband.'

James and Sophie, who had been frantically searching for Anne close to the spot that had seen the Kirbys swallowed up, were hurrying over.

'Who is that man?' Sophie gasped. 'There was another – I thought they had come to help – James, he's gesturing. Has he found Anne?'

'That man, Sophie, is Kommissar Voegler, can't you recognize him?' James was grim, fearing the worst, for there was no sign of Anne. Then Voegler moved. He stepped forward, disclosed the inert body of a man, and reached down. The next moment he had brought Anne to her feet. Sophie let out a cry of great relief, and James lost his grimness. They ploughed forward, skis tramping the yielding surface of the swamping snow and ice, exhaustion forgotten in their relief, determination uppermost concerning the Gestapo officer. They were certainly not going to allow him to rearrest Anne.

Voegler took Anne's hands between his own to rub and massage them. Her woollen hat was gone, her fair hair disordered, her face marked with tiny little cuts, her bottom lip bruised, her eyes uncertain. She glanced and saw James and Sophie moving towards her. They were some fifty yards away, and well beyond them it looked as if Carl, Josef, Vicky and Nicholas were bringing the Kirbys up out of the snow.

'Herr Voegler, is Ludwig dead?'

'Not in the least, Baroness, although he might prefer to be when this incident is investigated. At the moment, he's merely unconscious, and will be for another five minutes. He has a stunned nerve.'

'Herr Voegler, you're a very strange Gestapo officer,' said Anne.

Voegler smiled wryly.

'I must tell you, Baroness, that I've just been forced to resign. My own fault, but there it is, none of us can ever say exactly how each day will go.' A familiar buzzing was heard. 'Ah, I thought it would be back.'

The biplane was there again. Ludwig was still unconscious as Sophie and James arrived. Sophie, emotional, flung her arms around Anne, and James stared down at Ludwig before eyeing Voegler in curiosity.

'That's Ludwig Lundt-Hausen down there,' he said.

Ludwig had not stirred a muscle.

'Yes, but he'll recover,' said Voegler.

'What happened?' asked James.

'I will tell you,' said Anne, allowing Sophie to dab at her little facial cuts with a damp handkerchief.

'Permit me, Baroness, to advise all of you to go on your way at once,' said Voegler. 'The plane is back, as you see, and I think another detachment of paratroopers will be here in a very short time. The first detachment – ' Voegler winced. 'The avalanche took every one of them.'

'My God,' said James.

'Yes,' said Voegler drily, 'who but God could explain why courageous adherents of National Socialism died and its enemies survived? Most odd.' He shook his head. 'Baroness Anne, do you understand it's now necessary to my safety for me to come with you and your party?'

Anne looked at Ludwig, now fitfully stirring.

'Herr Voegler, I understand very well,' she said, and smiled.

'I'm damned if I do,' said James.

'I think Kommissar Voegler is questioning some of his beliefs,' said Anne, 'but yes, we must go now.'

'Anne, I'm not sure if all of us are fit to travel,' said Sophie.

'Try force of will and waste no time,' said Voegler. 'If you need help, I'll give it.' He stooped and picked up Ludwig's revolver. He glanced at Anne. She was marked by the avalanche, but her colour was returning, and if there was a suggestion in her expression that she still could not quite make him out, she was definite in her acceptance of the fact that he had saved her life.

'Come, Herr Voegler,' she said, 'come with us, then. To Italy.'

'Anne,' said James, 'I'm not sure we should – '

'Ludwig meant to shoot me,' said Anne. 'Herr Voegler made sure he did not.'

'Jesus Christ,' said James.

They all made the necessary effort, and were across the border a little later. A trek of half a mile then put them only a similar distance from the nearest village. They were on the soil of Italy, a country of happy-go-lucky people who respected the Pope, went to Sunday Mass in the north with their neighbours, in the south with the Mafia, cheered Mussolini loudly, called him 'Il Duce' to his face and 'Big-bellied Benito' behind his back.

For the moment, in the first advance of twilight, the refugees halted to draw breath, while trying to come to terms with the wonder of having survived the avalanche. Bodies were bruised and aching, Kirby had a gashed arm, Josef Meister a sprained wrist, and everyone showed facial cuts and grazes. However, there were no real casualties, and Carl and James were passing their brandy flasks around. Voegler stood apart from them, but did not look uncomfortable about it. They were discussing him, he knew it and accepted it as reasonable.

'Can we trust him?' asked Josef.

'Good question,' said James. 'He's armed, and has anyone heard of a Gestapo leopard changing its spots?'

'But how can he be against us if he saved Anne's life?' asked Vicky.

'Another good question,' said Nicholas.

'Does anyone like him?' asked Carl.

'No,' said Sophie. 'I remember his contempt for all of us on the morning he arrested Anne.'

'Is he a Bolshevik or not a Bolshevik?' said Karita.

'A Nazi or not a Nazi, you mean?' said Vicky.

'What is the difference?' asked Karita for possibly the hundredth time in a week. 'You cannot like or trust any of them.'

'What does Anne say?' asked Kirby, who thought that as she knew more of Voegler than any of them, her opinion was the only one worth serious consideration.

'I trust him and like him,' said Anne.

'Like him?' said Sophie.

'One could trust a man who saves one from being executed,' said Vicky, 'but you don't have to like him, Aunt Anne.'

'I don't have to,' said Anne, 'but perhaps what I mean is that I no longer dislike him.'

'Ah, then he is not a Bolshevik,' said Karita, 'and because I like you very much, Anne, I will try to like him too. So will Nicholas and Ivan.'

'Little Mother,' said Nicholas, 'I can make up my own mind.'

'Tck, tck,' said Karita, 'you are still cutting your front teeth.'

'Back,' said Kirby, 'back teeth.'

'Front or back, it is all the same,' said Karita. 'Come, tell Herr Voegler we accept him and trust him, but will blow his head off if he deceives us. I am getting cold and we have rested long enough.'

'Herr Voegler?' called Anne.

'Baroness?' Voegler joined them. 'Your discussion was frank, of course?'

'Yes, indeed,' said Anne, 'and if I say we're all ready to trust you, will you mind if I also say not everyone is ready to like you?'

'I assure you, Baroness, I have never asked for anyone to like me,' said Voegler. 'My old but respected mother, who swears she happily gave birth to me, nevertheless insists I am the most unlikeable man in Austria. I accept that, even if only for the sake of avoiding an argument with her.'

Carl laughed. Karita laughed. Kirby smiled, and Anne regarded Voegler wonderingly.

'Do you honour your mother, Herr Voegler?' asked Karita.

'Of course,' he said.

'Would you denounce her if she opposed Hitler?' asked Kirby.

'She does oppose him, but no, I would never denounce her, only suggest she talks to her mirror and not to her neighbours.'

'Then my wife will tell you you are not a true Bolshevik,' smiled Kirby.

'I think your wife is the Greek woman,' said Voegler.

Karita laughed again.

They all moved off then to reach the village and an inn before darkness fell. Voegler said he hoped he would be able to make a phone call. James and Carl thought that might entail something suspicious. Others were too tired to care.

The new detachment of SS mountain troops came down from the sky before daylight had run its course. Ludwig was waiting, but when he spoke to them about crossing the border into Italy in pursuit of a group of suspected criminals, they countered by asking him where their buried comrades were and how it was that the avalanche took them. His answers made no sense. In fact, he sounded like a raving idiot, foaming at the mouth about the treachery of a Gestapo officer, one Kommissar Voegler, who had, he shouted, been responsible for the deaths of the Alpine troops. There will be an inquiry, they said, and then did what they had come to do. They searched for the bodies of the dead.

Chapter Twenty-six

'What? You have done such a crazy thing as this?'
Frau Voegler at sixty-three could still deliver
herself loudly enough to make ears ring.

'Don't shout, Mother—'

'Shout? Shout? Who is shouting? You are telling me you're in Italy, that you have torn up your
National Socialist Party card, and have exiled
yourself?'

'Exactly,' said Hans Voegler from the residents' phone box of a hotel in the little Italian
border town of Tarvisio.

'Have you gone mad?'

'You could say I'm slightly off my head,' said
Voegler.

'Crazy, I tell you,' expostulated Frau Voegler,
'and at last I am proud of you. National Socialism,
bah, I spit on it.'

'Not in public, old one,' said Voegler. 'Listen
carefully. I don't think headquarters will have
received news of my defection yet, but when they
do they will surely call on you and take you as
hostage against my return.'

'Yes, they would do that, such swines they are,

and what a disgrace you've been to me as one of them. But good, you have gone off your head and are forgiven. I—'

'Go this evening to your old theatre friends, the Gunthers, stay the night there and in the morning take a train to Switzerland. Stay with your other friends, the Ostermanns, in Geneva, and I will contact you there as soon as I can.'

'What, am I a performing monkey? Go there, go here, and all in less than a day?'

'Do it, old one, or someone will knock on your door.'

'I am to gather up my belongings in five minutes?' said Frau Voegler.

'Gather up enough for your immediate needs, and no more.'

'I will need my jewellery to begin with.'

'I rely on you to use your good sense, of which you have enough for six women,' said Voegler. 'If they arrive within the next twenty-four hours and break in, don't let them infer you've permanently vacated the apartment, or they'll smell a large rat and put out a wanted notice immediately. Leave a note addressed to me saying you've gone to Salzburg for two days. Is that clear?'

'It's clear I shall arrive in Geneva destitute of belongings and dying for want of breath. We are both crazy, but good, you are my son again. There is blood in your veins, after all. We must both say goodbye to Austria. Ah, well, it isn't what it was, and you aren't what you were, either, God be thanked.'

'Goodbye, Mother, for the time being.'

'Wait, what caused you to go splendidly off your head? I demand to know.'

'I came into contact with something far better than National Socialism.'

'Something? What something?'

But Frau Voegler's cryptic son had hung up.

He then went by arrangement to join Kirby, James and Carl in a private room of the hotel. He had promised to tell them something, and they were waiting for him. He first gave them details of his phone conversation with his mother.

'Very wise,' said Kirby.

'We can believe it, I suppose?' said James.

'You mean in similar circumstances, you'd not have warned your own mother?' said Voegler.

'You have to understand you're an extraordinary surprise to us,' said James.

'My old mother has just said much the same thing.'

'What was it you had to tell us?' asked Carl.

'That Lundt-Hausen made several phone calls today,' said Voegler, 'and it's almost certain that your arrival at the house of Baron Carl's mother-in-law will be noted by a certain section of the Italian Secret Police, the section that is always willing to unofficially co-operate with Himmler's SD. Lundt-Hausen is noted for extending his options. If you're arrested here in Italy, you can expect to be quietly escorted back to Austria. Lundt-Hausen, I presume, knows the location of your mother-in-law's house, Baron Carl?'

'He knows,' said Carl.

'Then be prepared,' said Voegler, and that

prompted a discussion, after which Carl phoned his mother-in-law's house.

Mariella took the call, reaching the phone in advance of rushing young people.

'Hello?'

'Pia?'

'Carl! But no, this is Mariella. Where are you? Is everything and everyone all right?'

Carl said everyone was fine and that they were in the little town of Tarvisio inside the Italian border. They were staying the night at a hotel and would take the first train to Trento in the morning, except for Josef Meister, who would be departing for Genoa and a ship to England.

'You'll be here tomorrow?' said Mariella.

'Yes,' said Carl. 'Let me speak to Pia. Oh, before you call her, I've a message from Karita Kirby. I believe you've a Sergeant Wainwright with you, is that so?'

'Yes. Fräulein Kirby insisted I needed a protector.'

'Well, the lady wants him to know he's free of that duty now, and can spend a few days in Rome, if he'd like, before returning to England, where she and John Kirby will contact him.'

'I see,' said Mariella. 'Hold on, Carl, and I'll call Pia.'

Pia was happily on the line moments later, while Franz, Lucia, Paul and Emma Jane kept the phone close company, hoping to speak to Carl themselves. Mariella went to the drawing room to acquaint her mother and Carl's parents with the glad news that Carl and the others had crossed the border and would arrive tomorrow. Sergeant Wainwright put his head in.

'Good news?' he enquired.

'Yes, they'll be here tomorrow,' said Mariella.

'Any message for me?'

Mariella came out and took him into the living room.

'Yes, when you are free of your duties, Frau Kirby says you may spend a few days in Rome, if you want to,' said Mariella.

'That means I can push off first thing in the morning.'

'You're still on duty,' said Mariella.

'I don't think so. I've only been waiting to hear if they're all right,' said Sergeant Wainwright.

'But don't you know there are two men watching this house? There was only one this afternoon. There are two now. Paul has been keeping an eye on them.'

'Well, here's a fine thing,' said Sergeant Wainwright, 'the Italian Mafia on your doorstep and I've only just been told?'

'I didn't know myself until five minutes ago,' said Mariella. 'Paul didn't want to alarm us. Where are you going?'

'To take a look at these men,' said Sergeant Wainwright.

'But it's dark now.'

'All the better,' said Sergeant Wainwright, and disappeared.

That's it, she thought, talk to yourself, Mariella. Sometimes I might as well be a stick of furniture.

Meanwhile, Pia in her conversation with Carl

had arrived at a point of mentioning the two men. Paul, standing beside her, had prompted her to.

'What men?' asked Carl, thinking immediately of Voegler's warning.

'Speak to Paul,' said Pia, 'I haven't noticed them myself and he's only just told me.' She handed the phone to Paul.

'Uncle Carl?'

'What's this about two men?' asked Carl.

'There was one at first, strolling up and down the street,' said Paul. 'Just before dark, another one turned up.'

'Are you sure they're watching the house?' asked Carl.

'Well, I only know they kept giving us shifty looks,' said Paul.

'Shifty looks?'

'If you know what I mean,' said Paul.

'Don't do anything,' said Carl, 'I'll call you back.'

He hung up, found James and Kirby at a table in the hotel bar, and spoke to them.

'Looks as if we've still got problems,' said James.

'It looks as if we can believe Voegler,' said Kirby. 'If so, and the Italian Security Police are co-operating with the lunatic Lundt-Hausen, then yes, we've still got problems. You two have to pick up your wives and children, and your parents, Carl. The lunatic knows that, so how would his mind work if help from the Italian Security Police had been promised? Might he not get them to arrest your wives and the baron and baroness on some pretext, and release them only if we handed ourselves over?'

'He's enough of a swine to think of exactly that,' said Carl.

'Well,' said Kirby, 'my suggestion is that we stick to the arrangement of going to St Francis tomorrow, except for Josef Meister.'

'Carl and I certainly mean to rejoin our families,' said James.

'Which is what the bloodhounds expect,' said Kirby. 'I think arrests of your relatives will only be made if we don't turn up. Call your wife back, Carl, and tell them all to sit tight.'

Carl made the call. He spoke to Pia, asking if she knew whether or not the two men were still watching the house.

'Yes, yes,' said Pia, sounding hot-blooded. 'Sergeant Wainwright has been outside to check. It's dark, but he says they are there. Mama is furious. She phoned Emile Viccenti, the police chief here, and made bitter complaints about her house and her family being watched by Gestapo men from Austria.'

'Are they Gestapo?' asked Carl.

'No-one knows, but Mama decided to say they were.'

'Bravo to your mama,' said Carl. 'What happened?'

'He rang back a few minutes ago,' said Pia. 'He apologized, but told her it was not a matter for the uniformed police. Mama informed him he had let the *fascisti* turn him into a coward. He put the phone down.'

'So? Problems, then,' said Carl. 'But do nothing

until—' He checked at the sound of an interruption at the other end. 'Pia? Pia?'

'It isn't Pia this time.' The voice was mellow, if vibrating a little. His mother-in-law was on the line. Signora Amaraldi was very philosophical for an Italian, and could be calm in a storm while others shouted and flapped in a mere squall. But she had very strong principles about what was right and what was wrong. 'What is this trouble all about, Carl?' she asked.

'The story, Mama, is a long one,' said Carl.

'Long or short, you are out of Austria yet still in trouble.'

'It seems to have followed us,' said Carl, 'and the fact that your police chief refused to help confirms it. But the last thing I want is to bring the trouble to you.'

'Ah, you think I should not share your worries?' said Signora Amaraldi. 'You're forgetting you're my son by marriage. You're forgetting my husband – God rest his burdened soul – tried to murder you when you were in this house during the war, and that for the sake of me and my daughters you did not denounce him. So he went free. You are also forgetting he was a comrade of Benito Mussolini, and helped Il Duce become what he is today. When he was killed by the Communists, Il Duce gave him a hero's funeral. If you have forgotten these things, my son, I have not.'

'I haven't forgotten,' said Carl.

'Good. So you must share your worries, and not ask me to sit and do nothing for you and Pia and all of you. Pia has spoken to me about why you have left Austria. Tonight I shall go to Rome, taking Franz with me to keep me company. Tomorrow I shall speak with Benito Mussolini, who knows me as the widow of a fascist hero. Ah, these *fascisti* and their secret police, they aren't the best thing Italy has ever known, and I shall tell Benito so. He'll laugh and pat my hand, but he won't like it that my family is suffering their attentions. So be here tomorrow. Everyone is waiting for you.'

'What can I say to all that?' asked Carl, an admirer of his mother-in-law. 'Well, I would suggest trying to phone Mussolini instead of making a tiring journey to Rome.'

'Speaking on the phone to Benito isn't the same as speaking to his face,' said Signora Amaraldi.

'If he knows you as the widow of an old comrade and hero,' said Carl, 'it shouldn't be necessary to go and see him. If you can't get through to him on the phone, speak to his wife. I believe Signora Mussolini is always at home.'

'Ah.' There was a sigh from Signora Amaraldi. 'I had forgotten something myself, that you are a man who can think. Yes, I will speak to Benito's wife at once. Give me your hotel phone number and perhaps I'll be able to talk to you again this evening.'

Carl gave it to her, and she said goodbye. Carl then spoke to James and Kirby again. They both declared Carl's mother-in-law an asset.

Karita and Sophie appeared.

'We are up against the impossible,' said Karita.

'Something must be done,' said Sophie.

'About what?' asked James.

'Is that a sensible question?' said Sophie. 'No, it isn't. We have taken baths, and now Nicholas tells us we're to dine in a little while. How can we in these clothes? They're for skiing, not for dining, but we have nothing else.'

'I only have a scarf and a handkerchief,' said Karita. 'Can I dress for dinner in a scarf and handkerchief? No, something must be done.'

'Find out if the shops here stay open late,' said Kirby.

'Yes, reception will tell you,' said James to Karita. 'If the answer's yes, take Anne and Vicky to the shops with you, but don't spend all evening there.'

'Men,' said Karita. 'Do you notice, Sophie, how easily words come from them?'

'Actions speak louder,' said Sophie, 'so let's go to reception, Karita. If I don't like the answer, I shall take dinner in my room.'

Hans Voegler, having taken a bath, was in the hotel lounge drinking coffee and musing on the predicament in which his incomprehensible behaviour had placed him, although perhaps it was more incomprehensible to others than to himself. His growing contempt for Ludwig, a hero of the Austrian National Socialist Party, had made him query National Socialism itself. If its ideals were embodied in the principles of a man willing to murder his ex-wife for no reason except that he seemed unable to look her in the face, such ideals were for cynics and thugs. He himself had made use of thugs, which put him among them. His contempt for men who could obtain results only by thuggery began to be directed at himself, and at Himmler, who looked like an intellectual and posed as one, but master-minded the indoctrination of SS recruits. How-ever, he freely admitted his sudden defection had been governed more by his admiration of Baroness Anne and the ideals she represented than by his mood of disillusionment. It had also been made necessary by what he had done to Lundt-Hausen.

'Herr Voegler?'

He looked up. The woman herself had in-terrupted his reflections. She was still in her ski outfit. He came to his feet.

'Baroness?'

'Why are you here by yourself?' asked Anne.

'I've never quarrelled with my own company.'

'Well, too much of it will turn you into a querulous hermit,' said Anne, 'a sad fate for a man who probably considers himself intelligent. How do I look?'

'I'm being asked to comment on your looks?'

'Yes, I've had a bath and repaired my face,' said Anne. 'At least, I hope I have. Is it now passable?'

He examined her and saw how a bath and make-up had made all her facial marks near to invisible.

'Baroness, under no circumstances could I criticize your looks, now or at any other time.'

'Thank you,' smiled Anne, thinking him an altogether better man than Ludwig, even if he had served the Nazis as single-mindedly as

Ludwig. The clear eyes that had been so clinical during his interrogation of her seemed even kind now. They held her own, and a little flush disturbed her. 'I can do with some flattery,' she said lightly. 'The men are looking for you, by the way. We ladies are looking for help. The dress shops in the town are shut, and we shall have to take dinner in our rooms. We can't appear in the hotel restaurant dressed like this.'

Voegler smiled, and the smile was warm too.

'Does dress matter when all of you must be starving?' he asked.

'Herr Voegler, that is quite the wrong attitude,' said Anne. 'It matters to the manager, and it matters even more to us.'

'There's a dress shop in the hotel,' said Voegler, 'off the lobby.'

'We've been there, and Karita Kirby is positive she wouldn't be seen dead in anything they have on offer,' said Anne. 'She prefers to take dinner in her room.'

'Greek women, I believe, are fussy as well as dangerous,' said Voegler whimsically.

'Now now, Herr Voegler, all that is forgiven, isn't it?' said Anne, and watched the way the light of amusement crept into his eyes. It made him look quite a humane and companionable man.

'Not by Ludwig Lundt-Hausen,' he said.

'A soulless creature who hates me,' said Anne.

'Baroness, he now hates us both,' said Voegler.

'He'll hunt you,' said Anne. 'You will have to come to St Francis with us and plan your escape there.'

'I think your menfolk intend to keep their

eyes on me until all of you are quite safe,' said
Voegler.

'It's natural that they find your sudden conversion questionable,' said Anne. 'Are you going
to invite me to share coffee with you?'

'Do you want to?' Voegler looked astonished.

'It would be polite of you to ask me to,' said
Anne. 'Dinner isn't for another thirty minutes.'

'Please, sit down,' said Voegler, and drew out a
chair for her. He ordered more coffee from
the waiter. 'Do you know, Baroness, why your
brother and the other men are looking for me?'

'Yes, to tell you that the house in St Francis is
being watched by two men believed to belong to
the Italian Secret Police,' said Anne.

'I'm not surprised,' said Voegler.

'I think—' said Anne, then checked as the
waiter brought fresh coffee. On his departure,
she said, 'I think they want to be sure you come
to St Francis with us.'

'Yes, to keep their eye on me,' said Voegler,
'which you think natural and I think reasonable.
I'm not complaining. Well, if they're looking for
me now, I'll go and find them.'

'Now?' said Anne. 'But I haven't finished my
coffee yet. In fact, I've hardly started.'

'Baroness – '

'There's no enjoyment in drinking coffee by
oneself,' said Anne, 'so kindly stay where you
are.'

'You astonish me,' said Hans Voegler.

'Do I? Why?'

'It's the last thing I'd have expected of you,
drinking coffee with me.'

'Oh, I share with Karita Kirby a belief that your conversion is genuine,' said Anne. 'Tell me, during the interrogation, was it your own belief that I was guilty?'

'Of passing something to Herr Kirby?'

'Yes.'

'Baroness, I firmly believed that. The coincidence of your meeting with him so soon after being seen close to the man Gibbs was too much to make me feel you were innocent.'

'And you still believe that?' said Anne.

'Yes,' said Voegler, 'but I forgive you.'

'Forgive me for what?' asked Anne.

'For looking so serenely innocent,' said Voegler.

'I haven't said I was guilty.'

'That doesn't concern me now,' said Voegler, 'and when the time comes to say goodbye to you, I shall wish you good luck and happiness. I think your ex-husband gave you very little happiness. Ah, and here are your menfolk, come to make sure I haven't slipped away.'

In they came, Carl, James and Kirby. Carl regarded the table, the coffee cups and the seated couple in surprise.

'Anne?' he said.

'Herr Voegler and I are having a delightful conversation,' said Anne.

'Delightful?' said James. 'Well, damn me.'

'Twists and turns plague all of us,' said Kirby good-humouredly, 'but not always in a miserable way.'

'Join us,' said Anne, and the three men drew up chairs and sat down. There were only two other people in the lounge, a married couple absorbed in a whispered argument. 'Carl, I've told Herr Voegler there are two men watching your mother-in-law's house,' said Anne.

'Would you know about them?' asked James of Voegler.

'Herr Fraser,' said Voegler, 'I only suspect that Lundt-Hausen almost certainly persuaded a section of the Italian Secret Police to co-operate.'

A discussion ensued on the implications, after which they all retired to their rooms to take dinner there. Voegler smiled when invited to join Carl, Anne and Meister. James, Sophie and Vicky dined together, and the Kirbys by themselves.

Chapter Twenty-seven

'Ah, Benito, to have you call me is more than I expected,' said Signora Amaraldi.

'Maria, Maria,' said Benito Mussolini, 'if you can believe me incapable of picking up the phone to speak to you, you will make me sad. Nor did I need Rachele to take hold of my ear.' Rachele was his long-suffering and placid wife.

'She is an old friend of mine, as you are,' said Signora Amaraldi, 'and always sympathetic. So I spoke to her first.'

'Now you are speaking to me, Maria, and if I can help I would do so not merely for fond memory for your husband Pietro, although how would my Squadre d'Azione have been as brave and efficient without his inspiration?'

The Squadre d'Azione had made its name during the 1920s. It comprised armed gangs of fascist thugs, its purpose being to destroy Socialist, Communist and other republican organizations. The fact that her husband had helped to engineer this murderous force was not something Maria Amaraldi remembered with any pride. It eventually cost him his life, but Mussolini gave him a hero's grave and held his widow in affection. He had an affection for many women, especially those who nurtured his ego by expressing themselves favoured when invited to share the bed of Italy's greatest man.

'Benito,' said Signora Amaraldi, 'I've never been sure how many of your Blackshirts were brave and how many were thieves and ruffians.'

To which dry comment, Mussolini responded with a throaty chuckle.

'Ah, you were always one to speak your mind, Maria,' he said. 'I remember how cross you were with Pietro at times, and even with me. Now Rachele tells me your family is in trouble with the Austrian Gestapo, but not for being Communists, eh? Eh, Maria, not for being Communists?' Again the chuckle. Mussolini was in a good mood.

'Always you like to have your jokes,' said Pia's mother. 'It's my family and their relatives and friends, and not one of them is a Communist.'

'Tell me, what is it all about, and what do you want of me?'

Signora Amaraldi said her family and their relatives had Jewish friends they wished to protect and had protected. For this they had been forced to leave Austria to escape imprisonment, and were now in Italy. Some were staying with her, the rest would arrive tomorrow, when all of them wished to make arrangements to go to England. But the house was being watched by the Gestapo.

'The Gestapo?' said Mussolini.

'Or your own security men,' said Signora Amaraldi. 'It's a disgrace and has come about from the conceits of that performing clown in Berlin.'

'Tck, tck, Maria.'

'A clown, yes,' she said. 'Why do you suffer yourself to shake hands with a man who has no dignity? Look at you, Benito. You are a great leader. He's a circus performer, but will consider himself your equal if you shake hands many more times with him. But no, he will never be the man you are.' Signora Amaraldi's approach was faultless. 'Is it with your permission that he has arranged for the Austrians to put men outside my door, or has he done so out of conceit and insolence?'

'How busy your tongue is when you are vexed, Maria,' said Mussolini. 'It sings in my ear. No, no, we need not believe Germany's Fuehrer had any hand in this. And in politics, it's sometimes necessary, even wise, to suffer clowns. I'll see to the matter, I'll see that the men on your doorstep go quietly home, and make arrangements to ensure your family and relatives are allowed to depart peacefully for England. I'm only thankful you're not asking me to go to war. Eh, Maria?'

'I'm glad, Benito, to know you are still a friend.'

'How many are they, your family, their relatives and friends?'

'Oh, no more than sixteen,' said Signora Amaraldi.

'Not six or seven? Sixteen you say?' Mussolini chuckled again. 'Almost, for so many, one might have had to go to war. But we must arrange something simpler. One of my secretaries will phone you later and write down the details, their names and so on. Then I'll see what to do for their safe departure.'

'They will be very grateful, Benito. So will I.'

'Could I do less for the fine widow of Pietro Amaraldi? No, no, Maria, I could not.'

It was after dinner at the hotel that Carl was summoned to the residents' phone to speak to his mother-in-law, who at once gave him details of her conversation with Mussolini.

'If he actually does arrange our safe departure, I'll think more charitably of him than I have in the past,' said Carl.

'I have his promise,' said Signora Amaraldi. 'You must let me know exactly who is coming here. I have to give this information to one of Benito's secretaries.'

'It's endemic to dictatorships, the collection of every kind of information,' said Carl.

'We have to trust Il Duce,' said his mother-in-law.

'Yes,' said Carl, and gave her the required details. He did not mention Voegler.

Kirby and Karita were vastly intrigued by Mussolini's offer of help.

'Ivan,' said Karita in bed that night, 'what do you think of Mussolini?'

'Once an effective revolutionary, now a dressed-up dictator existing in the shadow of Hitler,' murmured Kirby. 'But he still has craft and guile, and must be given credit for not regarding Italy's Jews as a problem. What do you think of Voegler?'

'A man shell-shocked by his decision to defect,' said Karita. 'An intellectual Gestapo officer whose intellect suddenly fell to pieces. Poor Hans Voegler, enamoured of Anne.'

'That's it, is it, little peahen?'

'A terrible thing to happen to a man whose god was Himmler,' said Karita.

'In rejecting Himmler, he's no longer a Bolshevik?'

'He will try to purify himself of the ideals that embrace persecution and murder,' said Karita. 'Love can be scourging. Alas, poor Hans Voegler.'

Voegler did not consider himself a poor man at this moment, but a reborn one. Further, his mother, safely out of her apartment and ready to depart for Switzerland in the morning, had phoned him to say she had hopes for him now.

The ladies had new outfits, the men new wear for the rail journey to Trento. Everyone had shopped before leaving. A warm goodbye had been said to Josef Meister, who found it impossible to express fully the extent of his gratitude.

The train was not far from its destination now, winding and snaking amid the sun-sharp Tyrolean landscapes, little white clouds dancing on the peaks. Vicky, in the corridor, turned as Nicholas approached. He smiled, and she wished she didn't have to wear hideous horn-rimmed spectacles.

'Hello, bright eyes,' he said.

'Mind your language,' said Vicky. 'Who have you been talking to?'

'Your mother,' said Nicholas.

'You're on very familiar terms with my mother, Mr Kirby,' said Vicky.

'I'm making progress,' said Nicholas, surveying the daughter with frank admiration. She looked sweet, he thought, in a beige costume purchased that morning. Vicky removed her glasses in a casual way.

'I think you're inspecting me,' she said.

'Well, so I am, and you're well worth it,' said Nicholas. 'I salute you, Victoria Fraser.' He kissed her fresh-looking lips. Vicky didn't know whether to kick him or ask for more. Her body swayed as the train entered another bend. Nicholas steadied her and that allowed her to draw breath.

'Well, really,' she said, 'don't you dare do that again.' Nicholas risked his luck. He did it again. Vicky came out of it with a slightly flushed look. 'What a shocker,' she said, 'I suppose you make a practice of kissing young ladies in every port or on every train, do you? Lucky for you my parents aren't around.'

'Yes, golden opportunity, I thought,' said Nicholas.

'If it happens again,' said Vicky, 'I'll get my father to flog you.'

'I hope he'll allow me to plead my case first,' said Nicholas.

'What case, you dissolute kisser of helpless women?' demanded Vicky.

'Helpless women? Um, yes, I see,' said Nicholas. 'Well, my case is that I'm so weak and you're so kissable.'

'All I can say is heaven defend one from a weakness like that,' said Vicky. 'Don't you know a gentleman should fight it?'

'I am fighting it,' said Nicholas, 'but my weakness keeps winning.'

'Lord,' said Vicky, 'I hardly dare be alone with you any more.'

'It's a risk, I suppose,' admitted Nicholas.

'Hello, you two.' Vicky jumped as her father appeared. James smiled, noting the closeness of one to the other. 'Who's winning?' he asked.

'Winning what?' replied Vicky.

'I've no idea,' said James, 'but it's a lovely day for being young. Where's your father, Nick?'

'Gone to take up a watching brief,' said Nicholas.

'Near the front end of the train,' said Vicky.

'The front end, I see.' James smiled again.

'He told me he wants to take a good look at the station and platform, all of it, as we arrive,' said Vicky. 'Mrs Kirby is at the back end. Oh, she said it would be best if we didn't move until she or Mr Kirby gave us the all-clear.'

'Understood,' said James. Noting Vicky's mouth looked dewy, he smiled yet again and returned to the compartment.

'He knows,' said Vicky accusingly.

'About what?' asked Nicholas.

'That you've been kissing me, you philanderer,' said Vicky.

'Well, as he didn't flog me, I think I'll do it again,' said Nicholas.

'Let me warn you, sir, that I'll scream if you do,' said Vicky.

But she didn't, especially as she'd taken her glasses off.

In one compartment, Anne was talking to Sophie. Opposite sat Hans Voegler and Carl. Voegler was quiet, a faint smile on his face, as if he found his situation amusing. Anne wondered if that meant he had a surprise up his sleeve, if, in fact, his stated conversion was a charade designed to fool everyone. She hoped not. She was coming to find him an interesting man, even enjoyable to talk to.

The train began to slow down.

At Trento station, passengers were alighting. Kirby and Karita were taking their time to make a careful inspection of the platform and barrier, having moved to the centre of the train after viewing the platform from beginning to end.

'No invisible jackboots?' said Karita. 'No men who look as if they usually wear them?'

'What kind of a look is that?' asked Kirby.

'A stiff-legged look with feet apart,' said Karita.

'I see nothing like that,' said Kirby, 'at the barrier, beyond the barrier or anywhere on the platform. However, let's send Nicholas in search of a couple of taxis. He's probably the least known of us.'

'We are to throw our son to lurking wolves?' said Karita.

'Only if the challenge appeals to him,' said Kirby.

'Well, it won't be long, I think, say in a year, perhaps, before the free peoples of Europe will either have to face up to the wolves or be eaten by them,' said Karita.

'Hitler will make war inevitable,' said Kirby.

'Ah, tyrants of his kind aren't happy unless his followers are soaking the earth in the blood of those who oppose them,' said Karita, and went to fetch Nicholas.

Nicholas detached himself from Vicky at a moment when she was letting him know that if he didn't give up all his other girlfriends, even if there were fifty of them, he was never to darken her door on arrival home. He left that matter up in the air to obey his mother's command. He was to find two taxis that would take the party to St Francis, several miles away. Everyone else waited on the platform.

'Baroness, it will be England for you and the others as soon as possible?' said Hans Voegler to Anne.

'Yes,' said Anne. 'Perhaps you would like to know we had all decided to move to England before the Gestapo became so interested in us, and in the supposition that we were dangerous enough to bring your Fuehrer down. Ah, should I have said that if he's no longer your Fuehrer?'

'His ideals are no longer mine,' said Voegler, 'and that means I'm more of a refugee than you are, since I doubt if Mussolini will extend a helping hand to me.'

'Well, you must plan a very intelligent escape, perhaps to America,' said Anne. 'I'm told there are places in America that take one's breath and where you can be alone for a whole year except

419

for the eagles. Myself, I have a liking for England and its quiet little places. I have a longing for peace and quiet. There has been neither peace nor quiet in Vienna since the end of the war.'

Voegler issued a sigh, and Anne thought then what a fine-looking man he was, and how he had betrayed his intelligent self and even his common sense by choosing a career with the Gestapo.

'Perhaps I might find a small chicken house in England more to my liking than sharing a vast space in America with eagles,' he said.

Anne laughed.

'Herr Voegler, you are fond of chickens?' she said.

'I've yet to find out,' he said. 'What can you say about English chickens, Baroness?'

'Oh, the cocks are noisy, but the placid hens only cluck,' smiled Anne. 'Herr Voegler, there is nothing to stop you asking for asylum. The country of James and my sister Sophie has received many refugees from Germany.'

Karita interposed.

'What are you two discussing so earnestly?' she asked.

'Chickens,' said Voegler.

'If it's the weather next,' said Karita, 'you may count yourselves as eccentric as the English. Now, where is that wandering boy of mine?'

On cue, Nicholas appeared in the station hall and spoke to his father through the barrier.

'Two taxis at your service, Pa. They're waiting outside, and there's no sign of Geronimo and his Apaches.'

'Good gracious,' said Vicky, peering, 'is that a cowboy out there?'

'That is Nicholas,' said Sophie.

'Really? How sweet,' said Vicky, as they began to pass through.

'Nicholas is not sweet,' said Sophie, 'he's a young man of sound character.'

'Well, young men of sound character shouldn't go around kissing helpless young ladies,' murmured Vicky. 'One alone, yes, but not all of them.'

'What was that?' asked Sophie.

'Oh, just an unimportant observation, Mama.'

The party emerged from the station into crisp sunshine, Carl and James close to Voegler. They were still not absolutely sure of him. Everyone experienced a little tension, much as if they were expecting some kind of enemy to materialize and spring.

'I suppose,' murmured Kirby, appearing beside Voegler, 'I suppose if your old friends are waiting for us anywhere, it'll be in St Francis, where the children are.'

'That would be the tactical choice in my book,' said Voegler.

'Of course,' said Kirby equably.

The two taxis moved off when everyone was settled, and the drive to St Francis began.

'Paul, my young cavalier, where is Sergeant Wainwright?' asked Mariella. The house was no longer being watched.

'He's just gone out for a walk,' said Paul.

'Sergeant Wainwright is a swine,' said Mariella.

'Is he, Aunt Mariella?' said Paul. 'Why?'

'How do I know, except I have an instinct for swines.'

'Does that mean you like them?' asked Paul, but Mariella had whisked away.

She was wearing no coat when she caught up with her particular swine.

'Where are you going?' she asked.

'To find out the best way of reaching Rome by train,' said Sergeant Wainwright.

'What a fool,' said Mariella, 'you could have phoned Trento station for the information.'

'A walk to the information kiosk is more to my liking, don't you see,' said Sergeant Wainwright. 'You hop off back to the house. I'll manage.'

'Hop off? Hop off?' Mariella was incensed. 'What am I, a flea?'

'Now, marm, you know as well as I do there's a world of difference between a flea and a woman, especially a full-bodied woman.'

'*Mama mia*,' breathed Mariella, 'never have I met such an insolent pig of an Englishman.'

'If I buy you a coffee and myself a pot of tea, will that make up for it?'

'But Carl and the others are due to arrive any moment,' said Mariella.

'They've probably only just arrived at Trento,' said Sergeant Wainwright, 'and they'll have a forty-minute drive from there. That's according to Frau Signora.'

'Frau Signora?'

'Something like that,' said Sergeant Wainwright.

'Oh, you fool,' said Mariella. He glanced at

her, and she saw the grin on his rugged face. She laughed. 'You can't go to Rome without me,' she said.

'Why can't I?'

'I won't let you,' she said, and laughed again.

Chapter Twenty-eight

The drive from Trento took time, but it was brilliantly picturesque in the afternoon light, and they arrived in St Francis without incident. Voegler and Nicholas noted the attractive appearance of the small town, set in the heart of the Italian Tyrol, its houses protected by heavy sloping roofs with overhanging eaves. Spring was feeling its way in on the disappearing heels of winter, and where snow lay its surface sparkled with the changing facets of a thaw.

Signora Amaraldi's house was situated in a charming street, and the moment the taxis pulled up outside, the front door opened and Lucia and Emma Jane came running, Franz and Paul close behind them. The taxis began to disgorge their passengers. Emma Jane hugged Sophie.

'It's been ages,' she said, 'and aren't you a multitude? Never mind, there's hot coffee and biscuits, or tea and hot rolls.' She stared at her father's bruised face. 'Now what have you been and done, Daddy? I can't leave you alone for a single minute.'

James assured her it was nothing serious.

Lucia, in happy communication with Carl, said, 'I'm so glad you're here, Papa. So is Mama. She saw the taxis from the window and swooned with relief. Oh, what do you think? We're all going to go by plane from Milan to Paris. It's with the compliments of Signor Mussolini.'

'By plane? Are you sure?' Carl looked sceptical.

'It's what Grandmama said.'

'Who's that?' asked Paul as Voegler alighted. 'Here, I know him, he's—'

'He's with us now, Paul,' said Sophie, 'he saved your Aunt Anne's life.'

'That's a hard one to swallow,' said Paul.

'You can believe it, however,' said Anne.

Carl led the way into the house. Pia swept into his arms. Her mother appeared. Signora Amaraldi, a handsome woman of sixty, had grown stately. Given to tolerance and common sense, she was always prepared to see the other person's point of view as long as she was not expected to deny the Pope's infallibility or, because she was practical, to accept that Mussolini had contributed more to civilization than the anonymous plumber who had first introduced water directly into a house by means of a pipe and tap.

She embraced Carl without reserve. He had a special place in her affections. She made a pleasure of welcoming Anne, Sophie, James and Vicky, and of being introduced to Kirby, Karita and Nicholas. It was Carl who introduced the odd man out.

'Hans Voegler, ex-Gestapo, Mama,' he said.

Signora Amaraldi raised her fine eyebrows.

'Who is joking?' she asked.

'No-one,' said Vicky, the dialogue in German.

'Signora, it's quite true,' said Voegler, who appeared not in the least embarrassed.

Franz, a muscular boy who seemed more physically equipped for playing rugby than a violin, said, 'How can anyone be ex-Gestapo? Aren't such men Gestapo for life?'

'I'm an exception,' said Voegler, and that brought about explanations from Carl and Anne, Carl in not unfriendly fashion and Anne in a sympathetic tone. It succeeded in confusing the young people, and bewildering Pia and her mother. Voegler put his case in his own way.

'I had the interesting experience of interrogating Baroness Anne at the request of her former husband,' he said. 'Her former husband disillusioned me when he attempted to execute her, and at a time when I was already questioning the ideals he represented. I defected and placed myself in the hands of your relatives and their friends, Signora Amaraldi.'

'I see,' said Signora Amaraldi. 'Then you had better enjoy some refreshments, along with everyone else, for I can't think why you shouldn't. A redeemed soul is more deserving, in fact.'

'Well, that's settled, then,' said Paul, as practical as the handsome lady herself.

'Where's Mariella?' asked James.

'Out somewhere with Sergeant Wainwright,' said Paul.

'And going hammer and tongs, I expect,' said

Emma Jane. 'He tells her not to argue, but she always does.'

At which point Mariella arrived back, rushing in to celebrate reunion in extrovert fashion before checking to stare at Voegler.

'Impossible!' she breathed, and that required a repeat explanation. 'Well, who can believe it of such a monster?' she said. 'But it's true, he saved Anne's life?'

'Quite true,' said Anne.

'A Gestapo man has turned into a hero?' said Mariella.

'An exaggeration,' said Voegler.

'Holy Maria,' said Mariella, 'Ludwig will kill you.'

Sergeant Wainwright came in.

'Well, hello there, Colonel Kirby, and hello, Mrs Kirby,' he said breezily.

'Why aren't you on your way to enjoy yourself in Rome?' asked Karita.

'I needed him here for my sense of security,' said Mariella.

'I pointed out,' said Sergeant Wainwright, 'that my duties—'

'He is confused, poor man,' said Mariella.

'So am I,' said Emma Jane.

'Come, the refreshments,' said Signora Amaraldi.

'I want to hear more about this plane to Paris,' said Carl.

'Yes, can it be true?' asked Karita.

Over refreshments, Pia's mother explained in detail. One of Mussolini's secretaries had phoned last night for the particulars of all people concerned, and had phoned again this morning to say cars would be coming to drive everyone to Milan airport, where a plane would be waiting to take them to Paris. From there they could make their way to England without trouble.

'This from Il Duce himself?' said Kirby.

'I am overwhelmed,' said Karita.

'We all are,' said Pia, 'we didn't expect such magnificent help.'

'Benito can still be generous to old friends,' said Signora Amaraldi.

'Generosity at that level speaks volumes for his friendship with you, Mama,' smiled Carl.

'His wife Rachele spoke in my favour,' said Signora Amaraldi. 'She is even more an old friend than Benito.'

'The old Italian fox is actually providing a plane?' said James.

'Give thanks,' said Sophie.

'In Russia,' said Karita, 'we say a fox will part with nothing but its fleas.'

Everyone was standing around the refreshments table, helping themselves. Sergeant Wainwright, having lost the gist of the German dialogue, poured himself a cup of tea, took a hot buttered roll, sat down in a corner and retired comfortably from the arena of many voices.

Carl drew his mother-in-law aside and asked her if she had thought of going to England herself. He left unspoken his opinion of Italian fascists. Signora Amaraldi expressed herself touched by his consideration, and asked to be allowed a month in which to think about such a drastic move.

'Herr Voegler?'

Voegler, sipping coffee, turned to find Kirby beside him.

'Herr Kirby?'

'You must forgive us for standing apart from you,' said Kirby.

'To give me what the English call the cold shoulder?' said Voegler.

'We'll come to terms with the situation some-time,' said Kirby. 'What's your opinion of this gesture of Mussolini's?'

'I can only say that if I were still a dedicated Gestapo officer, I'd report the gesture to Himmler, and Himmler, of course, would take a very angry view of help given to enemies of the Third Reich by Hitler's chief ally.'

'But would you see it as suspect from our point of view?' asked Kirby.

'If Mussolini is an old friend of the grand-looking signora, why should it be?'

'Yes, why?' smiled Kirby. 'Have a biscuit. I'm told you're fond of them.'

'Ah, Herr Brummenger, the grocer, who did not know Frau Kirby was the Greek woman,' said Voegler, and laughed. 'You're a devious pair.'

'Only when deviousness stands between us and disaster,' said Kirby.

'Frau Kirby did not go to England, after all,' smiled Voegler. 'My compliments to her for out-witting Lundt-Hausen and leaving him painfully mortified. The account gave me pleasure.'

'You'll be with us on our drive to the airport,' said Kirby.

'As a hostage?'

'As a friend, I hope,' said Kirby.

Someone sat down beside Sergeant Wainwright.

'Listen to me, English blockhead,' said Mariella. 'I have money left to me by my father, and I also earn well from my paintings. There will be enough for me to buy a house with a studio in London, and because you're not such a bad protector, I will hire you as my manservant, if you like. If you are good at it, I will pay you generous wages, but if you're no good I shall have to fire you.'

'Well, I've never before heard the like of such a handsome offer,' said Sergeant Wainwright.

'Good, I will hire you, then,' said Mariella.

'Unfortunately—'

'I don't like that word.'

'Unfortunately, marm—'

'I don't like that even worse,' said Mariella.

'Correctly,' said Sergeant Wainwright, 'you like it even less. Where was I? Yes, the fact is, there's my government work, running errands for departments various, which prevents me accepting your handsome offer. But I'll remember you as handsome yourself and a lively lady as well, even if you do go in for a lot of argufying. If you'll kindly pass me the teapot, I'll pour myself another cup.'

'I'll pour it myself, all over your silly head,' said Mariella, and flounced away.

Paul and Lucia were talking about the excitement of flying to Paris. Paul pointed out it could mean they'd be home in England by tomorrow.

'Tell you what,' he said, 'once you and your

family get settled, I'll teach you how to put a wireless set together.'

'Yes, but couldn't we go to the cinema sometimes?' asked Lucia.

'I'll be pleased to take you once a week,' said Paul. 'After all, you are my cousin.'

'Perdition,' breathed Lucia in passionate Italian, 'who wants to be your cousin?'

'Come again?' said Paul, his Italian limited. 'What was that, Lucy?'

'Anyone can be somebody's cousin,' complained Lucia.

'You're not anyone,' said Paul, 'you're my assistant car mechanic. I suppose you wouldn't like to be my girlfriend as well, would you?'

'Oh, I thought you would never ask,' said Lucia.

Franz was making conversation with Karita, the subject, rifles and violins. Karita said that violins and violinists were necessary to bring beautiful music to people, and that rifles and brave hearts were necessary to save the world from Nazi Bolsheviks. She produced her rifle, wrapped in her windcheater.

'You see, it's one thing to be driven to Milan airport, and another to arrive safely,' she said.

'Well, because of everything, I agree,' said Franz. He went and found a spare violin case in his grandmother's attic. Karita placed the rifle in it.

'I suppose even Mussolini might not be able to make the Gestapo give up the chase,' mused Franz.

'It isn't the Gestapo gentleman, Franz, but the

431

man who used to be your Uncle Ludwig,' said Karita. 'He's the one who will not give up. Also, he has a Greek bone to pick with me.'

'A Greek bone?' said Franz, mystified.

'You are puzzled?' Karita smiled. 'Who would not be at the actions of such a lunatic?'

'You're a mystery to me, Frau Kirby,' said Franz, 'but I can't help liking you, and will take care of this violin case.'

'Good,' said Karita. 'Your father is a fine man. You will be one too.'

Cases were packed and ready, and everyone was waiting for the promised cars to arrive. Sophie was hoping that all the luggage left at the house in Vienna had been collected by carrier. Heinrich and Hanna were very reliable.

Kirby was talking to Anne.

'It's been a horrible time for you, regrettably,' he said.

'A little harassing,' she said.

Kirby, who shared Voegler's admiration of her serenity, said, 'Matthew Gibbs has a troubled conscience about you, you know.'

'Where is he now?' asked Anne.

'Back in England, I hope. He went while the going was good. Voegler's a surprise packet, isn't he?'

'Indeed he is,' said Anne.

'Will he be able to adjust, I wonder, to life on the ground floor after his time in the upper echelons? He spent two years in Germany, you know, and had the pleasure of meeting Himmler himself.'

'Is it a pleasure to meet a mad dog?'

'An honour and a privilege for some men,' said Kirby, 'but not for the disillusioned. In coming down to earth, is our new friend wondering if he can adequately cope with the feelings that probably finalized his decision to throw himself overboard?'

'What feelings?' asked Anne.

'If you don't know,' said Kirby, 'then I'll say nothing, just in case I'm wrong.'

Paul's voice was heard from the hall.

'Fall in! The cars are here!'

There were four long black Italian limousines parked outside the house. The drivers belonged to a Blackshirt unit, an officer and three NCOs. The officer spoke to Carl in the hall, while his men began moving out the stacked luggage.

'I am Captain Gabrielli, detailed to report first, signor, to a lady, Signora Amaraldi.'

Carl's mother-in-law emerged from the drawing room.

'I am Signora Amaraldi.'

'Good afternoon, Signora Amaraldi, I am favoured.' Captain Gabrielli, sleek and handsome, cap under his arm, bowed, then cracked his thumb. One of his men appeared with a huge bouquet of flowers, which he handed to his officer, who in turn presented them to Signora Amaraldi. She received them with an enquiring smile. 'With the compliments and good wishes of Il Duce, signora.'

'I shall write and thank him.'

'We have four cars, signora, and instructions to

receive such passengers as are listed, with valid passports.'

'Plus one more, a late addition,' said Carl.

'Ah,' said Captain Gabrielli. 'I'm not sure, signor – '

'My son-in-law is Baron Carl von Korvacs,' said Signora Amaraldi.

'So?' Captain Gabrielli was still not sure. Beside him, the NCO whispered excitedly into his ear. He beamed. 'The racing driver of fame and excellence? I am favoured again. An honour to meet you, Baron, an honour. But the addition – '

'Il Duce assured me one more, one less, no matter,' said Signora Amaraldi airily.

'Ah, good. It is necessary to have everything right, you understand, and to avoid too many formalities at Milan.' Captain Gabrielli handed his cap to the NCO and produced a list. 'With your permission, signora, I will read out the names and ask your relatives and friends to identify themselves and to show their passports. Thank you.' He began to read from the list. 'Signorina Amaraldi?' Mariella came forward and showed her passport. He gave it a courteous inspection. 'Thank you, signorina. You may go and enter a car.'

Mariella looked at her mother. Emotion was evident.

'I'll come and say goodbye to all of you outside,' said Signora Amaraldi.

Captain Gabrielli, entirely pleasant, continued. 'Baron Ernst and Baron Teresa von Korvacs?'

Carl's parents, dignified and quite calm,

stepped forward, and the Italian officer acknowledged their standing with a little bow, and only a brief look at their passports. 'Thank you. Please proceed.'

He made progress with the list, giving the younger people a kind smile, and looking with interest at the two violin cases Franz was carrying.

'My grandson is a student of the violin in Salzburg,' said Signora Amaraldi, who had no idea of what was lodged in one of the cases.

'I wish him success, signora.' Captain Gabrielli reached the last name on the list, with Carl and Kirby standing at the door waiting for Voegler to pass inspection. 'Josef Meister?' said the captain. Kirby glanced at Carl's mother. She knew about Meister, and that he was no longer with the party.

'There's a mistake,' she said, 'there's no Signor Meister here, nor did I give his name to the secretary.'

Captain Gabrielli looked at Voegler. The Austrian defector, handsomely austere and with the air of a professor, held his ground.

'Ah, of course, I understand.' The Italian officer smiled. 'No Josef Meister. On the list, but not here. The extra gentleman instead, yes.'

Kirby and Carl exchanged glances. The inclusion of Meister on the list was inexplicable. Kirby gave Carl a little nod.

'Captain Gabrielli, may I see the list?' asked Carl.

'Not necessary, no, I assure you,' said the captain. 'I understand.' He looked at Voegler again. 'You are, signor?'

'Hans Voegler.'

'Well, that is as good a name as many others, eh?' Captain Gabrielli used a pencil to add it to the list. 'Your passport, please?' Voegler produced it. It was inspected, smiled at and nodded at. 'Good. You may proceed. We are ready to go now.'

Voegler emerged from the house in company with Carl and Kirby.

'Do you two gentlemen also understand?' murmured Voegler.

'Yes, he thinks you're Josef Meister,' said Kirby.

'He was happy to fool himself,' said Voegler.

'Well, if it means you can board the plane with us,' said Carl, 'you can ask for asylum in France. Or in England, if you travel on from Paris.'

'I'm forced to choose France or England, Baron. The hunt for me will be on now. I don't complain.'

'In you get, my friend,' said Kirby, and Karita materialized as he watched Voegler entering the car containing Pia, Mariella and Sergeant Wainwright. Then he spoke quietly to Carl while Captain Gabrielli was saying a profuse goodbye to Signora Amaraldi. 'Carl, Meister's name was last on the list. Someone added it. Captain Gabrielli, I suggest, on instructions from someone else.'

'Thinking, perhaps, to catch us out?'

'Perhaps,' said Kirby, and Carl entered the car.

Karita murmured to her husband, 'Well, I shall be sitting with Franz, and we'll both be cuddling violin cases. So if more games are going to be played, they won't be too one-sided. Also, we have Sergeant Wainwright in reserve.'

She and Kirby then entered the car occupied by Franz and Anne. Signora Amaraldi proceeded along the line of limousines. Windows were down and goodbyes were exchanged with her, emotional in some cases, boisterous in others.

'*Arrivederci*, Grandmama, *arrivederci*!'

'Ciao, Grandmama! Come to England!'

'I will see you all again soon,' she said, as if the farewells were helping her to make up her mind. She saw Mariella. 'Ah, there you are,' she said. 'Remember to make something of your life in England, or you'll have nothing when you're old except a paintbrush.'

'Mama,' said Mariella, 'tell that to Franz too, or he'll have nothing when he's old except a violin.'

Signora Amaraldi shook her head. It was always hard work trying to persuade Mariella to marry and settle down.

With Captain Gabrielli at the wheel of the first car, the four limousines began to move off. Signora Amaraldi, eyes moist, waved a final goodbye. Benito Mussolini, she thought, had been almost too good to be true in providing such splendid transport to Milan, and a plane to Paris. But, of course, he liked to do some things in a flamboyant and expansive way.

Chapter Twenty-nine

It was a five-hour journey to Milan airport. Once they were on their way, some members of the party relaxed. Their Blackshirt drivers were friendly, and Sophie supposed they were protective escorts as well as chauffeurs. If James, like Carl and Kirby, felt Mussolini was nobody's fairy godmother, he kept his suspicions to himself. He and Sophie were riding with her parents, and the conversation was generally about what kind of a life the elderly baron and baroness could make for themselves in England. They were to live with Sophie and James to begin with.

The limousines made smooth, purring progress towards Verona, where there was to be a stop for an evening meal. Carl, in the leading vehicle, knew the route to Milan, and checked unobtrusively that Captain Gabrielli kept to it. Pia mused on the possibility that the reputed stability of English society might mean a boring life. Voegler ventured to address Mariella by bringing up the subject of her painting techniques. Provoked, she conducted a lively argument with him, during which she accused

438

him of having a philistine approach to art. Voegler admitted his preference was for the traditional. Every form of art eventually becomes traditional, said Mariella. The argument induced Sergeant Wainwright to absorb himself in a cloak-and-dagger novel, *The Prisoner of Zenda*. This unsocial behaviour made Mariella so ratty that in crossing her legs she managed to kick his shin.

'Oh, so sorry,' she said.

'Don't mention it,' he said, and returned to his novel, as if it was the only real interest in his life.

Mariella asked herself a question. Why do I want to kill him?

'Is it possible I'm naive in expecting a tree to look like a tree?' asked Voegler.

'Yes,' snapped Mariella.

'Ah, so?' smiled Voegler.

'That is, you have no imagination,' said Mariella. 'I know other men equally dull.'

Sergeant Wainwright, who was the reverse of dull, read on.

Kirby, in the last car, took an occasional look at following traffic. His only impression was that all such traffic was speedily left behind by the powerful limousines.

Verona was reached without incident, and a welcome meal was taken in company with the very agreeable Captain Gabrielli. From Verona, they took the main road west to Milan. The limousines, comfortable at all speeds, ate up the mileage.

In the third car, occupied by Vicky, Paul, Emma Jane, Lucia and Nicholas, Emma Jane was talkative. She asked Vicky and Nicholas if they were dying to get to Paris.

'Is anyone dying to?' asked Vicky. 'I'm sure our distinguished Mr Kirby isn't.'

'I'm not asking him, he's not here,' said Emma Jane, 'I'm asking you and Nicholas.'

'Nicholas?' said Vicky. 'Oh, I suppose you mean this young gentleman here, Mr Kirby's son.'

Emma Jane, lethal for her age, said, 'Well, fancy you. Fancy having your life saved by Nicholas that day in Vienna, then going through fire and water with him to get to St Francis, and then not being sure who he is.'

'Sometimes children should be seen, not heard,' said Vicky.

'Nicholas, have you ever been up in a plane?' asked Emma Jane.

'Can't say I have,' said Nicholas.

'Daddy has,' said Emma Jane, 'he flew them during the war, and we've all been up for a flip around Hendon aerodrome. It costs five shillings. Mama said it was like taking wing below clouds enchanting. Mama's very poetical, you know. So's Vicky sometimes. I'm just a gasbag myself.'

'Passed unanimously,' said Paul.

'Mind, you've got to have a gift for gassing,' said Emma Jane.

'It's not a gift,' said Paul, 'it's a complaint.'

Emma Jane giggled. She never took offence.

Darkness had fallen when the convoy arrived at Milan airport untouched and intact, Captain Gabrielli cheerful at the good time they had made. His men unloaded the luggage. Franz carried one violin case, Karita the other, as the Blackshirt officer led the way to the reception lounge.

'Everyone please be seated,' he said, 'and if you will let me have your passports I'll look after all the formalities for you, then escort you to the plane.'

The passports were produced. Karita was not sure about entrusting hers to any Blackshirt. She was a naturalized British subject of His Majesty King George VI, proud of her passport and fixed in her loyalty. She was beginning now to mutter about fascist Bolsheviks. However, when her husband handed his passport over, she followed suit. Captain Gabrielli acknowledged receipt of every passport with a smile, and disappeared. His three NCOs stood guarding the luggage. There were only two other people in the lounge. Air travel was mainly for persons of importance.

Kirby, James, Carl and Voegler grouped together, while the others sat down. Kirby told James that Josef Meister's name had been on the list.

'Fishy,' said James.

'Who would have been responsible for that?' asked Kirby of Voegler.

'Someone who suspected Meister was one of you,' said Voegler. 'I also suspected. The name might have been added simply to reassure you he could travel with you, that there was no need to disguise his identity.'

'In other words to make sure that all the

people wanted by Ludwig and the Gestapo took the plane to Paris,' said Carl.

'Mussolini might have used his informants to get hold of all the facts,' said Voegler, 'and to be the reassuring factor. Except why not simply have phoned Signora Amaraldi to ask for clarification?'

'So we're not looking at Mussolini,' said James.

'I would look at Lundt-Hausen myself,' said Voegler.

'Does that mean we can expect a detachment of SD men to burst in on us while we're stuck here?' asked James.

'Perhaps,' said Voegler.

'Would the Italians allow that?'

'A blind eye might be turned if the right kind of order had been given,' said Voegler. 'Note the absence of witnesses, gentlemen, except for these Blackshirt NCOs.'

The two people had gone.

Nor was there anyone at the reception counter. Sergeant Wainwright unfolded himself and came over.

'Trouble, Colonel?' he said to Kirby.

'Not yet,' said Kirby, 'but stand by.'

Mariella looked at the seat vacated by the sergeant, and shifted herself to it. That put her beside Karita and a violin case.

'Frau Kirby, that man is impossible.'

'Sergeant Wainwright?' said Karita.

'I have never known such a swine. What is his work? Is he a porter?'

'One could truthfully call him a servant of the British government,' said Karita.

442

'Yes? Well, he's still a swine,' said Mariella.

'Ah, he has tried to seduce you?' murmured Karita. 'Well, he's a very healthy man and as you are a very alluring woman, he's bound to try his luck with you.'

'No, no, nothing like that,' said Mariella.

'Nothing? Ah, I see.' Karita smiled. 'Well, it's disappointing for you, perhaps, to have him indifferent to your appeal, but – '

'Frau Kirby, you're mistaken if you think I want such a stupid man to make love to me. I'm speaking of his irritations.'

'He doesn't take enough notice of you?' said Karita. 'Well, he's what the English call a discriminating man and will only fuss over a woman he finds interesting.'

'I am uninteresting? I myself?' Mariella bristled. 'I have had the most discriminating men in Vienna beg for my favours.'

'Perhaps he knows that,' said Karita, 'and being a proud man refuses to simply be one of many. You must take on the modesty and sweetness of a shy virgin who has never allowed any man to undo a single button of your blouse. Then perhaps he'll find you the most interesting of women.'

Mariella gaped. She stared at Karita. Karita gave her a sly wink.

'Frau Kirby, you are impossible too!'

'You mean ridiculous?' said Karita. 'Well, we are all absurd creatures, aren't we? That is why we enjoy life more than men do. Come, confess it, Sergeant Wainwright vexes you because he won't make love to you.'

'That man?' breathed Mariella. 'He has as much appeal for me as a turnip.'

'It's extraordinary that a turnip should vex you so much,' said Karita.

'Frau Kirby, you're laughing at me.'

'Not at you, my dear Mariella. Everything is really quite fascinating, and you must let me know when the situation is more to your liking.'

'I must tell you, Frau Kirby, this conversation is driving me mad. And why are we having to wait like this?'

'We shall see,' said Karita, the violin case on her lap.

James, becoming impatient, let the other men know he didn't like kicking his heels.

'I've heard you can't hurry Italians,' said Sergeant Wainwright.

Captain Gabrielli reappeared. Smiling, he returned the passports to their owners.

'They are now stamped,' he said, and nodded to his men, who began to wheel the trolleys containing the luggage. 'We can proceed now. Please follow me. I shall be travelling to Paris with you. Come, everyone.'

He led the way into the departure hall and out onto the illuminated tarmac. A plane was just taking off, its lights flashing, and the young people watched in fascination as it sped along the runway and lifted into the air, its engines roaring as it began a slow climb into the night sky. Captain Gabrielli then marched briskly towards a Douglas DC-3, owned by Italian Air Lines. It was fifty yards out on the tarmac, and the distance represented to Anne the final little journey of escape from Ludwig's venom. Once aboard the plane, freedom lay ahead, and in England she could begin again. Even at forty-one, a woman could enjoy a new beginning, even a new love.

'You are in good spirits, Baroness?'

Voegler was suddenly beside her, walking with her.

'Exceptional, Herr Voegler.'

'I don't ask you to forgive me – '

'Forgive you? You saved my life. Everything else is forgotten, and I'm pleased you've chosen to exchange the sadness of Nazi Austria for a new life in Britain.'

'Pleased?' said Voegler, astonished.

'Yes, I think you'll turn out to be a quite likeable man,' said Anne.

'Good God,' said Hans Voegler.

Arriving at the plane, Captain Gabrielli stood aside as the passengers began to mount the little flight of steps. A uniformed attendant smilingly received them. The cabin was quite empty, and there were, he said, no reserved seats. They could sit where they liked. Anne and Pia drew long breaths of relief at being aboard. Mariella took a window seat, and Sergeant Wainwright sat next to her. There was a book in his hand. If he tried to read it all the way to Paris, she'd snatch it from him and hit him with it.

Franz and Karita, each carrying a violin case, reached the cabin.

'Ah, musicians?' smiled the attendant in English.

'My young friend is brilliant,' said Karita, 'I am only ordinary.'

'You may play during the flight,' said the attendant.

'Being ordinary, I hope I don't have to,' said Karita.

'Move along there, little Mother,' called Nicholas.

Emma Jane was disappointed to find the flight deck closed off. It meant she wouldn't be able to see the pilot flying the plane. She said so.

'I don't think the pilot will take a wrong turning,' said Sophie.

With everyone finally aboard and seated, the attendant made sure all seat belts were fixed, then supplied blankets to keep knees and legs warm, and finally handed out boiled sweets to help counteract the effect on the ears of air pressure. The cabin door was still open, Captain Gabrielli not yet aboard, while the door to the flight deck remained shut.

'What are you thinking about?' whispered Karita to her husband.

'About the time Captain Gabrielli took to get our passports stamped,' murmured Kirby. 'He assured us in St Francis all airport formalities had been taken care of. And did you hear Sophie tell Emma Jane she didn't think the pilot would take a wrong turning. Supposing he did, how are we to know?'

'Ah, yes,' whispered Karita amid the noise of many conversations, 'and I also think Captain Gabrielli smiles too much. But James might know about wrong turnings. He was a fighter pilot during the war, and has flown light planes since. Sophie told me.'

'And Emma Jane remarked she'd like to see the pilot,' mused Kirby.

James was alert, Carl was alert, and Voegler had his ears pricked.

Captain Gabrielli came aboard. He stood at the door, his smile an apparent permanence, his uniform fitting him like a glove, and his boots gleaming with polish.

'You are all comfortable? Good. We shall be taking off in ten minutes. It will only be three hours or so to Paris.'

'A moment, Captain Gabrielli,' said Kirby. His seat belt undone, he came to his feet.

'Please sit down, Herr Kirby, then you may ask your questions.' Captain Gabrielli's German was faultless.

'My young friend there.' Kirby pointed to Emma Jane. 'She wishes to present her compliments to the pilot.'

'Oh, yes, could I?' Emma Jane was eager.

'So does Herr Fraser, a fighter pilot during the war,' said Kirby.

James caught on.

'It would be a privilege,' he said. Unlocking his belt, he too came to his feet.

Captain Gabrielli, blandly agreeable, said, 'Perhaps during the flight. There's no time now. Please sit down.' He closed the cabin door.

'Yes, do sit down, James,' said Baroness Teresa. She and her husband had been remarkably composed all the way from St Francis, but since neither of them had seen the inside of a plane before, or ever contemplated flying in one, she was now a little on edge.

'A moment,' said Kirby again, certain that this was where the trap was. The plane itself. Mussolini, whose alliance with Hitler probably meant far more to him than the widow of a long-dead fascist hero, was quite capable of double-crossing Signora Amaraldi, and of allowing the plane to be flown to Vienna, not Paris. Any moment, no doubt, the engines would fire. 'You'll allow some of us a look at the flight deck.' He moved forward. So did James. While the young people only seemed curious, their elders, sensing sudden drama, held their breath. And for the first time, Captain Gabrielli lost his smile. The attendant spoke up.

'You must return to your seats.'

'Sit on that man, Jack,' said Kirby, and Sergeant Wainwright, up out of his seat in a second, placed himself between the attendant and the flight deck.

Captain Gabrielli, his leather holster unfastened, marched up the aisle.

'Go back to your seats, go back,' he said angrily.

'Let's have a look at the flight deck first,' said James.

Captain Gabrielli, uncompromising now, drew his revolver.

'You're under arrest,' he said.

Voegler was the next man on his feet.

'Very good, Herr Captain,' he said, 'I'll take charge now. Give me that.'

Anne turned white. Captain Gabrielli glanced at Voegler and his smile came back.

'Ah, yes, you are – ?'

'Kommissar Voegler of the Vienna Gestapo. Your weapon, man.'

'Of course,' said Captain Gabrielli, 'although it was not supposed to be like this.'

'New orders,' said Voegler.

A violin case was being pulled from its lodgement as the Blackshirt officer placed his revolver in Voegler's hand. Voegler strode to the flight deck, put his back to the door and faced the passengers.

'You wish to pay your compliments to the crew, ladies and gentlemen?' he said.

'You swine!' shouted Mariella.

Voegler opened the flight-deck door, then moved to one side.

'Here they are, Herr Colonel,' he said.

Shock numbed Anne as Ludwig, seated behind the navigator, stood up, turned and came to the open door, expression dark with malice and triumph, body clad in a thick grey jersey and black trousers.

'I cannot tell you how happy I am to see you all,' he said. 'Thank you for your help, Kommissar Voegler, a very pleasant surprise to me.'

'Unfortunately, Herr Colonel,' said Voegler, 'the surprise isn't quite the way it seems. These people, some of whom I hope to be able to call my friends, will be flying to Paris, as they expect, and not to Vienna, as you planned.'

'Jesus Christ,' said James.

Ludwig, livid, shouted over his shoulder to the pilot.

'Start the engines! Take off!'

'I can't,' said the agitated pilot, 'not until the plane from Rome touches down.'

'Take off!' shouted Ludwig again.

'Don't be a fool,' said the pilot, 'I have no clearance.'

Ludwig turned, blocking the doorway with his back. He produced a revolver, and Lucia and Emma Jane emitted frightened gasps as he pointed it at the pilot's head.

'Take off,' he said, quiet with menace this time.

'Herr Colonel, unless you give up these useless dramatics, I shall shoot you in the leg,' said Voegler, 'which will upset the young people and do you no good at all.'

Ludwig swore violently and made a blasphemous reference to Voegler's ancestry and his acts of treason. Most of the passengers sat rooted, while James, Kirby and Sergeant Wainwright made no attempt to interfere with the way Voegler, a man full of surprises, was handling the situation. Midway along the aisle, Captain Gabrielli, recovering from shock, slipped a hand into his jacket pocket. Something dug into his back. He stiffened and turned his head. Karita smiled at him and dug deeper into his back with her rifle.

'It is not your day, after all, Herr Captain,' she said.

At the sound of her voice, Ludwig turned again in the flight-deck doorway to face the passengers. He saw her, the woman who had called herself Greek and robbed him of the satisfaction of arranging for his ex-wife to disappear into a concentration camp.

'Bitch!' he hissed and brought up his revolver. Captain Gabrielli ducked, leaving Karita exposed. Voegler reacted as fast as he had on another occasion. He pistol-whipped Ludwig's hand with a lightning strike. Ludwig shouted at the instant savagery of the pain, and his revolver dropped. Sergeant Wainwright swooped and picked it up. Karita kicked the backside of the bending Blackshirt officer.

'Fascist Bolshevik,' she said, 'you are a disgrace.'

Ludwig, rage in his eyes, nursed his swollen hand and looked at Kirby.

'You,' he said, 'are the husband of the Greek bitch who is Russian.'

'Greek women play games,' said Kirby, 'Russian women don't.'

Sophie thought herself a spectator of the unreal. There were strange actors and strange lines, and everything was appalling and unbelievable. Anne was looking at Voegler, the strangest of all participants in the drama. He glanced at her. She wanted to give him a smile of relief and gratitude, but her facial muscles were too stiff.

The pilot's radio crackled. From the south came the sound of an approaching plane. Ludwig unclenched his teeth.

'When that plane has landed,' he said, 'we shall take off for Vienna.'

'Herr Colonel,' said Voegler, 'losers forfeit the privilege of giving orders.'

'Captain Gabrielli,' said Carl, 'this plane was due to fly where?'

The Blackshirt officer sighed. His orders had

been specific. See that the plane lands in Vienna, not Paris. It must look as if the pilot is at fault, as if he misconstrued his flight instructions. Only Italian personnel are to show themselves before and during the flight. In Vienna, the authorities might very well detain certain of the passengers for crimes committed against the State. Il Duce, of course, could not be held responsible for such detention. The other passengers must be flown from Vienna to Paris, if that is their wish. Under no circumstances are Signora Amaraldi's daughters, son-in-law and grandchildren to be detained or left with the impression that Il Duce was at fault. If during the flight the operation is tarnished by any incident detrimental to the objective, then the pilot's apparent error is to be corrected and he must change course for Paris. It will then be up to the Austrian authorities to ask for extradition of the suspected criminals.

Tarnished was now very much the operative word, and Captain Gabrielli knew it.

'This plane will fly to Paris,' he said.

'It will take off for Vienna,' insisted Ludwig bitterly.

'I have to inform you no, it will not,' said Captain Gabrielli. 'It will fly to Paris. Do you hear me?' he asked the pilot.

'Heard and understood,' called the pilot.

'I am forced, then,' said Ludwig, 'to allow everyone to go to Paris, except Herr Kirby and his wife. They must be arrested and Vienna will apply for extradition.'

'My orders will not allow me to permit their arrest on Italian soil,' said Captain Gabrielli.

Carl spoke to the shaken attendant, who made his way to the cabin door and opened it. Carl then looked at Ludwig.

'You're free to go, Ludwig,' he said with fine irony.

Ludwig's breath escaped in a hiss. His dark eyes travelled to reach Anne. He saw the look on her face, a sadness. A sadness for him, for both of them, for the bitter dregs of their years together. They had been young once, and at a time when life in Vienna was a carnival for their kind.

It seemed to Anne as if the lines and hollows of his drawn face resembled grey haunting shadows. His compressed mouth broke apart, he drew a painful breath and walked from the cabin. He released the exit door, thrust it open and called for ground staff to wheel back the flight of steps. They did so, he descended in silence and limped away. He did not look back.

It was over.

'Please, can we go now?' asked Emma Jane.

They left seven minutes later.

Chapter Thirty

The plane, high in the night sky, was flying
north-west to Paris, and most of the passengers
were glad of their blankets. Lucia remarked that
planes ought to have central heating. Generally,
however, adrenalin was high, the atmosphere
expressive of a multitude of emotions – wonder,
relief, incredulity and shock among them. Every
tongue was at work, and the actions of the
man who had defected from the Gestapo were a
source of interest to everyone. He was sitting with
Kirby, and they were in deep discussion. Captain
Gabrielli, having rid himself of any embarrassment, put himself at ease with the turn of events
before joining the pilot and navigator. James
went with him to make sure no deviation to the
course was attempted.

Not until they had cleared Switzerland and
entered French air space did Anne venture from
her seat to ask Kirby to change places with
her. Kirby and Voegler were occupying front
seats.

'With pleasure, Anne,' said Kirby.

'Thank you, John,' said Anne. When she was

seated beside Voegler, and the conversation among other passengers was still noisy, she said, 'So, you were true to your conversion, Herr Voegler.'

'You thought for a few moments I'd deceived all of you?' he said. 'That was to trick our devious Italian into letting me take charge. It became obvious, I thought, that we were going to be tricked. While I didn't know Lundt-Hausen was aboard, I suspected he was directly involved. The refusal to let the girl pay her compliments to the pilot triggered the suspicions of Herr Kirby as well as myself. When I opened the door to the flight deck and called on Lundt-Hausen to show himself, that was – guesswork, shall we say? Captain Gabrielli thought I was Herr Meister at first, but changed his mind in a split second when I announced myself as Kommissar Voegler. He saw me then as a conspirator working for Lundt-Hausen. So here we are, Baroness, you and yours to go on to England as free beings and I as a seeker of asylum.'

'When we shall say goodbye to each other,' said Anne.

'Well, you have seen more than enough of me,' said Voegler.

'You have never been to England?' said Anne.

'Never.'

'But you have heard of Victoria railway station?' said Anne.

'Yes.'

'And have you also heard of its famous clock?'

'Yes.'

'Then, Hans Voegler, I shall be under the

clock at noon on the first day of May,' said Anne, 'and unless the English have locked you up, perhaps you'll be there too.'

'Baroness?' said Voegler, astonished.

'I shall be quite happy for us to get to know each other in a country where people do not have to look over their shoulder,' said Anne.

With landing time only half an hour away, Mariella, having delivered a variety of comments into Sergeant Wainwright's ear, took a different tack.

'Sergeant Wainwright,' she said, 'I wish to speak to you seriously.'

'Very good, marm, go ahead.'

'Will you stop calling me that silly name?'

'With respect—'

'Shut up. It's true you have no wife?'

'Never had time to—'

'Or a mistress?'

'Having been brought up in a Church of England family, and accordingly given a clip round the ear just for looking at a lady's legs on a tram, it's not in my nature to keep a fancy woman. I'm—'

'Did I ask for your personal history?'

'No, I can't say you did, you asked—'

'Anyway, what is wrong with a lady's legs? I have very good legs myself.'

'Is that gospel, marm?'

'Gospel? Gospel? What do you mean?'

'Is it a fact you've got very good legs?'

'You've seen them, haven't you?'

'I've seen your ankles and calves, but wouldn't

456

say that means I've seen your legs. But I'll take your word for it.'

'I'm not going to pull my skirt up for you. So, you have no wife and no mistress. Is that what makes you such a dull man?'

'Give me a minute to think about that,' said Sergeant Wainwright, and sat back, closed his eyes and took up an attitude of deeply thoughtful repose. Mariella waited, while all around conversation still buzzed. She kept waiting. In the end she poked him with her elbow.

'Have you gone to sleep, you swine?' she hissed.

Sergeant Wainwright opened his eyes.

'Sorry, marm, what was the question now?'

Instead of hitting him, she put her mouth to his ear.

'Would you like me to be your mistress?'

'Well, I'm a dull old army type—'

'Shut up.'

'If I grew a moustache, would that help?'

Mariella put her mouth to his ear again.

'I like you just as you are, you fool. Will you sit for me?'

'Sit for you?'

'Yes, I would like to paint you.'

'I see.' Sergeant Wainwright chewed on that. 'In a costume? Say in a suit of armour?'

'No, you idiot, without your clothes on.'

'Marm, I regard that as highly improper.'

'But you have a good body, yes?'

'So-so,' said Sergeant Wainwright.

'I think good,' said Mariella. 'And yes, I do like you, and will be your mistress.'

'That being the case,' said Sergeant Wainwright,

'and you being a fine figure of a woman with very good legs as well, if I can take your word for it, I daresay we could go to Hyde Park together on Sunday afternoons and listen to the band.'

Mariella laughed.

That was over too now, her infatuation with Carl.

'You're very quiet, Vicky,' said Nicholas.

'Yes, I feel very upset by everything,' said Vicky, 'and what's worse, I also feel life is going to get terribly unpleasant for all kinds of people unless the French, the British and yes, the Scandinavians, get together and act together to knock Hitler's head against a brick wall and stop him forming rotten organizations that are full of thugs and bullies. I can't think why the German and Austrian people get hysterical about him.'

'Probably because they like his promises to right the wrongs the Allies forced on them with the Treaty of Versailles,' said Nicholas.

'If you've read modern history,' said Vicky, 'you'd know the Germans forced even greater wrongs on the Russians in 1918. If they could do that to the Russians, why do they think the Treaty of Versailles was so unfair to them? Sauce for the goose is sauce for the gander, that's what France and Britain should tell Hitler. It's like that boxer Jack Dempsey handing out awful hidings to other boxers, then complaining because he received a hiding himself from Gene Tunney.'

'That's a speech, Vicky, and a rattling good one,' said Nicholas.

'I feel better for it,' said Vicky, 'and, anyway, not everything that happened was frightening. You must have realized there was something very nice as well.'

'And what was that?' asked Nicholas.

'You had the pleasure of meeting me,' said Vicky.

'That might turn out to be the happiest meeting of my life,' said Nicholas.

'Yes, aren't you the lucky one?' said Vicky.

Captain Gabrielli appeared, smiling as if he was everybody's friend for life.

'Ladies and gentlemen, all seat belts fastened, please,' he said. 'We shall be landing in the enchanting city of Paris in five minutes.'

England. The day was cloudy, the land green with lush spring growth, a green that was shot in many places with the bursting gold of daffodils. The beauty of nature in spring, however, didn't prevent Mr Neville Chamberlain, the Prime Minister, from suffering the confusions of an old-fashioned gentleman who could make neither head nor tail of Adolf Hitler.

In his study at home, John Kirby was looking at a blow-up of a photographic negative. The painting, *English Cottage*, had arrived yesterday, and the negative had been extracted from the label stuck to the back of the frame. The print was headed with the words, CASE WHITE, and marked for the attention of General Goering. The instructions were as follows:

'The present attitude of Poland requires the initiation of military preparations to remove, if necessary, any threat from this direction for ever.

'The aim will be to destroy Polish military strength and create in the East a situation which satisfies the requirements of Germany's national defence. The Free State of Danzig will be proclaimed a part of the Reich territory at the outbreak of hostilities.

'It will be the task of the German army to destroy the Polish armed forces. To this end a surprise attack is to be aimed at and prepared.

'The plans of the German army and the details for the timetable must be submitted by May 1 1939.'

That, however, was not the only item on the negative. Below it was another, a small sheet of lined writing paper headed '3'. Staffler had photographed them together. The letter contained part of the final paragraph.

'. . . and what you and many other people know, my dear friend, is that Hitler's father Alois was the illegitimate child of Maria Anna Schicklgruber, and that she married the man called Hiedler five years after the birth. He then declared himself the father of her child, but there are still people who will tell you the father was Maria's employer, a Jew. That is what you don't know, so what do you think now of our Aryan Fuehrer, dear Helga? Love as ever, Rolf.'

'Yes, and what do you think?' asked Kirby of Karita, who was reading over his shoulder.

'That Hitler cares no more for people than Stalin,' she said. 'Stalin has eliminated thousands of Ukrainians simply because they're Ukrainian, and Hitler is going to murder Polish people simply because they're Polish. But that he has Jewish blood, I'm to believe this?'

'It's questionable,' said Kirby. 'The writer of the letter may only have been passing on gossip to his lady friend. All the same, I'd guess the letter came from Himmler's file on Hitler.'

'Himmler has a file on Hitler?' said Karita.

'Your guess is as good as mine,' said Kirby. 'Well, it's obvious now why the Austrian Gestapo, under orders from Himmler, badly wanted to get their hands on the envelope that found a place in Baroness Anne's coat pocket.'

'For the letter as much as the Polish document,' said Karita.

'Chamberlain may dismiss the letter, but the Polish memorandum represents a warlock's brew for him to swallow,' said Kirby.

'Poor dear man, he's very sweet,' said Karita, 'but this will make him ill.'

'Not if he refuses to believe it,' said Kirby. 'But Matthew Gibbs will like it. It's as sensational as he hoped.'

'He's home, of course?' said Karita.

'Yes, he dodged into Switzerland,' said Kirby.

'A newspaper editor would offer him a small fortune for this and the story he could write about it?' said Karita.

'Whitehall would slap an immediate silencer on any editor willing to publish,' said Kirby.

'But the negative belongs to Matthew more than anyone else?'

'You'd say so, and I'd say so.'

'You're not going to cheat him, Ivan, are you?'

'I'm not, but Whitehall might pull a fast one,' said Kirby.

He presented the negative to his superior the following day. His superior ordered a print to be made. Kirby did not say he had a print of his own. He supplied the story of how the negative had come into his possession and how it had reached his home.

'We can now regard it as ours?'

'Definitely not,' said Kirby. 'Ownership still belongs to Mr Gibbs.'

'Don't be funny, old man. Leave it with me, and we'll see if there's anything in it that'll cause a headache.'

Kirby received an official phone call the following morning.

'I thought I'd let you know there's no need for any further action.'

'No need?' said Kirby.

'None. It's a fake.'

'Is it?' said Kirby.

'Some kind of a hoax. It's of no consequence.'

'Then explain to me,' said Kirby, 'why the other side went to a hell of a lot of trouble over something of no consequence.'

'Storm in a teacup, old man.'

'We can let Matthew Gibbs have the negative back, then?'

'What's got into you? Two funnies in two days?'

'He's hoping to make it the centrepiece of his story on the late Nazi bureaucrat who lifted the document and part of a letter, and ran away with them.'

'He won't get it published.'

'Then you'll have to make him an offer for it. He has a print.' Kirby was talking of the print he had himself, which he felt, in all fairness, belonged to Gibbs.

'Tell him it's classified information and that the Government's slapped a notice on it. Tell him, if he's thinking of selling it in the United States, that he can't leave the country until he hands the print over.'

'For how much?' asked Kirby.

'Find how much he has in mind.'

Kirby phoned Gibbs that evening, and Gibbs named a sum.

'A thousand.'

'I'll ask for five hundred on your behalf,' said Kirby.

'I said a thousand.'

'You'll get five hundred, so settle for that.'

'Five hundred means the Government isn't taking it seriously,' said Gibbs.

'Oh, they're taking it very seriously,' said Kirby, 'which is why they don't want even a small whisper to reach anyone's ears. In any case, it's the kind of thing Ministers and their Civil Service advisers always like to keep to themselves.'

'Pity,' said Gibbs, 'it's a damn good story, and hot. By the way, the Gestapo defector you told me about – Voegler – do you know what the Home Secretary is doing about his application for asylum?'

'Yes, arranging for him to be given a new name and a job in a department where he'll be useful as soon as he's been cleared,' said Kirby.

'I see,' said Gibbs, 'you'll be passing him in the corridor from time to time, will you?'

Later, Karita said, 'One would have thought Mr Chamberlain would have wanted the whole world to know what Hitler's planning to do to Poland.'

'He's probably made up his mind that he can make Hitler see reason by talking to him as one gentleman to another,' said Kirby.

'Hitler is a Bolshevik,' said Karita, 'and you can't talk to Bolsheviks.'

'Well, you know that, my little Russian chicken, and so do I,' said Kirby, 'and I only hope that by the time Mr Chamberlain comes to realize it, it won't be too late.'

On the first day of May an elegant fair-haired woman dressed in a dark blue costume and hat entered Victoria railway station in London. The time was twelve noon. Underneath the clock stood a man in a trench coat and bowler hat.

They met and spoke together.

They left together.

THE END